THERE'S

NO APP

FOR THIS

THERE'S NO APP FOR THIS

138 STORIES BY SIXTH-GRADE STUDENTS OF BERKSHIRE MIDDLE SCHOOL

EDITED BY

Daniel Fisher
Barb Babich
Deana Straub

CONTENTS

Animal Farm

Crime Spree

Good Sport

Intruder Alert

Lifelike

Look Back

Puzzle It Out

What Happened

World Beyond

World Beyond (continued)

To the Authors

Your editors are proud of you for the work you have done.
Keep writing what *you* want to write.

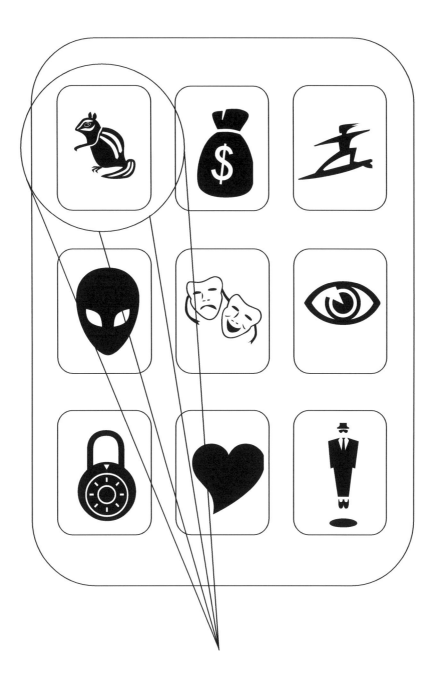

Animal Farm

The 39ᵗʰ Day

A puppy needs to find a home, but no one wants her because she only has three legs. Will she find a home before her 39ᵗʰ day is done? Find out in **THE 39ᵀᴴ DAY** *by **Jilly Wainer.***

I jumped, barked and wagged my tail like all the other dogs, but everyone ignored me and moved on. The reason this happened was because I only had three legs. But that wasn't all I had. Couldn't they look at my dark brown puppy eyes or my black, white and brown fur? They could pretty much look at any other part of my body and be amazed.

Today was the second to last day before "it" happened. No dog knows what "it" is, but they do know no dog ever come back from the room. The room is where "it" happens. None of the dogs have ever made it back to tell the others what the room looks like, but we all agree that it probably has blood all over the walls and dogs fur along the ceiling.

I was lying down when a little girl walked back with her mom and the owner of the shelter, Mary. The little girl had long, brown hair with dark, brown eyes. She looked at me once and snarled.

"This is your only puppy!" she screamed loudly. "Mom, why do you hate me so much? I'd rather get one of the dogs up front!"

"Okay, sweetheart we'll get one of those ones, but why don't you like this one?" her mom asked calmly.

"Look at her! She's missing a leg!" the girl exclaimed.

Mary whispered very annoyed, "You can't judge a book by its cover."

"Let's go to the front and buy another dog, okay?" her mom whispered to the girl.

"Okay," the girl repeated.

The girl left me, and Mary whispered, "Better luck tomorrow. That was the last of the day." Then she shut off the lights.

Next thing I knew, I was staring up at a little girl. The little girl had short, blonde hair, freckles and deep, blue eyes. She was with her mom who looked exactly like her except her short blonde hair now had some silver in it and her freckled face was now a bit wrinkled.

I kept looking up at them and barking when the little girl yelled, "Oh, mom she'd be the perfect gift for Jessie!"

"Are you sure, Maya?" asked her mom.

"Yes, yes, yes!" yelled Maya.

While her mom signed the adoption forms, Maya held me and explained how it was her older sister's birthday, how they woke up at six A.M. and they would give me to her when they got home.

It didn't take long to get home from the shelter. When we pulled in the driveway, Maya and her mom reviewed the plan of waking up Jessie, by putting me on her stomach to lick her.

Jessie looked exactly like her little sister, except with longer hair and several years older. They put me on Jessie and waited. First she smiled, then she laughed and finally she woke up.

"Oh, my gosh!" she yelled. "Oh my gosh, you guys got me a puppy!"

"Yep, straight from the pound just like you wanted it," explained Maya. "I know she's missing a leg, but we thought she was cute anyway."

"She's perfect in every way," Jessie smiled. "I think I'll call her Riley." I loved my new name, my new home and most importantly my new family!

Gorillas Vs. Humans

When the gorillas get mad at the humans for hunting them so much, they choose to rebel. Will they have a war, or will the humans stop hunting the gorillas? It's **GORILLAS VS. HUMANS**, *by Zavier Warren.*

It was the worst day you could ever think of in House Africa. Everybody was doing the regular: trying to stay alive.

This was a poor town. They did not have any money, and everybody hunted alone. The population was about six hundred, and there were not a lot of animals. The people hunted any animal they could find because it was hard to find animals. But they hunted the gorillas the most, and the gorillas were really angry. The gorillas don't like to see family members being killed, but the humans don't care. The people hunted the gorillas because they were the biggest animal to eat, meaning more meat for the humans.

During the prior ten days, there had been exactly thirteen kills from gorillas. They could tell the kills were from gorillas because of the gorillas' footprints around the area. These killings occurred at night, so no one knew about them until the morning after. This town does not have any guards, so no one could protect the town.

The humans had a town meeting to try to stop the gorillas from killing the humans. The humans' plan was to get rid of the gorillas by killing the gorilla population. The humans killed many gorillas, and they used the leather for clothes. The humans killed about 20 gorillas.

The gorillas started to fight back, and the next thing you know there was a war between the humans and the gorillas. There were only about 70 gorillas, but they were much stronger than the humans. However, the humans had bows and arrows. All that the gorillas had were their fists.

This war lasted about ten days. There were about ten kills a day. This was because the gorillas were faster, so they could run away and hide.

The war finally ended. The humans ended up winning the war because they had better weapons and way more people. Also, all of the gorillas there were left started moving south because the population was so small and they wanted a better life.

The humans celebrated their victory every day of that week, and it became a national holiday in Africa. The people had lots of meat and leather, but then they realized that they would not have any more gorillas to hunt. So the people did not live happily ever after because about ten people starved to death.

Latté

When Latté loses his mom, will she come back or is she gone for EVER! Find out in **LATTÉ**, *by* **Paige Baccanari**.

*M*OM! *Where are you? Come back! Please, I need you,* he thought. *I'm going to need food and water, and I'm going to need it soon!* Puzzled, he wondered how to take care of himself. *Maybe I can catch up to her. No, that won't work.* He keeps thinking and thinking about what to do, but he can't think of anything!

I got it! I will just wait there, and then she will come back for me. Now I should get some food and water, he thought. *Now where is a river? I can get a drink out of there. Oh here is one. I will get a quick drink out of there and go right back to where I was.* He keeps thinking that his mom will come back, but will she?

He has been waiting for a long time. She still has not come back. *Where is she?* he thought. *But where am I? All I know is that I am under a tree and scared to leave.*

The puppy's mom is long gone by now, but he doesn't want to believe it. He won't leave because he thinks she is coming back, but she is not. She is never coming back. Then he thought that if he was a human he would get out of this mess. But he is not a human. He is just a dog, confused about where he is and where he really wants to be.

He rethought about where he really wants to be. Does he want to be with a mom who leaves him there, or does he want a loving family that will take care of him and love him?

He heard a noise and wondered, *What are those footsteps? They're coming my way. Oh no!* "Woof, woof!"

"Hey, look what I found. It's a dog just lying here," said the dogcatcher. "He really needs food and water. Hurry, go back and get him some water and food. No more time to look for others. He is too sick to wait. He is nearly dead. Come on. Let's go! It looks like he was thrown out of a car into the woods because he has a lot of scratches all over him."

"Hey, Mom, I found the perfect puppy," said Paige, walking into the kitchen with a puppy in her arms.

"Yep, he is the one for us, but how was he found? Is he sick, or does he have a problem?" Mom said.

"No, the dogcatchers said they fixed him all up and he is ready to go. Now we have to find a name for him," I said.

My brother looked at my dad's coffee and said, "That's his name: Latté."

"What!"

Everyone said, "Yeah! His name is Latté."

"Perfect," my mom said. "Now all we have to do is get Latté set for the rest of his life."

Lily's Adventure

In **LILY'S ADVENTURE** *by* ***Camryn McIntyre***, *a boy named Trystan takes his dog Lily for a walk in the park when Lily runs away. She finds herself in a strange city…alone and afraid. Will Lily ever get home?*

"Come on Lily! Come!" Trystan said, in a high pitched voice to his black, furry puppy.

"*Ruff Ruff Ruff…*" Lily barked, as she wagged her tail as fast as a race car.

"Let's go on a walk!" As Lily and Trystan rounded the corner, their brown brick house and black Chevy car went out of view and the park was now visible.

Lily was pulling and tugging as hard as she possibly could when finally her front paw touched the expertly manicured green grass. That second she settled down as if to say, *"That's better!"*

Trystan had a loose grip on Lily's leash when Lily caught sight of a plump squirrel. Lily had managed to struggle out of her collar and jolted into the woods, as fast as lightning. "LILY COME BACK! LILY!" Trystan shouted, but it was too late.

Lily was gone, out of sight, too deep in the woods to find her. As the cool, crisp autumn air began to surround him, Trystan was left alone, with his face drenched in tears.

Deep in the woods, Lily was chasing the squirrel so fast, she felt like Supergirl. Her face was being scratched by leaves and branches but she didn't care. She wanted that squirrel, and she wasn't going to stop until it was in her possession. In Lily's most determined state of mind, she was about to clench down on the juicy squirrel's tail when she heard a loud rumble. The food train was coming! Every Sunday the train was transported to an outlet where restaurant owners go to buy supplies for meals. Lily crouched, ready to leap for the train. She took her final breath of anticipation…and jumped! *I'm on! I'm on the FOOD TRAIN!* Lily thought to herself.

There must have been tons and tons of food on there! She ran around frantically smelling at the crates of food, until she found one that smelled like apple pie. She stuck her head in the box and nibbled at the pie, savoring every bite. She felt like she was in heaven.

Soon her dream ended and she heard the train's metal wheels screech against the rusty, neglected railroad tracks. She hopped off the train and ran for the closest alley. Suddenly, she pictured Trystan lying on the park grass or worse…with another dog! Lily knew she had to get home, but her question was how she would get home. She made her way to a map of the city, but when she got there she realized she was miles away! Now what would she do? *Here are my choices: hijack a car, steal a plane, or skydive my way home.* She pondered to herself.

When suddenly, two dirty hands grabbed her sides and whispered in a raspy voice, "I could really use myself one of them fluffy lil' puppy dogs."

Lily wiggled and kicked but she couldn't get away from the man. She barked, whined, and cried but no one paid any attention to her. Finally her instincts told her to settle down. Soon she had fallen asleep.

When Lily woke up, she stretched then looked up. What she thought had been a cruel dream had been reality. She scanned the room and noticed the dirt floors and a filthy sheet with holes in it being used as a ceiling and walls. It was rather crammed and there were few items in the "shack." There was a pair of shoes with duct tape holding them together, a scratchy looking blanket, and a brownish colored pillow. The small area reeked of expired tuna and body odor. She got back to her feet and walked outside. What she hadn't noticed before was that she was in Hobo Land.

Hobo and was located in the woods! She could probably make it home for dinner. The human food had been nice, but she missed her kibble. Lily was just egger to get home. She crept around the corner making sure she was out of sight when she heard the abductor's voice saying "Oh today was amazin'! I gots me a pupper dog, oh, she's very pertty. It's got some fluffy fur, and a pair of big brown eyes!"

"Can I see the dang dog already? What are ya waitin' for?" a new voice snapped.

"Oh, yessir!"

By now Lily had heard enough. She knew it was time to run! She passed an old lady reading a newspaper from a couple months ago, and an old man knitting with yarn that was covered in filth. Lily heard the dognapper yell, "Which one of ya old geezers stole my pupper dog?"

Lily was running so fast she felt she could have outrun the train. She could see the hill in the park! A few more feet and she would be out! *Come on Lily! LET'S GO! I HAVE KIBBLE TO EAT!* She thought to herself, exhausted. *Almost…there!* And within seconds she was fast asleep on the cold grass.

The sound of leaves crunching woke her, but by then the only glimpse of light she could find were the stars. Lily heard the two hobos whispering, "Come to papa ya lil' rascal." Lily started to panic. She started to crawl toward the exit of the park when of course; she stepped on a crisp leaf making a small crackling sound. Now her only option was to run out of the park as fast as possible. She zipped out the exit with the hobos trailing a few meters behind. Down Churchill, Lily ran, sprinting past Old Man Bill's house, with the hobos panting and gasping for air, but not giving up. Lily couldn't keep running down streets so she had to find a place to hide. She searched frantically for a good place to hide. That's when she caught sight of an overgrown bush. She sprinted for it, trying to be sneaky and leaped into the prickly bush. The hobos stopped. Confused, they looked around. Neither of them thought to look anywhere but a tree, so they both just shrugged and headed back to Hobo Land.

As soon as they were out of sight, she dashed down Warwick, then to Chelton. She could see her house! She sprinted faster, and overjoyed began to scratch the door, when Trystan opened it. Lily was safe, Lily was home, and Lily had a great big bowl of kibble calling her name!

Puppy Love

*In **PUPPY LOVE** by **Timara L Harper,** a girl finds the most important things to her. Those things are her dogs. But when her mom sells one, what'll happen to her?*

At first there was one. When we got her, her name was Rosy. She was several months old.

We probably wouldn't have been so sympathetic to the idea of getting a puppy from that bunch if the lady (I think her name was Angela) hadn't said they were orphans. But that's not the only reason we got her. She was so hyper; she was actually bouncing off walls when we walked through the door. She also had a unique color. All of the puppies were either black or white. But Rosy was a pepper color.

My mom wanted the pure white dog. "We would have to wash that dog quite often, you know," I said. Then she pointed at the obsidian black dog. I shot that idea down in a second. "In my mind that black dog would turn right into a black cat!" I'm very superstitious. So Rosy came home with us. We renamed her Lily.

A few weeks later, my mom and I went to the store. When we got there, I saw the cutest outfit for Lily. I knew she'd never wear it, so I put it back. But then a thought popped into my head. Maybe if I had a more calm dog I could dress it. Of course that's not the only reason to get another dog. It'd be nice for Lily to have a play pal, too. So I asked my mom.

"I'll think about it."

I groaned. I knew "I'll think about it" only meant no.

When we left the store, I noticed something. "Do we have more errands to run? We're not heading the way home."

"Yup, we've got more errands."

"What?"

"I think it'd be best to get a new dog. For Lily to have fun with."

"Yes!"

When we got to the Humane Society, my mom's eyes were led to a certain place. Then mine were too. We saw a cage with a sign that read, "Hi! I'm Petey!" About five to six people were gathered around. I was thinking that if everyone was over there, he had to be awesome, right? But I was completely WRONG.

When we came home with him, Lily automatically thought; Play! Play! Play! She jumped on top of him, bit him, and rammed into him, but he stayed there. It was weird. He was adorable. He seemed perfect. But one thing he lacked was energy! He didn't seem like the type that wouldn't play. But he wouldn't.

I was kind of disappointed, but just as I started to get disappointed, he bit Lily back. Then she did. Then they played! I guess he's not as lazy as he seemed at first. I say "guess" because right after they played, he fell asleep.

After a few weeks of having Petey, my mom's friend called. "Beloved daughter!" my mom called after she hung up.

"Yes, beloved mother?"

"Marcela called and said she'd pay us $150 dollars for one of our dogs!"

"WHY IS THAT A HAPPY THOUGHT TO YOU? I DON'T WANNA GIVE UP MY BELOVED DOGS!"

"I'll give you some of the money…!"

"No!"

It was kind of too late to protest, because Marcela was already here. I stayed in my room until she left, and when I came out, I couldn't believe my eyes. Lily was GONE. The first dog I'd ever had, my favorite dog, had just been bought. My mom said that obviously Marcella already knew that Lily was the best dog. So when she came in, she automatically took her.

I was heartbroken. Everything reminded me of Lily. Every time I was reminded of her, I cried. When I saw Toto in the *Wizard of Oz,* I cried. Every time I saw a black cat, I cried. But in one day all that changed.

Marcela called. She said that she couldn't deal with Lily's whining. She wanted to return her. "Also, since I bet you guys have already spent the money, I don't want a refund." Yup. She really said that. She said we could actually HAVE Lily back.

When Lily came back, Petey barked with glee. They were so happy! It was funny to watch them play. I wanted to see that forever. Two is how it should stay.

Snakes

SNAKES, *by **Lance Collins,** is the story of a boy who has three snakes. It tells us what you need to watch out for.*

A boy named Nick got one of his snakes on his seventh birthday. The first one Nick got was Snaky. He is a Red Tailed Boa Constrictor. He is now four years old. He doesn't bite, and he is very friendly. When Nick gets him out, he squeezes Nick around the neck. When he gets around Nick's neck, Nick just touches his tail, and he gets off.

Nick got Harry and Tiny on the same day a couple of years ago. They are also snakes. Harry is a green tree python. Tiny is a winter boa. Harry sometimes bites but not very often. Tiny doesn't bite at all.

They all eat two mice every month or so. Snaky and Tiny live in the same cage. They like each other because Snaky is a boy and Tiny is a girl. Also, they are both boas. When Nick first got them, Nick didn't have cages, but Nick bought them some a couple of weeks later. They just had to live in a box for a couple of weeks. Snaky and Tiny live in the living room. Harry lives in Nick's mom's room.

When Nick didn't have cages the snakes stayed in their boxes. They don't get around the house. But once Nick got an idea. Nick was going to put Tiny on the ceiling fan just for fun. So at the right time Nick got Tiny out and put him on the ceiling fan, and Nick forgot about the snake.

He went to his grandma's house, having no idea that Tiny was still on the ceiling fan. When he got back from his grandma's he looked in Tiny's box, but Tiny wasn't there. He was still on the ceiling fan.

Nick's dad said, "It's hot in here," and turned on the fan. Nick looked on top of the fan. There was Tiny.

He shouted at the top of his lungs, "Dad, turn off the fan!" The fan stopped. Nick said, "Are you ok?" Tiny was fine. Nick wiped his forehead and said, "That was a close one." Nick still has all three snakes and continues to take care of them.

The Thanksgiving Lesson

In **THE THANKSGIVING LESSON** *by **Amber Durrell**, a young hamster doesn't want to play with her owner's cousins. But when she hears a story from a friend, she learns an important lesson.*

"I don't want to play with your cousins," Avery whined. Avery was a panda bear hamster who could talk. But the only one who could understand her was her owner Cameron who Avery was whining to. Avery and Cameron were on the patio arguing about Cameron's cousins.

"Oh, come on," said Cameron. "They aren't that bad."

"Are you crazy?" said Avery. "Last time they almost killed me."

It was Thanksgiving, and Cameron's cousins Erica and Mark and Matthew, the twins, were coming over. The last time they came over they nearly killed Avery. They put scissors in her cage, tried to duct-tape her to the floor, and threw her running ball around while she was in it.

Before Cameron could protest they heard the sound of a car door opening and closing. Cameron's cousins were here.

"Quick, open the sliding door," Avery yelled. Cameron got up and opened the sliding door. Avery ran out just as Erica opened the door that led to the patio.

As Avery walked around outside she ran into her friend Max. Max was a hamster who didn't have a home. Well, at one time he did, and according to Max the reason he left home was because his owner didn't care about him. Avery had found him last winter, cold and hungry. Cameron had asked her mom if they could keep him. Her mom said yes, but he had to stay outside. Max had been happy about that. He liked the outdoors better anyway.

"Hi, Avery," said Max.

"Hey, Max," said Avery.

"What are you up to?" Max asked.

"Just trying to get away from my owner's cousins," said Avery.

"Why?" Max asked.

"Because they nearly killed me last time," said Avery. "But that's not important. Besides, I would rather be out here than in there."

Suddenly they heard the sound of crying. It was Erica. She was sad because Avery was not there and she really wanted to play with her.

"Avery, I really think you should go back," said Max.

"Why?" Avery asked.

Max was silent for a minute. Then he said, "Let me tell you the real reason I left home."

Max sat down, and Avery sat down next to him. Then Max told the following story:

"A long time ago I had an owner named Amy. She and I were best friends. But she also had young cousins, and every time they came over they would try to kill me. One day I couldn't stand it anymore. As soon as Amy's cousins came I went into the backyard. Unfortunately while I was walking around I fell into some mud, but I didn't think too much about it. When I finally went back in the house, I went to Amy's room. But instead of hugs and kisses, she started throwing books at me. I guess with all the mud on me she probably thought I was a wild hamster. So I had no choice but to run away. I ran and ran and ran until finally I reached your house." After that there was silence for a while. Then Max said, "Well I've got to go. Think about what I said."

Then Max left, leaving Avery all alone. Avery did think about what Max had said. Then she realized something. Sure, Cameron's cousins hurt her, but why should she run away and hide rather than deal with it? After all, they were young and Cameron was there to watch them. Avery knew what she had to do. She headed to the patio and knocked. Cameron came to the door.

"What are you doing here?" she asked.

"I changed my mind. I want to play with your cousins." Avery said. Without asking, Cameron let Avery in. Avery walked over to Erica who was still crying. When Erica saw Avery, her face lit up.

Before she could grab her, though, Cameron said, "If you want to play with Avery you have to be gentle, okay?"

"Okay," said Erica.

When Cameron said that, Avery knew she had made the right choice. After that Erica, Mark, and Matthew played with Avery. In fact, Avery had lots of fun. Avery realized that she was lucky that she had a home full of people who loved her and cared about her. And from then on, Avery always played with Cameron's cousins.

The Turtle Eggs

When Emma does her job to save two baby sea turtles in **THE TURTLE EGGS** *by* **Emma Peake**, *will her rescue pay off?*

"What is that?" I thought to myself as I was walking on a white sandy beach in Florida, near my home. I had been looking for sea turtle eggs to save from the many dangers of a public beach when something pearly white caught my eye. I noticed two small, white sea turtle eggs. I did not want anyone to step on the eggs, so I picked them up and put them into a bucket full of sand. I took the sea turtle eggs home and put the eggs deep under the sand on the beach in my backyard. I put them where I usually bury sea turtle eggs that I had found in the past. Being a marine biologist who specializes in turtles, I love taking care of these special creatures.

The next day I went outside to check on the sea turtle eggs. One of the eggs I had found the day before was hatching! All of a sudden the other egg I found was hatching, too. They both rocked back and forth until small cracks appeared. A small, wet head popped its way out of the shell. Then the second one followed, first with its nose, and then with head and arms pushing the rest of its body out of the shell. The two turtles hatching reminded me of baby dinosaurs coming out of their eggs like I have seen in the movies. I watched as the baby sea turtles struggled to come out of the sand.

When they finally came out of the sand, I picked them up and put both turtles in my two-foot by four-foot big tank full of half salt water and half fresh water. This mixture closely matches the turtles' preferred habitat. I watched as the baby sea turtles started swimming around the tank. The baby sea turtles were diving underwater and biting the water as if they were trying to catch something. They must have been as hungry as piranhas.

I gave the baby turtles a minnow. They gobbled the fish really fast and loved every bite.

One of the baby turtles started to blow bubbles underwater. The other turtle began to splash around in the tank. I also noticed that both of the turtles were male, because the sea turtles each had a dark brown stripe on his head.

As the turtles learned how to use their flippers to swim, I felt happy that I had saved them and even more glad that I did something wonderful while doing my job. I got my camera and took a few pictures to put in my journal.

While I was watching the baby sea turtles I decided that their tank looked plain. It was just a big clear tank with sand at the bottom and a few underwater plants. I decided to go to my friend Sammy's store to buy a few interesting and colorful shells to decorate the tank.

When I went up to the counter to pay, I told Sammy all about the baby sea turtles and showed her my pictures. "Wow, Emma, they are really cute. You did a really great job caring for the baby sea turtles," said Sammy.

"Thank you," I said.

"How old are they?" asked Sammy.

"They were just born," I said with a smile. "I rescued them just yesterday." As I was leaving with my new shells, I invited my friend to visit anytime.

"See you soon," Sammy said.

After one month of caring for the sea turtles I took them down to the beach at my house and let them go into the ocean. While the sea turtles swam away I decided to think of them as Bubbles and Splash, because of the way they blew bubbles and splashed the water in the tank the day they hatched. I felt happy as I watched Bubbles and Splash swim off into the golden sunset knowing that they would live a happy life, where they belonged, in the ocean.

The Zoo

In the mall something always goes crazy! In **THE ZOO** *by* **Aliyah May**, *a girl goes to the mall, and everything goes crazy from there on!*

On Saturday, I needed to go to the mall. I wasn't thrilled about it because the mall in my city is old and dull. The walls of the mall are painted gray in color. The window displays are old and dull. There is no music or interesting decorations. Nothing interesting ever happens there. In fact, many of the stores were closing due to lack of business, which made shopping dull. Even though I wasn't happy about going, I dragged myself out. I needed to buy Christmas presents for my family. I also needed to shop for a new TV since mine was broken.

When I arrived at the mall I went to the local television store. There were only a few people there, and the store seemed depressing. I struck up a conversation with Josh Yale, a boy that I knew from school. He was also looking at the televisions. We agreed that our mall needed to be remodeled and made more exciting. He suggested that new stores should be brought in, and I thought the food court could be more attractive. While we were standing there complaining, we suddenly felt movement. At first we thought it was an earthquake. "OHHH MY GOSH!" someone yelled from across the mall.

I grabbed the Josh's arm, and we both looked up at the television I had been thinking about purchasing. The news was on. The newscaster was talking about the zoo. He said, "The animals at the Detroit Zoo have escaped." He also said, "The zookeepers are frantically searching for all the animals that are loose." He warned the public that the lions and other dangerous animals were running free. It was suspected that a zookeeper had accidently left the cages unlocked. The zoo manager told everyone to stay in their houses.

Meanwhile, at the mall I heard *BOOM, POW,* and *SMASH.* People started running past us in all different directions. Then Josh looked at me and said, "We gotta get out of here." He started to pull me toward the exit where the few shoppers that remained in the mall were pushing and shoving, trying to get out. I started to follow him, but my curiosity got the best of me. I broke away from his grip and started running back toward chaos.

I peeked into the mall and at first saw nothing unusual. I wondered why everyone seemed to be in a panic. Suddenly I was overcome by a shadow. I looked up and standing next to me was the biggest animal I had ever seen. It was an elephant drinking water from the fountain next to me. I screamed so loud it frightened the elephant who then turned and squirted me with the water from the fountain. It felt like a cold shower. I was so scared my knees started to shake and my heart began to race.

The next thing I noticed was that a monkey opened the door to the entrance of the mall, letting in 50 more monkeys. It was as if 50 *Curious George* books came to life. All of the monkey s ran past me as if I wasn't even there.

I forgot about my fear and ran after them. The next thing I knew a big smile came over my face and I started to laugh! I felt as if I were The Man in The Yellow Hat from the *Curious George* books. The monkeys ran through the stores. They tried on hats, shirts, and anything else they could get their hands on. Then, dressed in hats and scarves, they ran toward the food court.

In the food court they found uneaten food. The tables were covered with the food that the customers had left behind in their hurry to escape from the mall. As the monkeys started to eat, more and more animals came to the food court. The animals that were there just amazed me. There were lions, tigers, bears, giraffes, sloths, and every kind of birds that you could think of.

Suddenly I noticed that some of the animals were in the kitchens cooking food. The lions were cooking pizza. The sloths and the monkeys were preparing subs from Subway. The birds were making salad, while the bears and giraffes were flipping burgers. Others were sitting at the tables and appeared to be socializing. I couldn't believe my eyes! It was as if the mall had transformed into a café for the wild animals who were surprisingly not being wild.

I walked slowly and cautiously. I didn't know what to expect. I walked past each station. At each station an animal or two began to jump up and down, waving their hands (or paws) in my direction. The monkeys screeched as they waved their hands in front of my face and pointed towards the food, and the elephants trumpeted and pointed their trunks in the direction of the tables. The lions began to roar, and the birds began to frantically chirp! I screamed, "OMG!" Finally all I heard was the song "The Lion Sleeps Tonight."

As they were making the noise in the tune of the song I started to think I was going crazy. So the part of me that was going crazy started to sing along, "In the jungle the mighty jungle…" Walking past them, I felt like I understood what they were trying to tell me! I thought they were trying to tell me, "Eat my food please."

I was starting to feel pretty brave. I walked to the Subway and asked for a ham and cheese with lettuce, tomatoes, and ranch. The monkeys made me the sandwich. It was the most delicious thing that I ever had. The monkeys watched me taste the sandwich and clapped their hands as I smiled and said it was good.

Then I sampled burgers from the bears and the giraffes. They were also delicious. Next I had a salad that the birds made, and it was delicious.

Suddenly I felt like eating dessert. I walked around the food court. The next thing I knew there was ice cream, cake, and pie flying over my head. Some of the monkeys were trying to make combinations. They made me a ten-course dessert. The first was chocolate ice cream. The second course was vanilla ice cream. The third course was strawberry ice cream. Chocolate cake was next, followed by vanilla cake. The pies came next. There was pumpkin pie, apple pie, and cherry pie. Then I had a banana split and finally a hot fudge sundae.

My stomach started to hurt. I screamed, "Ouch!" Everything stopped like I had just pressed pause on my TV. I fell and hit the ground.

The animals got me up and took me to a lion that gave me Pepto Bismol to settle my stomach and held my hand until I was better. I was feeling pretty tired, so I decided it was time for me to head home.

As I left the mall the news reporters ran toward me. They shoved microphones in my face and all started talking at once. They were pushing and shoving and were very rude. I felt just as frightened as I had when I first saw the elephant. The chaos of the reporters all talking at once made my ears hurt and my head spin! As

I ran away I couldn't help but think how all the animals had made me feel much safer. All the people were rude and inconsiderate. The animals were very nice and somewhat polite in their own way.

I finally got away from the crowd of microphones and screaming people and went home. Later that day I agreed to give a press conference. I gave the press conference because I thought the media was reporting that the animals were wild and harmful. I totally disagreed. I felt I needed to defend the animals. I felt like they were my friends.

I was nervous because I knew I was going to be on television. During the press conference I told everyone how kind the animals had been. I also said that I felt that the animals had made the mall a lot more interesting than it was before they came.

The mall manager asked me if I would return to the mall with him to talk to the animals. I agreed. Even though I was tired, I agreed because they were my friends and I believed in them.

When we got to the mall we were surprised to see how orderly things were. The merchandise was displayed beautifully, and the singing of the birds filled the air with music.

Over the next week or two the mayor decided to have the animal rights people come in and decide how to handle the situation. The animal rights people went to every food area and every store. They were very satisfied with the results. They felt the animals were safe and that they were very, very happy. They thought that it was right for another reason. That reason was because they thought the animals were better off free and making their own decisions than being in a cage locked up all day.

Then people from the community came and went to every store and food area, and they were very satisfied. They were pleased with the results and thought the same thing. They liked the liveliness the animals brought to the mall.

Next a group of about twenty people came together and decided that they didn't want the animals to take over the mall because it would take away jobs from people who needed them. Everyone in the town had his or her own opinion. People were found talking about it all over town. Finally the mayor told everyone at a town meeting that they would let the people have a vote.

The voters decided that the animals won by a large majority. It was decided that the animals would stay and run the mall. What was once a dull mall with little business turned into a wonderful place to shop. The mall became more successful than ever, and to this day it is known all around the world. People talk about the day of Thursday, October 15, 2009 as the day of liberation of the animals.

I will always be proud of what I did to help the animals that day.

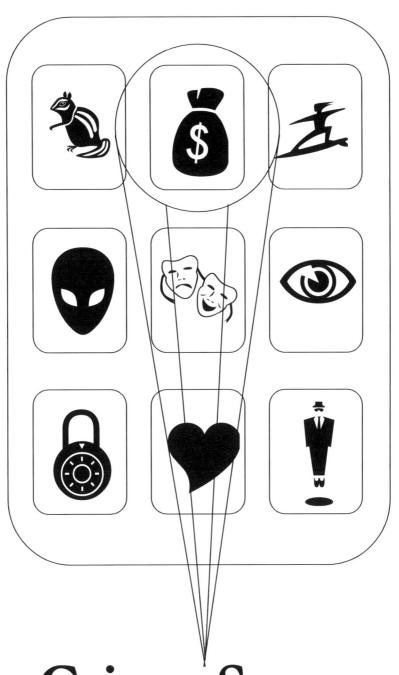

Crime Spree

Bobby and Clyde

This story is about an unsuspecting murderer named Clyde who has killed multiple people. Little does he know that he will be caught very soon in the story called **BOBBY AND CLYDE** *by* ***Bradley N.***

One day two men named Franklin and Chris were at their jobs at a Ford car factory and saw a human hand coming down the conveyer belt. When the hand got closer to them, they realized that the hand was not attached to the body. They called the police but a man in a black suit appeared behind them and killed them both. The man in the black suit forgot to hang up the phone so the cops still got the call. When they realized that the man was not answering them, the cops immediately drove to the factory. Meanwhile, at the factory the man in the black suit had already cleaned up his mess.

The cops arrived and were searching the factory when the cop named Parrish found a spot of blood on the ground and a hair. The cops brought the hair back to their lab and identified it. The hair belonged to a man named Clyde Franklin. They did some research on Clyde Franklin and found out that he worked at a fish market and that he had been charged with murder before. The cops went to the fish market and saw him. They could not arrest him without solid proof that he killed the men. So they waited and waited until they saw him going for his next kill. They jumped in before he could kill the women and arrested him for first-degree murder.

Two years later…

Clyde found a spot on the electric fence that was not connected to the wire. Clyde snuck up behind the watch guard and killed him. Clyde then ran to the spot on the fence and climbed it. He escaped and managed to hotwire a car and drive to Mexico. Clyde went to Mexico because he knew that no American cops could get him once he had crossed the border. Once he got across the border, he went on a huge killing spree. He killed two men, a woman, three kids, and a dog. After he killed all of those people, he stopped for a little while and started living a normal life.

He had gone for about a year without killing anyone. One day, he was at IHOP and a homeless man asked him for some change. Clyde refused to give him change. A man named Bobby overheard Clyde say, "No!" to the homeless man and got mad.

He said, "Why couldn't you have just given the man some change?"

Clyde said, "Because I didn't want to!"

Bobby got so mad that he just blew up and shot Clyde in the head. Bobby instantly left the IHOP and drove away. Bobby did not know that the bullet only skimmed Clyde's head so he did not die. Clyde chased after Bobby and tried to kill him, but the bullet hit and killed somebody else. Now that he had killed someone in the United States and in Mexico he had nowhere to go.

After Clyde attempted to run away from the IHOP so that he could not be put in jail, the Mexican police arrested him and put him in jail for life. When Clyde got to the jail he realized that Bobby was his cellmate. Clyde did not like this, so he talked to the head of the jail to see if he could move cells. The head of the jail said no, so they put him back in the cell with Bobby. Clyde figured that if he had to stay with Bobby for the rest of his life, he might as well make the best of it. So he tried to be friends with him for a while.

One day Clyde caught Bobby sneaking out without even telling him. While Bobby was sneaking out Clyde followed behind him. Clyde saw a guard. He knocked the guard out and took his gun. He then shot Bobby and killed him. After killing Bobby, he could not take it anymore, so he took his own life, too.

The Christmas Eve Kidnap

Three children go to the store to get their grandma a gift for Christmas. Suddenly, one of the children is in an unknown place and doesn't know how to get out. Find out what happens in **THE CHRISTMAS EVE KIDNAP**, *by* **Brent Asmar.**

On Christmas Eve, three children named Charles, Lauren, and Mark realized they had forgotten to get their grandma a present for Christmas. They went to the store and tried to get her something wonderful! They had two things to pick from: earrings or slippers. They put their money together, but they only had fifty dollars. The earrings were seventy dollars and the slippers were thirty dollars. Obviously, the children had to buy the slippers.

As the children walked outside the shop, a big black van pulled up. A hand popped out of the van and snatched Lauren by her t-shirt.

Once the van arrived at a house, Lauren found a computer under a bunch of dust. Very quietly, Lauren opened the computer. She didn't want the big, scary guy who pulled her into the van to hear her. Lauren was grateful the computer worked. "I'm saved!" she whispered to herself.

She went to a website called Splash Face. Luckily, her brothers, Mark and Charles, were on Splash Face as well. She wanted to chat with them to let them know what was happening. But, Lauren had to do this all very quietly because she did not want the big guy to hear her. She didn't know what he would do to her if he found out what she was doing. So she chatted with Mark and Charles as quickly as possible.

> *Dear Mark and Charles,*
> *I am trapped in an unknown place and I don't know the address, but please call for help and tell them that we were at Somerset to get Grandma a present for Christmas and then when we got out of the mall a big black van pulled out right in front of us and quickly reached and grabbed whatever was right in front of him. Please, I'm in desperate need, and don't tell Grandma about this, she will get really mad and she won't trust us anymore. Thanks. Lauren*

Mark did not answer, so Lauren got worried. No one appeared that night to save her. Lauren was hoping and praying that someone would come and save her. Suddenly, she heard a noise. Her face turned red, her cheeks turned rosy, and she was as red as a tomato. Her heart was pounding, and she heard a loud *SMASH, BOOM, CRASH, SMASH*!

The door opened, but it was the big, scary guy.

"What do you want now?" Lauren asked.

The guy answered, "You know, I have a name. My name is Jesse."

He quickly threw something at Lauren, but she didn't know what it was until she picked it up. It was food. He left the room saying, "Eat up!" She looked at what Jesse gave her. There were apples and oranges. She ate them slowly.

Then her door opened again, and Mark and Charles barged in! They were there to save Lauren. She was so happy! Mark grabbed her by her feet and Charles grabbed her arms. They picked her up and took her home. She was saved!

Before she knew it, the day was Sunday, December 26, 2010. She was upset that she had been trapped in a messy room for Christmas without any of her family. But it wasn't as big of a deal as she thought. Her family celebrated Christmas on Monday, December 27. Lauren was able to celebrate with her family. They didn't forget Grandma's present, either. Grandma was very excited; she loved her new slippers. The kids had tons of fun, and everything turned out well in the end.

The Circus Taking

In this story, two girls go to the mall with their aunt. Suddenly, a mysterious man takes them into his car and drives off. Will they ever see their family again? To find the answers to these questions read **THE CIRCUS TAKING** *by* ***Candace Brown.***

I'm Candice Candi. My twin, Candace, and I were ten when we were kidnapped in the mall. Let me tell you the full story.

My sister and I were with my aunt at the mall. She gave us both 50 dollars each to go shopping. We went in a magazine store so we could buy an *American Girl* issue. When we were looking at the new issue, a guy in a red shirt and black hat suddenly came out of nowhere. He put us in his car and drove off. We screamed! *I wonder if anyone heard us scream or if our dad would be looking for us.*

DAD

"It has been two hours! They were supposed to come home by now! I told you not to let them go with your sister!"

"Honey, they will be home soon. Don't be worried, they should be home."

All of a sudden, a yellow car pulled up. Then a police car came. We were so confused at this moment. I kept thinking, *why is Gloria coming in with a policeman? Why is she crying? Where are the girls?* "Hello, may I help you with something officers?" I asked making sure I didn't sound worried.

"Sir," the officer started off, and the way he said it sounded serious. "Your daughters, well, your daughters, we can't seem to find them in the mall."

As soon as he said that I was speechless. "What do you mean they are not in the mall? I thought they were supposed to be with you, Gloria! Why weren't they with you, Gloria?"

I couldn't stop myself. She lost my kids, what else am I supposed to do?

"I know, I know. They were inside of the magazine store while I was in the grocery store. When I went back they were gone. I found Candice's phone on the ground next to an *American Girl* magazine. I knew Candice wouldn't just leave her phone anywhere, so I looked around the store. I couldn't find them. I asked everyone in the store if they saw the girls, but they all said no. That is when I called the police. I am so sorry, please forgive me." Gloria pleaded.

I couldn't believe her. She lost my children and now she wants to cry and beg for our forgiveness.

"Um, sir, we didn't just look in the store. We looked in the whole mall knowing how young girls can be…" the officer trailed off.

I could not believe this. "Well that might be some girls, but never my girls! My girls would never leave a place without calling or telling one of us!"

"Sir, I know you're upset but…"

"Upset? Upset? You don't even know the half of it!"

"Ok sir, you need to calm down. Now if they don't come home by 8:00 A.M. tomorrow, then call us ASAP."

"Will do, officer."

CANDICE

We stopped at this house and the mysterious man pushed us inside. When we got inside, the house was colorful and had circus animals all around. Finally, the circus man told us that we needed to be in his circus. At first, we wondered why he just didn't hire people to be in his circus. He told us (more like yelled) that people in Michigan don't want to be in circuses, and if we didn't do what he said, something bad would happen. We didn't know what that bad thing would be, so we didn't take any chances.

It had been one year, two months and thirteen days since we had seen our family. Sometimes we thought that our family had given up on us. On July 7, 2011 we were on tour for the CIRC BABOON BALLOON performance and we saw a familiar looking lady, man, a little baby in the woman's arms, an older lady in her sixties and a little girl about two years old sitting in the front row. They looked like such a wonderful little family. We both thought that they were our family.

Then when we got on stage to do our act, I saw them more clearly in the light. The scent of the older lady's perfume smelled recognizable. The dad's cologne smelled like heaven, just how I remembered my dad smelling when he would go out on a business meeting or dinner. I knew for sure that they were my family now. Backstage, we kept questioning how we would escape. Then all of a sudden, Candace saw the trapeze bar, ran to it and swung out of the door. Mom followed her and hugged her.

Now it was my turn to escape. I didn't know how I would leave, but I had to figure it out soon. Just then, the elephant show began. As the elephants circled the ring, I knew I could ride out of the door on Bubba.

As soon as I got on her back, my kidnapper screamed, "No! Get those girls and her family!"

As soon as he yelled those words, the police came and arrested him. Then I got to leave on Bubba. My family was so happy to see us. We had a bonfire and a barbeque to celebrate us coming home.

The Gold Rush 2011

In **THE GOLD RUSH 2011** *by* **Ryan Hafen**, *four friends try to find a prize of gold under dangerous circumstances.*

"Darn it," said Bill when he found out he had gotten a word wrong on the newspaper crossword as he checked it on his porch. Once he finished checking the crossword, he scanned through the articles, hoping there was an interesting one.

One article caught his eye with the title "The Gold Rush." It was about a competition where people all across the town and maybe even some people from different states would come searching for a three-pound brick of gold that someone had hidden in a cave. Everybody wanted to have the prize for themselves. The prize was to keep the gold or to trade it in for thirty-five thousand dollars. He scanned quickly through the article trying to find key things to tell his friends, like where the cave is, who can participate, and when the competition starts.

Bill ran out to Joe, Bob, and Suzy (his best friends), who were playing at the park down the street.

He said, "Hey, guys, guess what! There is going to be a competition starting tomorrow. It is going to be in the cave right next to the creek that we would always play in when we were younger. The competition is to go digging for gold in the cave. To get in we need to pay $90 as a group. Do you guys want to do it?" They talked about it for a while.

Then Joe finally said, "Sure, we'll all do it."

"All right! See all of you tomorrow then," Bill said.

That night they all went to bed early so they would not be tired the next day.

The next day they all woke up, ate breakfast, and got dressed in clothes they didn't really care about. Then they met each other down by the creek near the caves they would be searching.

They were waiting in line for a while. When they finally got to the entrance of the cave Bill got the money out and handed it to the sponsor's assistant.

Then they walked into the main area of the cave, and Bill said, "Joe and I will take the first cave, and you and Suzy can take the last one." Then they took off with their flashlights, water bottles, kneepads, and shovels.

Bob took one side of the tunnel he and Suzy were in, and Suzy took the other side. Joe and Bill did the same. They would take a break every few hours so that they wouldn't get tired and dehydrated.

That day they had no luck and found no gold. Luckily nobody else had found it, either. They got the same thing that entire week. They were annoyed.

By week's end, they were about to quit when Joe was digging and saw a sparkle in the pile of rocks he had just dug out! They weren't sure if it was gold. They took it with them, and they all ran back to Bill's house. Bill snatched up the newspaper searching for the article. When he found it, he looked toward the bottom of the article for the contact information. Then he found it: "32795 Barley Street. Come here to claim your prize."

They all ran a few blocks down to that house.

When they got there, they were so excited they just ran into the house. They startled a man sitting at a desk, who they recognized from the article as the sponsor of the competition. He asked who they were. They said they were competitors in the competition in the newspaper. They showed him the newspaper and the mineral. He looked at it for a while, and then he finally told them the news. The news was bad. It was pyrite – fool's gold. Joe, Bill, Suzy, and Bob were frustrated.

Then the man gave them a clue. He told them that they were looking for a brick of gold, and that it had an imprint on it saying "Good Job! You have won the competition." They all walked slowly back to Bill's house. They all took a few days off from the competition to relax.

A couple of days later they started searching again because it sounded like more people were joining the competition. Then after lots of pyrite was found and a month or so later, Suzy was digging in the cave and saw something like Joe had found, but this one had an imprint on it that said, "Good job! You have won the competition." Before she could turn around or say anything, she got kidnapped by another competitor in the same cave who wanted the prize.

Bob didn't notice because he was too busy searching for the gold himself. A couple of minutes later Bob turned around and couldn't find Suzy, so he started calling her name. Then Joe and Bill heard Bob and ran to him. Just after Joe and Bill got there, they heard a loud, thundering noise. Big boulders were covering the exit of the cave! Bill, Joe, and Bob were all trapped with lots of other competitors, and Suzy was gone.

Bill, Joe, and Bob, with the help of other competitors, started digging their way through the boulders. It took days. It was a good thing they all had flashlights, food, and water. Once the opening was big enough for all of them to fit through, they climbed through the hole.

They suspected that it was one of the competitors who had kidnapped Suzy. So while all of the other competitors went home Joe, Bob, and Bill went to the sponsor and asked if someone had already won the prize. The sponsor said no one had come to him yet. He told them when someone came to him that it would be in the newspapers all over town.

A couple of days later, the newspaper came, and Bill ran outside to go read it. But this time he didn't go straight to the crossword. Instead he started ripping through the pages trying to find out if someone had claimed the prize, even though barely anybody dared to go back into that treacherous cave after hundreds people had been trapped in there. After scrambling through the newspaper, he couldn't find the article.

It had been weeks since the kidnapping, and Bill was furious. He decided to go back into the cave and wondered if Joe and Bob wanted to come along with him. Bob agreed to come along with Bill, but Joe refused. There was no way he was going back into that cave ever again.

That day they got all the tools that they needed to go digging in the cave again. Then they got as much sleep as they could. The next morning they woke up and got ready to go digging. Then they met by the cave. They got digging right away.

A couple of days passed by, and there was still no sign that anyone had found the gold. Then the sponsor called Joe's phone number that all of them had given to him in case he needed to call them. The sponsor sounded frightened! He had gotten a call from an unknown caller telling the sponsor to send him the thirty thousand dollars and in return he would send him the gold. He would only send him the girl if the sponsor had given him an additional fifteen thousand dollars. Right as Joe was about to call Bob he came zipping through the door with a tiny piece of gold in his fist.

At that point Joe called the sponsor back asking if there was anything that he could remember about the gold.

Then he responded saying "I put a tracking device on the gold." Then Joe asked if he could come over and they could track down the gold together. The sponsor said that they could.

Once they all got there they started tracking the gold and finally it led to Joe's house. They all went over there with the location of the tracking device set on a GPS and found the little speck of gold that Bob had found. They thought that it was over and that they would just have to pay the kidnapper money, so they decided to get the police involved.

A few days later the case wasn't solved, and then the GPS beeped. There was another tracking device on the gold. They let the police handle the rest, and Suzy was rescued. Suzy was awarded the gold for herself, but she decided to split it with all of them. Suzy was safe, and the gold was recovered.

The Hero of Bethlam

Never underestimate an 11-year-old boy. In the story **THE HERO OF BETHLAM** *by* **Ernest Allen**, *how far does young Spartamis go to save the king's daughter from the evil ninjas who kidnapped her?*

I was an 11-year-old boy named Spartamis in the sixth grade who had many talents. I could do many things like create movies on the computer, practice karate, and also sword fight. I took a class for these things, which I am really good at. I grew up in a country called Bethlam. It was named after the last name of the king and his daughter. My dad, who was a servant for the king and his daughter, Sophia, had worked 24 hours for them. I did not like the king or his daughter because they would always say mean things about my dad while he was working hard for his family late at night. I did not know why they despised my dad, but he always told me to not let people discourage me no matter what.

I had a thing for movies and the bad guys in them. I always dreamed of being a crime fighter to save the country just like my grandfather had done. It was fun to get taught how to use the sword of my grandfather. One day while we were training, my grandfather handed me a black box. I opened it to see what it was, and he told me it was his favorite sword he used in every battle. I thanked him for the sword and went to put it up. It was late, so my grandfather had to go home. I was hoping that he would be okay walking home by himself, but he wasn't.

He knew the ninjas had been following him the whole way home but didn't do anything. He knew he was going to be outnumbered by the ninjas, so he just stood there and let them take him away. We never heard from him after that incident. We soon found out that he had been kidnapped by the ninjas and killed. This was terrible. I was much crushed. I asked myself, *What would they want with him?* I wanted revenge on them badly.

One day while I was practicing with the sword my grandfather gave me, I heard a terrible scream in the palace. At first I thought, *Why should the king and his princess get help from me? After all, they despise me and I despise them too.* As I started to turn around and continue what I was doing I heard the king's voice saying, "Can anybody help me?" When I heard that, I ran to the palace as fast as I could.

It took a while to get into the palace because I had to go through lots of gates, which made it hard. The palace was very nice inside, and everything was solid gold.

When I entered the room of the princess, I saw the king on his knees, crying. I asked the king if he was okay, but he said, "Go away!" I waited for a second and then walked out. As I walked out the king said, "They kidnapped her."

I said, "Who kidnapped the princess?"

The king responded, "The ninjas and their master did."

I asked, "What did they want with the princess."

He said, "Ever since we went to war with them they've been trying to take away my most valuable things."

I asked, "What can I do?"

He said in demand, "You are going to go rescue her and bring her back to the palace safe without any wounds."

I said, "Why would you want to send me when you have an army?"

But he stopped me right there. He said, "If you want to see your family again, you will do it."

I said, "I will do it, but only for my family."

"Okay, then go get your things prepared and leave. I do not want you to return to this palace without her."

I ran out of the palace on my way home. I had to explain to my parents what I had to do. At first they weren't going to let me go until I lied to them, telling them that the king was going to give me an award. They went along with it, so I picked up my bag and headed out the door.

I walked for several hours, but I didn't arrive at the location of the ninjas. It was torture because I didn't have any food, water, or clothes.

As I was walking I stumbled upon a campground full of trash and ripped-up tents. It was very dirty there, but that didn't matter to me because I was on a mission to save the princess of Bethlam. I saw that no one was there, so I took some food, clothes, and water. I knew this was wrong of me, but I was starving.

As I was about to walk out, I ran into one of the people who lived there. He took out a gun and almost pulled the trigger until I told him I didn't have any food or anything. I also told him where I had to go, and when I did he offered me a ride to my destination to help me with my adventure.

On the way there I asked why the campground was all torn up and trashed. He answered, "My ancestors went to war with another group and they trashed the campground with all the bombs." I was so thankful for the ride he gave me that I gave him my best wishes in return. When we arrived there I got out of the camel carriage and said, "Thank you."

The stranger said, "Be careful" as he drove off.

I walked for about an hour and finally arrived at the ninja's palace. There were ninja bodyguards surrounding the palace. Luckily they had to go around the other side of the building. I looked around the corner of the building to see if they were out of sight, and looked around for an opening. A ladder was on the side of the building, so I climbed up. As I was walking around I stepped on a secret brick and fell through the roof of the palace.

When I got up I went looking for the princess and found nothing until I finally saw a door on the floor that led to the secret basement. I heard the princess screaming, which led me to her voice.

When I reached her, she started to kick and push until I took the rag off of her eyes. She was surprised to see me and asked what I was doing there, but instead of answering I told her we needed to get out of there before the ninjas came.

It was too late. The princess said, "Look!" and I saw a circle of ninjas around us.

I said, "Princess, stand back," and she did. I pulled out the sword my grandfather gave me and told them to bring it. Three of the ninjas came at a time. They kept trying to sneak up on me. While I was fighting one ninja, the other came. The princess kept telling me they were coming, though. The ninjas were climbing on walls, and it was hard to keep track of them. More ninjas started coming, and I was starting to get tired, but I didn't stop swinging my sword.

The battle lasted a long time, but after a while their master told them to stop coming at me. I didn't know where he was or why he stopped them, but I had to be aware of any trick he might play. All of the ninjas backed off except the head leader who was coming down the stairs as the rest backed up. I had to stay aware of the leader who came walking down the stairs. He came close and said to me, "You win."

I said, "I know you won't give up that easily," but he did. He dropped his sword and everything. He said the princess and I were free to go.

I stepped back slowly and told the princess to come on, but as soon as she got over to me he stabbed me through the chest with my back turned away.

The princess of Bethlam could not believe that her rescuer was stabbed. She was terrified that she would never leave this place. When she came to see if I was okay the ninja pushed her out of the way, not knowing the sword was in the direction he pushed her in. The ninja came up to me where I was bleeding to death and said, "Your time is up." He raised the sword behind his head, but as he was about to jab the sword in me for the final stab, the princess came out of nowhere and stabbed the ninja master. He dropped to his knees and died. The princess came over to me quickly, and I passed out.

When I woke up I was in the medical house where they had sand beds. I was all bandaged up. When I looked up I saw almost the whole city in my room bringing me thank-you baskets. I asked what was going on, and the king spoke and said, "This is a ceremony for the honor and bravery you showed to all of us."

I saw my dad by the side of my bed saying, "Good job." Everyone in the medical house was happy that the princess and I had returned. The king of Bethlam brought the princess in to say a few words.

The princess said, "Thank you for rescuing me, good brave one. For that we shall honor you with great wealth and riches. Thank you again. We are also sorry for despising you and your dad when you didn't do anything to us."

I said, "It's okay."

After all of this everything turned out for the best. I was honored as the hero of Bethlam. I brought great riches and wealth into our life. I also saved the princess, which is a big accomplishment, and it all turned out well. So after all of the chaos, everyone lived happily ever after.

Life or Death

When everything is on the line in **LIFE OR DEATH** *by* ***Mackenzie Stabile***, *everyone wants a chance to live. When two twins are fighting for their lives, every choice counts.*

Thump, thump, thump. My heart was racing, and my mind was soaring. All that matters is that Maya and I get out alive.... A close friend once told me when I said my life was ruined that life goes on, but life can't go on if you don't have a life to live. The day they came for us didn't compare to how I felt now.

It all started when there was a knock at the door. There was no screaming, yelling, or even a gunshot. There was just a knock. My mom went to answer the door, but before she opened it she checked who was there. Standing on the porch was a man completely concealed in a black cloak. Just looking at the manmade chills run down your spine, and when the cloak was blown by the wind it reminded me of a ripple forming on the kind of black, icy cold water you only see in nightmares.

Without warning our mom told us to get in the attic as fast as we could. At the moment we had no clue what was happening, but we were about to find out. Before she could hide anyone else the door was no longer attached to its hinges. Seconds passed feeling like hours before anyone spoke.

"Where are they!" the man in the black cloak bellowed.

"They're at a friend's house. They'll be back in the morning. You can come back in the morning. They have keys. They'll come in if our cars are in the driveway," our mom said.

"Fine, I'll be back, but if they're not here there are going to be consequences for all of you," he answered.

"I don't understand," our mom said.

"And what would that be?" he asked.

"Why not kill us? You only want the girls," she replied.

"Bait," he simply answered.

"Bait? What is that supposed to mean?" she said.

"Fools. If they find out something happened to you they'll come. They always do."

"Nicki, I'm scared," Maya whispered next to me.

"So am I, Maya. So am I," I replied.

He grabbed our brothers, dad, and mom. And then with screams from my little brother Max they were out of sight.

We didn't move for several minutes just to make sure they had left. When we were sure they were gone we climbed down and gathered our cellphones, blankets, food, money, and clothes. All we knew was that we couldn't come back.

I opened the front door, and we left, never turning back. We kept hoping that everyone was ok, but we knew that it was unlikely.

That night Maya and I slept at a neighborhood park. In the morning when I woke up I saw the same man in the black cloak walking through the street.

As I was ducking back under the shelter of the trees I saw him drop something. I waited until he disappeared behind a house before grabbing it. The piece of paper read:

> Take the family to the old licorice factory. Once the girls are dead get rid of the rest of the family.

"Maya!" I screamed.

"Nicki, what is it? What's wrong? Is he coming?" she asked me.

"I know where they are!" I replied.

"Where?" she eagerly asked.

"They're at the old licorice factory. Come on, let's go," I said.

"We can't," she said.

"What? What do you mean we can't?" I exclaimed.

"I mean exactly what I said. We can't, Nicki. He wants us to go. It's a trap," she whispered, clearly wanting to scream it at me.

"Maya, he knew we would come because it's what we have to do," I answered.

"All right," she replied.

And with that we were at the bus stop waiting for the next bus. When the bus let us off it was only a short distance away, and in a short time the factory was looming overhead.

Maya and I slowly crept up to the door. I went in first to make sure it was safe. We could hear voices echoing off the walls. We stopped at every door and listened. Finally we found the room we wanted and when we pressed our ears against the door a gunshot rang out. There was moaning, screaming, crying, and the feeling of sadness hung in the air. That second I understood what had just happened. Max was dead. We turned on our heels and sprinted away.

Maya screamed, but never stopped running. It wasn't a scream of terror. I could make out words: "Why are you doing this?" Then there was a laugh, eerie and terrible. It reminded me of nails scraping down a chalkboard.

"Don't you understand? You didn't find that piece of paper by accident. You were meant to find it on purpose! Someone wants you dead. I'm not supposed to tell you who, but since you're about to die, I really don't think it will matter. He hired me to kill you two. You see, he had a twin sister, but then he murdered her. His sister was a show-off. Well, actually he thinks all girls are show- offs, but back to the point. He wished she had never been born, so now he targets twin sisters. Well, honestly, he really only wants you two dead, but your family knows what happened, so I have to kill them, too," he answered.

We were too stunned to answer. Maya went right, and I went left. He was following me. That meant Maya had a chance to get the others and escape. But knowing Maya, she would never leave me, being the stubborn person she is.

I was cornered. My only option was going into a room, so I did. The room was white: the walls, floors, and even a small table with a small white box on it. I slowly walked toward it, and when I opened it there was a small hand mirror. I looked at it, but it was too late. He was behind me with a gun.

"He knew one of you would be forced to come in here. Also, you might want to know that your family is going to hear all of this," he said tauntingly.

I forced myself to keep the mirror steady in my hand. I couldn't look away. I wouldn't. I could not let him gain power over me. But inside fear was washing over my body like waves lapping against the sand on a beach, spreading like wildfire. I didn't want to listen to him anymore. It was too painful.

He pulled out a cellphone and dialed a number. Almost immediately a man on the other line answered. The man in the black cloak said, "I have her. Turn on the speaker." Just then a smile crept across his face as he flipped the phone closed.

I knew what was about to happen. Then he held the gun to my head and pulled the trigger. There was searing pain, and then there was nothing.

Nicki was dead. Maya had heard him pull the trigger because a loudspeaker had turned on. She had heard him walk up behind Nicki, load the gun, and pull the trigger.

Maya ran into a dimly lit room. She searched the floor for something, anything, to help save her. For a second a small spark of hope lit up her mind. At first she thought she was imagining it. There was a small bright patch of light on the ground. When she looked up there was a window with the curtains partially drawn. Perfect, she thought.

Sitting in the corner of the room was a small wooden chair. It was facing the corner like it would be when you get in trouble and have to sit in the corner. She ran at the chair knowing she didn't have much time left.

Maya grabbed the chair, but something fell to the floor as the chair flew into her arms. The object on the floor kept drawing her attention toward it, making her want to pick it up. She dropped the chair and reached for the object. In her mind she was screaming: Why did you drop the chair? Pick it up! Pick up the chair! Then she was suddenly aware of the object in her hands. Now Maya fully understood what the object was.

It was a hand-carved wooden doll, but at first it looked like it had chunks missing. Slowly, Maya realized that the chunks missing were actually names carved into it: Anna, Mary, Clarisse, Elizabeth, Sarah, Madeline, Nicki, and Maya. All the names had been familiar, and Maya knew why: they were all pairs of twins that had been found murdered.

She heard him walking in the hallway, looking for her and getting closer and closer. Through the window Maya saw her mother, father, and older brother break through the doors that led outside. They knew Max was dead, and either Nicki or Maya was dead and the other trying to escape. That moment Maya knew she had to get out. It was now or never.

She grabbed the chair, and she ran with all of the strength she had left. As the window and chair met, the glass shattered into a million shards. The footsteps grew louder and closer. Maya brushed away the pieces of glass that clung to the window frame. Maya lifted one leg out the window, and then tried the other, but she couldn't. The man was so close now, and she was almost out the window, but her shirt was stuck. Maya didn't even hear him come up behind her. She was too busy tugging at her shirt. The next second she was falling out the window. Maya was so happy. She thought that she had made it, but when she was halfway to the ground he shot her. The truth is he pushed her out the window.

The police never found the man who killed them, but remember: If you ever see a man concealed by a black cloak, run. And that is the story of Maya and Nicki.

Lost in Vegas

Jack expects to live it up in Vegas and have a good time. Most kids would expect that too, but in **LOST IN VEGAS**, *Nick Quenaudon makes a thrilling suspenseful story where things don't go quite as Jack had hoped.*

One cold, brisk, winter morning at home I was asleep, and then…

…*BEEP, BEEP, BEEP!*

"Oh, shut up, stupid alarm!" It was Christmas break, and my family and I were going to Las Vegas. I heard my mom shout for me to get up, but I just pulled the covers over my head and acted as if I had never heard her. I wanted to go, but I hated waking up so early the first day of vacation.

It took me about fifteen minutes to get out of bed. Then I pulled on some jeans and rummaged through a pile of dirty shirts trying to find a clean one. I pulled on my favorite shirt, which had a small stain. I looked into the mirror, and saw my blue eyes, and blond hair.

I staggered out of my room and crashed into my little blond-haired, blue-eyed, three-year-old brother, Andrew. I yelled at him and shoved him out of the way. He silently slipped past me.

As I walked downstairs for breakfast, I thought to myself "What if something happens to me while we are in Vegas?" I just moved that thought out of my head, and let it pass.

When I got downstairs, my green-eyed, brown-haired, teenage sister, Courtney, was at the table eating, so I decided to wait for breakfast. As soon as she left, I got some cereal. I brushed my teeth, and before we left, I grabbed my knife and threw it in my suitcase, just in case I might need it. Friends have told me that Vegas can be rough.

About thirty minutes later, we left for our plane. When we got to the airport, it was very close timing, so we just boarded the plane.

About four hours later, we landed in Vegas. We called a cab and went to our hotel to check in. My parents were going to see a show that night, and Courtney, Andrew, and I were staying and walking around Vegas. Luckily, Courtney would be in charge of Andrew. Mom had told us a million times to stay together at all times.

Our parents left around 8:00 P.M., but just before they left, they gave Courtney and me each thirty dollars! I was thrilled because they don't usually give us much money, but here in Vegas, we were living large.

We went out right after they did. I wandered off with Andrew following me. Courtney chased after us and grabbed Andrew, but I still kept going. I turned around and didn't see them, so I walked back, but could not find them. I walked to the park thinking they were there, but they weren't anywhere in sight! Oh no! I can't lose them, especially not here in Vegas.

I started to go back to the hotel, but I couldn't remember which one we were staying at. I kept trying to find them, and I thought I saw Courtney, so I chased after her, shouting for her to wait for me. When I caught up with her, I tapped her on the shoulder. She turned around, but it was just a wrinkled, old lady, who was smoking.

I was going to call my mom and ask which hotel it was. As I reached into my pocket, my phone wasn't there. "Oh darn, I left my phone back at the hotel!" I decided to just walk down The Strip and enjoy the moment, or at least try not to panic.

There was a club in front of me, so I popped in to have a look, because I thought my parents might be in there. But then I saw the sign which read "Strip Club," and I thought to myself, my parents would not go in there. I headed back out into the bright night of the Las Vegas Strip just as a bouncer came bounding toward me.

I saw a tall building that said Stratosphere Tower. I walked into an elevator, looked at the buttons for the floors and hit "Roof." About two minutes later I got off, and saw three amazing rides. One was a roller coaster, another, a bungee cord, and the last, a ride that brings you sixty feet over the edge of the building.

At a booth, people were selling tickets. I reached into my pocket and realized I had the thirty bucks my parents gave me. I walked over and asked for one ticket for Insanity, the ride that brings you over the edge. I got on and the ride started. Five minutes later, I got off. The ride was so scary and exhilarating. I wanted to go again, but I didn't have enough money. I left and went back to The Strip thinking about Courtney, Andrew, and how annoyed or angry my parents would be with me.

Just then I saw a dark silhouette in one of the alleyways. I turned and looked at it, but then I just kept on walking. I turned around once more and saw the silhouette coming closer toward me. I started to walk faster and noticed it, too, was now walking faster. I started sprinting and then… I tripped on a rock and hit my head.

Later I woke up in a strange, dark, large, musty-smelling, humid environment. The ceiling was really low, and it was hard to see, but I could make out the figure of a man talking on his phone. He was about 20 feet from me. I could not understand what he was saying. I wanted to try to make a run for it, but I realized I was tied up.

Then I thought of my knife! I struggled to wiggle my hand free, and finally I grabbed it. Good thing I took it out of my suitcase before we left the hotel!

I swiftly and quietly worked at cutting the ropes and eventually managed to get my hands free. My wrists hurt like sandpaper was being rubbed against them. He heard me, and turned to look at the chair. I hastily hid behind a pile of empty boxes. I saw him pick up a gun.

I thought back to my mixed martial arts classes. He started to look around, and I jumped out and stabbed him in the hand. He dropped his gun, and I grabbed it and pointed it at him. He slowly moved back still clutching his bloody hand. I told him to turn around and he did without questioning it. I ran up to him and smacked him in the back with the butt of the gun. He gave a quick shudder and dropped to the floor. I checked his pulse and he was still alive, but unconscious. I wished I didn't have to do that, but it was just self-defense. I wrapped his hand to stop the bleeding, and searched him for his phone. I found it and ran outside.

I looked at the street names and then dialed 911. A voice answered. "911, what's your emergency?"

"A stranger kidnapped me!"

"What streets are you on?"

"I'm at the intersection of Las Vegas Boulevard South and Las Vegas Boulevard West. I'm near a warehouse. Can someone please come help me?"

I gave the operator my name and hung up. I was just starting to dial my mom's number, when a police officer walked up to me. "Are you the boy who was kidnapped?"

"Yes, officer." I started to explain how I got separated from my sister, but he seemed to already know the whole story.

He asked me for my mother's cell phone number, and I gave it to him. He called her and told her that he had me and was bringing me back to the hotel. He asked her for the hotel name, and I heard her say, "The Mirage." If only I had remembered that before all this trouble.

He gave me a ride back to the hotel. I rushed upstairs and saw my mom, dad, brother, and sister waiting for me. I ran up to them and hugged them. It felt like I had been gone forever, but it had really only been four hours. I was so happy to see them again.

We went home a few days later, and boy, was I glad to be home. I ran upstairs, pulled off my shirt, jumped into bed, and pulled the covers over my head. Then I fell asleep until … *BEEP, BEEP, BEEP!*

"Oh, shut up, stupid alarm!"

Money Gets "Almost" Everything

Sean's life is finally right once he is free of his alcoholic father. But when his father's blood is put in his hands, everything changes. Killing his father was not on his agenda for a fresh start in the story **MONEY GETS "ALMOST" EVERYTHING**, *by* **Tim Brown**.

"Dad, I'm moving out!" exclaimed Sean in a vivid voice. "You messed up my life; first you make me work at a bait shop for my whole summer just so you can buy your whiskey and cigars. Second, you got the house foreclosed on by taking a loan and gambling it on the Colts when I told you a thousand times the Saints were going to win. We didn't even see the game. I had to ask my friends," said Sean, finally letting all of his rage burst from him.

"Son, I...," Sean's dad whispered in a raspy, scratchy voice.

"Don't call me your son," said Sean. It brought pleasure to his lips. He had always wanted to say those words. Sean had been looking at houses and apartments ever since his dad got drunk and got his mom killed in a car accident.

Stroking his beard and trying to hide his scar on his neck from the accident, Sean's dad managed a sentence through his quivering lips. "Fine, we'll see how long you can last without me," his dad said, reaching a cockier tone with each word.

Sean left without saying another word. He was simply overjoyed. He was too happy to see this place go. Sean couldn't wait to get out of this rat nest of a "stable foundation," as his dad put it. He had already rented a place in Nebraska with his secret stash of money he had made on the side as a pirated-DVD seller. He got in his car and left his deadbeat father to rot the rest of his life in homeless shelter.

When he finally got to his place in Nebraska, he loved it. It had a full kitchen, laundry room, and bathroom. Plus, the grocery store was a block away and the places he loved were practically next door: A motorcycle shop, a 7-11, and a Subway!

He was in his room watching who would go to the 2011 Super Bowl when a casino commercial came up. He was mesmerized by the money. If there was one thing Sean knew how to do, it was gamble. He had learned a lot from his dad: Do the opposite of what his dad says.

So he made his way to the casino. Most people were making bets on the Steelers, including someone very familiar: his dad! Sean avoided him and managed to make a bet for $100. Sean left the casino and headed back to his apartment. What was his dad doing here?

Sean decided to go to bed and think about things the next day.

Sean woke up to a burned foot and a ruined apartment. He could barely see his possessions and the money he was too dumb to keep in a bank through the burning rubble of what was supposed to be his fresh new start. All he owned was being consumed by a massive, hope-burning inferno of yellow flames, looking menacing as the flames licked the ceiling of his apartment.

His first response was to get out. He limped out his door to see ashes of the building as he was going down the stairs. He saw his father and the man who Sean had made the bet with, and a gun in the hands of the man he was pointing it at Sean's father.

"There ain't no way I'm paying the two million dollars you cheated me out of," said the man. Sean couldn't make out his features through the fierce flames.

"What two million dollars?" Sean said as a trickle of sweat ran down his head.

"The ones we bet. I'll give you one chance. You let me loose of the two million and I'll let your daddy go," said the man as if he were enjoying this.

There must have been a mix-up. Sean only bet $100. How could that be interpreted as TWO MILLION dollars? Sean didn't know what to do, his mind racing with the two choices in his head: Let him keep his two million dollars, or basically kill his father. Either way the man was most likely going to keep the money.

Sean couldn't take it anymore. He came to a decision. "Fine, keep the money. Just let him go," Sean exclaimed angrily. He didn't like anyone that does business this cruelly and humiliatingly.

"I'll let him go, but I never said nothing 'bout you." He gave Sean one last smirk and raised the gun. "*Adios, muchacho.*"

Stranger

STRANGER, *by **Kayla Cornett,** is a story of two girls locked in there basement with someone who they don't know. What will happen to the girls?*

" Amber, where are you?" shouted Leah. Leah heard a noise coming from the basement. Leah walked down the stairs to the basement.

When she got down the stairs, she saw a fast movement, kind of like a person running to the heater. Leah walked over to the heater. It was Amber hiding. Before she could say anything, there was a noise. The noise was coming from the stairs.

Leah walked over to the stairs to see who was there. When she got there, there was a person that had a mask on. The person said, "HELLO."

Leah screamed and ran back to Amber and said, "There's a person down in the basement and I don't think he's here to be nice." When Leah got her breath she pulled Amber's arm and ran to a better hiding please.

Leah explained more of what she saw to Amber. When Leah got done telling Amber what happened, Leah told Amber to run up the stairs and push and pull on the door on the count of three. "1, 2, AND 3!"

They both ran up the stairs, but found the stranger had locked the door so they couldn't get out. The stranger must have heard them hitting and pushing on the door because they heard a noise behind them. A voice said, "Turn around!" so the girls turned around.

There was the stranger. The girls looked at each other and knew what each other meant. They were going to run around the stranger and run in separate directions.

They ran past him. When Amber got to the bottom, she was off the hook because the stranger didn't see where Amber went. But when Leah got to the bottom, the stranger was behind her. Fortunately he was a little ways back, so she could find a hiding place before he got her.

Leah heard footsteps coming to her hiding place. She knew they weren't Amber's because they were hard footsteps. Leah turned around and saw the person turn the other way because there was a noise. He went in the direction of Amber.

Amber saw the stranger walk past her, and she heard other footsteps behind her. She knew they were Leah's.

When Leah got to Amber, she whispered a plan in Amber's ear. When Leah said, "GO," they both ran up the stairs and started banging on the door.

The stranger heard them. He ran up the stairs and said, "Turn around!" so the girls turned around again. They saw that he had a knife in his hand and was about to hit Leah with it. But Amber got another hit on the door, and the door fell down.

Amber pulled Leah out of the way. They both ran to their next-door neighbor's house and called 911.

When the cops got to their house, the stranger was in the two girls' bedroom. The last time the girls saw the stranger was when he got put in the cop car.

Good Sport

Baseball Season

The team from Rochester has a shot at going to the Little League World Series. That's where the fun begins in **BASEBALL SEASON** *by* ***John Kowalchuk.***

It was near the end of the season. We had a very good record. In fact, we had a perfect record of 40-0. We were at our last two games, and we were going to play teams that were 35-5 and 40-0, just like us.

We won the game against the team that was 35-5. Its name was the Michigan Red Sox. We played our last game and won against the 40-0 team called the Motor City Hit Dogs. We had won all of our games, but we had to be the best in Michigan, and the judges had to pick one team in Michigan. The judges said they would have the results next week Monday on Channel 11 at six o'clock P.M.

It was the next week, and my family and I were watching and waiting to see the results to see which team would make it the Little League World Series. First the newscaster announced the teams from America. They named the teams from the West, East, South, and then North. What we were waiting for was the Mid-West.

"The team for the Mid-West is the Rochester Recruits."

At that moment everyone in my family was going crazy, saying, "We're going to the Little League World Series!" We started packing our bags to go to New York.

The plane ride was fun. When we got there we went to our hotel and unpacked all of our items.

Our team went to go see the fields we would be playing on the next day at four o'clock P.M. When we got to the field we were amazed at how nice they were. There were so many things to buy there. There were hot dogs, souvenirs, uniforms, and hats. They had everything a professional park would have.

We went back to the hotel. We all played around in the pool. After that, we all went to bed to get ready for our game.

The next day when I got up, I put on my uniform to go to practice before the game. When I got my uniform on I told my parents and sister to get up so we could go. The park was only one mile away, but we drove instead of walked to keep my energy.

When we got there we were almost ready to start. At practice we did hitting, infielding, outfielding, catching, and pitching. We did not want to practice too long so we would not be tired for the game. Before the game I was warming up and going over the signs with the catcher in the bullpen getting ready to pitch in the game. I told the catcher Ryan that I was ready, and then I ran out of the bullpen to the pitching mound. After a few minutes the umpire said, "Play ball!"

The first inning I pitched I struck out the side on nine pitches. I pitched four innings without a run. When I was done pitching the other team got two runs off our other pitcher Benny.

We had Chase on third base in the very last inning of the game. He stole home on a wild pitch, and we won the game.

The next team we played was 7-0 just like us. In the fourth inning it was 6 to5; they were winning. We had Andrew on second, and I hit the ball. I watched it go over the fence. We won on a walk-off homerun by the score of 7 to 6.

We went back home and had a huge party celebrating our perfect season and perfect Little League World Series win. Then the coach said, "Let's do this again next year."

We all said, "Bye! See you next season!"

Basketball

A young boy finds his hopes and dreams in an epic story, **BASKETBALL**, *by* **Louis Forman**. *Will his team win the biggest game of the season?*

"He shoots; he scores! The Raptors are going to the finals!" said the announcer with enthusiasm. Then the team yelled as one, "WE'RE GOING TO THE FINALS!"

That night they had a huge party at Mike's house. The team had a party at his house because Mike's dad is the coach. "Hey, Mike, your old man didn't do too bad this time," John said to Mike. The more people came, the less food there was.

The next day the team went to practice. On the way to the court John said, "I don't feel so good from all that food I ate last night." After that they made teams. The first team was John, Billy, Mike and Dave. On the other team it was Brice, Collin, Joe and Jack.

When the game started, John's team had the ball first. That's when Brice ran up as fast as he could into John and they both fell to the ground. John was hurt. First there was a moment of silence, and then everybody looked at Brice, and then at John. Billy and Mike carried John home, and from there Billy walked home alone.

When he got home his mom said, "Hi, honey. How was practice?"

"Bad because John got hurt and can't play in the game this Saturday," said Billy.

"What else is bad is your grade in math. You went from an A- to a C+," said Mom with disappointment.

"Mrs.Prasario said she will bring my grade up to an A- if I do well on my test Tuesday," Billy said like a three-year-old kid.

"Well, go study then," said Mom.

Billy studied all night and the night after until the test day.

On the test day he woke up early to eat breakfast and get ready for school. On the car ride there he studied, and that's all he did until his mom got him there. At fourth hour (his math class) he studied for his test until his teacher said "Class, clear your desks. It's time to take the test." She went around the room passing tests out to kids, and when she got to Billy she handed him his test and said, "Good luck."

On Thursday the class got their tests back, and Billy was in shock because he was so scared. The teacher went around the room one last time to give the tests back. When she got to Billy he was scared but happy at the same time. His test said A+ with a smiley face and words that said "Nice job."

Now that it's Friday, Billy has one day to practice and find a way to adjust to the whole John situation. He made a plan called "The Plan That Might Work." He biked up to Mike's house and explained it to Mike. He went back home and went right to bed to wake up in the morning.

When everyone got to the gym they started, and Raptors got the ball first. At about the end of the fourth quarter the score was 98-97 with the Raptors down by one. There were five seconds left, and they needed to score or they would lose. So Billy decided to do the play. He looked at Mike and nodded, indicating that it was time to do the play.

Billy passed the ball to Mike, and ran up to the rim. Then Mike passed the ball to him and Billy jumped to the rim and slammed the ball through it. "The Raptors win the finals!" said the announcer.

They won the finals as a team, and not as a one–person job.

It's On!

A soccer team has a chance at an undefeated season, but the team has to play against one that is also undefeated. Will they beat them and finally have an undefeated season? Find out in **IT'S ON!**, *by **Nellie Chalem**.*

We had five minutes to get to the soccer field so there was no time to spare. We were playing an undefeated team and we knew that we could beat them. I know we have a chance! Paige agrees that we are good team and reminds us that we just need some confidence.

We just arrived at the soccer field and we knew we were ready. We were five minutes from the kickoff. I was starting at center, Cappy was right, and Paige would play the center next.

Beep! The whistle blew and I ran up and kicked the ball. Cappy got it so she ran toward the net. She shoots and scores! Everyone went crazy. The score was 1-0. We were winning!

Now it was the other team's kickoff and almost the second half. *Beep!* They kicked the ball. I got it and dribbled up the field, passed it to Lindsay, and she passed it back to me. I took a shot in the left corner of the net and scored. Now the score was 2-0. We were still winning and thirty seconds from the second half.

Beep! It was halftime and we ran off the field with confidence. We knew that we were going to win and have an undefeated season!

It was the second half and Paige took the kickoff. She passed it up to Jenna, dribbled up the field, and passed back to me. I gave it back to Jenna; she took a shot and scored. Everyone went wild! We never thought we would get this far and it was even more exciting to be undefeated. The score was 3-0. We were still winning!

It was the other team's kickoff. They kicked the ball up field. Sarah stopped it and kicked the ball up to Cappy. She kicked it to Jenna who shot the ball but missed. Paige got it back and scored. We couldn't believe the score was 4-0 and we were winning by four points.

Beep! The whistle blew and the game ended. The final score was 4-0. We were finally undefeated!

A Normal Day in the Park... That Is, the SKATEPARK!

When a group of skateboarders from California have to build a super skate park, they get right to work and get the job done in **A NORMAL DAY IN THE PARK... THAT IS, THE SKATEPARK!** *by* ***Jonah Kamoo.*** *They learn a valuable lesson about skateboarding and their community that affects their career for the rest of their lives.*

It was a normal, beautiful day in Sacramento, California. In the city, there was a local skateboard team called Element. It consisted of five team members: Levi, Ryan, Tony, Correy and Matt. Levi was the manager of the team, or the captain in other words.

"Come on," said Tony. "I can never get that nose blunt to 180 out down pat."

"Dude, it's like one of the easiest tricks in the book," said Correy.

"Well, it's not always easy for someone who does vert more than street," said Tony. "And besides, you do street, so don't be laughing when I can't land a nose blunt. I'll be crying from LAUGHTER when you DIE attempting a 900."

"Fine, we're even," said Correy.

"Good," said Tony. They shook hands on it.

"Hey, guys, Levi's about to five-o the staircase," said Matt. "Come on over."

The two ran over to the others. Since Levi was the team captain, he usually did all the hard tricks and showed off a lot to the other crew members. The whole crew was in front of an entrance of a building. They were doing tricks on the staircase that led to the building. Levi was about to try a trick that nobody in the crew had tried that day.

"Okay, Levi, you can do this," said Ryan. "Just keep your balance and let your skateboard slide all the way down the rail." As Ryan was talking to Levi, a man came out from the streets and started to walk by the crew. The crew did not notice the man because they were too busy giving Levi advice for his trick attempt.

"All right, guys, I got this," said Levi.

The whole crew was watching and waiting for him. Levi attempted the trick but fell and stumbled onto the shoe of the man who was walking by. After he recovered, Levi looked up and saw a grin on the man's face.

"Hello," said the man to Levi. "Are you all right?"

"Yes," said Levi.

The man helped Levi up. "Oh, well, thank god. My name is Chad. Do you skate for Element?"

"Yes, yes I do," said Levi.

"Well, that's just what I needed to hear to brighten up my day. I work for Baker Skateboards. I am the lead designer of all the decks that Baker has been making lately. Do you know them by any chance?"

"Yeah, you guys have a great team. It's a pleasure to meet the guy who makes all of Baker's decks. I'm Levi. Nice to meet you." They shook hands.

"I was wondering," said Chad, "I was assigned to film a new movie called *Riding Again* for my manager. Shooting is going really well so far except that I'm kind of short on people for the street part of the flick, and I was wondering if you and your crew could maybe help me put that part together? I was thinking that you and your crew could build a skate park and then film you skating in it. You wouldn't need anything except you and your friends. I would arrange to get all the money needed to buy the supplies, and I will also arrange to hire workers to help you build it in less than two months! After everything is built and you have the film, you will return it to me in exchange for quite a bit of money from Baker Skateboards. You will also be invited to the after-glow for the movie and anything else that is related to it. Everyone will be happy in the end. Are you in?"

"Um...let me ask my crew. That sounds like a great idea to me, but I don't know what the other's opinions will be. You know, why don't you just come over and I'll introduce you to them. We'll talk it over."

"Sounds great," said Chad. They walked back up the flight of stairs.

"Hey, man, are you okay?" said Ryan.

"Yeah, I'm fine," said Levi.

"Who's your new friend?" said Tony.

"Guys, I'd like you to meet Chad. He's the manager of Baker," said Levi.

"Nice to meet you guys," said Chad.

"Chad wants us to be in a part of his new movie, and was wondering if we were interested," said Levi.

Ryan replied, "Yeah, that sounds cool. What about you guys?" The whole group talked and agreed on a contract.

Chad said, "Let's meet so we can sign the papers and clarify."

"That's sounds great," said Levi. They all decided to meet up on Saturday.

Saturday came quicker for the crew than they had expected. They all met up at Chad's office to review the papers and sign the contract. The contract said they had to make the skate park out of the materials that they would buy with the money they would receive from Baker. They would then work with professional workers and build the park in a certain amount of time. By doing this, they could make the skate park popular by having an autograph session and spreading the word about how good the new movie is. They all shook hands on it and clarified for sure about everything.

The next day, they got straight to work on buying the materials they needed. They went to professional wood shops and stores and talked with specialists about what materials were the best to build the unique skate park. When the crew had bought all the materials needed to create the park, they went to the site where Baker told them to build the park and dropped off all the materials in a small warehouse. They then met up with the workers that Baker hired, and they built the enormous park in a short amount of time. After a lot of *very* hard work, the crew and the workers had built a park that would probably be in the hall of skateboards *right* when it would have its grand skate opening.

The crew members were very proud of themselves. They had built a quality skate park so that now people and kids would not be chased off of property for skateboarding in places that they were not supposed to. They had built a single hangout that made both skateboarders and landowners that need their space very happy. They all worked together and got the job done well. In approximately two months after the contract was signed, they had built the *enormous* park. The park contained ramps, rails, bowls, fly boxes, staircases, mini-ramps, wall rides and quarter pipes. It was a very high-quality park. The crew was now ready to skate in the contest to complete the contract's rules.

The big day finally came when the park opened and the first contest aired. Hundreds of people had come to see the park all the critics were talking about. At the time, they had not thought of a name for the skate park. That had planned to name it after the contest was over.

It was an exciting, but nerve-racking day for the crew. They were all prepared for this day after working *very* hard for many months. They hoped that they would skate well that day.

Luckily, that exact day, the crew skated the best they had in a long time. They did five-o's, nose-blunts, dark slides, pressure flips, kick flips, tre-flips and much, much more. Overall, the crew won first place in both the vert and street competitions.

The following week, the crew met up with Chad and gave him what he needed. Chad was impressed at what they had done and he gave them 200,000 dollars in return. He also gave them the skate park to keep, just to be nice. Chad and Element were both very happy and hoped to see each other again soon.

EPILOGUE: *One Month Later*

The crew named the skate park *Riding Again* after Chad's movie. The skate park was very popular from that point on and was named the number one skate park in Sacramento by critics. Chad's movie did very well in the market, and the Element and Baker crew became big "movie stars." Both Chad and the team were very successful after that point in skateboarding for the rest of their lives.

Soccer Madness

Never stop trying, and always believe in yourself. One girl could never imagine that trying out for soccer would be this hard in **SOCCER MADNESS,** *by* ***Allison Lammers.***

I grasped the envelope tightly as I walked down the driveway about to put it in my mailbox. It was an application for a worldwide soccer team, and this was just for conditioning.

I really wanted to make the team. I would be able to meet, interact with, and befriend girls from all around the world. I also love soccer; it is my passion. Every time I am in a game running for the ball, or fighting for it from another girl I feel empowered.

A week later the mail came, and I practically ripped it out of my mom's hands. I tore open the envelope that said whether I qualified for the conditioning process, and guess what? I did! Relief washed over me, and I felt like I didn't have to worry about anything. Little did I know the experience ahead was going to be physically draining and strenuous.

The next day would be conditioning for the first time, and I was really nervous. Even though this wasn't the tryouts, this was the first time the coaches got to see how well you played. I would call myself a decent player. I wasn't great, but I wasn't horrible either. I had only been playing for a year or so.

The next day right after school, I got on all my soccer gear, and instantly I felt a lot more confident.

"Sammy, it's time to go," my mom yelled from downstairs.

"I'm coming," I yelled back as I pulled on my second sock. I filled up my water bottle and jumped in the car.

In the blink of an eye I was at the soccer field. There were tons of girls there, and I couldn't even begin to count. The coach sat us down and told us what we would be doing for the next couple of months. We would be doing all different kinds of drills: passing, shooting, stealing the ball, and much more. It sounded like a lot of fun, and I couldn't stop bouncing because I was so ecstatic.

We started passing and dribbling up the field. To tell you the truth, it was really easy, and I wasn't worried at all anymore. I had already met three friends; their names were Emily, Sara, and Chrissy.

"So where are all of you girls from?" I asked.

"We are both from here," Emily and Chrissy said at the same time.

"I am from Australia, mate," Sara said. All three of us loved the accent and giggled every time she said "mate." Trust me, she said it a lot.

Just when we had started to talk, Coach Barry decided to pick up the pace a little bit. We ran up and down the field for what felt like hours. Then we did pushups, sit ups, and suicides; they aren't called that for nothing. I was completely exhausted. When we finally finished, sweat dripped down my face, and my muscles ached. I wanted to go home and fall asleep. Unfortunately I couldn't do that because I had math, science, and social studies homework.

When I got home I went straight to work. While I was doing my math I fell asleep, and I woke up three and a half hours later. I was so mad that my mom hadn't awakened me. She claimed she thought I was working. It was already ten thirty, and I had barely finished my math.

I worked for as long as it took me to finish up. I finished at twelve in the morning, and right after I wrote the last word I collapsed on my bed.

I woke up in the morning, and I couldn't stand because I was so tired. I practically fell asleep in all my classes. Then it happened again. I had to go back to conditioning and do the same stuff all over again. This went on for the next two months, but I refused to quit. I would finish what I started.

In my classes I felt mentally exhausted, like I couldn't think straight. Soon enough my grades started to drop, my A's went to B's, and my B's went to C's. My parents started getting on me about my grades slipping, and I would just tell them I was trying my best. I was eating, sleeping, and breathing soccer.

My days all went like this: wake up, go to school, and go to soccer for an hour and a half. Then I would wake up the next day and do the same thing all over again. I felt like a zombie because I was completely stressed out and tired. My friends got mad because they told me all I ever cared about these days was soccer.

Finally conditioning was over, and we had tryouts for the next couple of days. No worries, though, because tryouts were nothing compared to conditioning. Then the day came, and Coach Barry handed out envelopes that said whether we made the team or not.

I opened up mine and held my breath. My face felt hot, and my eyes swelled up with tears. I didn't make the team.

I just sat down on the grass and looked around; I saw sad and happy faces. A tear rolled down my cheek. I had done all this hard work for nothing? I went home that night feeling crushed.

A couple of days later I had gotten over it. Even though I was disappointed in not making the team, I wasn't disappointed in myself. I think I would try out again next year. Even though getting my grades up and my friends back felt good, so did soccer. I would never lose that feeling of wanting to be there on the field with my teammates.

Swish!

When the Bulldogs make it to the basketball championships, and their top scorer is under a heap of pressure, what will they do? Find out if they win the championship in **SWISH!**, *by **Faraz Ahmed**.*

"The Bulldogs shoot the three with two seconds left and make it! They are going to the championship! I can't believe it!" yelled the announcer.

"Nice job!" the team said to me.

"Excellent performance, Zachary," said Coach Smith.

It was fun making all those shots, but my team always wants me to take the shots. When I don't take shots, my team gets mad at me and adds a lot of pressure. I changed my clothes and met my parents by the gym door.

"Good job, Zachary!" said my mom.

"I loved that last shot where you turned around and shot the three right as the buzzer rang," said my dad.

"Thanks," I replied.

My dad kept on going on and on about how we are going to the championship and how good my team was and about the championship trophy.

When I got home, I went straight to my bedroom because I was so tired. I better get a goodnight's sleep for tomorrow.

The next day, I went to the gym just to shoot baskets and my coach happened to be there too. "Maybe I should go and tell the coach how I feel," I thought. I walked over to my coach.

"Good morning!" said the coach.

"Hello," I said. "Umm, the whole team practices together and you probably know who shoots well."

"Yes, what are you getting at?" he asked.

"Well, why don't we let other people shoot the ball?" I continued.

"That's a good question," the coach replied. "It is probably because no one else is confident enough to shoot."

"I actually was hoping you can talk to the team since we are going to practice before we start the game, right?" I said.

"Yes, we are and I most certainly will," said the coach.

"Thank you," I replied.

RRRIIIINNNNGG! School was finally over! I headed toward the locker room.

"Okay, guys! Let's win this and get that trophy. In all of the teams I have coached, we have never been able to win, but let's try our best!" encouraged the coach. "Also, when we start the game each of you should take at least three shots, okay? We can't only have one main shooter. You all need to step up!" encouraged Coach Smith.

"Yes sir!" the team yelled.

"Let's go warm up!" demanded Coach.

It's the second quarter and so far almost everyone has made three shots and we have a decent lead by six.

"Timeout!" called Coach Smith, "Okay everyone huddle up, we are doing great so far, tighten up the defense and they won't be able to do anything."

"ONE, TWO, THREE, BULLDOGS!" We all ran out and started playing again.

It's the third quarter and we are up by only one. Jake has stepped up with eighteen points, five steals, and three blocks.

"Will the Dragons take the lead?" said the announcer. "They make the point now are up by one point!"

By the fourth quarter and were down by five points; 98-103. I got the ball and shot the three and swished it! Now we need another three-pointer to win this game.

Coach called our last timeout, "Let's bring it home!"

I stole the ball and passed it to Jake and he passed it back to me. I had a few seconds left so why not let someone else shoot? I passed the ball back to Jake. He looked confused and looked at the clock and saw that he only had three seconds. He shot the ball, eyes closed, and it had bounced in! He made the three-point shot!

"Wow! That was an amazing shot! The bulldogs showed no mercy," said the announcer.

We won the game by one point! My team and the coach were in high spirits. The coach held up the trophy and the entire team was surrounding him and the whole crowd was cheering for us. I changed my clothes and my parents ran over when they saw me.

My dad chanted along with everyone else, *"Bulldogs! Bulldogs!"* My parents were so proud of me. I went home relieved in knowing that we won the championships and we got the trophy. I felt that I made the right choice by giving Jake the ball. I went to sleep thinking that next season our team was going to be a more confident and even better! In my sleep the chanting went on, *"Bulldogs! Bulldogs! Bulldogs!"* That was the best basketball game!

Intruder Alert

The Amazing Time Travelling Xbox 360

Richard is sucked back in time to help an American Indian Tribe from 1827. He has a plan to get back, but trouble shows up and ruins his plan. Can Richard help the tribe and get back in time? Find out in **THE AMAZING TIME TRAVELLING XBOX 360** *by* **Colin Jones.**

On a warm and, humid day, Richard was playing his new Xbox360. Out of the corner of his eye, he saw three of the indicator lights on the Xbox 360 go from green to red. Then all of a sudden the TV went white.

"Mom the TV went blank, again!" exclaimed Richard. There was no answer, as his mom had already left to go to work. "I know why it's not working," said Richard. "It's because that family who always has garage sales ripped me off again."

Richard bought the Xbox 360 from a family that lived down the street who was in the process of moving. So he thought he might help them out, although he knew they had some pretty crazy stuff like poison arrows and a collection of Indian Chief's teeth. While he was thinking about what could be wrong with the TV he heard someone talking, Richard was stunned to see it was the Xbox 360 that was talking.

"Thank you for entering the Xbox 360 time machine. We will make you travel through time forwards, backwards and to the sides," said the Xbox 360.

Richard was drawn inside the TV. As he was rushing through time, he saw colors and pictures of the past and future combined. He heard bullets and paintball guns. Then Richard heard, "Help, help!" He wondered who or what was calling for help. Finally, he stopped traveling through time and discovered he was in the mountains. He didn't know where he was in time, but had a feeling it wasn`t present 2011 anymore. Richard saw no roads, factories, cars, trains or airports in sight.

"Help, Help! I'm lost!" hollered Richard.

Nobody responded, so he started to walk. After what seemed like hours, he saw a town. It looked like a Native American town because it had fifteen teepees and a big town center. He also saw a bunch of campfires and many people dressed as Indians. He continued walking and when he was about to get to the town, he saw his Xbox 360 on the ground. It was sitting there a little banged up, but not seriously damaged. He picked it up and continued walking. When he reached the town an Indian Chief greeted him with water and food. As Richard was eating, he asked what year it was.

The Chief replied, "This is the year 1827 and you are welcome to stay with us."

All of a sudden, Richard heard a deep breath and then a little sob that went, "Boo woo boo woo" coming from one of the tents. A man with a runny nose and tears streaming down his nose walked in the tent.

He said, "My name is Jerry and I am the medicine man. I have dreams that tell me what will happen in the future. One of these dreams involved a boy that looks just like you." Jerry began to describe the dream to the Chief and Richard. "It started off with some of the people from our village getting captured by the Englishmen. Eventually, we were all captured and forced to be slaves for them. So we were sold and beaten for days. Richard also appeared in the dream. He snuck into where we were being held captive and cut all of us free and helped us to escape. But that still didn`t stop them, so we had to learn how to protect the people of the tribe because Richard had to go. We did and then we were free for the rest of our lives."

The chief said, "We have been afraid that only one part of Jerry's dream would come true. The Englishmen are already here and have taken several of our people. One of them escaped and told us they tortured him. Then he said that they will come one day. Now it appears that all of the dream will take place. Will you please stay and help us get them back?"

Richard thought about it for a few minutes. Finally, he answered the Chief, "I will help you get your people back if you will help me get back home. I arrived here through my Xbox360 and I was in the time 2011."

It was getting late so they decided to go to bed when all of a sudden they heard someone yell for help. Richard, Jerry and the

Chief ran out of the teepee and saw Englishmen all over the town. The Englishmen were capturing the Indians and putting them in wagons to take them away. One of them yelled," You will never become a bigger town than ours now!"

Then the Chief yelled to Richard, "Run north to find the Englishmen's town. We need you to save us all."

Richard ran out of the town. Once he was a ways away from the village, he began walking north, taking care to stay out of sight so he would not be captured. After he had been walking for most of the night, Richard spied the Englishmen's town in the distance. He snuck into the town, taking great care not to be seen, and hid in a shed. Richard decided to stay hidden until it was dark when most people would be asleep. Then, he would find where the people from the Indian village were being held.

Once it was dark and the town had quieted down, Richard scouted the town looking for the wagons that held the villagers. He found them by a large building that was locked. There was a guard stationed outside the door. Hanging from the guard's belt was a key that would open the door. Richard looked around for a big stone that he could throw. He found one and waited until the guard was not looking and threw it at his head. Luckily, Richard's aim was good and the guard was knocked unconscious. Richard carefully took the key off the guard's belt and unlocked the door. He stepped inside.

Richard said to the Chief, "You should leave in groups of five so that the Englishmen don't see you all leaving at the same time." Richard started cutting the rope that was around all of their wrists. Silently, the villagers started leaving in small groups. Each group carefully made their way through the town without raising the alarm. Outside of the town, all of the groups gathered together. They carefully made their way back to the village.

Once they had made it home, the Chief said, "Thank you Richard for saving our people. We will have a big feast to celebrate."

The next day the feast was enjoyed by Richard and all of the villagers. After the feast, Richard and Jerry got together to talk about how they would get Richard back home. They knew they would need to make a power source so that the Xbox 360 would work. They decided to build a windmill. Many of the villagers helped

Richard to make the windmill by gathering the wood needed to make the frame and by providing hides that would be used to make the blades.

In a week, the windmill was complete and Richard was ready to see if it would work to charge the Xbox 360. He hooked it up to the windmill and saw three of the four lights on the indicator glow red.

"Thank you for entering the Xbox 360 time machine. We will make you travel through time forwards, backwards and to the sides." said the Xbox 360.

Richard was suddenly pushed forward and sucked into the Xbox. This time when he travelled though time he heard nothing. All of a sudden, Richard saw a blank white screen of a TV coming towards him and he shut his eyes. When he opened them, he was in the same spot in his room when he left. Then he heard footsteps in the hall heading for his room. His mom opened the door and saw Richard on the floor in front of the TV.

His mom said, "Richard, why are you on the floor? I told you not to play on the Xbox 360 all day long!"

Richard replied, "I have an amazing story that you will never believe. I will tell you at dinner. You won`t believe me at all, Mom."

His mom exploded saying, "You are grounded for a whole two weeks and try this again and I'll make it a month!"

American Angels

*In **AMERICAN ANGELS** by **Lamar Dimitry**, France has established a new law and Britain doesn't agree. They call out the American Angels, a task force to assist in the retaliation of the dead Prime Minister of Britain. Mackov and his brother Chankov are leaders of this squad. Will they find who issued the assassination?*

It is Monday, October 31, 2242. Many things have changed. One thing that has changed is France. The government has instituted a new law for their country. In France, starting 2243 January 19, it will be legal to buy, sell, and own slaves. The British were trying to stop them and doing everything they could. France didn't want another country telling them what to do. The French had attacked the British, and the British would have to retaliate. The French had threatened the Prime Minister of Great Britain over this law.

The Prime Minister was shot by a troop of French soldiers disobeying the President of France, but illegally obeying the French General…

Detroit Metropolitan Airport: Hangar 56, Detroit, Michigan

At a private military company (PMC) named Task Force of America; (TFA) Mackov is the lead pilot in the TFA Air Force along with his squadron Sidney, Parrish, Chankov (Mackov's brother), Albert, Jerrome, Vandall, and Juan. Their squadron's name is Double A, for American Angels. This squadron is on a mission, a mission to help the good, not the bad. They are assigned the contract of assisting the British in their war against France's slavery laws, and the retaliation of the dead leader of their country.

After leaving Detroit, the men jump on an aircraft carrier from the US to Great Britain. They are three quarters of the way to France to help the British when they encounter a problem. The French wouldn't want an attacking aircraft carrier anywhere near them, so they send out a squadron of fighter jets. The aircraft carrier wasn't ready, they hadn't even known about the enemy fighter jets until they saw them. Their defense networks were down. Their fighter pilots were nowhere to be found. Even the captain of the carrier was out of sight. Soon enough, the TFA fighter jets appeared on the carrier and were ready to take off!

"All right, are you guys ready?" asked Chankov.

"As ready as I've ever been captain!" shouted Jerrome.

"I'm good to go!" confirmed Parrish.

There were many enemy fighter jets, maybe too many. If the AA squadron didn't get there in time, many things could go wrong. Since there were so many of them they could sink the carrier, and its fleet. There was a big chance that the AA fighter pilots wouldn't come home that day, and there were hundreds of enemy aircrafts out there. They wanted to take the chance. They knew they could do it even though one of them had a little problem. The second they looked up it was like a sea of deadly metal. Finally, everyone rid their fears of getting hurt and went to defend themselves.

"It's a fifty-fifty chance, guys," announced Mackov.

"More like a hundred-zero for me, guys," shouted Chankov.

"Yeah, but there's a hundred percent chance you don't get there in time," Jerrome laughed.

They had seen many enemies trying to shoot them down.

"Enemy fighter jets closing in fast, watch out!" screamed Mackov. Then one of the enemy fighter jets shot a missile at one of the squadron pilots.

"Pilot Mackov, someone's fired a missile! Drop throttle and brake. EVADE, EVADE!" yelled the aircraft carrier GPS manager. Mackov tried to get loose of the missile, but he hit the water while doing that.

"Pilot Mackov is down! I need an immediate search and rescue! Now!" roared Chankov. Soon enough, the mad flight leader finished off the French fighter jets by himself.

As they started to land, Pilot Vandall fired a missile at Chankov. "Take this!" Vandal screamed. "The TFA can't pay me as much as the French do. *Au revoir, Monsieur* Sucker!"

"I've had a bad day kid. I always knew you were bad, kid, but not this bad," Chankov replied. They had landed and the flight leader went straight to his cabin in the aircraft carrier, and he didn't say a word.

The group went to Parrish's cabin on the ship to talk without Chankov, of course.

"Guys, do you really think that Vandall actually shut down our defense networks and tried to sabotage us?" Parrish wondered.

"Well, it's obvious he tried to!" Sidney argued. "He intentionally tried to shoot down Chankov. Doesn't that tell you something?" Sidney continued.

"Yeah maybe he did, but he was my friend Sidney!" Parrish exclaimed.

"Oh yeah? Well, he's not your friend anymore," Sidney said as she left along with the others.

The next day they had to search the air for any aircrafts invisible to radar. That day AA went out to help, including Chankov. Chankov had refused to go home. After Chankov took off, he saw a flare. The flare was light pink, a unique color, which would show that it was a flare from a TFA member that had been lost. No other members had been lost in that area, other than Chankov's brother. The flight leader knew it was his brother. He went back to the ship and on to a boat and soon enough he saw the flare again.

"It's him, I know it!" affirmed Chankov. Chankov saw him and two guards ready to shoot him. The TFA members heard a gunshot, but not from the French. It was from Chankov, to save his brother.

Chankov and his brother were safe and ready to help the British. The aircraft carrier and its fleet headed straight to France to retaliate the death of the prime minister of England. Now the TFA had gone to France and they were going to provide air support for the British invaders.

As soon as they got to their boat, the AA squad was sent out on a mission to provide air support for the British army. They had taken off as usual and flew to Paris in search of the French army general. They started looking at different bases around France until they found him at a base in Rodez. They called ground troops to look at it, and after a small amount of gunfire, where no one had gotten hurt, they found the French general!

"Finally, we found him," Chankov happily said.

"Yeah, now let's go home brother," Mackov cheerfully added.

The British army had now found the general of the French army and took him to England to be prosecuted. The TFA Air Force members of AA were discharged and sent home to their families, safe and sound.

Destination: 1650

Have you ever dreamed of traveling to a new place in a different time? This seemingly impossible fantasy becomes two best friends' reality in **DESTINATION: 1650** *by **Olivia Reeves**.*

I was lying in bed trying to plan what to do when my best friend Kelsey came over later, when suddenly there was this cry of happiness from my brother in his room. Curious, I dragged myself out of bed and walked down the hall to see him.

"Toby, it's early! What are you yelling about?" I yawned.

Toby grinned from ear to ear. "I have just completed the only working time machine in existence!"

"No way! You couldn't have!" I dramatically gasped in mock surprise, when underneath I was trying not to crack up.

"I did, but I need two people to test it, so when Kelsey comes over later, you can try it!" Toby answered.

"Okay! Whatever you say!" I said, still holding back giggles.

I can remember the day like it was yesterday, even though it was almost a year ago. I will remember the day forever. It was the day I traveled back in time. The day didn't start as crazily as it ended, though. In fact, it started off as just another lazy Saturday morning.

As I wandered back to my room, I was thinking about what Toby had said. I didn't think he had really built a time machine. I mean, come on! He's thirteen! It just wasn't possible! Then again, Toby has invented a lot of other things before. Who could forget the solar-powered curtains, or the heated boots? It almost seemed possible, in some crazy sci-fi way.

Later that day, when Kelsey came over, I filled her in on the morning's happenings. By the time I had finished telling her, she was smirking.

"Seriously, Ella, do you believe your brother built a time machine in his room?"

"I don't know, Kelsey," I responded, "because my first reaction was thinking it was a joke, but then… well, it kind of seems like something Toby would try to do. Don't you think we should give him the benefit of the doubt?"

"Well," Kelsey sighed, "there's only one thing to do. Let's go."

We hurried up the stairs to Toby's room where we found Toby surrounded by tools, working on a machine that looked like an upside down washing machine. The only difference was that a normal washing machine isn't the size of a truck.

"We're ready to test your time machine," I said, feeling completely ridiculous.

"Great," Toby grinned. "Just step in here."

He opened the door of the weird washing machine creation and motioned for us to step inside.

"You're kidding," Kelsey snorted. "You want us to step into an oversized washing machine?"

"Do you want to travel through time or not?" Toby retorted.

We climbed into the machine, feeling silly. Inside we saw thousands of glowing lights flickering on the walls like fireflies. I glanced up and saw what looked like an air vent. Two seats that looked like they belonged in a car from the sixties, newly equipped with seatbelts, occupied the center of the machine.

"Strap in!" Toby called as he shut the door.

I had barely clicked my seatbelt into place when there was a monstrous roar from the vent above our heads. Lights flashed all around us, and the machine quaked and shook. The roar lasted for about five minutes before the machine fell silent. Toby's time machine stayed put. Kelsey finally broke the silence.

"Well, so much for a time machine."

"Yeah," I agreed. "Come on, let's go."

We hopped out of the machine expecting to see Toby's crestfallen face. Instead a new sight greeted our eyes. We were in some sort of Native American village! We stood on a large, green plain. In the distance I could see a handful of cone-shaped houses, which I knew were teepees. Smoke curled from the tops of the teepees, which were decorated with feathers and paint. I couldn't believe what I was seeing. Was I hallucinating? The time machine worked!

"Oh my goodness!" I shrieked. "Kelsey! We're time travelers!"

"Ella!" Kelsey cried. "Calm down! There's a problem!"

"What's wrong?" I asked, still explosively happy from our success.

"We can't get back!" choked Kelsey, close to tears. "Toby used a control panel to bring us here! We don't have it! We can't go home!"

"Calm down!" I said, trying to convince myself to do the same. "Toby won't leave us here!"

During this scene, a crowd of people gathered around us. A man with an ornately feathered headdress approached, and the crowd parted to let him through. Kelsey and I stopped talking and gazed in awe at this man, who seemed to emanate power. This was a man you didn't want to mess with, that was for sure.

"I am Abooksigun, chief of the Algonquins. Who are you and why are you here?" asked the man in perfect English.

"I'm Ella and this is Kelsey. We came from the future in that machine," I said, pointing to the abandoned machine.

"Ella and Kelsey, are you from another tribe?"

"No, we don't belong to a tribe," said Kelsey. "We just need somewhere to stay until we can go home."

"You may stay, Ella and Kelsey, until you are able to go home. You are welcome in the Algonquin tribe," said the chief.

Before we had a chance to respond, there was a familiar roaring behind us. We dashed to the machine.

"Thank you!" we called.

Again the roaring lasted for five minutes. As soon as it had stopped, we dived out of the machine. The machine was in the exact same place as when we stepped inside it.

"You guys did it!" shouted Toby, white in the face. "I just sent you back to 1650! I thought I wasn't going to be able to bring you back!"

"You did, though! We just talked to the chief of an Algonquin tribe! It worked!" yelled Kelsey.

Within half an hour, word had leaked out about my brother's invention, thanks to one call to my mom, who works for the local newspaper. The street was lined with reporters, news vans and people from all over. That day, I was probably interviewed at least fifty times!

The actual time machine was moved to a government lab in Washington, DC for safekeeping. We had to go to Washington to give the scientists the machine, and Toby got to demonstrate the use of his machine. Kelsey and I were sent back in time again to Chief

Abooksigun and his people to explain where we were from. To make a long story short, they didn't believe us!

Before we gave the scientists the machine, we were allowed one last trip. This time, Toby came with us. We traveled to the thirteen colonies in 1772. He was taking notes and photos the whole time, so he could help people have a better record of history.

On our last night in Washington, we were invited to the White House for a banquet celebrating our success. At the banquet, Toby was given a grant from the government to help fund plans for a new idea of his: a teleportation device. Kelsey and I were awarded full scholarships to the college of our choice, even though college is seven years away.

Later, as I sat on the airplane watching Washington get smaller and smaller, I felt a sense of remorse, because our adventure was over. Suddenly I broke into a smile. I realized: Who knows? Maybe we'll be back soon so Toby can demonstrate a teleporter he invented!

Is Everything Normal?

A boy is the only one who can save the world. Will he succeed? Find out in **IS EVERYTHING NORMAL?** *by* ***Trent Pitser.***

It was a normal day, just like any other you could imagine. What Sean didn't know was that everything was about to change. But let's not get into that quite yet.

When Sean woke up he walked downstairs and grabbed a bowl of cereal. He grabbed his books and got ready for school. He walked to the bus stop and as usual sat with his best friend, Tyler.

Sean asked Tyler, "What are you going to do for the talent show?"

"I don't know," Tyler replied. "I'll think about it. I might just do something on the guitar."

When they got to school everything was normal. But on the way back home Sean saw something shining right by the big oak tree. They walked over to it, and it was a necklace. They picked it up, and as soon as it touched Sean's hand it glowed blue.

Sean thought, "I'll bring it home to Karen. She loves shiny things." When they got to Sean's house, Tyler said goodbye and walked on down to his house.

When Sean gave Karen the necklace she screamed in joy. She yelled so loud that Sean would have bet Tyler could hear it. "Thanks, Sean! You're the best brother ever!"

When Karen finally let go of Sean he went downstairs to watch some TV. There wasn't anything good on, so he decided to watch the news. Fifteen minutes into it he saw a story on aliens. Some guy had reported that he had seen a U.F.O. Scientists all around the world were investigating this story. Sean was very confused. He just thought it was a bunch of bologna. "Everyone knows aliens are just a myth," exclaimed Sean.

It was getting late, and Sean had school tomorrow. When he was finally asleep he dreamed about aliens. There was fire everywhere and people screaming left and right. The aliens had taken full power over the world. Obviously it was a nightmare. He woke up startled, and he was panting and sweating like crazy. Then he realized that there were footsteps coming up the stairs. They were getting louder with each step. The creature grasped the door knob and turned it.

"Honey, time for school," said Sean's mom. A big sigh of relief came over Sean. She seemed pretty laid back, probably because she didn't know about the aliens everybody was talking about. Sean's mom, unlike other moms, didn't care about the news a lot. She would probably find out at work this morning.

Sean got ready for school but had a bad feeling in his stomach. He wasn't hungry and had some time, so he watched TV. He heard on the television that same story about the aliens, but with startling new details. The alien ship had landed right next to the big oak tree where we found that necklace! The door of the rocket ship had opened, and the aliens stepped out. Everyone had pictured them to be green and have enormous heads with six or seven eyes. They didn't look like that at all. The aliens looked almost exactly like humans, except that they always had white workout clothes or something on.

Their leader stepped out in front of the other aliens with bodyguards standing on either side of them. The bodyguards had enormous guns, which probably shot lasers. Everyone was shaking. The whole news team and all the people of the town were frightened. The alien leader said, "Where is the necklace? If you don't bring it to me I will kill everybody one by one." His bodyguards pointed their guns at the townspeople.

Sean ran into his sister's room. "Karen, do you still have that necklace I gave you yesterday?"

"Of course I do. It's on my dresser over there," replied Karen. Sean grabbed it, but Karen refused to let him take it.

"Sean, give it back!" screamed Karen, but she wasn't strong enough.

On his way a man stopped him and told him, "Don't give them the necklace. They need it to take over the world."

"How do you know?" replied Sean.

"This isn't the first time this has happened. Long ago the same thing happened. It was a rainy, winter night. The news crew was reporting the story like they are now. They didn't know what the aliens were going to do. The aliens landed right in front of that same tree, and they said they needed that necklace to take over the world.

Nobody knew where it was except for one little boy who found it by the tree on his way home from working on the farm. He gave it to his sister for Christmas. When the aliens found them no one ever saw them again. I don't want you to make that same mistake. You need to put that in military hands. The only one who can stop them is the one who it rightfully belongs to. When you found that necklace, did it glow blue?"

"Yes, it did," Sean replied. "Who are you?"

"I am that little boy in the story. I'm the only one who still remembers this because I was not hypnotized. Before they left, they brainwashed everybody so they could not remember it, but I was the only one not hypnotized. You need to get that into military hands, or you could make a really bad mistake. Your choice."

Sean ran to the nearest troop of men clearing the people out of the way. Everyone could hear the aliens counting down before they were going to blow everything up.

"3, 2, 1" BOOM! Crash! The aliens fired their weapons. Sean and the troops ran back to the plane. Half the troops were still clearing the people out and got incinerated by the alien weapons.

The aliens saw them getting away and tried to attack them, but the plane was too fast. The plane was heading toward one of the military bases. One of the troops said to Sean, "We'll hide it here till we know what to do with it."

"Ok, but this is where they will expect it the most," replied Sean.

"Don't worry. It's physically impossible to get through these walls," said the soldier. They flew to a different military base just to make sure the aliens weren't following them. They left a whole troop of men to protect the necklace.

"Let's call your mom and let her know that you're ok."

"Mom, are you there?"

"Yeah, sweetie, I'm here. Where are you?"

"I'm at a military base. I'm going to save the world."

"YOU ARE WHERE! WHY ARE YOU AT A MILITARY BASE? I'M FREAKING OUT TRYING TO FIND YOU! YOU HAVE TO COME HOME RIGHT NOW!"

"I'm afraid he can't," said one of the soldiers. "Your son is the only one who can save us right now."

"NO, NO, NO! I'M NOT GOING TO LOSE MY BABY IN THIS WAR. YOU BETTER BRING HIM HOME RIGHT- "

The soldier cut her off saying, "Ma'am, calm down. We can't bring your son home. It's too dangerous, and we need him to save the world. Now can we please go and carry on with our investigations?"

Sean's mom started to weep through the phone. "I will not let my baby be a part of this war! I need him now," said Sean's mom.

"Wait a second," Sean paused, "that's not my mom's voice! GET OFF THE PHONE. IT'S AN ALIEN TRYING TO TRACK US!"

They ran to alert the troops of an attack.

Meanwhile, the scientists were still working on the case about the aliens. They had to hurry up before the aliens blew up everybody and everything. They had to move to a new location before the aliens got there, so they moved to the military base where the necklace was, and they began on schedule.

The war had been going on for days, and people were hiding in their homes and dying of starvation. On the streets dead aliens and creatures were just lying on the floor. The cold wind blowing against people's faces made it seem that no one would be able to stay alive.

While people were dying Sean was figuring out a plan to stop the aliens at the military base. "That's it!" Sean yelled. "We can turn the aliens' technology against them. We need some scientists to investigate their lair. If there is anything that would be helpful let us know."

"Nice plan, Sean. We'll get some scientists working on it as soon as possible," said one of the scientists.

The military sent a troop of soldiers to the spaceship. They went inside, and the first thing they saw was the enormous time portal. The only way to activate it was with Sean's necklace. They called back to the base, got the necklace, and started heading toward the ship.

They couldn't get too far or else the aliens would see them. It was Sean's time to shine. He would be the one to take the necklace to the ship.

He ran as fast as his legs could take him. He had sweat dripping from his face. Sean was getting more and more tired with every step.

He was dodging explosions and jumping over dead bodies. The military had his back and were covering him every step.

Finally he got to the spaceship. He plugged the necklace into the portal and then *ZZIINNGG*! A laser hit Sean right in the shoulder. The aliens had found him! Still conscious, he dropped to the floor. His shoulder was gushing blood. Luckily, he had plugged in the necklace right in time. The aliens disappeared, and since there were no aliens, there was nobody who had shot him so his shoulder was healed. On the aliens way out there was a big flash, and everyone was wondering what they were doing here except for Sean.

Sean ran home and saw his mom making dinner. He ran to her and gave her the biggest hug in the world. Of course his mom didn't know what it was for, but she liked it anyway.

That night Sean went to bed, and this time he didn't dream about aliens.

Legacy

Jannik awakens to find himself imprisoned by an evil guard threatening to kill him. With no one to save him, Jannik must find a way to escape and survive in this futuristic world. Can he overcome the challenges working against him in **LEGACY***?*

J*annik*

Year: 3245
Time: 12:00 P.M.

I awoke to see only darkness. It was a very cold room. I could feel the icy metal of the shackles on my wrists. I looked down at the shackles and I searched for a keyhole. There wasn't one. A noise sounded at the door of the room. I saw a gun and I started to laugh.

"What's so funny, kid?" The guard sounded aggravated at the laughter. He waited for an answer, and I finally I gave one.

"You're just a soldier and they sent YOU to watch ME." I saw the guard raise his gun. The guard held his gun at the exact level of my head. "They should send someone with a higher rank, stronger, and good with a plasma sword." That's what set him off.

"That's it, you're dead," he dropped his gun and pulled out a plasma knife.

He started coming at me, but I swung up into the air, high enough to wrap my legs around his neck. Finally, I snapped his neck. Before the plasma knife dropped to the floor, I kicked it up to my hands. I grasped the knife with twists of my hands and expertly cut the metal off my wrist. I grabbed a dark black suit with black boots and black gloves from the floor. There was a slot on the back for an assault rifle, a pistol holster on the right side, and plasma knife holder on the left. I grabbed the assault rifle and headed down the detention level.

Every five minutes a detention guard passed by. The first one that passed by noticed I wasn't a soldier and tried calling for backups, but I was too fast. I stabbed him with my knife. I saw a bridge above me, and then a ladder. By the time I climbed up the ladder, there were two squads on it. "Uh, hi," I said and I scurried down the ladder. They were coming down, closer to where I was. A few went down, but most stayed up. I threw some sticky grenades under the bridge. *BADOOM!* There were shrieks of pain. Even I was knocked around some.

There was one soldier that landed close to me; pure fear was in his eyes. He wasn't a soldier either. Instead of a black suit he had on a white suit, now red from the surrounding scene. "Who are you?" I shouted at him, which I had to do because of everyone screaming.

"Don't worry, I'm the good guy," he shouted back.

The next thing we heard were soldiers shouting, "Get them, you idiots!" Then everyone bounded up to get us. It turned absolutely nuts.

"The White Knights are here!" the stranger in white screeched, and leaped up firing his gun like he was crazy. Some White Knights picked me up and carried me to a craft. The last thing I remember was soaring up in the air, flying into the dark night sky where the stars and moon were as bright as they could be. I could barely see over the grassy plain, and my body ached from all the flying we were doing. Soon, we arrived at their base.

When we landed there, I was rushed to a doctor to treat my wounds. Finally, I was sent to the observatory where a man greeted me with "Welcome, your training starts now."

Lite

When a kid named Lite ventures into space he finds planets he has never seen before. Find out if Lite gets back home to Earth or not in **LITE**, *by* ***Seth McGhee***.

A young boy named Lite, who is 11 years old, has great fighting skills. He could fight anyone. One night Lite woke up in the darkness wondering about the sky. He saw a shooting star, so he made a wish.

The next morning Lite went down the stairs and he watched the news. The government was sending people to outer space to look at the stars in a big ship. Lite wished he could see what space looked like. So he packed his bags and went to the big ship.

When he got there the place was packed with people. Soon people began boarding the big ship called *Clay Star*. He got on, and the ship took off into space.

Lite found his assigned room, unpacked his bag, and sat next to the window.

Lite looked out the window and saw the stars. He was enjoying the view, seeing all the stars and planets he had read about. As Lite looked out the window he saw the Earth moving far, far away. He asked himself, "Why is the Earth moving so far away?" Lite hadn't thought about how big space was or how far the stars were when he decided to get on the ship. Lite became a little afraid, so he decided to take a nap, hoping he would feel better when he woke up.

Lite woke up from his nap and did feel better. He decided to look out the window and see how far away Earth was now. The ship had come to a planet called Pyro. Pyro was a planet that had blue people called Pyroians. They could kill everyone who stands in their way. They are very strong, but Lite could fight them if he put all of his strength into it.

Lite heard the captain say through the speaker system, "Before you can get off the ship, you must put on the special suit that is in the closet." Lite found his suit and put it on. He then headed to the area where people were getting off.

The people that were living on the planet came to see what had landed on their planet. Lite saw the blue people attack some passengers because the blue people thought that the passengers were hostile. Lite had to do something. He grabbed a pole that had been broken off by the blue people. He ran after the blue people, knocking them off of the passengers and running them off. Lite and the passengers ran back to the ship to yell at the captain to take off.

Lite was sort of freaked out and wanted just to go back home, but he has more planets to visit before that could happen.

*　*　*

I have traveled to many planets, but I'm not sure we will make it back.

Lite stopped writing and got off of his computer. As Lite looked out the window, he saw many planets come past and wondered if he would find Earth or not. Lite left his room and walked down the stairs to the second floor and the food court.

As Lite watched TV about space, he had an idea. Lite ran back upstairs to his room to plan the idea. Lite's idea was to use the ship's map of the universe to try to find Earth. Lite already knew the ship had a map of the universe.

There was Earth at the very end of the map. Lite was very happy that he had found Earth. But Lite has a problem. He has to get there without getting killed by the starks. Starks are dangerous aliens. They find ships with other beings on it and eat them.

The Lost City

People always wonder if there is another world that has not been discovered. **Talon Gibson** *has always wondered if there was another world underground, and considers the possibility in* **THE LOST CITY**.

It was dark in the Lost City, but then again it was always dark in the Lost City. Bob wondered for the millionth time why there was never any light. He was on his way to work at City Hall where he worked for the mayor. The mayor was always happy and always had a smile on his face. The mayor always had new stuff that many had never seen before. This made people very suspicious about him.

When Bob arrived, the mayor asked him to deliver a message to a friend. He would only give Bob the address and not a name. Bob set off with the message. He became very suspicious and decided to open the letter.

"Deliver the cash to the special room."

Deliver the cash? If the mayor was hiding something then why wouldn't he make the delivery himself? So, he kept walking and finally arrived at the address. It was a huge building. The biggest Bob had ever seen! When he knocked on the door, a tall man answered.

"Message from the mayor," Bob said. He handed the tall man the letter and went back to the office. The mayor was gone. Since he was gone, Bob decided to leave work as well and walk home.

When he got home, he went to his grandma's old room. Every day he goes to his grandma's room to think about her. He pulled out an old note from her closet. It was the same note he pulled out every night. Something in his head told him that it had something to do with his delivery today. If only he had more clues.

The next day, he left for work again. The mayor was not in his office again. Bob heard something under the office floor that made him wonder what was going on. He wondered if that was the room where the cash was going to be delivered.

He knew how to get underground, but he was afraid to go there because it was even darker than the Lost City. He asked his friend, Lena, to go through the office floor with him. Lena and Bob took the staircase underground. It was pitch black down there and very scary. They heard footsteps walking very slowly. They heard a screech as if a door was opening. They waited a few minutes and heard faster footsteps. They thought that someone must have had the cash and had just gotten rid of it.

They carefully slid against the wall until they found the opening of a door. They turned the handle, and the door opened. What they saw made them gasp. It was another city. It was bright. They went into the new city where they found all types of new things, like fruit and vegetables, televisions, and cars.

This was what Bob's grandmother had been trying to tell him all along. There was another world outside of the Lost City. The mayor must have been using his money to buy things from this newer, brighter world. Bob and Lena stepped out into this new world to begin a new life together.

The Rock

Floyd finds a special rock that gives him and his friends superpowers. They are put to the test when aliens come to invade in **THE ROCK** *by* **Charles Jones.**

Floyd is playing in a basketball game with his friends Derrell and Geon and his sixth-grade team. It's in Chicago where Michael Jordan used to play. "I can't wait to play in the tournament on Saturday," said Derrell.

"I know the competition is tough, but I think we have a shot at winning," said Floyd.

"Yeah, I am excited, too. Those teams don't stand a chance against my skills," said Geon.

The games were fierce, and there were ten games going on at once. During their last game they were down by one point with 14.8 seconds left on the clock. They had to win or else the team wouldn't get the championship trophy. Derrell inbounded the ball to Floyd, and he lobbed the ball down to Geon who made the game-winning basket. Everyone jumped off the bench and ran to Geon, picked him up, and carried him to the locker room.

The bus ride back to the school was loud and exciting. Derrell and Geon decided to spend the night over Floyd's house. All of a sudden they heard a big thump. The bus driver told the coach that everyone had to get off the bus. The coach stood up and said, "Boys the driver wants us off the bus. When you get off the bus stand over by the tree near the bus and we will let you know when you can get back on."

The boys got off the bus and went to stand by the tree. Everyone was talking when Floyd noticed a rock glistening in the sunlight a few feet from the tree. Floyd looked over by the bus where the coach and the bus driver were looking at the tires. Floyd slowly walked over to the rock. He picked up the rock and looked at it. The rock was clear blue in color with blue and red stripes. Quickly Floyd put the rock in his pocket.

After about forty-five minutes the coach told the boys the bus had had a flat tire, but it was fixed, so they could get back on the bus and continue back to the school.

Finally, after two hours had passed, they made it back to the school. Floyd and his friends went to his house. They couldn't wait to start playing when Floyd's pocket started to heat up and glow. Floyd took the rock out of his pocket, and it exploded into three pieces. Out of thin air a hologram appeared of a beautiful girl. She appeared to be about the same age as the boys and said, "My name is May. My father is an evil man, and he is planning on killing all the adults on the Earth and holding the children of your planet as slaves to help him rebuild Earth the way he wants it to appear. I have a looking glass that lets me see what is happening on your planet. I was able to see the game you all played, and I was impressed with your athletic ability and sportsmanship, so I picked you three to help me save your planet and defeat my dad. The rock is the key to …." The hologram disappeared.

"The rock is the key to what?" asked Geon.

Floyd picked up the three pieces and threw one piece to Derrell and one to Geon, and he kept one for himself. "I don't know what this rock is the key to, or if this save-the-planet mumbo jumbo is even real, but somehow these pieces of rock must do something."

They ran through the house looking for Floyd's parents, but they were gone. They tried calling the police, but they, too, were gone. They ran outside, and cars were stopped in the middle of the street. No adults were to be found anywhere.

Floyd looked down the street and noticed a kid driving a car toward them out of control. With amazing speed he grabbed Geon and Derrell and carried them to the other side of the street away from the speeding car.

The driver and his friends jumped out of the car and ran over to the boys. The biggest boy stepped up close to Derrell and said, "I am taking over since the adults are gone. You and your big-headed friends have to do what I say, and I say you three need to get on the ground and kiss my feet."

"Not in this lifetime," said Derrell.

The big boy tried to push Derrell to the ground. Derrell told him to stop, but instead the big boy's friends jumped in to help. Without hesitation Derrell picked up all the boys at the same time and tossed them in the Dumpster.

Geon looked at Derrell and Floyd with disbelief and said, "Wow, how did you guys do that?"

Floyd and Derrell didn't know, so they said, "WE HAVE SUPERPOWERS!"

Geon yelled, "WHERE ARE MY SUPERPOWERS?" Then the sky turned completely dark and Geon said, "According to my calculations the alien ships are approximately two hours away."

Floyd and Derrell said, "How did you know that?"

Geon said, "The rock that Floyd found gave us all superpowers, and mine made me super smart."

Geon began to think of a strategy to defeat the aliens. After a couple of minutes Geon shouted, "I got it! I know how to defeat the aliens."

Geon ran to the laboratory in Floyd's basement. Derrell and Floyd ran close behind wondering what Geon had planned. Geon started putting things together and Floyd said, "WHAT ARE YOU DOING!"

Geon responded, "I am making a time machine to send the aliens back to prehistoric times where they will not have any technology to come back." Geon told everyone the exact location where they would land.

Derrell carried the time machine to where the aliens would come. They all hid, and waited for the aliens to appear. Within a minute the ships began to land on Earth. The aliens' leader said, "Come out. I can smell you!" The three boys stepped out of hiding.

They were surprised when they saw the aliens. They looked human, but they were very tall and muscular. They looked like giant football players. When the alien saw them he said, "I know my daughter told you of my plan, which is why I have put her in jail. I also know she gave you a special rock, and I want it back. Give it back to me, and I will not kill anyone."

"We are not afraid of you. The rock gave us superpowers and we will defeat you," said Geon.

The alien grew to twice his original size and said, "If you boys have the rock, you boys better give it to me, or we will start destroying every kid in our sight!" Without warning Floyd began to run around the whole alien fleet with super speed until a huge funnel was surrounding them. Derrell began to increase in size until he was strong enough to force through the high winds and toss the alien ships into the time machine. Quickly, Geon set the time machine and sent the aliens back to prehistoric time.

After the time machine was out of sight the sun came back. Out of nowhere another hologram appeared. It was May. She said, "Thank you for helping me defeat my father. Now that he is gone, we can live our lives in peace on my planet. I will send all the adults back to your planet, but only the three of you will remember what happened. I will also let you keep your super powers, but use them wisely."

The adults returned, and like May said, no one remembered anything that had happened except for the three of them.

Geon said, "It is going to be nice to have superpowers."

Derrell said, "Yeah, we'll be the best basketball players in the NBA."

Then Floyd said, "No, that would not be a wise way to use our super powers. We should only use our powers for good."

They all agreed, and went back to Floyd's house to continue celebrating their win and saving Earth from aliens.

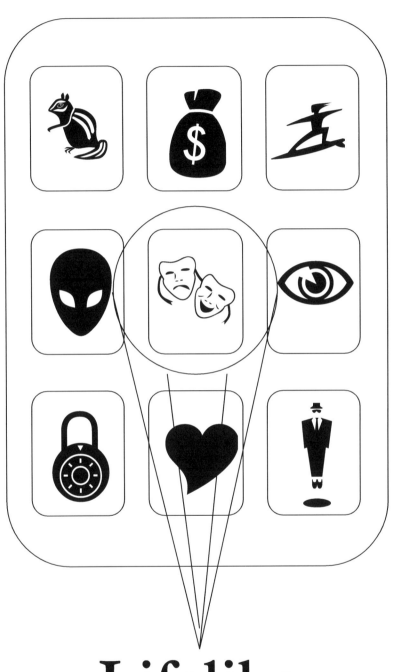

Lifelike

The Bad Lie

When a boy named Joe starts to struggle in school, he decides that his only way out is to lie. In **THE BAD LIE** *by* **Sean LePine,** *a boy learns that lying isn't the best way out of school.*

This story is about a twelve-year-old boy named Joey. Joey was just starting middle school, and was struggling. He used to be a good student, but he started to get bad grades and was trying to hide it from his parents by throwing away his tests and graded work.

Joey's mom, Meredith, found a couple of assignments in his trash can while she was cleaning his dirty room. Meredith waited until Joey's father, Paul, came home from work to tell him about Joey's poorly-done assignments. Meredith and Paul waited for Joey to come home from school, to confront him about his bad grades. Joey at first denied that the assignments were his. He must have thought his parents were stupid, because his name was on them, they were in his handwriting, and they were in his room.

Joey finally owned up to the assignments. His parents punished him immediately. He was grounded until he raised every grade to at least a B.

Joey knew this wasn't going to be easy. He didn't get the point of school. It's not like he was going to use it in life. He stomped away from his parents into his bedroom where he was sent for the rest of the night.

The next day Joey went into school early and told his teachers that his dog ate his homework, even though he didn't have a dog or any pet. None of the teachers bought into the lie. In fact, a few laughed so loud you would have thought Joey had just told the funniest joke ever.

Day after day Joey continued to lie at school. His teachers didn't tell his parents because Joey's lies got better and better each time. Joey told lies that were convincing, like, "My great-grandfather recently passed away," and "My parents are going through a tough time, so I had to stay with my aunt last night." None of the teachers got suspicious, except for his gym teacher.

Mr. Lopez, the gym teacher, was not a stupid man. He was a quiet, conservative guy, but knew tons. He is the eyes and ears of the school. He knows everything that's going on, but that doesn't mean he will tell you.

He fell for Joey's first couple of lies. But after a while he stopped believing everything Joey said. Mr. Lopez hates when people lie. One day Mr. Lopez stopped being the quiet guy. He started calling Joey "The Lying Boy."

At first, only Mr. Lopez called Joey The Lying Boy, but soon everyone knew him by that. Even his parents called him their lying son, because he lied to everyone, even though they begged him to stop. This story doesn't have a happily ever after, but no less of a lesson: Don't lie repeatedly, especially when you don't have to. Joey is still known as The Lying Boy, even though he stopped lying years ago. It's too late for Joey, but not for you.

A Bad Weekend

In **A BAD WEEKEND** *by* **Louie Nader,** *four brothers and a friend head north to take their speedboat on an interesting adventure to Charlevoix. As it turns out, this isn't the kind of adventure they had in mind.*

It was a warm night, the trees were still, the lake was warm, and the sand tickled Mr. Bubblebutt. Mr. Bubblebutt had been part of the FBI for 23 years. He was the Commander of the Troops until the "stupid move." He accidentally blew up the Empire State Building and killed innocent civilians, so he got fired.

Then he saw it, a sudden weather change. It started snowing and didn't stop until it reached twenty -four inches. Then he saw a glimpse of something he couldn't picture. It was a UFO. Then the UFO landed and changed into a car. Then Mr. Bubblebutt knew what to do. He went to the UFO and inspected it and found nothing. He had to call the FBI, but they would think he was crazy. "I have to do it," said Mr. Bubblebutt. He called the FBI and they came right away. They brought machetes, machine guns, tanks and the fighter jets. The FBI took it from there.

Mr. Bubblebutt felt lonely that night so, he decided to go to the MEC Mount Everest Casino. While he was driving, he felt a blast of wind whipping past him. He knew it could only be an alien at least that is what he predicted. When he got to the casino he saw this weird looking car. It was a car that was not out in any dealerships over the world. No one had even heard of a Fartwagon. He walked inside as a tingle moved down his spine. He first went to the blackjack table. There was this person that bet four billion and it was a perfect blackjack. Then that guy won again and again. That's when he knew that something was getting fishy.

He thought all night about this, afraid and sweating like a pig. Then he knew that he had to take a stand. He walked back to the car to suit up. He reached into his car and grabbed a gun and his old uniform from the FBI that was a bit too small around his butt. He marched right up to the alien. He stood tall and proud, the Alien morphed into a creature with green scaly skin. He ran for his life, going back to his house which was near Mount Everest. Then these green scaly claws came out from under his skin. The creature smelled his ship. *The creature has supersonic smell* thought Mr. Bubblebutt. The creature stopped chasing him and ran to Mount Everest where the ship was taken until something stopped him. An invisible force field was sealed around the whole place. The alien then ran back into town.

Mr. Bubblebutt had to warn the FBI about this, "There in an alien on the loose you have to stop him," said Mr. Bubblebutt. He returned to his house to take a rest, but something stopped him. He can't stop thinking of the fact that the alien could morph. It was like a dream, but it wasn't. It was all real live stuff he just saw. He thought it was a nightmare.

The next morning he went to town to investigate. He saw a trail of footprints in Mount Everest town. He wondered if it was the alien or just a human until he saw the weird design on the footprint. It was the alien. He decided to go have breakfast. He saw his best friend Billy from the FBI.

"Did you see the alien yet Billy?" whispered Mr. Bubblebutt.

Billy whispered back, "Do you mean that freakish guy at the casino?"

"Yeah, doesn't he seem like an alien?" replied Mr. Bubblebutt.

"I got to go, see you around," replied Billy.

Right when he was about to pay the bill, a gun fired and knocked down the whole casino killing thousands of innocent civilians. The FBI came right away and thought of a plan, but Mr. Bubblebutt thought that everyone should circle the alien in. The FBI listened to his plan and started thinking about it.

They decided to do the plan that Mr. Bubblebutt said. They circled the alien until the alien started getting angry and vicious. They requested back up. They brought tanks and fighter jets. But nothing worked! The alien already destroyed millions of dollars spent on those weapons. They tried to circle him in again. Right when the alien was about to attack, Mr. Bubblebutt jumped out from behind and Tazered the alien just at the right moment that the alien was lying on the cold, wet ground. They took the alien to the lab for further testing.

Afterward, Mr. Bubblebutt got an award for excellence and dirty work. The FBI decided that Mr. Bubblebutt should be promoted back to the commander of the FBI. The FBI wanted the alien alive for now. Knowing that the alien would soon be awake, they would be ready.

Later, the scientist dissected the alien. That was the end of the alien named Hulioricartosfiancodicastraes they found out later on but now, the alien is finally dead. They won't have to worry about him anymore.

Mr. Bubblebutt had a speech. "Fellow citizens, that was the most deadly and vicious creature, but we still defeated it, because we are the United States of America!"

The Best Summer Ever

Skateboarding is Eli's life. When he and his father move to California, he figures he will make friends and have a great summer skating in the California sunshine. Eli learns that fitting in and skateboarding aren't always as easy as they look in **THE BEST SUMMER EVER** *by* ***Joshua W. Yunker.***

There once was a boy named Eli. Eli was a small, skinny boy. He was twelve years old. His parents were separated. His dad was starting to warm up to the whole skateboard thing while his mom, on the other hand, was not. Eli was a class clown with his friends but that was about to change.

One day, the last day of school to be exact, he came running home from the bus stop to see a moving van in front of his house. He immediately sprinted to his dad and asked, "What is going on?"

His dad sighed, "Eli, we have to move."

Eli's jaw dropped he asked, "Why?"

His dad replied, "It's for work."

Eli started to cry and he asked, "So, where are we moving?"

His dad replied, "To California."

Eli broke down again. "Dad, what about our trip?" You see, every year Eli and his dad go on a fishing trip.

His dad said, "We're just going to have to hold off." Eli got mad and left with his skateboard.

Eli is a skater. He just started about a year ago, so he is not the best at it. His friend got him interested in it, but Eli was a street skater. That means he rode street obstacles.

Eli went to his best friend Tyler's house. When Tyler heard the news, he was pretty sad. Tyler told Eli that everything would be fine. Tyler gave Eli a hug and said, "Have a good summer."

Eli went back to the empty house and saw his dad sitting on the ground. Eli asked, "When are we leaving?"

"Tomorrow," Eli's father replied. It was kind of weird that night, because they slept on the floor.

Moving day was a long day. Eli and his dad arrived at the airport and boarded the plane. Eli's dad fell asleep before they got off the ground. Eli hated planes, so he tried to fall asleep too.

When they landed, Eli and his dad drove to the house and started unpacking. Eli was shocked when he saw how big the house was. When Eli was done unpacking he asked his dad if he could go to the skate park that he saw up the road. His dad gave him permission.

When Eli got there, all the boys were looking at him funny. So, Eli started to skate when a boy flung his skateboard at him. Eli fell and hurt his knee. Then, Eli confronted the boy, and the boy punched him in the face. The hot dog vendor saw that and told the other boy to go home. The man gave Eli a free hot dog and asked if he was ok. Eli said, "I'm all right."

The guy said, "Well, I'm John. My dad and I opened the skate park a few years ago."

Eli said, "Wow! It's pretty cool."

"Sorry about what happened earlier," John replied.

"Oh, it's okay."

"I'm going to try the half pipe. Do you want to come?"

Eli got excited. "Sure, I've never done it before."

When Eli got to the top, his nerves started kicking in. He set his board up and stepped down. He flew through the air! He landed it, and by the end of the day, he had met a new friend and begun a great summer.

The Camping Trip

In **THE CAMPING TRIP**, *by* ***Katie Lockwood,*** *two friends go on a camping trip together. What they did not know is that they are about to get lost in the woods and have an adventure that they would never have expected.*

Sarah and Nicole

Camping is normally fun with your friend, but for me, not so much. I was camping with my friend Nicole at a campsite near Grand Rapids. There were so many people camping that there were too many people to count. It was about 8:45 P.M. when most of the people started to go to sleep, but of course Nicole and I planned to stay up all night. We got a little bored sitting near the fire, so we decided to go exploring in the woods in the dark. We grabbed our green and purple flashlights, and then we ran out into the woods.

When we stepped into the woods, we could hear the water from the river rushing and splashing across the stones. We looked through the trees and we could see the river shimmering from the moon onto our faces. When we saw the river we were so excited that we almost jumped in the water, but then we heard a big splash and we did not know what it was, so we started running and screaming. About an hour later, we started to get tired and not so scared, so we grabbed our flashlights and walked back to the campsite.

Nicole and I did not remember the way back to the campsite. We tried to retrace our steps, but of course we had no clue where we were. Nicole quickly grabbed my arm like she found something important, but when I looked I only saw an old, wrecked tree house.

We ran up to the old tree house and climbed up the ladder. Suddenly, I had an idea that we could sleep there overnight for shelter. I told Nicole the great idea I had. She thought it would be great for shelter. I looked around in the tree house and saw old antiques like chairs, toys, blankets, and little lanterns. It seemed like someone lived there once.

Nicole and I slept in the old tree house, and we used the old blankets that were left there. For pillows, we used our jackets.

The next day we woke up to the sound of the swooshing of the trees and the chirping of the birds. Suddenly, we felt an ache in our stomach. We were really hungry. We started to search for some berries.

Nicole jumped and then shouted to me, "Blueberries!" I ran to her and saw bushes so loaded with berries that we would never starve. Nicole and I gathered as many blueberries as we could. I made a pouch out of one of the blankets in the tree house to carry our berries. After we ate most of our berries, we started looking for the campsite again.

Campsite

Meanwhile back at the campsite, the people that worked there were doing a routine search check that they do every two days. They walked around making sure everyone was there following the rules and were not lost. They came to Sarah and Nicole's camping area. They did not see anyone at the campsite. They even peeked into their tents. At that point, they realized the girls were missing because their reservation site had expired and their belongings were still there.

They looked through the beach and at the river nearby. They even asked all the people at the campsite if they had seen Nicole and Sarah at any time, but they all said no. They finally made a conclusion that they should call the search team and look in the woods.

Sarah and Nicole

We walked miles and miles until we were too tired to keep going, so we took a break. We sat on a big log, and we heard some rustling of the leaves. A voice called out, "Is anyone here, hello?" Nicole and I jumped up and started running toward the sounds.

We shouted and shouted "We're right here, we're right here!" but no one heard us. We were running and so excited because we were almost to the sounds.

All of a sudden, I heard a scream coming from behind me; it was Nicole. She had slipped down a steep hill while running and was lying at the bottom of the hill screaming in pain. I ran down to see if she was hurt badly. I sat down beside her in a panic.

She had hit her head, sprained her arm, and broken her leg. Nicole was screaming and screaming in pain as I called for help. I could no longer hear the voices we thought were people.

It started to get dark, and there was no one to help. I sat next to Nicole, trying to comfort her. It began to get darker, and it was going to be another night alone in the woods.

All of a sudden, we heard helicopter noises coming from the sky. The blinding headlight shined in our eyes as the rescue people came down a rope ladder in huge yellow suits. They picked Nicole up and brought her up in the helicopter. A large man walked up to me and asked, "Are you Sarah or Nicole?"

"I'm Sarah," I said. He helped me up, and then wrapped me in a blanket, since I was so cold.

"We've been looking for you and your friend for a long time. You're lucky you survived." I climbed into the helicopter and fell asleep.

When I woke up in the hospital, people were crowding around me and clapping, happy that my friend and I were found. Six weeks later, Nicole recovered and was back on her feet. We were on the news that day, and they wrote an article about us in the newspaper. Like I said before, normally kids like going on a camping trip with a friend, but for me, not so much.

The Cheater

Andie is at camp for the last year. Color Days is coming up. Andie and her friends all want to be captain. When somebody breaks the rules, Andie thinks that she will never be captain. Will she? Find out what happens in **THE CHEATER** *by* **Emily Lulkin.**

This is the story of Color Days. Color Days is five days of competition at summer camp. There is swimming, canoeing, singing, and anything imaginable that a camp would have. There are two teams: the Blue team and the White team. Four of the girls from Bryn Mawr, the oldest cabin, are chosen to be captain. There are two captains for each team. It was all fun and games until somebody's desire to be captain grew too strong…

The stage was set; it was twilight. Everyone was sleeping. The trees seemed to be like monsters about to strike. I heard a golf cart, so I turned my flashlight off. I couldn't see my hand an inch in front of my face. I told myself to keep going. I snuck into the office. Color Days would start tomorrow and I HAD to be captain. If my name wasn't on the Captain's list, then things were about to change. Nobody would suspect me. That's what happened the night before Color Days. Those were the words of the cheater.

Let's jump ahead to the next night. Andie, a Bryn Mawr, was hoping with all her heart to be Color Day Captain. She was, until last night.

Andie walked eagerly to the opening ceremony of Color Days. It was an exciting night because she might be captain. She sat down, smiling, and sharing anxious glances with her friends. Everyone except Natalie seemed nervous. The last five days of camp was always designated for Color Days! The counselors would put the whistle around the person's neck if she were captain. Andie hears one, two, three, four screams but none of them were hers.

Andie and all her friends walked back to the cabin together. Natalie and Jamie were captains for the White team. Lexie and Maggie were captains for the Blue team. Andie congratulated them for being captain, but on the inside she was crying. She was crying and screaming. She wanted to BURST! As much as she wanted to be captain, Andie knew she needed to go into this with a positive attitude. These were her camp "sisters." She had lived with them for two months every summer since she was nine. Instead of moping any longer, she went to bed. She knew tomorrow would be a long day.

The cheater's plan had worked. She was captain and Andie was not and nobody suspected a thing.

The next day, Andie woke up ready to face the day. She dressed in all white and ran to the White team meeting place like everyone else on the White team. Jamie and Natalie introduced themselves to everybody and explained to the new campers how Color Days would go.

Kaitlin, Andie's best friend, held hands with her as they walked to the mess hall together. They sat with the rest of their cabin. Natalie sat with the rest of the captains talking about how excited she was to be captain. Jamie decided to sit with the cabin instead though. She wanted to spend the last few days with her camp "sisters."

Later, Andie came out of the water soaking wet. She had just won the swimming race. She tried to find Jamie to tell her that she had won so that she could keep track of the wins and losses. Andie tried to avoid Natalie. She had been acting a little weird since she had become captain. It made Andie wonder if something unusual was going on. Andie and Jamie walked back to the cabin for rest hour when the activities were over.

Jamie sat outside the cabin that afternoon writing in her journal. "Jamie, come get your letters," yelled her counselor from inside the cabin. She set her journal down and went into the cabin. While she was gone, Andie couldn't help but look at what was written in Jamie's journal: *It worked! I am captain, and Andie isn't. I feel kind of bad that it had to be Andie, but at least nobody even gave it a second thought.*

"Oh my gosh," Andie whispered. "This has nothing to do with Natalie. It was Jamie."

Andie grabbed the journal and ran. She ran as fast as she could until she reached the office. Jamie was hot on her heels; she knew what was about to happen. Andie almost ran the door over. "SHE CHEATED!" Andie screamed.

"What?" everybody looked at each other, confused.

"Jamie cheated! It says right here in her journal," Andie argued.

"No, I didn't," Jamie protested. "I didn't cheat, but Andie should be in trouble for looking through my stuff!"

"Let me see that," Dayna, the camp director, said calmly. She read the page and asked, "Is this true, Jamie?"

"NO! I would never do such a thing," Jamie said grabbing her journal back

"I don't know," Dayna sighed, calming the girls. "If you can prove it, Andie, there will be consequences for Jamie."

Andie was almost in tears when she remembered, "The cameras! There are cameras in the office!"

"Okay then. Let's go check them right now," Dayna said walking towards the computers.

"I did it," Jamie cried. "I did it! I cheated! I knew nobody would vote for me because this was only my second year as a camper here. I changed the captain from Andie to me."

"I appreciate your honesty, but there are consequences for cheating," Dayna explained. "I will have to call your parents Jamie, and they will come here to pick you up. You will not be able to participate in the rest of Color Days."

Jamie sat on the bench crying. Andie felt bad. "That's a little harsh. Can't she stay?"

"I'm sorry, girls," Dayna said apologetically. "Rules are rules."

"I have an idea," Andie declared.

Jamie swept the floors of the mess hall. Andie walked up to her. "I'm sorry it had to end this way."

"It's okay. It's my fault, and it's better than leaving. We all got what we deserved. You're captain, and I'm sweeping floors...," Jamie said sadly.

"Hey," Andie said leaving. "You can call me any time when we get home."

"Really?"

"Ye-"before Andie could finish, Jamie had engulfed her in a hug. They were camp "sisters" for life!

Crazy Coaster

In **CRAZY COASTER** *by* *Haley Lemberg, a girl goes to an amusement park to ride one ride, Cobra 5000. She ends up having a crazier day than she thinks.*

"AAAAAAAAAAHHHHHHHHHHHHHHHHHHHHHH!" I heard as I walked into the old amusement park. I only wanted to go on one ride. I started walking past all of the old, small, wooden, rotting rides to the new, shiny, blue and gold Cobra 5000. That was all I was going to go on because it had a sign that said five hours to the front of the line. I got in line for Cobra 5000.

The line only ended up being two hours. Many of the people in front of me said, "This line is too long. I want to go on something else." This is the first time I have ever been on this ride.

Finally it was my turn. On this ride you can't sit next to anybody. So there is enough room. I buckled my seatbelt, put the lap bar on, and looked at the red 80-foot drop. I looked to my right and saw the 50 loops. To my left were the tunnels and big hill. I was scared, but it was too late to get off.

The operator announced, "The roller coaster starts at 90 miles per hour. Then the drop makes it 120 miles per hour for the loops. We turn the speed up to 150 miles per hour for the tunnels. Then the coaster crawls up the 350-foot hill. It stops at the top and goes 200 miles per hour down the hill." Just hearing that made it feel like I had been on the ride already. "We will be starting the ride in ten seconds," said the operator. "10, 9, 8, 7, 6, 5, 4, 3, 2, 1!"

"AAAAAAAAAAAAAHHHHHHHHHHHHHHHHHHHHH!" We had already made it down the drop! Now we are heading toward the loops. I tried to count them as they went by, but I got too dizzy. Suddenly I felt the ride slow down in the middle of the loops. Then it came to a complete stop when we were upside down.

"AAAAAAAAAAHHHHHHHHHHHHHHHHHHHHHHHH!" I screamed. I heard the operator say, "We are having technical difficulties; we will get you off the ride as soon as possible." I was starting to feel dizzy. Then people starting passing out. The park called ambulances. I couldn't keep my eyes open. Then I started to black out.

When I woke up I was in the back of an ambulance. I had a bad headache and was scared. They told me what happened and that they were taking me to the hospital to make sure I didn't have brain damage or memory loss. I was lying down, and my head was throbbing still. They said, "Who are you? Where do you live? How old are you?" I answered them correctly, so they knew I didn't have brain damage.

After about an hour they drove me back to the park so I could drive my car home. "Wow, that was a long day," I thought.

A week later there was an article in the newspaper. It talked about what happened that day at the amusement park. It said that on the ride before mine a person's hat and glasses were caught in the track. So my ride ran it over and got stuck. If the ride didn't stop when it did it would have flipped off the track.

Glass Jump

*Being stuck in a glass elevator seems harmless. Read **GLASS JUMP** by **Max Sandler**, and discover what harm actually happens.*

Having to get down to the first floor, I stepped into the glass elevator alone. The second floor was pretty far from the first floor, about three stories. I started to move down, but then the elevator squealed, eventually reaching a stop. I got kind of nervous and jumpy. I saw people walk out onto the atrium of marble below. They gaze up towards me, with a look that says "I'm glad I'm not you." I realized there was an emergency phone. I opened the small box that contained the phone. I called the main desk.

"Hello?"

"Hello, sir? Are you the man trapped in the elevator?"

"Yeah. Is there something you can do?"

"Unfortunately you are stopped at a distance directly in between floors. There is really no way to get to you. We are unable to fit a fire engine in this space. We are sincerely sorry for this situation. We'll try everything we can."

It was 2:00 P.M. Getting out of here is what I intend to do. But as of now, all I can do is wait.

It has officially been nine hours. Panic has already set in. The combined pressure of fear and anticipation made me roar with anxiety. I step up to the glass, and glance downwards. It seems as if I'm only about two stories from the floor. I can't take this. I stand back, grab my coat, and put it on. I take a deep breath, and close my eyes. I realize I have to jump in order to get out of here, and I know that there are dangers to this. I'm willing to take some risks.

The crash and the pain were both too extreme for me to handle. I screamed in agony as I headed toward the marble floor, shards of glass surrounding me. I landed on my shoulder, and I landed hard. People gasped in horror as they thought about the worst. I kept my head down on the floor, quietly weeping. I rose slowly, only to see everyone standing there, staring. After seconds of that position, I collapsed back to the floor from the throbbing misery. Eventually, the exhaustion got to me. My eyes started to shut. Everything just started to go blurry...blurry...black.

I open my eyes, only to realize I have been placed in a hospital. The nurse comes in.

"Sir?"

"Yeah?"

"The doctors needed to perform some emergency surgery on your shoulder. Your collar bone is fractured, but that should heal in good time."

"Oh. Well, thank you for informing me."

"No problem. It's what we do here, sir."

I hear some footsteps walk toward me. I'm very tired, so I just gently nod off.

My eyes ajar once again, I notice I have been put in the comfort of my own home. The pain is still in my shoulder, and frankly, my whole body, I start for the basement. Some aspirin should be somewhere down there.

Walking down the stairs, I get farther into the darkness. There are no windows, no lights, no food. I close the door behind me. Grabbing the medication, I turn around and head back upstairs. I get to the door. It has been locked from the outside. Here we go again.

Karl...Is My Life

Karl was a messed up kid who likes to annoy girls. Will Mikaela have to put up with Karl by her side every minute? Find out in **KARL...IS MY LIFE** *by* **Mikaela Kosik.**

Karl was a not-so-typical kid. He wore glasses, had a different hair cut every single week, and had a best friend who was my brother. Messed up, right? Well, he may be messed up, but so is his mom. She just collapsed after seeing Karl's new haircut and was rushed to the hospital.

"Ok, see you soon." My brother Evan closed his phone. "Mikaela, guess what? Wait, don't guess. Karl is staying here for the week!"

"You're joking, right? This was supposed to be my good week. I was going to hang with all my friends, but you always have to ruin it with Karl."

See, that would not be a problem if his number one priority were not to bug me. Unfortunately, it is his number one priority. I packed my things to run out to my neighbors and see if I could stay there for a while, but right when I ran out the door, it was too late. Karl had arrived.

"Ow! Move! I'm trying to run to Jane's house before Karl gets here," I shouted!

"Sorry, but Karl is already here," Karl whispered in my ear.

I screamed so loudly all the neighbors could hear! "Go home, please!" I yelled as I ran back into the house.

I started to think of a plan to get Karl out of the house. I heard crying from the room that Karl was staying in. I walked past his door thinking, *Wow, he's annoying already*. I had to find a way to make this week fun, so, before I went into his room, I got a water balloon, filled it with hot water and threw it right at his face. Oh, when I said fun? I meant for me.

Actually it turned out it wasn't him crying; it was his mom on the phone. After the water balloon incident, he ran upstairs into my room, picked me up, and threw me into the pool.

"Karl, what the heck! You don't just throw someone into the pool. I mean, who does that?" I yelled.

"Oh, I feel so bad; here, let me clean you off," Karl snorted sarcastically.

The week was finally over. It had many interesting and annoying turns including: me getting thrown into the pool more than 15 times, Karl getting bounced off the trampoline more than 20 times, Karl trying to give me a hug too many times, and many other trips in the water and on the dirt. Karl even got me when he said he was staying for three more days.

"Bye, Karl, have fun back home," I shrieked as hard as I could into his ear the morning I thought he was leaving.

"Oh, I'm not leaving. My mom might be home, but I want to chill here with you for a couple more days," Karl laughed.

"No, you don't. You just want to stay here to bug me and that's it. So just go." I almost cried.

"No, really, I want to stay."

Now we had a problem. He wanted to stay. I guess I'd have to deal with it for a couple of more days. But I couldn't; he was too annoying! He tried to hug me and always sat next to me.

Finally, we said our happy goodbyes and he left. Then, I realized something. Karl was crazy and different from other tenth-grade guys. He was a little out of the box, but Karl was and is Karl. And nothing will ever change that.

Kaylie's Cove

When Kaylie isn't allowed to see a visiting friend, they decide to meet in secret. Little do they know a dangerous adventure lies just ahead in **KAYLIE'S COVE**, *by* **Lexxe Lipsey**.

"What's he saying?" I signed.

"You don't want to know," James signed back.

"Stop that! Don't you know how annoying that weird hand thing is?" Dad said in his stern I-mean-business voice. "You can't be causing trouble like this! I don't have time to be watching over two ungrateful children every second!" I glared at him as I read his lips.

Why did Mom have to marry such a horrible guy? I just didn't get it. What did she see in him that was so great? She always tells me everything will work out in the end, but I don't see it. How could everything "work out" after I'm dragged to Florida to live with him in his boring, old private estate? After I am forced to leave my best friend Angie back home? After I'm forced leave my town, my school… maybe even my life. After I'm forced to live in a new home, new town, new state? After I am forced to try and find new friends?

"Leave her alone," James yelled back. He pulled me away, back outside, and I didn't resist. I was lucky to have James for an older brother. He was tall and muscular for fourteen, and he protected me from our stepdad, who was huge, with broad shoulders and dark brown hair. Dad had an unreadable face and serious blue eyes. I never saw him without a suit on. Whatever his job was must have been pretty tough, because he always seemed to be in a bad mood.

I was guessing Dad had said something back at us, but I didn't hear him. I never heard anyone, I couldn't. I was deaf. I didn't really care; I still got to speak in sign language, and I am good at reading lips. I don't speak a lot; it's usually hard to understand me when I do. I like the way I am, how I'm different. I like my shoulder-length brown hair, my hazel-brown eyes, and the way they sparkle like my mom's. I like my personality, and even my goofy smile. Dad, on the other hand, likes me about as much as I like him, and frankly, that's very little. He really isn't very accepting of me. I suppose he was expecting something great, because a deaf, twelve-year-old child didn't seem to make him very happy.

"Kaylie, you can't be getting us in trouble like that," James signed. He looked at me with disappointment on his face. I turned away, slightly embarrassed. I knew I shouldn't have freed the mice in the kitchen, but I couldn't stand and watch them suffer and die. Besides, that whole incident probably scared them enough to stay away. It didn't seem a big deal to me, but I didn't want to cause problems. I turned back and looked him in the eye.

"I'm sorry, I won't do it again."

I could see out of the corner of my eye, the maid, Samantha, from across the yard waving for me to come and finish my homework. I turned around and hesitated. I never wanted to go back there again, but what choice did I have? I walked towards the house.

The next morning I woke up late and quickly braided my hair. Samantha had already left my breakfast of scrambled eggs and toast on the huge oak table, meant to seat twelve people. My mother was sipping coffee as I sat down, and James had already left for baseball practice with his new friends Adam and Mose.

Lucky him.

I went outside to get some fresh air. Maybe I could find something to do on this lonesome Saturday. I passed through the living room on my way out the door. I saw Dad reading the paper silently. He didn't seem to notice me pass, or even the TV as a reporter went on about the bad weather.

The sun shone down brightly on my face as I sat down in the front yard facing the house. I have to admit, the place was beautiful. The garden was tropical and the white walls of the mansion looked freshly painted. The smell of sweet mangos lingered in the air, intertwined with the smell of salt water. The sky was a beautiful blue, empty except for the hot sun.

Someone tapped me from behind, interrupting my thoughts. "This is for you, Kaylie," Samantha signed with a smile. She handed me something and turned away to walk back to the house.

An envelope!

I shredded through it hastily. There was a card inside, neatly folded in two. It read:

Hey Kaylie! I hope you're having fun in Florida! I just got great news! I'm spending Thanksgiving break in Lido Key! Don't you live near there? I might be able to see you! I'm so excited. See you then. Love, Angie

I was surprised to see the letter. It felt like forever since I had last seen her. I went to tell Mom downstairs. I found her on the couch working on her laptop. She looked up. "Mom, Angie's coming," I signed quickly, "During Thanksgiving Break!"

Mom hesitated a moment, "That's great honey," she signed back. "Why don't you go tell Dad?"

Hmm, hadn't thought of that. She didn't seem as thrilled as I was expecting either, and I wondered why. I ran upstairs and hurriedly explained everything to Dad in his office. He didn't like me going in there, but I couldn't wait. His desk was neat, with thick stacks of paper in rows in front of him. He thought a minute, probably trying to decipher what I said. I was about to speak again, slower, when he said, "Kaylie, I really can't be having your friends over right now, I've been very busy, and can't be disturbed."

I stared at him, devastated and shocked. When I finally managed to speak, I spoke slowly, signing as I talked, "Dad, please. It would make me really happy."

He went back to his work, and spoke with his head down, making it very hard for me to understand him. He said something like, "You can't always get your way, Kaylie. Now leave, and don't waste my time."

I turned around choking back tears, but I knew this wasn't over. So what if he didn't want Angie over here? It sure didn't mean I wouldn't see her, and I had a plan. I ran back up to my room, thinking. I knew exactly what to do.

The next day after breakfast, I dug through my closet until I found the paper I had written Angie's username on, and logged onto chatroom.com, where I could connect and text her online.

Kaylie-roxs22: *Hey Angie!*
AngieAngel436: *K, u got my letter?! Do u want 2 hang out? How r u?*

Kaylie-roxs22: *That's the thing. My dad said I couldn't c u, but I know how we can see each other.*

AngieAngel436: *I don't know… what's ur idea?*

Kaylie-roxs22: *Well, I know this place. It's down a little way away from where I live, but I could bike there. I think u would be close, too, because you're staying at Lido Key, right?*

AngieAngel436: *Yes…*

Kaylie-roxs22: *So, u tell ur parents you're biking to my house, and I tell my parents I'm biking to the beach to hang out. We could spend the day together, and then will go back home, and they'll never know!*

Angie took her time before responding.

AngieAngel436: *I don't know, what if we get caught, or something happens?*

Kaylie-roxs22: *Nothing's going 2 happen and there is no way we'll be caught. It's perfect! I'll send you the address tomorrow!*

I logged off quickly, before she had the chance to respond. Everything was going to be great!

A week later, Thanksgiving break had arrived. Today was the day I would get to see Angie! I packed a backpack of two ham and cheese sandwiches, a few water bottles, my towel, and a flashlight, all the stuff we would need at our secret location. Then I headed out back where my mom was bathing in the sun. She already knew Angie wasn't coming over, so she was a little surprised to see me carrying my bag. "Hey Mom, I think I'm going to go hang out at the beach." I brushed my hair out of my eyes, and leaned on my side as I waited for an answer. I was pretty hot in my bathing suit and cover-up dress. I was thankful for the cool breeze.

"Alright honey, but be back by seven o'clock okay? Promise me that?" I smiled as I read her lips.

"Sure, okay, I will Mom." My guilt wrapped around me as Mom looked back at me for a second before going back to lying down and reading her magazine. Maybe I shouldn't do this, I thought to myself, but it was too late. I went back out into the front yard and hopped on my bike.

Before long, I had arrived at my destination. I had discovered the small beach the third day I moved here. It was out behind a cluster of trees. There was a small cave near it, and the sand was a beautiful white color. The ocean was a marvelous blue, as clear as the sky. I laid down my towel on the warm, dry sand and waited for Angie to arrive.

After a while I saw her appear, and realized it had been a long time since we were last together. Her red hair had grown out past her shoulders, and she was taller than I remembered her, at least two inches taller than me. She still had that pretty white smile and her bathing suit was covered with flowers. She wore a polka-dotted backpack and was carrying a towel. She laid it down beside me and sat down.

"What's up?" she spoke slowly, giving me time to read her lips and comprehend.

I smiled. It was just like before. We sat there together for a while, staring at the sea and taking everything in without saying anything. I finally decided to break the silence. "Still remember sign language?" I asked, signing as I spoke aloud.

She signed back and smiled. "Yep." I wasn't surprised; Angie had always had a good memory, even for sign language. Sometimes it's difficult because in sign language you don't always speak in full sentences, there just aren't enough signs for every word. It's quicker that way, and as long as people can understand me, it works.

We talked for awhile, catching up with each other. I felt great, like we had never left each other. The thought of her going back to Minnesota made my stomach sink, so I pushed that thought away. "Want to go on an adventure?" I shorted the sentence in sign language.

"Where to captain?" she signed, grinning. We used to play games like that as little kids. I stood up, and then pointed to the cave. "How?" Angie continued, giving me a questioning look. "Won't it be dark in there?"

I pulled out my flashlight and showed it to her.

"Nice. Let's go." Her eyes filled with excitement. I led the way, beaming the flashlight on the walls. Angie was right, after barely going anywhere, the cave became pitch black, but we kept going, enjoying ourselves and playing around. Angie grabbed the flashlight and turned it on.

"See any gold yet, Captain?" she mouthed.

"Not yet, Lad, be patient."

We smiled at each other. Twenty minutes into the cave, we stopped to take a break. I checked my waterproof watch I was wearing- 5:30. We didn't have much longer. I pulled out the sandwiches, and we ate them thankfully, gulping down water. Angie had brought Chex Mix and oranges too, but we decided to save them for later.

Just then, the earth began to rumble, and dirt fell down on our heads. I stuffed the sandwich wrappers into my bag and stood up quickly. "Hurry, we have to get out of here," I screamed. Angie didn't need the head's up, she was already packing up and standing too. We began to sprint, faster than I ever thought I could run. I saw the light at the end of the cave, but then...

Crack! Boom!

The rocks just above our heads plummeted downward. Angie and I ducked, diving out of the way. The cave became dark. I pulled out my flashlight and shone it in front of us. There was an entire wall of boulders blocking our path. We were trapped in the cave! The ceiling continued to crumble down as we ran the other way. The earth cracked and shook loudly, making earsplitting screeches through the air. I could feel the vibrations from the noise. The smell and taste of the dust flying in the air filled my nostrils. Then, suddenly, it stopped. Whatever it was, it was over, done. Just like that, as quickly as it had come, it was gone. I stopped running.

"Earthquake."

"What?" It took me a minute to register what Angie had said.

"Earthquake," she signed. "That was an earthquake."

The realization hit me. We were trapped in a cave, an earthquake had hit us, and there was no way out! My mind was racing. What if there's an aftershock? How will we get out? Will anyone find us? Will we survive? Did my family survive? What would they say?

Small rocks falling down had bruised my entire body, my cover-up was ripped, and my arm was stained with blood. For as bad as I looked, Angie looked even worse. Her left shoulder looked out of place on her arm, and across her cheek she had a bleeding gash. Her skin was turning black-and-blue all over from bruising, like mine. If one of us went into shock there would be nothing we could do. We would die. I couldn't speak. All of this, it was my fault, and there was nothing I could do to change it.

I looked at Angie, who had sat down. I couldn't look at her, so I spoke aloud. "I'm sorry Angie, all of this, it's my…" Angie grabbed my arm.

"This isn't your fault, you didn't cause that earthquake."

"No, but I did…"

"Kaylie, I don't blame you for any of this. We'll be fine. We just have to find a way out." She spoke with confidence on her face, but I saw what she had been trying to hide: fear. Even though I couldn't hear it in her voice, I saw it in her eyes. I realized how stupid this whole idea had been, and even how much stupider I had been to go into the cave without any real equipment, like extra batteries, or a first aid kid. I knew I had to find a way out and soon, because Angie was looking really pale. I wanted to keep walking in the opposite direction, but I knew Angie was too hurt to keep going right then. Instead, I lay down beside her and ripped off my cover-up.

The fabric was light, so it split in half easily. I dampened part of it with a little of our water, and then scrubbed away as much blood and dirt as I could off myself. Angie did the same, but even after she still looked beaten. Angie used the other half of the cover-up as a sling.

After a couple of hours, she fell asleep lying against the wall, but I couldn't. I stood watching shadows move that weren't there, and feeling more depressed than I ever had. The cave was darker than anything I had ever seen. Every little noise made me jump. Why hadn't I seen this coming, it was so obvious. I remembered walking through the living room, seeing the reporter giving warnings. Why hadn't I listened?

It was cold by now, much colder than I ever thought Florida could get. I pulled out our towels and wrapped them around us, thankful we hadn't gotten them wet swimming. A while later, Angie woke up, looking stronger. We ate the oranges slowly, savoring every bite. We had scarcely any water now, little more than half a bottle. This concerned me, but not half as much as how ghastly

Angie and I looked. Where our skin wasn't bruised, it was pale. That wasn't a good sign. It was easy to see we were both exhausted.

We stood up, barely capable of moving, but amazingly walked on, hoping to find a way out of the cave. By now it was most likely dawn. We had been in here how long, ten hours? Our parents were sure to be wondering about us by now. We walked slowly, never speaking, until we could go no further. We ate the rest of the food, and drank the last of the water. We slept more, and soon we had been in there over a day.

The earth shook again, but not as violently. Angie and I both hit the ground, without the energy to run. We covered our heads with our hands, and were pelted with small rocks from above. My heart sank. It was an aftershock. My head spun like crazy as I waited. I prayed the rock shower would just end, and be over. Soon enough, my wish came true.

My forehead was now gushing blood, and my leg hurt so badly I couldn't move it. Angie didn't seem much better. She was gasping for air and crying, and at that moment I realized I was too. All my emotions poured out of me at once, like a huge waterfall, until I couldn't cry any longer. I went over to sit next to Angie. I tried my best to comfort her, but she was comforting me more than I was her. Tired and defeated, I curled up into a ball and fell asleep next to her.

I gently opened my eyes sometime later, to see a bright light. There was a figure in front of me, big and tall. It picked me up gently, but I couldn't make out who it was. My eyes were adjusted to the darkness of the labyrinth cave, so I couldn't see through into the welcoming brightness. Small rocks fell overhead. "It's okay," whispered a familiar voice, and I knew they were right. I watched their mouth move slowly, as if they knew I needed to read their lips. I felt safe and was too exhausted to try and stay awake. Slowly, I closed my eyes and drifted back to sleep. The last thing I thought to myself was: *Who was that figure?*

I blinked as I awoke and tried to sit up. Where was I? What happened? Just as I thought these things, everything came back to me: the cave, the earthquake, the figure! I took in my surroundings and knew where I was instantly. The hospital! I was lying on a simple white hospital bed, next to Angie. She was okay, too! I took a deep breath of relief. Then I saw the last thing in the room. Dad was sitting in the hospital chair. Our eyes locked and all I could do was stare back at him.

It all made sense. Dad had found us, helped save us! He was the one who had carried me out, but why? Dad didn't like me, or so I thought. Seeing my look of confusion, Dad said, "You were right, Kaylie, everyone deserves to be happy. I guess I didn't realize just how much you meant to me until that earthquake hit. I was so worried you had been killed."

"How did you find us?"

Dad smiled, staring out at something I couldn't see. "You went to the place I went to as a kid, the cove. I had a lot of good times there, and when you didn't come back and the earthquake hit, I knew where to search."

I looked at him in disbelief, wondering if I had read his lips incorrectly. Then I turned towards Angie. She looked just as surprised as I felt. But I couldn't help the feeling of joy that bubbled up inside me at the thought of Dad trying to save us. I could see he was more concerned for me than upset by now.

The next day, Angie and I were both out of the hospital. Angie's arm was broken and I had twisted my ankle, but we would both be all right. Angie left after break, but at least we had gotten to see each other.

I never did exactly thank Dad for what he did for us that day. I'm not even sure I would know what to say. Being trapped in that cave for thirty-two hours had been a nightmare. What I do know is he loves me, and that's better than anything I could have ever asked for.

The Little Boy
Who Loved Candy

THE LITTLE BOY WHO LOVED CANDY, *by* ***Marvin*** ***McIntosh,*** *is the story of a young boy named Clifford who loved candy very much. But, Clifford's experience with eating candy did not end up so well.*

Clifford loved candy so much that he would dream about candy all the time. At night, he would sometimes hide candy under his pillow for a late night snack without his parents knowing about it. He would even hide the wrappers and throw them away when his parents were busy. Clifford did not want them to find out about the candy.

One day, his class had a Valentine's Day party at school. Clifford was so excited because there was lots of candy. There were so many kinds of candy that he didn't know what to eat first!

He began to eat so much that it made his stomach hurt. He was feeling so sick that he had to ask his teacher for help. Suddenly, he threw up. The teacher immediately called the office to let them know what was happening in the classroom. The office told his teacher to send him to the school nurse.

Clifford did not want to go to the nurse because he was scared of needles and did not like to see blood. The teacher told him that he must go so that she could check him out and hopefully give him something to make him feel better.

When he got to the nurse's office, she looked at Clifford and asked him about how much candy he ate today. Clifford looked down with a sad face and said, "Well, today, I think I may have had about ten pieces of candy, but maybe more."

"No wonder your stomach hurts and you threw up," the nurse said. "Oh honey, that is too much candy. I'm going to call your parents. I need to tell them what happened and that you are not feeling well so they can pick you up."

Clifford begged the nurse not to call because he did not want to get grounded. "Can't we leave this between you and me?" Clifford begged.

The nurse said, "I can't keep it a secret. I have to tell your parents. Sorry, honey."

When his mom got there to pick him up, he immediately told his mom that he was sorry for eating so much candy. He promised to never eat that much candy again. His mom looked at him and said, "Nope! You are grounded since I told you to stop eating so much candy. You did not listen so you are grounded for two weeks." Clifford's mom continued, "Candy can make you get yellow teeth and make you throw up like you did in school. That is what candy can do to you."

"I will try to never eat candy ever again." Clifford said finally, "I'm sorry, Mom."

"Okay," Clifford's mom replied. "I hope you keep your promise."

Lost in Alaska

When an Alaskan Moose hunt goes wrong, a young hunter is forced to live in the wild. Will he ever find his way back? Find out when you read **LOST IN ALASKA** *by* **Jack Hill**.

Day 1: Lost

I could see my breath in the crisp November air as a monster walked in front of me. My guide, Jimmy, gave me the signal to shoot. I released my arrow and hit the moose. It hit a little far back, but still a good shot. It didn't bring it down, though. Something must have clicked in it because it decided to charge!

It barely missed me, but it hit Jimmy in the chest. I thought it killed him, but he sprang back to life. The moose's nostrils were flaring, so I decided to run into the woods. The sun was setting over the treetops. I had to go into the Alaskan wilderness with nothing but a backpack and my bow.

I had run for miles, never looking back. I stopped in a clearing, and in front of me was a cave. I could stay there for the night. And that is what I did. I draped my coat over me and dozed off. I had a long trip ahead of me.

Day 2: Food

That night, the freezing rain fell outside the cave. I was able to find water, but I still had to find food. So I set out to find the moose that I shot earlier. With my arrowheads, I marked the trees as I went past. This was very helpful. It enabled me to find my way back to the cave. After marking my eighth tree, I looked over into a field of wildflowers and saw my bull moose.

I used my broad heads, or arrowheads, to gut the beast. Its musty odor made me gag. I took off my jacket and used it to carry the meat back to the cave. When I got back to the cave, I rummaged through my bulging pack for a book of matches. Once I found them, I made a fire, put a little moose meat over it, and had a feast.

Day 3: Bear

The next morning, I felt like something was watching me. The feeling was bizarre. It felt like something was breathing on my neck and watching my every move. When I decided to leave the cave to find some water, it happened. It felt like I was hit by a bus! However, this bus had sharp teeth and claws. It was a big brown bear.

He chomped down on my forearm and shook his head with locked jaws. Then I heard a loud *boom*, and the bear ran off. I fell to my side to see Jimmy with a pistol pointed in the air. He hobbled over to treat my wound. I was bleeding out fast so Jimmy wrapped his bandana around my arm. After that, I blacked out.

Day 4: Rescued

When I woke up, there was a helicopter outside the cave, and I was on a gurney. They rushed me to a hospital in Nome, Alaska. That was my first, but not last, adventure in Alaska.

Misunderstood

MISUNDERSTOOD *by **Sabrina Woo** is the story of a girl who feels forgotten by her whole family. It tells us the life of a single eighth-grader and how she fought for attention.*

As I am standing here today saying goodbye to my sister, Maria, before she boards her flight to California State University, I look back and see it didn't start this way. It all started at the beginning of the school year.

I was just starting eighth grade at O'Keeffe Middle School in Madison, Wisconsin, and my sister was a senior at Memorial High School in Madison. This year was like every other year: Come back in August from visiting our dad in Delaware, and then start the school year. But when we came back home our mom and John, our step-dad, gave their attention to Maria right when we got off the plane. They ran to her, hugging her a million times, and just said hi to me.

I thought, *Don't worry. Since it is Maria's last year at home then of course they would go to her first.* On the car ride home I didn't know what was happening because I was asleep the entire time until I got home.

When we got home, Maria and I asked our mom when we were going to go shopping for school supplies. John said that he could take us right now if we wanted. We checked the time and saw that it was only 3:30 P.M. When we got to the store Maria and I saw all our friends.

The next week school started, and I was so happy. On the first day of school when I got to my locker my friend Stephanie had the locker right next to mine. Right there when we saw each other we started talking about what we thought the school year was going to be like, and then Stephanie and I started talking about our sisters, who are also friends with each other. They had been friends since kindergarten. Then Stephanie said, "Well, Tori, soon everything is going to change. Alice already is the center of my family's attention, and everyone has forgotten about me."

"Steph, it's happening to me every day. They forget about me more, and I hate it!"

"Now you know how I feel."

"Well, that is true." Then the bell rang to go to first hour.

"Gotta go, Tori. See you at lunch. Bye."

"Bye, Steph." When I was walking to first hour I was thinking about what Stephanie had said. I had trouble understanding why. Before I knew it I was right in front of my classroom door.

It felt as if the day were over in two minutes. When I got home no one even said hi or "How was your first day at school?" This time they didn't even talk to me. I felt as if I were a ghost. Even my own parents didn't notice me. I thought it was really weird that whenever I called my dad nobody answered, but when Maria did he always answered. When I walked in the door and said hi, there was not one word from anyone.

That kept going on for months. When I made the honor roll no one said a thing, but when Maria brought her report card home and they saw she had raised an E to a B-, she got to have a huge dinner party. Well, I was happy for Maria, but I thought since Maria has some bad grades she shouldn't have a huge dinner party. I thought she should just spend her time studying to get better grades and get a small gift or something.

I got tired of my family treating Maria better, so I made an appointment with the counselor. When I told the counselor my problem, she asked a few questions like, "How long has this been going on? How did you feel?" and stuff like that. My counselor, Mrs. King, made a call to my mom, and it sounded like things were going okay. Mrs. King hung up the phone understanding why Maria was being treated better. Mrs. King said, "Victoria, if you would like to find out why your parents are treating your sister better, then wait 'til you get home, okay?"

I felt like everyone was keeping a secret from me, but I just replied, "Okay, thank you for your time, Mrs. King."

As I was walking out she replied, "No problem."

When I got back to my locker, I told Stephanie what happened. Stephanie said, "Well you better race home then."

At the end of the day when I got home my mom and John told me why. They said that Maria might not have the grades to go to college. I felt so sorry because I had treated my sister so badly and was mean to her.

In January, Maria got a full scholarship to California State University for volleyball. Our whole family was happy for her and was really excited that she was going to college. Now I am here at the airport saying goodbye to my sister and remembering the year that I had.

My Name is Semaj

Semaj gets injured from an argument with his best friend. Will this lead to death or a change in their friendship? Find out in **MY NAME IS SEMAJ** *by* **Sydney Patton**.

M*arch 29, 2010*

I'm walking home with my friend Wesinton. "Hey James," he said. The only reason he kept saying that is because the substitute said my name backwards. (Isn't that great the whole class laughed at me in sixth hour?) As we were walking I tried to cross the street. *BOOM*. I was hit by a car. The last thing I heard was Wesinton yelling, "Semaj!"

June 15, 2010

"Come on we're going to be late," I yelled. I flung open the door and ran to the car. I reached in the car and started to unload all of the chairs, blankets, and the net of soccer balls. Everyone came pouring out of the house including our dog Doobie. Doobie is an Alaskan husky with soft, thick, straight fur. She has brown eyes with dazzling white and golden brown fur. Her body looks very strong and she is very active.

Billie, my brother, had to chase her back into the house. My dad started the car and we were off to my championship game for soccer. My dad is the coach. I'm the team captain. (People ask me why I'm the team captain, it's not because the coach is my father, it's because I'm good at what I do.) We showed up at the soccer field just in time, ten minutes before the game was to start. Five of my teammates were already there.

"Ready to play?" I yelled to Wesinton.

"I sure am, James!" Wesinton replied.

"Stop calling me that; it's not funny," I hollered

"Ok, James," Wesinton called back with a sly face.

"It's Semaj," I mumbled walking away.

Nad came up to me and patted me on the back. "It's okay, he always calls me Dan," he said. I gave him a crooked smile back as if to say, thanks for cheering me up friend, but either way it goes, Wesinton is still a mean jerk at times.

I jumped in place to warm up some. This Wesinton, my so called best friend, was coming over to my house for the rest of the weekend. I'm sort of upset because I invited him over myself with my dad's permission.

Coach signaled the team to huddle together. "Okay team we're all in this together. Do your best and don't back down," he shouted with enthusiasm. We all got in place on the soccer field. The referee blew his whistle. I quickly passed it to Nad, he dribbled some with a couple of tricks then shot it to Oscar. I sprinted toward the net. The ball flew to me.

"I'm open! I'm open!" Wesinton shouted. I ignored him as I punted the ball into the net.

"Goal," the referee shouted.

"What's your problem?" Wesinton growled at me.

"What's wrong? Are you mad because you don't know how to score a goal?" I remarked.

For the rest of the game, I passed the ball to Nad and Oscar the most instead of Wesinton. We won the game. I scored six goals, Nad scored four, and Oscar scored one. Everyone had fun except Wesinton. I could tell he was furious. He only got five passes and he missed his shot when trying to score a goal.

We all went to Genn Jon's Pizza Palace. I saw Wesinton fooling around with Jereck and Willkin at the end of the table. At the end, Wesinton, Nad, and I stayed to the very last end of the party. I asked my dad if Nad could stay at our house for the rest of the weekend. He said, "Ask mom." She agreed. We all got into the car, Wesinton who looked surprised, sat up front with my brother. Nad and I sat in the very back talking.

We arrived at the house. I was so excited. This weekend was going to be great. We all went inside and packed for our trip to Lake City. We took the three hour drive to Lake. My mom stepped out with a load of bags in her arms. I helped her with them. Billie and Nad were racing to the door when Wesinton came behind me. He tripped me. I was real ticked off. I dropped all of my bags and tackled him. Wesinton rolled over on top of me. I reversed him back on his back. Nad's hands went under my arms and pulled me back. I was so angry I shouted, "I hate you Wesinton Polgeen!" I stood up straight and walked away.

"Coach, I mean Mr. Nackcin, can you take me home?" he pleaded.

"Sure thing, sport," my dad confirmed.

When we were all settled in, Nad, Billie, and I changed into our swimming trunks.

It was eight o'clock. I was sitting on the couch watching television. My dad came bursting through the door. We all went outside and caught fireflies. The rest of the weekend was great.

On our way home we dropped off Nad at home. We pulled up in the drive way and I saw Wesinton playing basketball down the street. Usually, I would join him, but all of the anger started building up. I wandered into the house.

Today is Monday, and Nad and I hung out for the whole day. We fooled around all week. We cracked jokes on Wesinton, Jereck, and Willikin the whole week.

Ding dong! "I'll get it!" I screeched. I opened the door.

"What are you doing here?" I mumbled. Doobie was standing right next to me growling.

"Oh nothing, James, I just wanted…" Wesinton was continuing right when the door was closing. He stopped in the middle of his sentence and stopped the door from closing.

"Wait, Semaj, I'm sorry. We've been best friends since first grade. I'm so sorry. Please stop avoiding me," he pleaded.

"Aaaannnnnndddd?" I added.

"I'll stop calling Nad, Dan," he muffled.

I flung open the door and smiled. He smiled back. I let him inside and we went to my room. There stood Nad by the Play Station remotes. Wesinton apologized, and we all went outside to play some basketball.

Ole' Carolina

An annual boat trip turns into a tragedy. When a young girl chooses to go on an annual trip on water with her parents, it takes a dismal turn. Find the answer to this twisting tale in **OLE' CAROLINA** *by **Daijeline K. Johnson.***

It all started on a cloudy, breezy summer day. Carolina was watching television in her room. It was time for the annual weeklong boat trip that Carolina's parents took. They usually would take this trip without her, but this year they wanted to take her along. It was time for Carolina to start packing.

While she was packing, she was scared because this was her first boat trip in her life. She wondered if the boat trip would be safe, if she was going to get sick, or maybe even arrive home safely. It was too much for her mind to comprehend, so all of a sudden Carolina fainted! She hit her head on the window and fell to the floor.

When she woke up she had a humungous lump and bruise on her forehead. Her parents ran into the room. She told them she was okay. That night she went to sleep with a boat ride on her mind.

When they left for their boat trip she was terrified! Her parents forced her to get on the fifty-foot yacht. She thought about it for a minute, and then saw her parents' faces, so she composed herself and slowly inched her way on to the boat. The captain, Robert, the First Mate, Denine and their daughter Raiylah met them. As soon as Raiylah saw Carolina she gave her a hug. Then she said,

"Do you like beef jerky?"

Carolina answered, "Yes!"

So then Raiylah gave her a piece. Once they were aboard, she sat down on the hull of the boat, to get a view of the lake. The boat took a little while to start, but that gave Carolina time to strap herself into one of the boat seats. The boat suddenly started. Carolina felt little drops of water on her skin coming from the splashing of the under-water propeller.

As the boat started to veer off into the lake, Carolina was worrying about sleeping on the boat. She was thinking about the *Titanic* and what happened to those people that night. As they traveled along the lake, Carolina soon found that boat rides weren't that bad. She was starting to get semi-comfortable on the boat. It was now 11:00 at night and it was time for her to go to sleep.

Two Hours Later

Carolina couldn't sleep, so she decided she wanted to go to the sky deck to look at the lake. Captain Robert made an announcement. He said, "We are running a little behind schedule so we are going to moor because it is getting dark and there is a closer dock a few miles east." Unfortunately, the announcement could not be heard on the sky deck, which Carolina was on.

Carolina saw a fish pop its head above the surface of the water. She was assuming the fish was hungry, so she reached in her pocket for a piece of beef jerky. She then leaned over the boat's starboard, and was about to throw the fish some food. Suddenly, the boat started to turn around. Carolina's pocket full of things was dumped onto the sky deck. Then she was thrown off the boat! One of her shoes came off as she was thrown off of the boat. She was torpedoed down. She flipped and hit her head on one of the windows, and then landed in the water unconscious.

First Mate Denine heard a thump above her. She was curious, so she charged for the sky deck. She looked around and saw a piece of beef jerky on the ground, a shoe, a cell phone, and a locket with a C on it.

She looked at the cell phone and flipped it open. The background of the cell phone had a picture of the girl, and it had her name, Carolina Divvits. Then Denine looked at the locket that had a C on it. It had a picture of a girl that was the daughter of the parents who chartered their boat, the Divvits. She looked out into the water and saw something moving under the water. She looked a little closer and saw bubbles coming up.

Denine immediately jumped in the water! Then she thought, *All of a sudden I collapsed through the surface, water's top and air's end. It was like I saw a blue portrait of never-ending water. I then saw a million particles of blue bubbles effervescing on top of me.*

She was back on top of the water. She saw a floating body, and charged for it. When she got to Carolina, she wasn't breathing! She hurriedly swam back to the boat and lugged her on top. She screamed, "Captain Robert, I need help, get the first aid kit!"

The Next Morning

Carolina was finally conscious. She awoke to a major headache and had a big gash on her head again. Her mother and father came to talk to her.
They asked, "Oh Honey, what did you do?"
Carolina replied, "Ma-Ma, Da-da?"
Her mom said, "Yes, it's us honey."
"Mama," Carolina replied again.
Her dad yelled, "Captain Robert, call a doctor!"

Three Hours Later

The doctor said, "We've determined that your daughter was in a coma, but now that she has awakened, she has retrograde amnesia. That means she may have a difficult time recalling past events and recent events. She may remember events from childhood, but not anything that happened recently. Just looking at her it appears she has regressed to her toddler years. I would suggest calling a doctor when you get home. It may take weeks, months, and even years to recover from her amnesia. You just need to take it a day at a time."

Fourteen Years Later

In South Carolina it was cloudy and breezy. Carolina was watching TV in her room while packing for her boat trip. She was scared because this was her first boat trip in her life. She wondered if she was going to get seasick or homesick. All of a sudden, Carolina was about to faint, but she caught herself. She wasn't injured so this time her parents didn't rush in. This all seemed somewhat familiar to her, but she didn't know why. That night she had a boat ride on her mind.

The next morning, they got to the boat. It was time to get on, but Carolina was terrified. Her parents urged her to get on. This time Carolina did not. She felt like something like this had happened before, but it was all a faded memory. She felt like this situation would end up having a dismal ending. She was a 28-year-old woman, and it was her choice to make.

Carolina said, "No," as she backed off the boat.

She said no because she was not going to be forced to do something she didn't want to do. Again, she had that feeling in her gut like this had happened before. Then suddenly, she questioned her parents, "Have you been hiding something from me?"

"No," her father said abruptly.

"Honey," the mother said in a stern voice. "Don't lie to our daughter."

"Dad, you lied to me?"

"Honey, don't worry about him now," she said as she walked Carolina over to the bench on the dock and told her. "A very long time ago, when you were fourteen years old, we took you on a boat trip just like this one. This is the same exact boat with the same exact people. We keep taking you this way hoping that it will somehow trigger your lost memory. So, it all started one night. You wandered up to the sky deck for some reason, and then an announcement was made. It could not be heard from the sky deck and the boat turned. You were thrown off and while you were going down, you hit your head on the boat and fell in the water. That day you went into a coma for a short while. When you came to, you weren't yourself. Then we called a doctor. He told us that day that you had retrograde amnesia. It works like this. What did your father do ten minutes ago?"

Carolina answered, "Well…umm…well… I, he… I forgot."

"So that's the whole story of your tragic childhood," her mother said.

"Thanks for the truth, Mom." She gave her father a scowling look. She walked off the boat and knew that she needed time to digest and reflect on this new information. She needed to decide how she would continue her life from that day forward.

A Ray of Hope

*In **A RAY OF HOPE** by **Lena Wachs**, a sixteen-year-old girl's parents die, and she has no other relatives that will take her. Being an orphan and surviving in a trailer, working two jobs, finding money for college and hiding her life from the government is nearly impossible. Can a young adult survive this harsh life?*

I slammed the door. It wasn't like there was a responsible mom home to hear my disgust and ask, "How was school, sweetie?" or "What's wrong, honey?" Nope. Mom was probably drunk at Rudy's place or getting high behind the bar. Rudy is mom's boyfriend. I trudged over to the crammed bathroom and looked in the mirror. My face was smudged with dirt and grease and my hair stuck out everywhere as if I had slept on the street. I went to the kitchen to find a crumpled bill on the table. Mom never pays the bills unless the bill collectors are at the point where they have to kick us out of the trailer. And Dad? He died of a heart attack when I was seven years old. It's been nine years since then. I'm not going to mourn over someone I don't even remember.

In the morning I realized I had been crying in my sleep. After taking a cold shower, I went to the kitchen. Opening the fridge, I noticed Mom wasn't screaming at Rudy. My ears liked the silence, so the first part of my morning was good. I devoured two pieces of bread and jelly and a glass of orange juice. I couldn't help being a little surprised that I hadn't heard my mom yet, so I walked to her bedroom. There was a motionless lump in the bed. I pulled the covers away and screamed into Mom's ear. She didn't move. I listened for a heartbeat. It was silent. I just stood there wondering what to do. I wasn't sad or happy. She was dead. I tried CPR and checked for a pulse. It had never been so quiet.

If the government found out, I would be sent to an orphanage. Foster parents would adopt me and I had heard terrible stories about how foster kids are abused. I didn't know how to cremate someone, so I went outside and dug a hole about four feet deep and six feet long. It wasn't very hard because the ground was soggy and soft. I walked back into the trailer and wrapped Mom up in her long sheets. I made sure the dead body wasn't visible and dragged her outside and into the hole. I took one last look at the lump in the ground and covered her up in dirt. My heart wasn't beating normally and I felt a little panicky.

It was really lonely even though if Mom were around I would be doing the same thing. I'm the type of person that only gets hungry when they know there isn't food, or when someone has to pee constantly when they know there isn't a toilet. It's the same thing with loneliness. At 8:00 A.M., I took advantage of the Sunday by staying in bed. Before I could take my socks off I was fast asleep. After about two hours, the doorbell woke me up. I pulled on my extra-large T–shirt and stumbled to the door. I opened it to find Rudy. There was a nasty look on his face to go along with his ripped jeans and stained shirt.

"Where's your mother?" he snarled.

"She went to the store," I replied casually.

"Tell her to call when she gets back."

"Here!" He shoved a check at me. I thanked him and closed the door. Part of the reason Mom was with Rudy was because he paid us $500 every month because mom agreed to help run Rudy's drugstore. I wasn't going to *not* accept it, because I needed the money.

I woke up at 2:00 in the morning and biked to Chick-fil-A. Chick-fil-A is a fast food restaurant sort of like McDonalds. Why do people want to have fried chicken at 2:00 in the morning? I don't know. The air was humid and foggy and it was warm outside, but shivers kept running up and down my spine. A soft, rainy mist sprayed into my face, so I started pedaling faster. Now the mist had turned into pouring rain. If I kept going I would be soaked, so I hopped off the bike and ran for cover under a tree. The occasional raindrop seeped through a branch. They made a pitter-patter rhythm on the soggy ground. There was a flash of light in the sky. It must have been lighting! I ran out from under the tree and chose the hilltop overlooking another neighborhood below it. I lay down flat so I would have a better chance of not being struck by lightning.

Suddenly, a wave of minty green and orange shimmered through the sky. The sun peeked out of the clouds and made the raindrops sparkle. It was the most magical thing I had ever seen. More colors rippled up above the horizon. This time they were pink and a dark blue and an even darker emerald green. Mist was still spraying lightly through the air, but it looked beautiful reflecting the painted sky. A rainbow was beginning to wash over the clouds. The humid air was now just comfortably warm with short breezes of cool wind. Everything smelled sweet like honeysuckle and lilacs. It was the perfect moment.

The birds stopped chirping. Everything went silent. Awed by the beautiful colors, my heart skipped a beat when dazzling bronze lightning sizzled in the distance. If these were fireworks then this was definitely the grand finale. Every color you could imagine was now spread across the sky's enormous canvas. Yellow billowed across the treetops while cream and purple and lavender flew across the clouds. A flaming orange licked the lining of the clouds like a hungry flame. Light blue danced across the houses' chimneys and left a dusty, pale pink behind it. As if they were watching, tiny, glittering, white stars blinked high above everything else. The show was over before I knew it. As if being sucked in, all the colors dissolved into the golden crack of dawn. The last to stand were the little stars. Eventually, the stars disappeared into the fog. I sat there waiting. I wished something would happen.

I returned home after work and leaned the bike against the wall. My legs felt shaky, my head was aching, my left eye was twitching, but worst of all I was craving a candy bar, so I walked down to the convenient store and bought a Milky Way, some Charleston Chew taffy bars, and stocked up on the 25 cent, just add water, macaroni and cheese boxes. I headed up to the checkout line. People were crowding around the newspaper rack. What was all the commotion about? I stuck my hand into the crowd and pulled out a paper. It read:

Tech TV Stock Soars!

I recognized the name. Mom had bought 5,000 shares for only $1 for each one. I continued reading. I couldn't believe my eyes when I read the next sentence. Now each share cost $100! I did the math in my head. If I sold all 5,000 shares for $100 per share… $500,000! I purchased everything as the cashier stared at me strangely. I walked home, went to the Tech TV website, and sold every single one on the shares. I called the managers of both my jobs and quit. The minute I stood up, the phone rang. It almost never did. I answered, "Hello, who is this?"

"This is Uncle Ray."

I loved Uncle Ray. He seemed like the only sensible one on my mother's side of the family. He was a genius too. One day, he just left his mansion and drove away. He said it had to do with work, but he never returned. "Uncle Ray? Where have you been?"

"I've been working on a top secret job with a few of my clients in Singapore. I wasn't allowed to tell anybody at the time, but I'm back at the house and done with the job." Even with the $500,000 I had, it could only afford a small house and I would have to figure something out for food and the water and lights bills and college. Should I risk telling Uncle Ray that my mother died?

"Uncle Ray, my mom died a few months ago. I didn't want to go to an orphanage or foster parents so I kept it a secret." I told him the rest of the story and there was a long pause when I had finished.

"I'll pick you up and you can live at my house. I'll just go to the social services and sign the guardian papers."

I told him what street I was on and hung up the phone. That was the most unexpected thing that could've happened! I ran into my bedroom and took all my clothes out of the drawers and put them in my bag. That was all I would need. I put my coat on and took the bag outside. Yet again, the sky was cloudy. Uncle Ray pulled up in a shiny, black, Porsche. Next door, Mrs. Smith stared at the car in awe. Other neighbors were also staring too. I got into the car and shut the door. The seats were soft and leathery and the car smelled like the new car smell. Uncle Ray drove away taking one last look at the trailer park asked, "How did you live like this?"

"It wasn't easy."

The rest of the way was silent until we pulled up into a long curved driveway. There were black iron gates. They opened up and an enormous mansion towered over us. It was like a palace. Long, leafy vines webbed the white stone towers. The grass was lush and manicured. It had little lavender flowers lining the trees that evenly lined up across the landscape. Uncle Ray parked the car in his four-car garage and we got out. He unlocked the back door and opened it. I walked into the house. There were rectangle shaped windows everywhere that let the sunlight pour into the kitchen. Everything was covered in a marble countertop. The walls were minty green with a tile splash back. The floor was a smooth maple wood. Before I could take everything else in, Uncle Ray led me upstairs. "Before I get back to my work, I will show you your bedroom. Feel free to tour the house and if you get hungry, ask Maria, my housekeeper, for lunch."

He left me at a paneled French door and briskly walked away. I opened the door and gasped. I was in the most beautiful bedroom a girl could ever have. The walls were purple and the carpeted floor was cream colored. There was a big queen sized bed that was covered in a velvet purple duvet cover. Over the bed, a crystal chandelier sparkled. Plush cream-colored beanbag chairs were sitting on a fuzzy, purple, rug. Velvet drapes hung over another window. As for entertainment, there was a Mac desktop computer, a 60-inch, flat screen, TV, and a stereo system with speakers.

I jumped onto the soft bed. All of the pillows were the kind with goose feathers in them. My head sank into them. I was too excited to sleep though. I walked downstairs into the bright kitchen. Maria was cutting onions and tomatoes. I waved to her. She smiled. Somehow, I found my way to Uncle Ray's office. Through the double French doors, I could see it was a mess. Papers had found their way on to the bookshelves in stacks, and pencils and pens were scattered randomly over the faded Oriental rug. I knocked on the door. Uncle Ray looked up from his work. "What school am I going to go to?" I questioned.

"You will go to Westleaf High. It's only two blocks from here." He handed me some textbooks and a lunch card.

"Thank you so much, Uncle Ray. Is it okay if I make a quick phone call?"

"If you ever need to call someone there's a phone in almost every room," he smiled

I jogged up the main staircase, passed through the marble hallway, stopped and got a soda at the upstairs kitchen's wine chiller, and finally reached my bedroom. Sure enough, there was a pager on my desk and a telephone attached to the wall. I dialed Rudy's number. "My mother is dead."

"I know." He hung up.

That actually didn't go as bad as I thought it would. Later on that day, I drove to the Westleaf High school in my new black BMW. The school looked really nice. There were lots of windows and huge, spacey lockers. I had everything I ever wanted. The $500,000 was being saved up for college and Uncle Ray was happy to pay for everything else. I made a few good friends and I was somewhat popular and not invisible to the kids in school. My life was actually turning out good. Even better, Uncle Ray got a job in Singapore to design advanced oil drilling systems and I got to go with him. I was inspired to be just like him when I grew up. There was a glittering future waiting for me, and for once I had something to look forward to.

Running with Avalanches

A young girl's adventure turns out to be a fight to save her dog from a destructive avalanche. To see what happens, read **RUNNING WITH AVALANCHES** *by* **Sarah P.**

School is the last place I would want to be on a Saturday, the absolute last. I was assigned detention from a 10th grade teacher for running in the hall. As I stared aimlessly at the ceiling of the detention room, I remember I was being allowed to go on a rescue mission with my dad tomorrow. He is head of the first aid on a mountain that has a lot of avalanches. He also has a sidekick, Starr. She is a three-year-old Siberian husky. *Brrrrrrrrrrring!* I cover my ears as the detention bell interrupts my daydreaming.

As I walk home, I call my best friend Katie. "Hey Katie."

"Hi April, how was detention?" We both laugh, knowing how horrible detention is. "I heard you get to see Starr tomorrow. Could you send me a picture?"

"Sure! I've got to go but I will see you on Monday."

"Bye bye."

I opened the door to my house and flung my backpack into the corner. "Daaaad! Have you brought Starr ho…?" I started. Starr ran in and jumped up to lick my face. I stroked her soft fur and gave her a big bear hug.

Starr and I then walked into the living room to see my dad. The TV was on the news, and my dad was sitting on our big red couch. Starr and I jumped onto the couch with my dad. Just as we snuggled in, a news report popped on the screen.

"We're here at Winter Frost Hill in Denver, Colorado where an avalanche just buried one person, who we think may still be alive under the heaps of snow. Rescuers will be arriving momentarily, hopefully with the help of some rescue canines," the reporter announced.

My dad sprang up off the couch and ran to his room with Starr right behind him.

"Dad! Where are you going?"

"We need to go to that hill today, not tomorrow. April, you're going to have to help me."

"Ok."

"Go get the rescue materials on the tall shelf in the garage."

"Ok." I ran over to the garage, grabbed the bags, and tossed them in the car. I ran back in and grabbed Starr's leash. "Starr, sit." I said. She sat right away. I clipped on the leash and we jumped into the car.

At the hill we put on Starr's rescue coat. It let anyone on the hill know that she was doing a job and to let her do it without distraction. Dad took Starr to get a scent of the person we were looking for. Then we started up the hill. I made sure my phone was on, just in case. Starr and I were hiking for at least ten minutes when I heard a few rumbles. I moved quickly off the trail and pulled Starr's leash close to me. When the rumbles grew louder, Starr, even being a search dog, got scared. She darted out from under me and started running across the trail. The snow piled down the hill in a giant roar, burying Starr under it. I picked up my phone and was about to call my dad when it rang.

"April, are you okay?" yelled my dad.

"I'm fine, but Starr just got buried in an avalanche!" I yelled.

"What? Can you see her?"

"No Dad, please come quickly!"

"I won't make it there in time! You need to find something to use as a digging tool, like a thick stick or a rock." I looked around and ran over to a tree. I found a loose branch and pulled it off of the tree.

"I found a branch! I am digging, but the snow is getting hard," I puffed.

"Keep going!"

I hung up the phone and dug as hard as I could. I dug and dug. I dug so long my fingers were getting numb. I kept digging and finally after ten minutes I got to Starr's legs. Then I found her head and body. She was lying helplessly on the ground. She was freezing cold and her eyes were closed shut. I took my backpack off my back and dumped it out. It only had a blanket, some food, Band-Aids, a rope, and a jacket. I wrapped Starr in the blanket and picked Starr up and put her on the side of the trail. I began to build a snow fort so we could try to stay warm. *Come on Starr, You have been with my family since before I was born and I am not going to lose you now.* I picked up my phone. Dead, *oh so it worked thirty minutes ago when I barely needed it, but it can't work now?* Then, I continued building the fort.

Two or three hours went by and I heard a rumbling again. I stayed where I was with Starr. To my surprise, a rescue helicopter was hovering over the trail. A harness fell down and I paused a moment to make sure it was a rescue helicopter. Then, when I was sure it was, I secured Starr in the harness and then fastened myself. The man in the helicopter brought us up.

In the helicopter, my dad was waiting.

"Dad!" I cried.

"April, are you okay?"

"Yes, but Starr isn't," I sobbed. "She can't be that hurt, can she?"

"I don't know; avalanches have killed many people on this hill before, so we'll have to wait and see. Let's get her to a hospital."

Hospital I thought for a moment as I stared at Starr lying limp on the floor of the helicopter. Her eyes were still shut and she was breathing very lightly.

Years later, we sit at home on the red couch with Starr at our heels. We look back at that day of the avalanche and remember how lucky it is to have Starr here with us. Luckily, she survived with only minor injuries. Just remembering that avalanche is scary, but we still do what we love best, running with avalanches.

A Sad Goodbye

In the story **A SAD GOODBYE** *by* **Maya Rosen,** *Jake cannot understand why his dad would break a promise in order to go to work. In response, Jake does something terribly wrong.*

I was in the seventh grade and my little sister Chloe was in the fourth grade when the events occurred that changed our family life forever. But I felt it changed my life the most.

I couldn't wait. My dad was coming home from his big business trip in less than a week. But he could only stay for two days, and then he had to go back. I was so excited to see him. On Saturday I had a baseball game, so he could see me play.

A week passed and it was time to get him. "Everybody in the car, we are going to get Dad!" Mom yelled. She was even more excited than me, it sounded. I jumped in the front seat, and Chloe sat in the back.

We arrived at the airport. Then I saw him. My dad walked out of the airport with luggage in his hands, his blond hair sticking out in the crowd. Before the blink of an eye, Chloe was running toward him. She was crying very hard, and I could see from the distance a tear roll down her face. Then Mom and I hurried over, and he gave us both a big hug.

Mom and I took Dad's stuff from him, and he was holding Chloe's hand as we walked back to the car. He was telling us all about his trip to China and what he had to do there. He reached in his work bag and pulled out a lot of really cool pictures. I told him about my baseball game the next day, and he said he was coming for sure. That made my day.

When we got home Dad wanted to cook for us. It was the first time in a year that Dad had cooked for us. He is amazing. He made homemade macaroni. Then he walked me to my bedroom, and we had a little man–to-man talk. "You have my genes, Jake," said Dad. "You like baseball and girls and you have blond hair and blue eyes!"

"Oh, Dad," I said.

"Anyway, Jake, talking about those girls, do you have a girlfriend?" Dad asked.

"No, Dad, I don't, but there is this girl I am asking to the dance. She is really pretty," I said. When he left my room he went to Chloe's room to kiss her goodnight.

The next day rolled around. I woke up at 9:30 and went downstairs. I had a bowl of cereal. Chloe was already in front of the TV with Dad. "Hey, buddy," Dad said as I came to sit with them.

"Are you excited for my game?" I asked.

"Yes, what do you think? I can't wait! Well, I am going to go out with mom for a little bit now," Dad said. Mom walked downstairs all dressed up, and I suddenly noticed Dad was, too. They must be going somewhere fancy. *Oh, well I better start on my homework,* I thought to myself.

By the time I was done with Math, Science, Social Studies, and English, Dad and Mom were home, and it was time for the game. I walked downstairs with my uniform on, but Dad was not ready. He was in his suit. My mom was standing next to him. "Dad, what's going on? You are coming, right?" I asked.

"Jake, I love you, and I will make it up to you, but I was called for an emergency at work, and I won't be able to make it. I am sorry," Dad said.

I stood there for a little while in shock. He had promised to come. "I hate you!" I yelled.

"Jake, you get back here and say you are sorry right now!" yelled my mom.

"NO!" I yelled back and ran out the door.

On the way to the field I was crying. I got there late because I had been walking slow and thinking about what I had said to Dad. My coach yelled at me. That made me even angrier. I did not want to play my hardest.

We lost the game all because of me. I am the star player. I'm the only one that could hit a home run.

I ran away at the end of the game. I did not stay to hear what the coach had to say.

When I got home I wanted to say I was sorry to Dad, but he was still at work. But my mom came up to me and asked me what had gone through my mind. I pulled away from her and went upstairs.

The next day Mom asked me if I wanted to go say goodbye to Dad and watch him go back. I said yes, but I did not say anything to Dad. When it was time for him to go, he whispered in my ear, "I love you." What was I supposed to say? But before I could say anything else, he hopped on the airplane. It seemed like he left so fast. I probably had a ton of time, but I couldn't figure out exactly what I wanted to say. I wanted to say something back, but it was too late. That thought kept running through my mind over and over.

I tried not to cry, but as soon as we walked away tears started to pour down my face. They were hot and full of forgiveness. I thought to myself as we walked back to our car and drove home that he was gone and I might not see him for more than a year. The last words I said to him were "I hate you."

A few hours after we came home from dropping him off at the airport, we got a phone call. After a few minutes of talking to the person on the other end, Mom hung up the phone and started crying. I did not know what to think. Why was she crying? Mom yelled that there was a family meeting. I ran to her, and so did Chloe.

She took a deep breath and said Dad's plane was on the way to China and crashed. Chloe wrapped her arms around Mom and started crying. I ran to my room and hid under my covers.
My last words were "I hate you," and now he's dead. I can't say anything else now. He's gone forever. I can't see him anymore. He's gone.

During the next week we had lots of visitors. Soon it was time for Dad's funeral. I cried and cried and never stopped, and then I yelled, "Dad hates me! My last words were 'I hate you' and now he is gone!"

Mom ran over to me and told me that Dad knew I was angry and that I loved him. She told me that if I told God that I was sorry, Dad would hear me. I did that over and over, but it made me feel worse. I could never say it to his face again.

Every day I regret what I said that day. I miss him more than ever, more than anybody could ever miss anybody in the world. He was the greatest person. He did everything he could for his family and his friends.

What I learned is that you can't always take your words back, so you should be careful about what you say and think before you say it. Maybe he did hear me say that I was sorry, over and over again; maybe he didn't. I will never know if he really heard me.

Shirtless Boy

You can see some crazy stuff when riding the school bus. The kids of bus eight were riding the bus home from school when they noticed a boy. Find out what happens in **SHIRTLESS BOY**, *by **Andrea J. Williams.***

Another school day had ended, and the kids of bus eight were riding the bus home. The bus stopped to let Jayden, Ryan, Abby, and Cole off the bus. The remaining students looked out the window and noticed a boy who just ripped off his shirt and started dancing. Then he jumped in his garage and pushed the button to close it. But as the garage door was closing, he started dancing and kept dancing lower and lower to the ground so we could continue to watch him. We thought it was over, but he jumped out of the garage side door and kept on dancing. Most of the remaining kids on the bus were laughing; he looked so weird.

A few weeks passed, and, although it was the start of spring, there was still snow on the ground. The bus stopped to let Jayden, Ryan, Abby, and Cole off, and we couldn't believe that we say the boy again. He was outside and started dancing again, but this time he kept his shirt on. The kids of bus eight started laughing. The bus pulled away from the stop, and the boy ran after the bus. He didn't get very far because he tripped over some snow and fell flat on his face. Now the kids were laughing even harder.

The boy still comes outside every now and then. When he comes out the kids of bus eight always call him "Shirtless Boy"! He hates the name we gave him. Now he runs after the bus every single time we call him that.

It was Tuesday, and it had been a week since we had seen Shirtless Boy, but he was out today. He was putting bricks around his plants when we yelled, "Shirtless Boy!" That was a bad idea because he picked up a brick and ran towards the bus. Just in the nick of time, the bus started to pull away, but he still chucked the brick at the bus. Luckily, he doesn't have a very good aim, and the brick fell short. All the kids on bus eight were laughing. The bus driver didn't see anything that had happened.

Still today, Shirtless Boy really hates it when we call "Shirtless Boy." Sometimes he gets so mad that his face gets red. Or he looks like he is about to cry. He says that he will get his brother to come talk to us, but that never happens. One thing is for sure: The students on bus eight will always remember "Shirtless Boy"!

The Ski Trip

Over Christmas break, two girls take a skiing trip to Crystal Mountain. Will they survive the blizzard on the iciest day of the year? Read **THE SKI TRIP** *by* **Lindsay Thomas** *to find out.*

On New Years of 2011, my friend Mikaela and I went skiing at Crystal Mountain. It was the first day of our vacation. That night it was very cold and icy to be out on the ski slopes, but Mikaela and I decided to take a risk. We were ecstatic when we saw the first Black Diamond; we couldn't believe how icy it was. We could see how shiny the ice was when we looked down from the slopes. At the top of the hill, the wind was blowing hard and fast.

While still struggling to stay at the top of the hill, it began to snow really hard, almost as if it were a blizzard. We were frightened that we were going to get hurt on the icy hill. While Mikaela was too scared, I put my skis on tight and began to ski down the intense hill. I was so scared, but wanted to be brave. I was thinking, *How can I keep my balance?* I looked back to see if Mikaela was skiing, when my skis became crossed. I lost my balance and started screaming. "AHHHHHH!" I screamed as I fell down the hill. I was terrified. Mikaela had no clue what to do, so she just stared, watching me fall. Everyone was looking at me. It was the most embarrassing moment of my life. I made a bad choice going skiing in this weather.

There was a paramedic at the bottom of the hill to help me. I was dizzy and felt like I was going to throw up. I had never felt this sick before. The paramedic helped Mikaela come down the hill by ski slope. The paramedic soon called an ambulance, because I was extremely hurt. They put me on a stretcher because I wasn't able to walk. I got many x-rays on my leg when I got to the hospital. I had a broken leg. I was so sad that I wasted my whole ski trip on one night, but I learned my lesson not to always take the risk.

Something Due

Three girls are lost in the woods with no food or water, and with temperatures dropping. In **SOMETHING DUE** *by* ***Kiara Giles****, the girls learn that they must stick together to survive.*

The best day ever was coming up. Everything was going great until the argument.

Carmen, Sam and I (Rebecca) were three best friends who were excited and ready to go to Camp Willow Beast in two weeks. It was also nearly Carmen's birthday, and she would be having her party at Zap Zone. When Sam didn't receive an invitation, she thought that Carmen wasn't her friend anymore. At the Girl Scout meeting that same day, Carmen and Sam weren't speaking to each other.

By the week of camp, Carmen and Sam still weren't speaking to each other, and we would leave in three days.

Three days came and went. It was the day we would leave for camp. At 4:30 in the morning everyone was in the car and ready to go.

We all dozed off in the car, and were awakened by Troop Leader Jill's bullhorn. When everyone woke up she assigned us our cabin, and gave us one hour to unpack and get situated for our four-day camping trip.

The first activity was a nature hike. We had to get all geared up in our snow pants, boots, hats, gloves, scarves, and coats. "Hot and sweaty, but ready to go," Carmen said.

We met up with the rest of the troop and started our walk up the trail. Halfway through our legs were getting tired. Jill let us sit and rest for ten minutes.

While we were sitting we all heard a hissing sound. Scared out of our minds, Carmen, Sam, and I ran off the trail. We stopped to catch our breath, and still heard the noise. We started running again, and as the sound got more distant we slowed to a walk.

Thinking we were walking back to camp, we were going in the complete opposite direction. I figured that out when we walked by the Lake Candy Canes. Then it hit me. When we first arrived, Jill had told us, "If you go by Lake Candy Canes, you have gone 15 miles away from the campsite." That's where we were: Lake Candy Canes, 15 miles away from camp.

We tried to find any sign of camp. There was nothing anywhere but trees, dirt, bugs, and animals. We all began to cry and cry until I said, "We can't just sit here and cry. We have to do something." After I said that I felt really good.

We were thinking really hard on a way to get back to camp. Our stomachs were rumbling. We hadn't eaten in four hours, and we were starving. There was no food to be found. We were all very tired and very weak.

"We can't just go to bed hungry," Carmen said. So we all checked our pockets for mints, chocolate, or anything. We found nothing but two mints. We ate those like they were the last meal in life.

We were still starving, and very cold. The temperature was getting lower by the minute. Night was coming very fast. Our eyes were growing weak until ZZZZZZZ....

When we woke up the next morning, we decided that we would go north and see where we ended up. With our last bit of energy we started walking. We walked for 45 minutes, still starving, but we made it. We finally came upon a sign saying "Stay on the trail."

"We did it!" Sam said as she threw her arms around Carmen and me. "This whole experience made me think that we shouldn't fight over something as dumb as an invitation."

We got to the main part of camp, and as soon as we arrived we saw Jill running with the ambulance, police, and our parents....

"That's a great story, Sam," Carmen said.

"I hope none of that happens in real life," I said.

"I got an A on it so it must be good," Sam said.

"Your story made me think. We should all join Girl Scouts."

A Startling Surprise

A STARTLING SURPRISE, *by **Jadyn Broomfield**, is about a girl who is thrown a surprise party for her birthday. What she doesn't know is that she is in for one more surprise.*

Bang, bang, bang! Someone was banging on the door. The sound caused her to jump.

"Who is it?" Keylian asked.

Bang, bang! the person banged back.

All of a sudden the door flung open and the light went out. Keylian screamed. A cover was thrown over her head. Somebody pushed her out of the bathroom and onto the couch. When Keylian pushed the cover off of her head it was dark in the living room, too. She could sort of see figures moving in the dark. Suddenly, Keylian was having a flashback to earlier that day.

She was at school, and it was pretty much normal. The only difference was that everybody wished Keylian a happy birthday. A few of her friends even gave her gifts.

Keylian was really waiting for school to be over. She knew that after school she would go open her parents' presents for her. They always had the best presents to give to her.

"Finally," Keylian thought when the bell rang meaning that school was out. She grabbed her backpack, ran out to the buses, and hopped on her bus. The drive home was so long to Keylian even though she was the fourth stop out of eleven. To try and make time go faster, Keylian listened to her iPod.

When Keylian got home and opened the door to her house she yelled, "Mom, Dad! I'm home from school!"

Why aren't the lights on? Keylian asked herself.

She turned on the lights, and all of Keylian's friends yelled, "Surprise!"

Keylian was astonished. Her friends and family had thrown a surprise party for her. How nice of them. She wondered, though, how they had gotten home before her. Then she remembered that a few of her friends had been missing from the bus that day.

Her mom walked out of the kitchen with a pretty cake that said "Happy Birthday Lia!!" It had pink frosting on it and blue bows in the corners.

"You are all so sweet. Thank you so much," Keylian said.

All of Keylian's friends crowded around her to sing "Happy Birthday." When they finished singing, Keylian blew out the candles, and they all sat down to eat the cake.

"What did you wish for?" Jennie asked.

"I wished that everyone here could have as good of a birthday as I am having," Keylian explained.

While Keylian was finishing up her slice of cake, she yelled over to her mom with a mouth full of cake, "Thish cake ish delicious."

"What?" her mom said back.

"She said that the cake is delicious," one of Keylian's friends translated.

Next came the presents. The first present Keylian opened was from her best friend, Jennie. Keylian opened the box slowly and carefully. Jennie began to smile because of the suspense in waiting for Keylian's reaction to the gift she had given Keylian. Inside of the box was an expensive earring and necklace set. On the necklace were the letters *L*I*A* with stars in between. They spelled "Lia," which was Keylian's nickname. The earrings were the same way.

"Oh, I just love it!" Keylian exclaimed. "Thanks, Jen."

Most of the other presents were not as great as Jennie's present, but they were pretty great. Keylian got presents like nail polish, hair clips, makeup and other girlie things that fit her personality.

"These are great gifts," Keylian said. "You guys rock!"

There was, however, one other present that surpassed Jennie's gift. Of course it was from Keylian's parents. They had given her a 100-dollar American Express card. Now Keylian could go to the mall and buy the shoes she had wanted for as long as she could remember. They were white high heels with clear, sparkling gems on the top strap near the toes. She would wear them to special occasions if she had them. Now she could get them.

Millie, another one of Keylian's friends, was passing out goodie bags filled with older kid things like Claire's gift cards and mini lip gloss "cell phones." Meanwhile, Keylian grabbed the box with her new jewelry in it and went to the bathroom for a mirror. She got in there and had just opened up the box when there was a banging at the door....

Keylian was flashed back into reality.

The lights flicked back on all of a sudden, and sitting in front of the couch Keylian was on was a 52-inch television wrapped in a bright pink bow.

"Is that for me?" Keylian asked.

"It sure is," exclaimed her mother. "The gift card was just a little teaser!"

"But it does still have the money on it, right?" Keylian questioned.

"Of course it does, Sweetie," her dad reassured her.

"This is so awesome!" one of Keylian's friends said.

"I know!" said another.

"Thanks so much, you guys! This was the best birthday ever!" Keylian thanked her friends.

"Our pleasure!" said Millie.

The girls' parents came to pick up their children gradually as the night went on.

Soon everyone had gone, and Keylian's birthday was over. Still, her memories of this day would last a lifetime.

The Storm

THE STORM, *by **Sydney Mantua,** is a story about a girl who ends up in a situation where if she doesn't do the right thing her life could be changed. Will she be okay?*

As we were getting ready for school and work, my mom yelled to me, "Bailey, Dad and I are going out tonight, so you're going to be home alone."

I yelled back, "Okay, but don't be gone for too long." The door slammed. I ran to watch the news while eating my breakfast. "Watch out for storms tonight around 6 o'clock," said the weatherman.

When I got home from school I ran straight to the living room to turn on the TV. "A huge storm is coming and possibly a tornado. Keep watching for more information," the weatherman said.

I was looking outside at the scary green and black sky when all suddenly it became extremely windy and the tornado siren went off. My dog, Sprite, and I ran down into the basement. Luckily I had my radio, so I could listen to the weather report.

I was starting to feel safe when suddenly the power went out. I could feel the cold air rushing on my back, and hear scary noises. I grabbed my flashlight and hoped the storm would be over quickly.

Sprite started to whine, which at first scared me. I tried to calm him down by letting him know it was ok.

"Tornado reports in Horsedot," the weatherman said.

"Horsedot, that's where we live!" I told Sprite.

I waited patiently in the basement for fifteen minutes listening to sports and other news. "Today in sports, William Lewis won the first game of the season for the Jaguars…" Finally there was more news about the weather. The weatherman reported that the huge tornado had just missed our neighborhood and the storm had moved to the east. Unfortunately, it did hit our village, our town's grocery store, and a lot of neighborhoods close to ours.

When my parents arrived home, my mom exclaimed, "I'm so glad you're ok!" My mom and dad were so proud of how brave I was. They were also pleased I knew exactly what to do. I smiled happily as my parents gave me a huge hug.

There's a Shark in Lake Michigan

In **THERE'S A SHARK IN LAKE MICHIGAN** *by* ***Dylan Sutton,*** *Dylan is living in Boyne City when he sees something in the water, which he thinks is a shark. Dylan tries to prove to his brother that there is a shark in Lake Michigan. When Dylan tries to find the shark to prove his story, he encounters something unexpected. Is there really a shark in Lake Michigan?*

It was a bright sunny day in Boyne City. The temperature was 80 degrees Fahrenheit. I woke up, got dressed and went outside. Grabbing my inflatable raft and a rowboat oar, I headed towards the lake. I put my raft into the water and hopped on. I paddled into the middle of the lake. It took me about a half an hour to get to the spot where I saw something I just couldn't believe.

The thing that I saw was rising in the water. Soon, I could see a fin and then a body. I immediately knew what it was, but that didn't make sense.

There can't be a shark in Lake Michigan. A lake is fresh water and sharks need salt water to live, I thought to myself.

The shark disappeared under water. I heard a noise and I looked around. There was a duck swimming around in the lake. Then suddenly, the duck was pulled under water. I thought to myself, *The shark must have gotten it.*

The wind started to pick up. Waves were beginning to form. I knew I had to get to the shore soon, so I started to row back. My clothes and feet were wet. I looked down and realized that the raft had popped. I was sinking. I jumped off my raft and swam to the shore as fast as I could. Looking in front of me, I saw a fin. The shark was heading towards me slowly. I couldn't do anything but stop and start treading water. I closed my eyes, waiting for the shark to sink his teeth into me. Everything seemed quiet after that. I could feel my heart beating. I felt something on my right hand. I opened my eyes and saw the shark right in front of me.

Now, I knew that there was a shark in Lake Michigan because how the shark felt was exactly like what I had studied in fifth grade.

The shark came closer to me. I closed my eyes waiting to be devoured. I waited and waited. After five minutes, I opened my eyes. The shark was gone. I quickly swam to the shore. I ran to the condo.

"I don't believe that story," my brother announced. I had explained my ordeal to Cole who is three years younger than me.

"Fine," I said. "I will go capture the shark and bring it to you so you will believe me."

"There is no way you can catch the shark," Cole claimed.

I left the conversation and went outside. Then I thought to myself, *How in the heck could I catch a shark without a raft?*

I decided to take a knife from the kitchen. I ran as fast as I could to the kitchen drawer and grabbed the biggest knife I could before running outside. Just as I opened the back door, my mom said, "Dylan, what are you doing with that knife? You could cut yourself."

I said, "No time to talk, but thanks for the warning." She looked at me, puzzled.

I closed the door and ran down to the dock. I jumped into the lake. Then I realized why my mom had warned me about the knife. As soon as I hit the water, the knife flew out of my hands and struck my forehead before plunging under water. I had to retrieve the knife. I swam down to the lake floor and felt around. I went back up to the surface for air and then went down to the lake floor again. I felt the knife and grabbed it, swimming back up to the surface.

I saw the shark about twenty feet away. I swam as fast as I could until I was in knifing range. The shark was as still as me. I knew this was my chance to kill it, so I stabbed it. As I lifted the knife up to see if I got the shark, I saw a flash of blonde hair in the water. I pulled the knife up even more and watched the shark moving in the water. He was giving me a better look! I could see it was plastic. I could also see who was holding it . . . none other than my good-for-nothing brother.

"Hi bro," he said, smiling.

"That's all you can say is 'Hi bro' after you made me think that there really was a shark?"

"Okay, you got me. I am the shark of Lake Michigan," Cole answered laughing.

I was upset. But then I remembered the duck. "Okay then explain this: What happened to that duck?"

"I bought a stuffed duck at the hunting store," he explained.

"Then what popped my raft?"

"I stuck a needle in it and then swam under the water to the shore."

Cole and I swam back to the shore and went back to the condo. I made him tell my mom everything. Mom grounded him for a week. So I guess I gained the advantage there.

"Hey, Dylan," my mom said.

"Yeah, Mom," I replied.

"What happened to the raft and oar?"

"Uh, yeah, they sort of got lost," I mumbled.

"Come on, go grab your money," she ordered.

"Why?" I whined.

"You're going to buy a new raft and an oar."

"But—" I tried to protest.

"You are responsible," said my mom. We got into the car and drove to a boat store.

While we were in the car I asked my mom, "What if there really was a shark in Lake Michigan," I asked.

"There can't be, Dylan. Sharks don't live in lakes," she answered.

"I know, but I swear that I saw a fin when we got out of the water," I exclaimed.

"Oh Dylan," she muttered.

Then, as we drove past the lake I looked out of my window and I thought I could make out a small black triangle that looked like a fin....

A Trip to the Woods

When five kids travel to the woods on a field trip, they learn why you listen to people around you even if they are not your friends. In **A TRIP TO THE WOODS** *by* **Sabryne Fattouh***, when five kids get lost in the woods, they show each other how to cope with their surroundings.*

"We're trapped," Jessica whined.

"Oh, well," murmured Jake.

"We're trapped!" Jessica stated once more with exasperation in her voice.

"Just shut up for like three seconds, and let me figure this out," sputtered Mike. "You've been whining this whole time, and if I hear another word I'm gonna lose it!"

"Fine, but if you yell at me, when and if we get out of here, you'll be in so much trouble," Jessica said (with a whine behind her voice that made Mike want to absolutely strangle her).

That was it. Mike came at her cursing, and she defended herself, spitting out words she didn't recognize she'd even known.

"Enough!" cried Lila, "Can you two stop fighting, I'm pretty sure I found the tunnel Mr. Smith told us about…."

Earlier that day

"Okay," said Mr. Smith. "We are all going on a scavenger hunt for clues about the hunter who fell into his own trap trying to catch large animals." He had fallen and suffered a serious head injury. The hunter dug his way out only to be found dead by campers two hours later. Everybody thought it was a scam. There's no way anybody could be that stupid. "Now I'm going to pick your groups." Mr. Smith's eyes wandered to the back of the crowd. "Jessica and Mike, for the hundredth time, stop fighting. For that, you two are in a group."

Timothy and Jake snickered. "And you two, in the back, you can join them." A low "ooooo" came from the crowd except for the teacher's pet up front. "Aha, that still leaves one. Lila, you too."

"Teacher's pet," somebody coughed. A couple of people standing near coughed in agreement.

"Cute," Lila said with a glare that could cut straight through your skin.

Lila looked at her teacher with disbelief, as if it were a joke. "But I did nothing wrong," she said in the most nonchalant voice she could hack up.

"Yes, I can agree with that," Mr. Smith said, nodding. "But you need to break apart your little clique and meet some new people."

"Not fair," Lila growled under her breath.

"Next group," Mr. Smith said while Lila trudged over to where her group had all met up. Lila traced over her group with beady eyes, thinking that she deserved more than two arguers and a couple of Eminem wannabes. Lila sighed with disbelief and walked back to Mr. Smith to get the materials. Lila remembered them all: a compass, a list of items (tattered pieces of cloth, fake blood, and other things the teachers had planted there that morning), five canteens of water, and a map (which had a different route for each group).

When she got back to her group, Jessica announced that there needed to be a leader for the group, and she volunteered. "Great, we'll have the dumb girl lead us to Insanity Ville," said Mike, smiling, with his hands behind his back. "I, for one, think that Lila should be the leader," stated Mike.

Lila was flushed. "I second that," said Jake and Timothy at the same time.

"Fine," spat Jessica. "But when we get lost I'll say I told you so."

"But wait."

"What?" asked Jessica, clearly irritated.

"What if I don't want to be the leader of the group?"

"Then I'll be the leader," Jessica said with a smirk on her face and in her voice.

"Oh, be quiet, you self-centered…" was all Mike was able to say before Lila shouted, "Language!" Mike grimaced at Lila. Then he set his stare to maim Jessica while saying through his teeth, "Besides, I'd rather pick Timothy over there than have you lead us, Jessica."

"Thanks," Jessica snorted.

"You're welcome," said Jake to Jessica with a really fake polite smile, as if he had been involved in another conversation.

"I'll be the leader if you guys are gonna be so immature about it," said Lila.

Mr. Smith announced to the groups that they should be back to the picnic area by noon. Then they set off with Jessica in the back complaining that she had drunk all of her water. Lila, in the front of the group, almost fell into the river with her nose in the map. At the same moment she was caught by Mike. Once again she was flushed. Jessica snorted at Lila's reaction. "Never been touched by a boy before?" she said. Timothy mimicked what Jessica would do if she fell into the river.

Jessica filled her canteen and drank until her cheeks were filled like a chipmunk's and spit it in Mike's face. "Eww, it tastes like iron," said Jessica, staring into her canteen like somebody had just spit in it.

"Maybe the drama queen shouldn't have chugged all her water then," said Lila with a sarcastic what-should-I-do look on her face.

Mike gave her a high five while Jake fell into the water dying of laughter, and Timothy said between endless giggles, "Double whammy. Jake's in the water and Jessica's amazed by what you got in you." Just to top it all off, Jake came up behind Jessica and pulled her into the water. Jessica came out of the water sopping wet and ran away.

"Aw, come on, I didn't mean it."

"Yes, you did" said Mike, laughing.

"She'll probably get mauled by a bear," said Timothy. All of the laughing subsided when they realized what could happen to a thirteen-year-old city girl that has no experience in the wilderness whatsoever. They all ran in the direction Jessica had run.

There was no sign of Jessica for three hours, until they found her being chased by a fox, because she had tried to pet one of her cubs. Once she ran a safe distance away from the fox, she came back to the group, breathless. "You're so duuuummmmbbbb," said Jake.

"But I wanted to hold him. His little face begged me to," said Jessica.

"Okay, you guys, let's get back to the…" Jake's voice trailed off looking for the direction that they came in. "I can't find it," Jake stammered.

"What can't you find, Jake?" Timothy asked puzzled.

"The, the, the path, I can't find the path!" Jake stammered.

"Well, then just look at the map," Jessica snorted as if it was a no-brainer.

"But where is, is, iii…"

"Where's the map?" Timothy finished for Jake. They all dared to look sideways just enough to see that a baby fox was rolling in shards of a Michigan woods map.

"Oh god, oh god, what have I done?" Jake stammered.

"S' ok, man, we'll figure this out," Mike said.

"But I was the one that pulled her into the water and made her run off," Jake thought aloud, staring at nothing as if in a trance.

"Eww, I'm sweating," Jessica whined.

"Can you please stop whining?" Mike complained.

"But I've never sweated before, and I can see why, it's gross," Jessica whined.

"Like I said before… SHUT UP!" Mike shouted.

"Stop fighting, I think we went that way," Lila said over the arguing. They fell silent, and followed Lila. While walking, they all fell into a deeply dug hole, covered by leaves and a thin layer of dirt, made by the hunter that Mr. Smith had told them about. They fell onto moss. It hadn't been touched in years because nobody had been down there. Thick and lush, it clung to their clothes and broke their fall.

They all screamed on their way down. Once the chaos died down they all threw out resolutions on how to get out. "Maybe I can climb my way out?" Timothy said with hopelessness in his voice.

"No, it won't work. The dirt's too weak," said Lila contemplating if it were worth a shot.

After three hours without water in a dirt hole, they started to lose their minds, not only from claustrophobia, but also from heat stroke from the sun. It felt as if they were sitting in a sauna.

"Kill me now," groaned Jake.

"We're trapped," Jessica whined.

"Oh, well," murmured Jake.

"We're trapped!" Jessica stated once more with exasperation in her voice.

"Just shut up for like three seconds, and let me figure this out," sputtered Mike. "You've been whining this whole time, and if I hear another word I'm gonna lose it!"

"Fine, but if you yell at me, when and if we get out of here, you'll be in so much trouble," Jessica said (with a whine behind her voice that made Mike want to absolutely strangle her).

That was it, Mike came at her cursing, and she defended herself, spitting out words she didn't recognize she'd even known.

"Enough!" cried Lila, "Can you two stop fighting, I'm pretty sure I found the tunnel Mr. Smith told us about…."

"You found the tunnel!" exclaimed Jake.

"Ooooo, leave it to the problem-solver to find an answer to everything," Jessica said jealously. Jake grimaced at her with disagreement.

"Better than you, Jessica. You're oblivious to the obvious. Even with brain damage and heat stroke, only Jessica can insult us," said Mike, talking to Jessica, but saying it like he was talking to somebody else.

"But who's that skinny to fit into that hole? It's like a half a foot by a half a foot," groaned Timothy. "You'd have to be anorexic."

"Leave it to me, boys," said Jessica (looking at Lila) wanting to be a part of the rescue herself before she slipped right through the tunnel.

She returned five minutes later, saying that she had dug an opening and gotten out, complaining that she ruined her manicure. "So now you can all get out," said Jessica cheerfully.

"One slight problem. We're not as anorexic as you, Jessica," said Timothy.

"Ooooo, bummer. Maybe you should have thought of something like this before you ate that extra bag of chips today," said Jessica.

Everybody glared at her. "Maybe someone should start digging a wider hole," said Jake speaking for everyone, as their stares intensified.

"Fine," said Jessica. "But wait. What should I do with the extra dirt?" said Jessica.

"Eat the dirt," Jake said flatly.

After that Jessica dug a wider hole in silence while everybody sat and watched. An hour later, Jessica crawled her way down the steep tunnel, exclaiming that it was big enough now.

They hurriedly climbed up the steep tunnel. Poking his head out and seeing that it was dark, Tim told everybody to hurry on up.

They wandered through the woods tripping and falling asleep. Keeping their heads straight and mouths quiet, they didn't fight. "Wait, you guys, look. I think I see something," said Tim, breaking the silence. Their eyes darted to where Tim was pointing.

"It... looks... like... chimney smoke?" Lila said puzzled. One quick eye conversation was all they needed to give, and then they ran toward it making all the noise they could conjure.

The owner of the cabin came out angry until he saw five ragged teenagers desperately running toward him.

His face softened as Jake told the story, while the rest of them added in here and there. The camper drove them down to the campsite where they had been told to meet.

All the kids and teachers sat at the picnic tables, looking down, thinking. The five climbed out of the van, and the other kids ran toward them shooting out questions until Mr. Smith broke up the crowd and told them to announce what happened. They hurriedly told the story, while desperately waiting for the food to warm up.

Just like that, the next day reporters came knocking on the kids' doors, and begging to tell them what had happened the night before. All five of them agreed to meet up at their favorite pizza place to tell the story together. Jessica, loving all the attention, would tell the story.

As soon as the reporters could they got the news truck to come down to the pizza place and broadcast it live. Proudly, the kids ran to mirrors in the restroom checking themselves out to make sure they would look good on TV. They told the story, and simply went home to watch the news. For forever they were popular, and forever they were telling the story of how they outwitted the hunter.

Vacations Strike Again

In **VACATIONS STRIKE AGAIN** *by* ***Megan James***, *two children wander away from their parent and end up in a dangerous position. The situation leads them to a big decision.*

First thing on a beautiful sunny morning in California, their mom said, "We have nothing to do. Let's go on a cruise."

"Are you sure, Mom?"

"Yes, let's go."

The kids weren't sure at first, but then they realized it was a good idea and she was right: they didn't have anything better to do. Next, after they drove to the dock the kids saw an ice cream truck.

"Mom, Mom, can we go get ice cream for a minute, Mom?"

"Not now, kids, I'm busy getting our tickets!"

"She won't answer me, Drew," said Natalie.

"Let's just go. She won't notice."

"Are you sure? I don't think she'll like this."

"She'll be fine. Let's go."

When they came back after ice cream, their mom was gone! They looked around, and a boat was leaving. They got on the wrong boat.

They realized they were on the wrong boat when the speaker announced, "We will be arriving on that island over there in one hour," as he pointed to a nearby island. They were supposed to be going across the bay! When they realized they were on the wrong boat, they were already two miles from the shore.

"We need to jump ship if we want to get back to Mom," said Drew.

"Yeah, I guess you're right," said Natalie.

As they jumped the ship, the shore didn't look that far, but they knew it was. It didn't take that long for them to get back to shore because they for sure didn't want to miss that ship.

When they got to shore, they saw their mom looking and asking people if they had seen her kids.

"Mom!" said Drew.

"Kids!"

"Mom!"

"Kids! I'm so glad I found you guys. I thought someone had kidnapped you!"

"No, Mom, we chased an ice cream truck and then got on the wrong ship."

"Why are you all wet?"

"We jumped the ship."

"What? That's so dangerous. You could have been killed!"

"Sorry."

"Oh, I'm so glad I found you guys!"

"Me too, Mom."

"Well, how about we go get on the right ship and have the rest of the day together?"

"Sounds good, Mom."

It wasn't the vacation they expected, but it was an adventure.

Zach Forner's Insane Story: Life and Being Rich

When rich parents leave their 16-year-old son home alone for the weekend, he decides to throw an insane house party. But it soon it turns into a disaster. Find out what happens in **ZACH FORNER'S INSANE STORY: LIFE AND BEING RICH**, *by* **Myles Earnest**.

Zach Forner's life was the best thing that a 16-year-old boy could have. He was revoltingly rich: He had a mansion and 900 million dollars! Right now he remembers the good times he had at his party.

It was Saturday night, and Zach was bored. He picked up his iPhone and called his friends Michael, Josh, Sam, Max, Jackson, Chris, Monique, and John. A few minutes later his best friend Mark kicked open the front door with a bag full of soda and food. "We're going to party," said Mark.

"I have some chips, I have some dip," said Zach.

"I don't mean to be a freeloader. I have some cups for the old-school soda," said Mark.

"I don't mean to brag, I don't mean to boast, I have some hummus for these mini-toasts," said Zach.

"This party is going to be awesome," said Mark.

"Since our parents are out of town, we get the weekend to ourselves," said Zach.

Around 8:45 P.M., Zach's friends arrived. "Everyone, I would like to thank you for coming to my first party. Now here's Eminem singing, 'I'm Not Afraid.' Okay, Mark, I need you to get my PlayStation in my bedroom."

"Okay," said Mark. "Hey, Zach, we've got a problem," said Mark.

"What is it?"

"You know how your toilet used to flush?"

"Yes I do."

"Now it's overflowing."

"Mark, we need to stop and fix the toilet."

"Hey, Zach, chill," said Chris. Chris was actually drowsy because he had taken some medicine for an upset stomach.

"No, I cannot 'chill'! I have a really big problem here." Zach was starting to feel drowsy, too. It was the medicine he had taken for a cold he caught from Chris, which made him sleepy. Zach fell asleep for six hours and 35 minutes.

"Oh, my head." As Zach rose off the ground, his jaw dropped. "Oh my god, Mark, what happened?"

The toilet continued to overflow and make strange gurgling noises. Zach called his parents, and they called a plumber to fix the toilet.

"Hey, Zach," said Michael, "that was a weird but the most fun party I've ever been to. I'll help you guys clean up."

"Thanks," said Mark. The three of them cleaned up just in time before Zach's parents came home.

"Bye, Michael. See ya later, Mark."

"See ya, Zach."

Zach shut the door and landed right on the couch. That was a pretty cool party after all.

Look Back

The Man in Black

It was the year 1855. Several banks had been robbed, including the bank of Oakbrook County. No matter who stood in his way, the sheriff was determined to find who did this in **THE MAN IN BLACK** *by* **Nicholas Ginopolis.**

The year was 1855. I was heading back home from my job at the sheriff's office, when suddenly I heard a loud sound. *Bang!* It sounded like it was coming from the bank. I ran to the bank to see what was happening. I saw my partner, Pete, lying on the ground outside of the bank. I realized that he had been shot in the leg. Pete yelled, "Someone just robbed the bank!"

I ran through the doors with my loaded pistol drawn, but the man who robbed the bank was not there. I asked the witnesses which way he had gone. One lady said she thought she saw him leave northward and that he was wearing black clothing and was riding a black horse. I went back to attend to Pete.

"How is your wound, Pete?" I asked.

"I need to go to see Doc to get the bullet removed from my leg," Pete moaned. Once Pete's leg was taken care of, we headed north in pursuit of the man in black.

It was approaching dark, so we decided to stop riding and set up camp. We pitched our tents and started a campfire. We warmed beans on the fire and went to bed.

It was early the next morning. "Wake up, Pete," I whispered.

"Go away, I'm sleeping," groaned Pete.

"We have a big day ahead of us. We need to get going if we are going to catch the man in black," I said.

"All right, just let me get my stuff together," Pete grumbled.

Pete and I loaded our stuff on the wagon and made our way to the nearest town, Armadillo. Once we arrived, we asked some people if they saw a man wearing all black come through the town riding a black horse. A tall man replied that he had seen this man and he thought that this was the same man who had robbed their bank and shot two bank employees. "Which direction did he head after he robbed the bank?" I asked.

"He went north," said the man. So, Pete and I headed north.

Several hours later, we arrived in a small town called Clayton. As soon as we entered the town, we saw a tall black figure off in the distance at the train station. It looked like he was waiting for the next train. Was it the man in black that we had been chasing? We called over to him, but he did not answer. Instead, he turned and fired his pistols at us.

Pete and I ran for cover, firing back at the man in black. We hid behind a parked wagon, screaming at the townspeople to take cover. The sheriff and his men heard the commotion and came to help. They came running out of the sheriff's office with guns blazing.

The man in black continued to fire back until he was struck in the arm by a bullet from my gun. He fell to the ground, but was still shooting with the gun in his other hand. We all were yelling, "Lay down your weapon and surrender or die!" The man in black threw down his gun and surrendered.

Later, during the interrogation, we found out that the man in black was a notorious gang leader. He and his gang had robbed over a dozen banks and had killed more than six people. He was wanted in more than three states.

Pete and I received a two-hundred-dollar reward for bringing in the wanted man in black. We also received a key to the city for our outstanding actions. I continued to remain sheriff of Oakbrook County for the next twenty years.

The Red Sands

Will the Americans and British take Hitler's iron grip away from North Africa and spoil his chances of reaching the oil fields of the Middle East? Join American WWII soldier Nolan Hollister in the fight for North Africa from 1941-1943 in **THE RED SANDS,** *by* ***Jaxon Bumbaugh.***

8: <u>*00 A.M., December 25, 1941, New York*</u>

Right now, British troops are fighting Hitler's troops in North Africa. This fighting started in August of last year. Hitler's storm troopers have been trying to control the Suez Canal to stop the steady food supply from India and to get to the valuable oil reserves of the Middle East for his war machines. In about a year, we are going to execute Operation Torch. We are just about done loading the supplies onto our ship and ready to fight in North Africa.

My name is Nolan. I'm 18 years of age, and I'm a recruit from Birmingham, Michigan. I was recruited in January of this year. My best friend from high school, Steven, is in the Pacific. He said he was being sent to Guam. So, as mentioned above, I'm going to North Africa to stop Hitler's troops from controlling the continent.

10:45 A.M., December 26, 1941, somewhere in the Atlantic

The seas sure are rough. For the first time, for Christmas dinner, I didn't have turkey or anything like that. Instead, I had just a biscuit and a piece of broccoli (there was water, though). So the plan is that we meet up in Morocco disguised as tourists from Spain due to axis control of the country. Spain is aligned with the axis and the other part of Morocco is under France, and that country is under Hitler's control. In November of next year, the allies of the North African front will put Operation Torch into action. Then that's when the real fighting starts. We will advance into Algeria and, hopefully, the Brits will run those gangsters out to Tunisia and we will have them cornered. They will have to evacuate the continent into Italy, and we shall win the war.

4:30 P.M., January 1, 1942, Western Coast of Morocco

We had just landed in Morocco, the French part of the country. I see Hitler's troop's flag fly on the capitol building. We are just commandos starting Operation Torch! Wow! I never thought New Year's Day could be this, well, this violent. The ship we went onto, _Morocco_, was an old cruise ship so Hitler's troops guarding the country wouldn't be startled and Operation Torch ruined. So, my new bud I met on the ship, Ed, is here with me and tells me, "Just don't look at them, it'll build up suspicion." The countries we will go into will be heavily defended, so that's why we are putting into action Operation Torch. But Algeria and Tunisia are what we're worried about. Anyway, by the eighth, we have to reach Algeria and meet up with British desert commandos and the French resistance.

3:30 A.M., January 5, 1942, somewhere close to Algiers-Morocco border

A skirmish just finished; we fought Hitler's troops' scout party. If we were reported, Operation Torch would've been jeopardized. So I grabbed a Thompson and did what I had to do! My bud, Ed, has a Springfield, and boy, he got two of the eleven. My other bud, Roland, did what he had to do, too. That night we saved Operation Torch.

1:30 A.M., January 28, 1942, Algerian northern coast

The free French are just getting unloaded from the last remaining ships of the French navy. However, I was told in the months ahead there will be heavy enemy resistance bombs, everything!

Noon, March 23, 1942, Algerian desert

Our company literally just survived a rain of fire. The Luftwaffe bombed us! Luckily our only car had a machine gun and we fired at I think uh…12 plane engines. We did the impossible! Anyway, I can't wait until Operation Torch. In February, Mussolini's and Hitler's troops launched a huge number of attacks on us; so far three are dead out of our 24 men. I got a letter from Steve saying he won the battle of Guadalcanal and most of the Solomon Islands are in American/Australian hands.

6:45 P.M., November 8, 1942, Moroccan coast near strait of Gibraltar

Operation Torch has begun; we need to help our brothers get to shore. This means destroying Hitler's troop's machine guns! So, this attack on the guns begins now!

2:30 P.M., November 10, 1942, Moroccan strait of Gibraltar

The battle is almost over; most of Hitler's ships guarding the strait are destroyed. We have the upper hand; however, we still have to destroy the resistance of 250 of Hitler's troops. We got most of the men on shore; 8,000 troops are on shore of the 10,000. By tomorrow, all of the troops will be on shore and the battle will be over. However, it is heard that Franco's troops will be reinforcing Hitler's troops, but we are going to bombard the coasts, and we shall sink the ships.

10:00 A.M., November 11, 1942, Moroccan strait of Gibraltar

The battle is officially over. All of Hitler's troops are dead or taken as prisoner, and we spared only 50 of them. We have little fatalities for us. Franco's troops were too frightened to even go near the strait. They thought the battle was over yesterday and thought it was pointless to attack the beachhead. By June, we should be able to take away Hitler's chance to control the Middle East.

4:30 A.M., January 1, 1943, Oran, Algeria

It is the New Year once again. I have been on this scarred landscape for a year now. In late December, British troops crossed into Libya after several attacks from Mussolini's troops on Alexandria. With our much larger force, we can take Algeria away from Hitler's iron grip. However, his storm troopers will be waiting.

7:30 P.M., March 10, 1943, Oran, Algeria

I got a letter from Steve, saying that he and his company are landing on Attu Island in Alaska. We have our own battle to fight; we are going to attack an axis-occupied city on the coast called Chlef. We start the attack on March 15 and should end by April 1. That is close to Algiers, the capital of axis-occupied Algeria, so we've got to win this battle. Afterwards, Algeria is ours for the taking. With our American manpower of 65,000, we should win. And with 60,000 British and her colonial territories, and about 1,000 tanks, we should win.

11:00 P.M., April 3, 1943, Algiers, Algeria

The storm troopers gave us a bit of a fight for Chlef. It was a moderate amount of opposition. However, by the 25th of March, the axis under Hitler was given the order by him to pull all of his troops in Africa and retreat to Tunisia. Even the troops in Algiers were supposed to pull back, which they did. And so the free French captured Algiers, and our troops were in Tunisia on the 29th. And Mussolini's troops also pulled back from Libya in early March. By June, we should have control of North Africa. However, I just hope that I don't die.

6:00 A.M., May 14, 1943, Tunis, Tunisia

The battle ended yesterday. Hitler was mad (as well was Mussolini). I missed all the action due to the fact I got hit in the leg by an artillery shell on the 9th. I was lying there in agony, but then an Indian commonwealth soldier helped me get to safety. My leg still hurts. I can barely write. Anyway, Hitler's troops along with Mussolini's are out of Africa, and in July we are going to invade the island of Sicily and then Italy. By then, I should be able to walk and fight. And what do you know, this diary is almost complete. One day, hopefully, my story will be published and people will read it.

The Ring of the King

In **THE RING OF THE KING** *by* ***JP DeRonne,*** *Zach goes on his best friend's family vacation to a little campsite in Colorado. But this little campsite holds the adventure of a life time for Zach and his friends.*

"Well, Mom. Can I go? Can I go? Can I go?"

"Maybe," said Mom. "You'll have to ace this upcoming math test."

"Ok, Mom, I promise I will! In fact, I'm going to study right now! For 45 minutes!"

Just one A, I thought. *One A and I get to go on Grant's family vacation.*

It turns out I got a B+ on the test. My heart was racing when I saw the grade. But luckily Mom still let me go because she knew I had studied hard. I packed that same night, even though the trip to Colorado was one week away.

Grant and his family, Uncle Jon and Ashley, came to pick me up to go to the airport. It seemed like just going through security would take as long as the plane ride. Just imagine how long the airplane ride felt.

When we arrived in Denver, we rented an RV so that we could go camping.

"Well, what campsite are we going to?" I asked. "I can't wait!"

"We are going to a small place called Camping in the Rockies," replied Uncle Jon. "There are lots of Jeeping trails around here, so I thought we could rent a Jeep."

"Cool! A Jeep!" said Grant and I simultaneously.

The next day, Uncle Jon left early to get the Jeep so we could have the whole day. He came back around nine. The Jeep was camouflage!

"But Dad," said Grant, "there are only two seats in this Jeep, and we have four."

"Well," Grant's dad replied, "I guess you and Zach will have to sit in the back!"

I could feel the wind rushing through my hair as we sped across the rocky terrain.

As we were approaching the end of the trail, we came across a big opening. It looked like an old abandoned town. We got out and looked around a little bit. I came across a boarded-up spot in the rocky mountains that towered over us.

"Hey, guys, I think I found a boarded-up mine."

"It looks pretty old," said Ashley.

"Yeah," said Uncle Jon, "it does."

"Hey, I think I see a crack in the wood. It looks big enough to see a nice distance into the mine."

"Good thing I brought a flashlight," said Grant.

I looked into the mine first. I saw lots of puddles and old, rusted candle holders. There was water dripping from the ceiling and specks of minerals on the wall. I even found a few bones. Eww.

"Wow, it's pretty big in he…guys, I think I see some sort of ancient writing."

Grant said, "Hey, let me look, I'm an expert. I've studied this before." Grant peered in. "Looks like Latin. Maybe I can make some of it out."

After about ten minutes, Grant finally said, "It says something about a mine entrance, ten paces east, and a chant."

"Looks like directions," said Uncle Jon. "Maybe we can follow them."

"Whatever," said Ashley.

"Well, what are we waiting for? Let's barge down this mine entrance!" I said.

After a few minutes of forcing the Jeep into the mine entrance, we finally opened it up. Then Uncle Jon drove the Jeep out of the mine onto the trail. We stepped into the mine and turned left. "Nothing." said Ashley. "Just a cave wall."

"Well, it did say something about a chant," I said.

"Hey, I think I remember an old Pueblo American Indian chant from my fourth-grade social studies book," said Grant.

"Well, let's hear it!" I said.

After he said what seemed like a forever chant and a bunch of gibberish, nothing happened. Nothing.

"Now what do we do?" I asked.

"Maybe you should try it again," said Ashley.

Still nothing.

"I bet this is all just a hoax!" cried Ashley. "This is a waste of our time!" Then she stomped her foot and stormed off.

But then, right in front where she stomped her foot, rocks started to crumble away at the wall. When the rock slide was over, in the middle lay a golden ring.

"Maybe I misread 'stomp' for 'chant,'" Grant said.

I went down to pick it up. Then the roof started to cave in towards the back of the mine. We all screamed and ran out of the mine as fast as we could.

"I'm glad I got out of that mine," said Grant as he was staring at the pile of rocks that had just been a mine we had been standing in.

I stared at the ring. "It has writing on it," I said.

"I feel like I just experienced an event from *National Treasure*," murmured Uncle Jon.

"Let me see," said Grant. "I think it says 'The Ring of the King.'"

"I wonder what that could mean," said Uncle Jon.

"Who knows," I said.

After that we drove back to our campsite and went straight to the nearest museum. The curator said the ring could belong to a king named Argas. He was a king who ruled a small empire around when the Native Americans thrived. They also said that this discovery could be worth $20,000. We couldn't believe our ears.

After other museum owners and historians heard about the ring, they bid higher for it. We gave the ring to the first museum because we consulted them first. We got $4,000 each, and the extra $4,000 paid for the trip.

When we were done giving the ring to the museum, *ABC Evening News* caught up to us before we got on our plane. I've never been on TV before, let alone live TV! We were interviewed by Diane Sawyer.

When we got home, my mom recorded the interview so we could watch it. Everyone at school saw the program, too, and thought it was pretty cool. They got a chance to see what an adventure we had in Colorado. It was quite an exciting trip that we will never forget.

The Savior of the Mississippi

A man named Rick in Wyoming is riding his horse when he realizes two men stole a train. Will Rick stop the train? Find out in **THE SAVIOR OF THE MISSISSIPPI**, *by* **Max Whalen.**

Click clop, click clop. Rick was riding his horse along a railroad track in Idaho in 1880. Rick had brown hair like chocolate milk and wore a black vest and a white button-down shirt. Rick was tall and thin. Rick was just coming home from a 7 A.M. rodeo. *Of course, I won first place*, Rick thought. Rick's horse was the fastest horse in the western United States.

Rick whispered to himself, "What's that noise?"

A train was next to Rick. Even though his horse just raced, Rick and his horse tried to beat it to the station. Rick looked inside and he saw two men with a map of the U.S. One of the men pointed along the railroad they were on and ended up pointing at the Mississippi River. Rick saw them laugh up a storm and could hear one say, "This train is ours!"

Rick realized they stole the train. He slowed his horse to find a good spot to hop on the train. Rick saw a good handle bar so he dug his spike into his horse. Rick's horse's hooves dug into the gravel. The train was too fast for Rick's horse so he slowed down. Rick decided to wait for the caboose. When Rick grabbed the train, he flew off his horse into the car. After this very long day, Rick hid under some benches. Rick went to bed after the sun went down.

Rick woke up at 8:00 A.M. and started making his way to the next car. When Rick walked into the next car, he found three men tied up. Rick cut the rope with his knife. He asked, "How did you get tied up?"

The men replied, "The two men who highjacked the train tied us." The four men worked their way to the front of the train.

At the end of the day they were in the car behind the engine and in Arkansas. The train workers and Rick made a plan to all burst in at once and tie the bad guys up. Their plan worked. Once they were tied up, the driver tried stopped the train. The break wouldn't budge. We yanked and pulled, but the break didn't work. Rick yelled at the robber, "What did you do?"

The robber laughed, "I'll never tell you."

After he finished laughing, a tall man jumped on the train and punched the driver. The driver flew right into the coal pile.

"This train is going where we want it," the tall man screamed, grabbing the engineer.

Rick picked up a hammer and yelled, "Not if I want it somewhere else," and slammed it into the brake.

The train pulled to a stop and everyone was sliding and falling down. Rick grabbed a rope and dove for the tall guy. Rick tied the rope super tight and heard, "AHHHHHH," from the man.

Rick tied up the bad guys and the three train workers and brought them to the sheriff. The sheriff hollered, "The bandits were on the Top Ten Most Wanted list. Thank you," and gave Rick one hundred dollars.

Puzzle It Out

Attack of the Germans

When Amelie meets a boy at the local high school, she doesn't know that he isn't what he appears to be. In **ATTACK OF THE GERMANS** *by* **Hope Lamphere***, Amelie has to figure out a way to save her family—and the whole United States.*

"M-o-o-o-o-m! I'm going to the high school on a field trip today, remember? I need a bag lunch!" I called as I rushed to put on my coat.

"All right, all right. Hold your horses already!" my mom called back.

I got to school, and what did I see? I saw the most humongous bus ever in human history! It was huge, almost 50 feet long! I guess I should have expected that since they were taking the whole eighth-grade class. I grabbed my bag and my coat, and hopped on. I headed down the aisle, looking around for my best friend Alyssa Mayer.

"Amelie! Over here!" I heard someone call my name. "Amelieeeee!" There it was again! Oh, wait, it was Alyssa!

"Alyssa, I'm coming! Where are you?"

"Over here, Miss Amelie Balder." Ah! There she was! I sat down just as the bus started moving. We held on tight, and off we went!

When we got to the high school, their principal was waiting outside for us even though it was below zero. We have had a *very* cold winter for Chandler, Arizona. We headed inside where it was much warmer, and the principal showed us where to put our coats.

Later, during lunch, I saw a ninth-grader sit down at the table next to ours. I really wanted to say "Hi," but I was afraid to; he looked like a nice person to get to know. Luckily, he started the conversation for me.

"Um, hi. I'm Finn Schröder. So, you're here from the middle school, right? What's your name?"

"Yes, I am here from the middle school. I'm an eighth-grader at Chandler Public Middle School. My name is Amelie Balder."

"Cool, I was, um, wondering if, um, you wanted to, um, go out sometime? Is Friday night okay? We could, um, go to, um, the movies, if you wanted to. Why don't you and your friend, there, come? I'll bring a couple of my friends, too."

"Um, well, I'd have to ask my mom, but I think I can go. What time will you pick me up?"

"Well, how about you be ready around 7:00. I think *The Outer Reaches* is on at 7:15."

"Great, I'll call you tonight if I can go!"

"Okay, have a good time on the rest of your visit!"

"Alyssa! Did you hear that? I have a date! You're invited, too, of course!"

"I'd love to come!"

Just then the bell sounded, signaling the end of lunch. Alyssa and I got up, and followed our class out of the lunchroom.

When I got home, I asked my mom if I could go over to Alyssa's house Friday night (not wanting to reveal that I had a date because she would say I'm too young).

When she said yes, I ran up to my room, flopped on my bed, and called Finn.

His grandfather picked up, "Hello? This is Aldrich Schröder."

"Hello, Mr. Schröder. This is Amelie Balder. Finn was expecting a call from me."

"Oh, yes. My grandson told me you would call! I'm sorry, did you say your name was Amelie Balder?"

"Um, yes it is. Is that a problem?"

"Uh, oh, no. Just wondering! Here's Finn for you."

"Hi, Finn. My mom said it was okay for me to go with you on Friday. Well, I'll see you then!"

* * *

After the movie, Finn helped walk everyone home. He walked me home last. "Thanks, Finn, for taking me to the movies. I had a great time! I think Alyssa did, too."

"You really think so? Oh, that's good. Well, have a good night!"

"Wait! I want you to meet my mom!"

"But, I thought you told her you were at Alyssa's?"

"I'll tell her that we went to the movies, and we met you guys!" We went inside.

"Hey, Mom! I want you to meet someone. His name is Finn Schröder. We met at the movies tonight."

"Nice, honey. Hello, Finn! Did she say your last name is 'Schröder'?"

"Oh, yes. I was born in Germany. I live with my grandfather, Aldrich Schröder."

"Did you say *Aldrich* Schröder?"

"Um, yeeesss. Is that a problem?"

"Is that a problem? Is that a problem? Why, of course that's a problem!"

Then my mother, of all people, Heather Balder, pierced the air with an ear-splitting war cry, and lunged at Finn, secret agent knives drawn!

"Stand back, *Finn.* You had better tell your grandfather that the U.S. is prepared for you! Germany might want to rethink its decision on trying to steal the U.S.'s plans for war! Out, I said. Out!"

What happened next was a sight to see. Finn opened the door, and in stepped his grandfather, followed by ten German agents, each with their knives drawn.

I raced to the phone and dialed 911. Busy! How can this be? The police have to answer! My mother is going to be killed! Finally, I got through! "Hello, police! There are German agents at my house. My mom is a U.S. agent! Help!"

I raced upstairs, and called Alyssa. I told her all that happened, and that she needed to get over here quick, but she'd have to use the back door. Luckily, Alyssa lived right next door so she was here in a flash.

I ran downstairs just in time. Alyssa was there, waiting, and we sprinted to the front of the house, just in time, too. Aldrich Schröder was advancing his small army into our foyer. I kicked my old banana peel across the room, and at the same time heard a sickening *THUNK* as Finn hit the floor. Score!

Phew! Now, I can relax, a little bit. I still have to keep the Germans busy until the police arrive. Oh, no! Aldrich's coming! Quick, got to find something to throw at them! Ah, ha! The old TV!

"Ha, ha, Aldrich! Why don't you watch something for me!"
BONK!

Wow, he really hit the floor hard. I hope he's okay. Actually, I hope he's not! Wow, all of them are going down hard. Finally! The police are here! Hey, it's the S.W.A.T. team! We're saved!

*   *   *

Well, that about does it. My mom is a secret agent, Germans invaded our house, now they're in jail, and I don't have a boyfriend anymore. Well, at least I have Alyssa!

Epilogue

So, once things slowed down, my mom explained everything to Alyssa and me. She became part of the U.S.'s secret agent force when she and my dad got divorced. The government knew that Germany was going to invade because we had a secret code that launched a nuclear missile at Germany. Although they didn't know exactly where, they knew they would probably come after my mom because she was in charge of the elite team of agents, having worked there so long. Also, she was the only person who had the code. It turns out my mom is pretty cool after all!

Charlie the Missing Boy

CHARLIE THE MISSING BOY, *by **Laura MacLean**, is a story about a boy who has to save his brother. Will he save him, or will he be lost forever?*

I woke up on a very foggy day, got dressed, and combed my short, curly, red hair. Then I did what I always did. I slowly and quietly went to my little brother's room. His name is Charlie. He was five. I walked in to get him ready for school. As I turned the doorknob considering how I should wake him up, I decided to push the door open fast and yell, "Good morning!"

To my surprise he wasn't there. I rubbed my eyes again and again, but he wasn't there. I also realized that the windows were broken, there was blood, and the room was a mess. I yelled for my mom and told her that Charlie had been kidnapped!

She called the cops. They were there in two minutes. As soon as they got there they were in Charlie's room looking for fingerprints. They were there all day. They told my mom and me that they would stay on this case. I was devastated. I wanted to cry, but I held it all in. It was time to go to bed, so I did.

When I woke up I saw caution tape all around my house. I went outside to see what was going on. I talked to the investigator. He told me that he found some clues, but they were minor. He told me he would keep looking.

As I was walking back into my house I saw that one house that was a block away had its lights on. That was strange because that house had been abandoned two years before. Throughout the day my thoughts kept returning me to that house. Finally I went to sleep.

When I woke up, something felt strange, like someone was watching me. Then I heard the door slam. Without thinking, I ran outside. I saw a dark shadow. I ran and followed it.

I felt like everything was going super-fast. I was scared, but I kept on following the shadow. I could tell he was cutting through the backyards of people's houses. I also could tell that he didn't know that I was following him.

He went into the abandoned house, and I followed. He saw me, so I screamed as loud as I could. I hoped the people at the crime scene heard me.

I was running around to find Charlie. The man tried to catch me, but I avoided him by jumping and doing fake turns. The house was super messy like he was a hoarder. As I was running he was yelling stuff like, "Get back here!" I was a few feet in front of him, but then I tripped on an old TV. As he was getting closer to me I could see the anger in his eyes and the sweat running down his face. Every footstep he took closer to me sounded like a bomb in my head, but right before he got to me, the door swung open.

The police came into the house and found Charlie doing the dishes. But right before they took the bad guy to jail they asked him why he took Charlie.

He said, "Because I wanted to have Charlie work."

I was so happy I simply picked him up and ran home to my mom. When I got him home my mom was so happy that I found him. She was crying happy tears. That night we all watched a movie and went to bed.

I woke up the next morning and ran to Charlie. We got ready for school. I rode my bike with him on the pegs, just like before.

Dead Toys 'R Us

Discover how a 13-year-old girl, taking her dog on an innocent walk, turns her life upside down forever. Read **DEAD TOYS 'R US**, by ***Parrish W. Roberts***.

One spring afternoon, a 13-year-old girl named Izzy (who had curly, short brown hair and hazel eyes) was walking her new dog, Fido. She found an awesome spot by a lake where she thought she and some of her friends could swim on really hot days during the summer. She went to the dock; sat down and put her feet in the water to see how warm it was. She was playing with Fido when she felt something scrape her feet. She wasn't sure what it was. She looked down and it was a hand. She thought it was a fake hand, but it was connected to a body. She thought she was dreaming, but it wasn't a dream. It was very, very real.

Izzy screamed hysterically. She jumped up still screaming, trying not to look at anything, but then her curiosity got the best of her. She saw the face that was not yet totally decomposed. One eye was gone; just a socket was there. The nose was gone as well. Izzy also saw what looked like intestines. They were sticking out of the stomach section that looked like spoiled three-month-old spaghetti. The smell was like no other smell Izzy had ever smelled before.

Izzy muttered to herself, "My stomach is doing backflips." The sight and smell of it all made Izzy shout, "I have to puke my guts out." And that's exactly what Izzy did! It was like a scene from a horror movie.

Izzy's dad was a detective for the local police department in the small town of Messmiana, Michigan. Izzy always wanted to follow in her dad's footsteps and be a detective, too. She never thought the opportunity to be a part of an investigation would happen so soon.

Earlier that day, Izzy read in the newspaper that the president of Toys 'R Us was missing. The president of Izzy's "still" favorite store (even though she was a teenager) was missing! Izzy said out loud, "I need to go to Toys 'R Us soon."

The president's name was Sisal Silverstone. He had a summer home, more like mansion, here in this little town. His mansion was located way up on the tip of Brown Edge Hill. Izzy wished she were way up on the tip of Brown Edge Hill now.

Izzy kept running and screaming trying to get that horrible picture that she had just seen out of her mind. Suddenly it occurred to Izzy that the body could be the president of Toys R Us. Izzy just sobbed, "I just want my daddy." As Izzy approached the house she saw her dad mowing the lawn. He could tell something was wrong with Izzy. He quickly turned off the lawnmower and ran up to his sobbing daughter and shouted, "Izzy, what's wrong? Why are you crying"?

Izzy gulped, "Dad I saw a…. a… a…. dead…dead body!" She began to cry some more. Dad hugged Izzy and they quickly went into the house.

In minutes, the police were everywhere. They were at the dock; they were at Izzy's house. Izzy told her dad all she could remember about what she had seen. Izzy was way past shaken up, but she felt proud to be working with her dad on this case.

Izzy did more and more research on Mr. S's case. Izzy could not figure out who would want to murder the C.E.O. of a toy store. She soon learned he was not a nice boss. She discovered during her research that Mr. S had stolen lots of money from his employees' retirement fund. Toys 'R Us had some financial problems, and Mr. S ripped off 75 percent of his employees. *It is so sad,* thought Izzy. The employees were tricked into believing their retirement money would double if they invested with Mr. S. The investment turned out to be worthless.

Izzy reasoned, *Some people have no retirement money, period. I wonder if one of his ex-employees killed him?* The case became more and more intriguing to Izzy. She could not stop thinking about it! Everybody thought it was one of the disgruntled employees who committed the crime. Izzy thought so, too. The employees were so hurt and very, very angry about Sisal Silverstone's stealing their money.

Izzy tried to talk to her dad about the case, but he wouldn't tell her much. Dad had become very tight-mouthed about the case. He knew she had a lot of issues to deal with after discovering the body.

Izzy's dad took Izzy to a professional to talk about her experience. Izzy was not sure she wanted to be a detective anymore. As summer wound down, Izzy's dad finally solved the case. It turned out that Mr. S's wife hired someone to murder her husband. She felt justified because her husband had hurt so many people. She also thought she would receive a nice life insurance payoff, too!

Izzy did not want to know all the details of the case like she thought she would. The details of that face were enough for her. Details were no longer important to Izzy.

Detective Lola

What would you do if somebody took your daughter's life? What if it was on a killing spree—would you do something about it or wimp out? It's your choice. It is just ahead in **DETECTIVE LOLA** *by* ***Amanda George***.

Detective Lola Franklin is a single woman who loves to solve murders. One day as she was watching the news, the reporter unraveled an interesting murder. "Three boys kidnapped a month ago have been found dead." Detective Lola wrote down every word she said. She had remembered in the past how her own daughter had been kidnapped and found dead in a ditch.

She drove to work with tears in her eyes. When she arrived at work, she told her associates and they got on the case. Three days later they officially started. It was only a couple of minutes before they got the first three suspects. Number one was Stephanie, the mom; number two their so-called uncle; and lastly the woman who was watching them when this happened, although the woman's child was fine after the boys were kidnapped.

It wasn't long before something horrible would happen. Detective Lola arrived home not knowing something was waiting for her amongst the shadows. As she was unlocking the door, she got plunked in the head with something hard and heavy. She woke up with a gag around her mouth and a blindfold over her eyes.

It talked. Her heart was pounding so hard she felt it might pop out of her chest. She couldn't make out the words it was saying, let alone if it were a girl or a boy. Its voice was disguised. The voice that she could once not understand suddenly became clear and admitted she was the murderer of the three boys. Detective Lola then realized this was also the murderer of her daughter. She'd recognize that voice anywhere. The murderer had an accent like maybe from Mexico.

Lola thought that one picture and voice on the 911 call was recognizable.

"Stephanie," she gagged.

"So how'd you find out? Oh, let me guess: the dumb little news lady?"

"No," Lola tried to reply. The gag fell off. "What do you want? You took my daughter's life and now three little boys."

"Do you know what I really want? Your perfect little life."

"Why do you want my life?"

Stephanie fell silent. Lola was terrified of what just happened, and then three gunshots pierced through the window, shattering glass everywhere.

Then the weirdest thing happened. She felt a warm hand on her face, and when she looked up, she noticed Charlie had taken her blindfold off. "Detective Lola, are you okay?"

Lola was stunned to see her co-workers standing there, each and every one of them surprised she wasn't dead,

"How'd you find me?"

"Remember, we have all those chips in our phone, and as soon as we couldn't locate you, we knew something was wrong. I suggested checking your house, but we weren't sure you would be there. Once we got here, we saw your car parked in the driveway and the front door of the house was wide open. We got scared and called the police."

"Well, that's a relief. What happened to…?" Lola pointed at the floor. "You killed…?"

"The police shot her when she moved in front of the window because she was holding a gun at you," Charlie explained.

"Well, at least you know the killer of your daughter and the three boys," Charlie said sadly.

Lola looked at him with tears in her eyes, "I love my daughter, and now I finally know who took her from me."

Forever Gone…Maybe?

There was a small town called Birmingham where a girl named Katy disappeared while at a party with her friends. Years later, they are still trying to figure out what happened to her. Will Katy come back alive? Find out in **FOREVER GONE…MAYBE?** *by* ***Isabella***.

In the town of Birmingham, there were four girls who have gone through something worse than anyone in the whole town. Three years ago, they were all at an end of seventh grade party with their best friend, Katy. They don't exactly know how they became friends with her because Katy was the most popular girl at school, and everyone wanted to be like her. She would walk down the hallway, her blonde hair flipping on her back, with the latest Burberry bag hanging from her shoulder. She always wore the charm bracelet her mom had gotten her for her birthday. All eyes were on her when she walked down the hall. While they were at the party, Katy said she was going to get some water from inside, but she never returned. The girls thought that Katy had just gone home, but no one actually knew what happened.

One day, Katy had two best friends, Bradley and Sloan, and then, the next day, Katy had four new best friends named Amanda, Meghan, Lexxe and Lauren. Nobody really knew what happened, but Bradley and Sloan were furious that she dropped them and wanted to get back at Katy. Amanda, Meghan, Lexxe and Lauren were not the most popular girls in school, so it was really strange that Katy had chosen them. Katy's life was pretty much like a movie… but it was real.

Now, they are about to start 11th grade and are trying to erase the memory of their old best friend, but they can't because there are still old signs everywhere saying, "HAVE YOU SEEN KATY WHITEHALL?" and had some old pictures of them hanging out by the pool, at her house, and the mall. That brought back terrible thoughts to each of their minds.

Lauren was walking down the hallway at school, trying to get to her next class before the bell rang, and noticed a man in his mid-twenties starring at her. He was wearing dark jeans and a gray hoodie. He looked very familiar. The man was wearing a nametag from the office so he must have had a way to get into the school. Meghan came up to Lauren and said, "Doesn't he look familiar?"

"Yeah, I think I've seen him around, why?" Lauren said.

"I don't know, it just seemed like he's been following us around," Meghan replied.

He glanced at them and gave them a little smirk so Meghan and Lauren both scurried down the first staircase they saw, which led them to the cafeteria. They met up with the others at their usual lunch table in the back corner and talked about all the things they did with Katy before she was gone. They all thought she was murdered, except for Lauren, who still believed she was hiding somewhere. Lauren was the closest to Katy out of all them. Lauren had told Katy EVERYTHING. Something that was always weird about their friendship was that Katy never told any of them her secrets, though she knew EVERYTHING about them.

Over the next two weeks there were TWO murders… but they ended up being suicides. It was Derek and Kaylin, two siblings who lived down the street who were always suspected of Katy's disappearance because they were good friends with Katy's family. They were jealous because she was so popular.

After more research, the police finally had a suspect. Katy's older stepbrother, Ethan, was always jealous of Katy because her parents always treated her better than him. He was the only person who didn't like Katy. Ethan was arrested and then two weeks later pleaded not guilty! And the suspected a killer was still on the loose.

Lexxe and Amanda were in their English class when they looked out the window and saw the guy with the gray sweatshirt and jeans. They heard Lauren and Meghan talking about him and now they were scared.

After lunch, the girls were called to the office because there was a policeman waiting to pick them up. The girls told the cop, Parrish, about the strange man, and he took a description of the man and asked some questions, and then drove them home just to be safe. When they were getting out of the car, they noticed a big duffle bag with the zipper opened just enough so you could see in it. Inside they saw a gray piece of soft material that looked exactly like the gray sweatshirt the man in school had been wearing. Something did seem suspicious about the cop, but the girls just couldn't figure it out.

Later, they called Meghan and Lauren and told them. The girls tried to report it to the cops, but they just wouldn't believe that Parrish might have had something to do with Katy's disappearance. Luckily, there was one cop who said that Officer Parrish was acting suspiciously. He decided to check out the bag when he wasn't looking, and sure enough, there was a gray sweatshirt and dark jeans in the bag!

The police kept a very close eye on him and one day, another officer saw him putting on the sweatshirt and jeans! Parrish was arrested, but the problem was that there was no proof that he actually killed Katy or that he did anything! After a couple of months, they figured out that Parrish had something to do with the murder (if it was a murder!), or if he was just searching for evidence.

The next couple of months went by… and still no evidence. The four girls went out to lunch and on the tiny TV in the restaurant the news headline read. "Katy Whitehall found alive in brother's basement"! The girls immediately put down their forks, left a small tip, and rushed out of the restaurant.

They tried to get to Ethan's house, but there were police cars surrounding the whole neighborhood. They managed to sneak in with a crowd and saw a frightened and pale girl on a stretcher being pulled into the emergency truck. They couldn't believe it. Katy was back, hopefully. Parrish was released and immediately started researching the case. Ethan was immediately arrested and taken into the police station. His story was that Bradley and Sloan forced him to keep her in the basement and not say a word. Nobody knows how, but she managed to live for almost FOUR years! You would think that she wouldn't survive in the basement, but when she was out of the hospital, she was taken to the police to tell them what happened. She told them he treated her fine, fed her, and gave her whatever she needed, but just kept her in the basement. The cops did not believe her at first because they had searched through Ethan's house many times and never found anything evidence that she was there!

Come to find out that was the true story. Bradley and Sloan were taken to court and days later pleaded guilty. This was finally over. Now, Katy, Amanda, Meghan, Lexxe, and Lauren promised they would never walk away from each other ever again.

The Kidnapper

In **THE KIDNAPPER** *by* **Gillian Tremonti,** *two girls' friends go missing, and it is a race against time to find their friends before it is too late. Will their friends be found or be lost forever?*

It was a normal day for Kenzie Smith. She woke up, put on her jeans and blue t-shirt and looked in the mirror above her dresser. She was not super pretty. She had wavy blonde hair with natural highlights of light brown. She had bright blue eyes and had lots of freckles. She went down stairs for breakfast and then got into the car so her mom could drive her to school.

When they arrived at the school, Kenzie went in and headed toward her locker. While she was at her locker, Kitty Rich walked by with her group of friends. Kitty Rich, the most popular girl at Pork Chop Middle School, was also the meanest. She had very curly, blonde shoulder length hair with hazel brown eyes. Kitty muttered, "Kenzie is a LOSER." Her friends giggled behind her. Kenzie didn't know why Kitty hated her; she just did.

After school, Kenzie worked on her homework. She focused on her math. She had a big test the next day in Mr. Quizella's class. He was the worst teacher at school. Kenzie thought he gave out F's for fun. The opposite of Mr. Quizella was Ms. Sweet. She was the principal at Porkchop Middle School.

That night it was Kitty's birthday party. She lived in a huge house that was as big as three, two-story houses put together. Kitty's cook came out with the cake; the lights went out and came back on. Kitty's friend Lemon Goldberg had disappeared. "Lemon, where are you?" Kitty said nervously. "I'm not joking, Lemon." But Lemon was nowhere to be found. Kitty was terrified.

That same night, at Kenzie's house, Kenzie's best friend Jess Blender was over. While they were in her room the lights went out, Kenzie heard someone whispering, "Shhhhhhhh!" When the lights came back on, Jess was nowhere to be found. Kenzie told her mom who called the police. They said, "Mrs. Rich (Kitty's mom) called earlier we will keep a look out for the girls."

At school the next day, everyone was there except for Lemon Goldberg and Jess Blender. Even Kitty said nothing, which was very odd for her. Kenzie told Ms. Sweet the next day about Jess and Lemon. Kenzie thought her reaction was odd when she nervously replied, "I don't know, pumpkin, just be careful."

In fourth hour, Mr. Quizella's class was going to take a test. "Begin the test. I will be back in a minute." Kitty gave Kenzie a note. Kenzie opened it thinking it would have harsh comments. It said, "I need to find Lemon Goldberg before it's too late. Meet me at lunch table five." Kenzie could not believe it was Kitty, the mean girl.

At lunch, Kenzie went to table five and there was Kitty. Before Kenzie said anything Kitty blurted out, "Where are they?"

There was a long silence. Then Kenzie said, "What if we work together to find them?"

"NO!" she replied.

"You can have the credit for finding them," Kenzie said.

"Fine, I guess."

"First, we need to find clues," Kenzie said.

"Let's meet back here tomorrow."

The next day at lunch Kitty and Kenzie met at table five. "Did you find anything?" Kenzie said.

"Yes, I did, I found a little bit of a red scarf caught on my jewelry box," Kitty said.

"Mr. Quizella was wearing a red scarf the day before Jess and Lemon went missing! Do you think it's him Kitty? Could it really be Mr. Quizella?" Kenzie said shocked.

"Maybe, I don't know. Let's find out," replied Kitty.

They walked to Mr. Quizella's class and said at the same time, "Why did you kidnap our friends? We saw you with this scarf on the day before the kidnapping happed!" Kenzie held out the piece of the torn red scarf.

Mr. Quizella answered, "I borrowed that scarf from Ms. Sweet the other day."

"No, it couldn't have been really," they both said.

"Really, I'm mean but I don't go kidnapping children!" Mr. Quizella then called the police. They all started to walk to the office.

Kitty, Kenzie and Mr. Quizella walked up to Ms. Sweet and said all at once, "Where did you put them? We called the police."

Then there was a little squeak; it sounded like a mouse. It was coming from the closet. Kitty rushed to it and opened the closet and sure enough, Jess and Lemon were in there. It was a huge closet, just like it was made to keep people in it.

The police took Ms. Sweet away and said, "That was Amy Phoenix. She is a crazy, insane woman that takes children for no reason. We have been looking for her a long time. Thank you for finding her."

After that, they never saw Ms. Phoenix (Ms. Sweet) again. Kenzie and Kitty learned never to judge a book by its cover. Kitty and Kenzie never became friends, but now Kitty never makes fun of or teases Kenzie again.

The Missing

In the story **THE MISSING** *by* ***Lexie Seidel***, *a girl's mother goes missing. Will she see her mother again?*

My name is Lisa. I'm in ninth grade, and I go to Lincoln Hills High School. My mom was working in the garden one day. She was planting some more flowers when out of the blue someone came up behind her. *BAM!* She is knocked unconscious. "Bring her to the headquarters," she heard just before going under.

Well, I was at school when this happened, but not long after I got home and said, "Mom, I'm home." There was no answer. I went to the kitchen to see if she was there. She wasn't. I looked around to see if there was a note. There was, but not from my mother. The note said *"If you want your mother back you must give me your money."* And that was it. There was no place to meet, no name, and no Mom.

When I read this note goose bumps came, and I felt hopeless. My mother is somewhere, and I have no idea who would do this. My heart sank, and I felt as if I would never see her again.

I called my grandma to see if I could stay with her while the police try to find my mom. My grandma felt the same way; she came to pick me up soon after. Before she came to pick me up I dialed 9-1-1. They said if she didn't return in 24 hours they would start a search party.

My mom woke up after being unconscious for quite some time. She found she was sitting with her hands and feet tied up. When my mom woke up she found herself in a sewer. Well, she found herself in a cellar-like room in a sewer. My mom looked around in confusion. The walls were greasy and muddy. My mom was disgusted.

It was dark and creepy because there wasn't any source of light. My mother heard voices, but she wasn't sure where they were coming from. She started to look around, when all of a sudden she put her hand behind her and felt something cool and hard. She looked back to find a full body skeleton. From the look of it the skeleton was obviously not real, but it was still cold and creepy. My mom screamed when she saw it. She heard footsteps coming near her.

"Well, well, well, look who's up," said one of the men.

"Why am I here? Why me?" my mom asked.

"Well you're *here* because no one will think to look in a sewer for someone. And why we chose you? Well, you just looked vulnerable," someone said.

"What do you want from me?" Mom asked.

"What do we want from you? Well, we want some money," another man said.

"Why would you guys need money?" Mom said.

"Well, we all lost our jobs, so we want your money," said someone else. Then they left her sitting in a little room with nothing to do.

Man, I'm hungry, my mom thought. "Hey, can I have some food please?" she screamed.

Someone was coming. "Why would we give you food?" asked a man.

"Because if I starve to death I won't be able to give you the money that you want," Mom said.

"Very well, you can have some food, but we are leaving you after this because it is just gross in here," he said. So he left again and came back with some food.

It had been three days since my mom had gone missing I am now staying with my grandmother who lives a few miles away for me I've been in my room most of the time I have been at my grandmother's. The only time she comes up to my room is to give me food. The rest of the time she is downstairs hoping my mother is fine.

I woke up to the sound of the phone ringing. It was the police. The police are coming to the house and are going to ask me some questions. I hung up the phone, and ten minutes later the doorbell rang.

The chief was there. A few other officers came along as well. When we were done the police officers drove back to the station. I was alone again until my grandmother came home, so I went straight to bed.

My mom was thinking of a way to get out of the little room. Just then she realized that the rope they used was tied very poorly. My mom was able to slip out and look for a way out. She started to walk around when she saw a door. My mother was so happy! But when she went to open the door, it was locked. My mother felt as if she were about to explode, because she was so angry.

My mother had a brilliant idea. *What if I walk to a sewer cap and climb out from there?* my mom thought. When she started to look around she went every way there was an opening. She was walking around as if she were in a maze blind-folded and trying to get out. When she was finished she found that all the walls that led to a sewer cap were sealed by cement.

Then, she realized that there was a sewer grate in the room she was in. She felt so stupid for not thinking of this before. She went to the room and screamed as hard as she could. Now it was probably hard to hear outside wherever she was, but soon enough my mom realized she was most likely on a neighborhood street because she could hear lots of screams from young kids.

My mom had to wait at the grate for about three hours until a little rubber ball rolled into the sewer. My mom could see little feet running toward the sewer. My mom thought that the little kid would be very frightened, but he was quite calm as if he had seen someone in a sewer before. My mom asked him to get his mother because she needed some help. The little boy did as my mother asked him to. About three minutes later his mother came running out.

My mom handed his mom the rubber ball, and started to talk to his mother. My mom asked her to call the police and come over as soon as possible.

The police came very quickly. As soon as they saw my mom they called the Water and Sewage Department to help them. The police told my mom that they would be there as soon as possible, but they had to go through the underground sewer. The police officers were there about five hours later. My mom was getting very tired of waiting, when suddenly, she heard loud banging on the wall. They apologized for a long time. Apparently they had not known about the sealed walls, so they had to go back and grab some sledge hammers.

Two policemen and one guy from the Water and Sewage Department walked my mom back to the Water and Sewage Department office.

The rest of the policemen and the other person from the Water and Sewage Department waited there until the bad guys came back to feed my mom dinner. The policemen only had to wait about an hour. As soon as the bad guys figured out that my mom had escaped, they looked around in confusion. Then they stumbled upon the police. The bad guys darted as fast as they could, but they weren't fast enough.

The police caught them and brought them to the police station. Then a policeman drove my mom to my grandmother's house.

"Lisa, are you here?" my mom screamed when she walked in.

"Mom, Mom! You're home! I thought I would never see you again!" I felt so overjoyed. I felt as if fireworks were going off in my body! It was great to know that my mom was safe, not injured, and with me.

The Missing Basketball

A boy wins a valuable basketball. If only he knew where it was! Read **THE MISSING BASKETBALL** *by* **Quinn Richter** *to learn where it ends up.*

One cold winter day I was walking home from school, kicking the snow and not really paying attention to what was going on around me. Suddenly, I noticed a bright green piece of paper lying on the ground. It looked suspicious, so I bent down to pick it up. The piece of paper was a raffle ticket for a Michael Jordan autographed basketball. The deadline to turn in the ticket was the next day, so I ran the rest of the way home and begged my mom to take me to the post office. My mom agreed to take me.

As I put the raffle ticket in the mail, I realized the drawing would be the following day. I knew my chances were very small that I would actually win, but I really wanted that basketball. Michael Jordan is my favorite basketball player, and all of my friends would be jealous. As I lay in bed that night, I was so anxious to see if I would be the winner I could not fall asleep.

The next morning I woke up and ran down the stairs to see who had won the drawing. When I watched the news, I saw the news anchor reach into the hat and pull out the winning ticket. As he read the name on the ticket I could not believe my ears. "And the winner is John Diamond." I had won the raffle! I screamed "OH MY GOD!" I could not wait to get my prize in the mail. The news anchor said it would come the very next day. It was going to be so hard for me to wait for the basketball to arrive.

I had to hurry and get dressed for school. I was so excited to tell my friends the news. When I got to school, I shared my amazing news with my friends. None of them believed a word I told them. They all wanted to see proof of the winnings. I told them the basketball was coming tomorrow and they should all come over after school to see it.

The following day my friends and I ran home to see my winnings. When we got to my house, the basketball was nowhere to be found. I asked my mom if it had come in the mail, and she said that she had not seen it.

We decided to go ask my brother Todd if he had seen the ball. Todd said he had not seen the ball, but he seemed to be a little nervous when he answered. My friends and I decided to go snoop in Todd's bedroom.

We searched for what seemed to be hours and found nothing! I was so mad that I slammed the closet door shut. All of a sudden we heard something hit the floor.

"What was that?" I said. I opened the closet door and looked at the ground. Out rolled the Michael Jordan autographed basketball. "I told you I won it," I said to my friends.

They could not believe it. "That is so cool," my friends said. I ran to tell my mom that I had found the basketball hidden in Todd's closet. She called Todd to the kitchen. "Thief!" I yelled at Todd. Todd explained that he was jealous that I had won the basketball all because I found a raffle ticket on my way home from school.

The next day I was the talk of the school. Everyone wanted to hear about how I had found the raffle ticket and won the Michael Jordan autographed basketball.

The Mystery of the Queen's Crown

When Queen Elizabeth's crown goes missing, it's up to the Mystery Solvers to get it back. In the story **THE MYSTERY OF THE QUEEN'S CROWN** *by* **Parker Tomkinson**, *they have to get her crown back before it is too late.*

"Ahhhhh," cried Queen Elizabeth. "My crown has been taken!"

We were just standing and watching the changing of the guard in London, England. All of a sudden someone was running with a black mask on and a bag. There were police chasing after him, and it didn't look good.

We are the Mystery Solvers. We are internationally famous for solving mysteries all around the world. I am Lila, who helps with all of the planning and researching. I have black hair and green eyes, and I usually wear things that are blue. Phillip makes traps to catch the thief. He has blond hair and blue eyes.

That night there was a big commotion. The queen's crown was taken. Phillip and I went to the queen's palace that night. We explained to the guards that we are the Mystery Solvers and we could help to find the crown. We had to go through security before we could see the queen. Once we were through, the guards took us to see the queen.

She explained the whole thing. Apparently the crown was in a showcase, and the person who stole it smashed into the showcase, took the crown, and ran off. The queen said, "Whatever you can do would be great."

The next day we talked to the guards who chased the thief. They said that he ran into the woods and tripped both of them. They also mentioned that he went through the mud so there are probably tracks.

Phillip and I went into the woods and went to where the mud was, and on the other side of the mud were tracks. We followed the tracks to an abandoned house. Phillip and I went inside.

Phillip and I went through the house looking for anything that could be a clue. We opened cabinets and drawers, too.

All of a sudden we heard a noise coming from upstairs. We dashed upstairs and went through all of the rooms. When Phillip went inside the last room, he found a bag. He dug through it, and he found the queen's crown! There were also muddy footprints leading up to the window where the bag was.

"The thief must have jumped out of the window!" I exclaimed.

While Phillip made a trap to catch the thief, I examined the fingerprints on the crown. They were very smudged like someone had tried to wipe them off.

I went to the palace that night and asked the queen, "Does anyone ever touch the crown with their bare hands?"

She answered, "Never. Everyone who touches the crown use a towel."

I was certain that the fingerprints were the thief's and that that one trap would catch him. When the thief comes back for the bag, he will jump out of the window again when he hears us coming. When he jumps out of the window he will fall into a net, which he will get tangled in. We will put a fake crown in the bag instead of the actual crown.

Exactly as planned, I went into the house and I heard noises like running across the floor. Phillip was outside waiting to set the trap. The guy jumped out of the widow just as Phillip unleashed the trap. We caught him!

I pranced outside to see if Phillip had caught him. I came over to the man and ripped the mask off of him. It was Boris Johnson, the mayor of London, England.

I asked him, "Why did you do it, Boris?"

He said he did it for money. Phillip called the police, and they came and took Boris to prison.

The queen was quite pleased to get her crown back. She said, "Thank you, thank you, thank you," repeatedly.

All of London thought that the Mystery Solvers were lifesavers and geniuses. They even threw a party because of us. We were very happy with ourselves after a job well done.

The Royal Thief

When royal riches get stolen from the Royal Family in England, what must they do to get them back? **THE ROYAL THIEF** *by* **Christian Sosa** *considers the case.*

The Royal Family has had a long and enduring history. Generations of leaders have ruled the English countryside for centuries, providing peace and stability through-out the region. However, just recently a scandal threatened to tarnish the name of the Royal Family. According to local authorities, the Royal Bank of England reported that some of the Royal Families most treasured jewels and artifacts had recently been missing. There was talk that among the many priceless items believed to be stolen was a 16th century jeweled dagger, reportedly belonging to King Henry the Eighth.

Word spread of the apparent robbery, and there was concern that the thieves would never be caught. Among those confused about the theft were the Royal guards. Such a robbery seemed nearly impossible as The Royal vault, where the treasures are currently held, is under remarkably tight security. There is 24–hour video surveillance, sophisticated motion and sound detectors, and heavily-armed guards patrolling its entrance. In fact, only a handful of people have direct access to it any given time. Among those is the Chief of the Royal Army, the King, The Queen, and their oldest son, Prince Richard. The locations of each of them during the time of robbery had all been verified, including the Royal Family who were vacationing in Switzerland.

So, the authorities began a more intense investigation. It was determined that such a robbery could've only occurred with some inside help. But a few questions remained. First, who could've been involved? And, if someone in the Royal Family was involved, why would they steal from their own treasures? In fact, many of the descending family members were very concerned. If these thieves were able to get into a highly protected vault, where would they strike next? The director of the Royal Police of England needed answers. He needed to solve this crime as soon as possible, as the longer it went unsolved, the worse it would be for the country of England. He knew that the media would have a field day with it.

A number of days went by, and still there was nothing. Countless people, including the families of the Royal Guards, were all questioned, and still there were no real answers. They had checked the video tapes and dusted for fingerprints in the vault to no avail. Whoever was involved in this heist knew how to cover their tracks pretty well. The police director kept going back to the Royal Family. He believed that someone had to know something. So, he called upon his crime unit and decided to give all those that had any access to the vault a lie detector test.

Such a test had never been given to a Royal Family member. However, the King and Queen all agreed that they had nothing to hide, and agreed to have one done. "The criminal must be caught, whatever the cost," said the King. When their Son Richard was approached he also agreed, although somewhat nervously. The test began, and both the King and Queen passed with no problem. When the tester sat Prince Richard down, the official began to notice how uncomfortable the prince suddenly became. In fact, sweat began to pour down his forehead, and before he could answer any questions, he suddenly stood up, looked at his parents, the King and Queen, and said "It was me. I was the one responsible for this so-called robbery."

The Queen looked at her son in disbelief and said, "We have given you everything and this is how you repay us?"

You see, as a child Prince Richard was a rather spoiled kid who spent most of his life in boarding schools and having bodyguard around him nearly everywhere he went. Although it seemed like Richard had a normal life, for much of it he felt almost imprisoned. As he got older, he realized how much he had missed and seemed to resent his parents for it. So, he devised a scheme to create the illusion that many of the Royal Treasures had been stolen. It would be the perfect crime.

With the help of one his closest bodyguards, Carl, Prince Richard made a replica fingerprint that would be ultimately used in the apparent heist. While the Royal Family was vacationing, Carl used the fingerprint given to him by Prince Richard to access the electronic panel on the vault. It was common for a guard to check on the jewels from time to time for security reasons. On a routine walk-through, Carl disabled the video cameras and managed to discreetly move some of the treasures from one vault to another. The Royal Family had a number of vaults, used to house various things. So, it gave the appearance that those precious artifacts had been stolen. They had planned it for months, and it all worked perfectly well.

The Royal Family was not at all pleased. When asked why he would do such a thing, the Prince simply said, "I did it just to get a little attention. I always missed a real adventure while growing up, and I figured this would be a lot of fun to pull off."

After the Prince's confession, the director of police approached the King and Queen and asked if they wanted to press charges. They chose not to do so, but vowed to punish Prince Richard by making him do community service at the local prison for the next year. Even his possibility of becoming King one day would be in question. As for the bodyguard Carl, Prince Richard had promised to protect his job. Unfortunately, it all backfired, and he was immediately fired by the King. He is now working as a crossing guard in a small town in England.

As the old saying goes, crime doesn't pay. Prince Richards will be reminded of that every time he has to serves lunch to all those prisoners who didn't get a second chance like he did.

Run!

Will a mystery lady end up ruining a very special day? **RUN!** *by* **Alex Bruner** *tells of how one girls' curiosity leads to a suspenseful and exciting birthday surprise.*

It all started on Monday, which happened to be my birthday. I was at the mall and had been looking forward to a leisurely day of shopping when I saw a suspicious lady dressed in a black outfit and dark sunglasses. Curious as to what she might be up to, I decided to follow her until she reached the outside of the mall. I watched as she entered a black limousine with tinted windows. Okay, maybe I shouldn't have followed her, but I had to find out what she was up to, and I had to know before my party.

The lady seemed very mysterious because of how she acted. Every two minutes, she would look behind her like she suspected someone was after her. I started to wonder if she was a criminal. Then she turned and looked straight at me! I tried to run home as fast as I could, but she was right behind me in the limousine. I needed to get away from her.

I decided to go to the nearest police station. When I got there the police told me that she was a secret FBI agent. I couldn't believe it was true! She told me her name was Raina. She was on a mission to help save animals and was investigating the pet store in the mall. I wanted to hear more about the mission, but I had to get back in time for my birthday party. I also wanted Raina to join us. It would be fun to have a spy at my party. I was thrilled when she said that she would be there.

By the time I got home, my mom was ordering the pizza. She reminded me that my party would start soon and that I should get ready. Raina ended up not coming to my party because, well, she *is* a spy. It still turned out to be one of the most exciting, yet scary, days of my life. Even if I had been a little too nosey!

That's Amore!

How relaxing it would be to vacation in Venice—especially if investigating mysterious art thefts is your idea of relaxing. **Annelise Fisher** *considers the possibilities in* **THAT'S AMORE!**

When the moon hits your eye
Like a big pizza pie
That's amore!

It was late at night, and a few of my cousins, my friend Rachel, and I were all in a little rowboat, the *S.S. BOAT*. We were just floating down a river, singing and goofing off. We were in Venice, Italy on vacation. My name is Elie Fisher, by the way.

"We better get back to the hotel," said Marie, my older cousin who was in charge of us. "It's 1:30 in the morning!" she said, glancing at her watch. We paddled as fast as we could until we got to the hotel. We got to bed before one of the adults woke up (luckily they are all heavy sleepers).

Next morning, I woke up to the smell of breakfast. I came downstairs to find my father reading the morning paper. And I could see why. The headline was "Crook Steals Famous Artwork from All Over the World! Where Will He Strike Next?"

After breakfast, we all went to the hotel lobby. A scrubby-looking man in his late 40's named Antonio showed us to our gondola. He was our gondolier, too. We came to stop at an Italian museum, and policemen were all around it. Some were in boats, but most of them were by the museum door. "What's going on?" I asked.

"Someone just stole *Starry Night* that was here on loan!" said one of the cops. "This is one of the biggest crimes of the year! And we think it's the same guy that stole *The Scream*. That was also on loan! We're gonna owe millions of dollars!"

"What do you know about the guy?" I asked.

"We don't know anything about him," said one of the cops. "We've heard a rumor that he's going to steal the *Mona Lisa* next, but we don't know for sure. We have the *Mona Lisa* here on loan and if the Frenchies don't get it back, they are going to make us pay big time!" he said.

We went back to the hotel, but my mind was buzzing with questions. (I was reading a mystery at the time, so I was all into crime scenes and playing detective.) "What kind of a person would steal famous artwork on loan, knowing that the museum would have to pay millions? Well, I'm stumped," I said.

"Elie, stop worrying! We're on vacation! You shouldn't worry on vacations," said Rachel. She always knows how to cheer me up.

"I suppose you're right Rachel."

I put in a good mystery movie to keep my mind off of things. About halfway through the movie, I fell asleep. I dreamed that I was at the museum. A shadow was creeping closer and closer to the *Mona Lisa* until two gloved hands reached out. That's when I woke up. I glanced at my watch. 2:05 A.M. I got out of bed and walked over to Rachel's bed. "PSST! Rachel, are you awake?" I whispered.

"I am now," she yawned.

"Well, get dressed. We're going to the museum. I've got a feeling that the thief is going to strike again. Maybe we can stop him."

Rachel didn't want to ask me questions at two in the morning, so she just did what I said. We snuck out of the hotel and got into the *S.S. BOAT*. We paddled down the street until we got to the museum.

I tried a side door. It was locked, of course. Luckily, I had a hairpin. One minute and forty seven seconds later (my personal best!) we were in the museum, sneaking around. When we got to the *Mona Lisa*, we both hid around the corner.

A few minutes later, we heard somebody walking around. Footsteps were coming closer. Then we saw him. He was dressed in black, and he looked like a ninja. I could only see his green eyes but he was coming closer.

Suddenly, Rachel collapsed. I turned around, and I was looking straight into the green eyes of the man. He smacked me on the head with a bat. The last thing I remember before I blacked out were two gloved hands reaching for the *Mona Lisa*.

I woke up tied to a chair, my hands and feet tied up behind me. Rachel was tied up too, right by my side. In the far corner were the *Mona Lisa, Starry Night,* and *The Scream*, just sitting there gathering dust. "Enjoy your little nap, girls?" said someone. I turned around and saw him: Antonio.

"YOU. What are you doing here?" I asked.

"SHUT UP!" he yelled. "Stay here, I'll be right back," he said with a devilish grin. He walked out of the door.

"Well, that's great. We found the artwork, but we don't know where the heck we are, and we are gonna die any minute," I said.

"Well, let's look on the bright side," Rachel said cheerfully. "One, we tried hard and two, we're still dear friends."

"Rachel, can it!" I said, "I have a plan. The green-eyed idiot left us in a room with several knives! Let's try to get to one." We started to move the chairs towards one of the counters where the knives were, but we fell over. "Crud," I said. On the bright side, one of my arms was free. I grabbed a knife and started to cut through the rope until Rachel and I broke free.

We started to sneak round until we found a trap door. We climbed up and found out that it led to the hotel lobby. We ran to the police station and told them all about Antonio. Rachel, the police, and I all ran through the trap door to find Antonio about to escape with the paintings.

Five minutes later, Antonio was in handcuffs and Rachel and I were being rewarded with medals for helping out Venice.

That night, which was our last night in Venice, my cousins, Rachel, and I were all in the *S. S. BOAT* again, drinking soda, and singing under the beautiful full moon.

I love vacations, and that's one vacation I'll never forget!

> *When the world seems to shine*
> *Like you've had too much wine*
> *That's amore!*

What Happened

Cancer

CANCER, *by **Spencer Lisabeth**, is the story of a six-year-old boy who is diagnosed with leukemia. It tells about the ups and downs of what happens during the time of his cancer.*

On Thursday, August 19, 2005, I woke up in the morning with severe pain in my left leg and a 103.5-degree fever. My mom had to take me to the emergency room at Beaumont Hospital where they took an x-ray of my left leg, knee, and hip to see if they were infected. I thought I had the flu or something but not that I had cancer. I was only five years old so I didn't even know what cancer was.

After several days of taking antibiotics, having my arm poked every six hours for blood, and running different tests, the doctors decided to perform surgery. On Tuesday, August 23, I was taken into surgery to have a piece of my left leg bone scraped and a bone marrow test. I had to be knocked out which was scary to me. The reason they had to do a bone marrow test was because my white blood cell count was going down every day. I found out on Wednesday, August 24, 2005 that I had Acute Lymphocytic Leukemia. It is a type of cancer found in the white cells of the bone marrow.

At 3:00 that afternoon, I started taking medicine that would kill my bad cancer cells but would also kill my good cells. This is how it was explained to me. This process is known as "chemotherapy". Two days later, I had surgery to put a medaport under my skin on the right side of my chest near my collar bone. A medaport is about the size of a quarter and has a rubber tube attached to a rubber bubble. This tube would then go into my vein and the liquid chemo would go into my bloodstream and then to my heart. The reason they had to put in a medaport was because some of my liquid chemo was too strong to be put into my tiny veins. After two weeks of chemo treatment, I was in remission which means no more cancer was growing. I was allowed to leave the hospital and continue treatment at home.

For the first month at home, I had an IV hooked up to my arm. My mom had to give me a new bag of antibiotics every six hours through my IV. This was I needed to continue to fight off the infection that I also had. A visiting nurse came every other day to take my blood pressure, test my oxygen level, and to make sure my IV was doing okay. I had to have my chemo pills crushed and put into capsules so that I could swallow them. Sometimes I had 13 different capsules to take in one day.

My illness was diagnosed five days before I was to begin first grade. I missed most of my first grade. My mom had to take a leave from her job and my brother had to go to school without me. I had to stay in the hospital multiple times for many reasons. If I ever had a fever over 100.5 degrees, I had to spend at least three days there to make sure I did not have any infections or that my medaport wasn't infected. I had to have my blood taken every week and every three months, I needed a spinal tap to make sure that I was still in remission. A spinal tap was when a long needle was inserted in the lower part of my back in between the vertebrae. The needle draws the fluid from my spinal cord. I was knocked out again for this and the pain in my back lasted for days. Sometimes I would get a major headache. I hated having them.

For three years and four months I received treatment for my leukemia and it was a horrible experience. The pain that I went through was very hard for me to understand and deal with. My family helped me and encouraged me to try and stay positive but it was very complicated. We cried a lot, and had many frustrating moments, and I felt like I couldn't be a kid or even play with my brother or friends. I ended treatment on December 21, 2009 which was the happiest day of my life. I continue to have my blood checked every three months to monitor my remission.

Leukemia had taken control of my body and my mind. I had difficult y making decisions and it seemed like everything was going against me. I was able to beat leukemia with the proper treatment, doctors, and support. When I am 15, I will no longer need to have my blood taken and I will be "normal" like I was before I had cancer. I don't even know what "normal" is because I was so young. The total number of days I had cancer was 1,208. I am truly a "survivor."

Cory

A normal day at school turns into a disaster. When a girl comes home from school she finds out terrible news. What will she do? Seek the answer in **CORY**, *by **Nicole Borovsky**.*

It was the middle of May in 2009. I was staring at the clock waiting for the end of the day in that dull gray room. I couldn't hear anything but the tick tock of the clock. My mind was blank. My teacher, Mrs. Ladd called me over to her desk. She said, "Nicki, here is the homework for the rest of the week."

"Why do I need this?" I asked puzzled.

"You will find out when you get home, Nicki," she replied. I walked back to my desk anxious to get home. The bell rang and as I walked out, I was thinking of reasons why I might need that much homework.

I pushed open the back door, tossed my backpack down and ran into the kitchen. "MOM!" I yelled.

My mom said, "Nicki, go get your sister. I need to talk to you girls." I looked at my mom. I could tell she had been crying. Without a word, I ran upstairs to get my sister, Danielle. My mom sat the two of us down on the couch. "Girls, last night your cousin Cory died." We burst into tears. "We will be going in for the funeral tomorrow morning."

When we got into Chicago the next day, I went to my cousin's house because we were going to be staying there. The whole entire day we talked about how sad we were about her dying. That night I couldn't fall asleep. All that kept coming into my mind was Cory.

The next day we went to the house of my cousin Robin (Cory's mom). We said we were very sorry many times. Then Zoey, Cory's daughter, came trotting into the room. She ran right over to me and gave me a BIG HUG! I just wanted to keep hugging her.

A couple of minutes later, we asked if my sister, my cousin Sarah and I could take Zoey on a walk. My sister asked Sarah about the night when Cory died.

She answered, "My mom was at A.J.'s house watching Zoey that night and then out of the blue Cory's brother, Adam, came in the

house. He picked Zoey out of the crib and hugged her real tight."
Wow, I thought.

The next day was the funeral. When we arrived at the funeral home, my mom asked me if I wanted to see her in the coffin. I responded no. The whole time I was thinking about her. She was so generous; I loved when I came to her house and hung out with her. I remember when she first became paralyzed and had the tumor. She was so strong through it all. If she wanted something people would offer to get it for her, but she proudly responded no. She didn't want anyone to treat her differently just because she was sick.

Later, we went to Robin's to sit Shiva. I didn't go downstairs; I just sat upstairs with my two baby cousins, Zoey and Emme. I know that Zoey didn't understand anything that was going on right now. She would start asking questions when she was older like, "Where is my mom?"

The next day I left to go home. I said my goodbyes and said I was sorry again. I will never forget what had happened that day. I will always remember you Cory. I love you!

Dakota

Some people think that a dog's life is boring, but it's not true for all dogs. **DAKOTA**, *by* **Cameron Camp**, *takes you through the life of a loved dog in a happy home.*

Before I was born, and when my sister was just a baby, my mom bought a dog. My sister wanted to name him Bingo. My mom insisted on the name Dakota, and Bingo would be his middle name.

By the time I was born, he was finally trained. Whatever—and I mean whatever—we did to him, he wouldn't growl or bite us. Dakota would only playfully bark when we played with him. And he would bark when people were at the door. In this story, I will tell you about all of the good times that we had with him.

One time, our dog, Dakota Bingo Camp, was lying on the dining room floor. I was only two years old. Since dogs never wiped themselves after using the bathroom outside, I dragged a roll of toilet paper out from the bathroom and tried to wipe his butt.

Another time my sister was bored and my mom and dad were half-sleep. My dad suddenly opened his eyes and saw that Cydney, my sister, had the stapler and was about to staple Dakota's ear. My dad yelled, "Stop! Don't do that!" Cydney jumped back.

Mom asked, "What is she doing?"

"She tried to staple Dakota's ear!" my dad replied.

In the winter, Dakota would pull us on our sleds in the front yard. At the dead end, there was always a small hill of snow from plowing the streets. At one point, Dakota was so big and strong that I would get on his back and ride him like a horse. But, of course, that was when I was a baby, and now I'm in middle school.

When my sister was still in elementary school, we were dropping her off, and I had about a hundred plastic Hello Kitty toys that I forgot to put away before we left. But I had brought my favorite one, a Hello Kitty bride. She had on a white gown and a wedding veil. When we arrived at my sister's school, I carried my Hello Kitty bride with me and must have dropped it. I didn't notice and I started crying when I realized that it was gone. When we got home, Dakota was laying down in the living room and chewing on the rest of the

Hello Kitty toys that were left out. All of my Hello Kitty toys were chewed up.

The next day, we were dropping off Cydney at school when I saw my favorite Hello Kitty bride. I was so excited until I noticed that it was crushed. I didn't know when or how it happened; I just knew that it was ruined. All of my Hello Kitty toys were ruined.

Another time, Dakota was eating some chalk from the chalkboard. The piles in the background looked like a rainbow!

As Dakota got older, he couldn't walk up the stairs. So, my mom helped him up by carrying him. We took him to the vet six months later. I was eight years old when we had to put him down. He had fluid in his lungs and he was very sick.

We know he lived a good life and he is in dog heaven. And this story is in memory of my dog, Dakota Bingo Camp.

Dino's Great Adventure

In the story **DINO'S GREAT ADVENTURE** *by* ***Tanner Reilly**, everything started with a simple family outing. Then something goes terribly wrong....*

It all started on a warm summer day in August, when the glowing orange sun was just rising. My family and I went to northern Michigan to enjoy the rest of our summer vacation. We decided to go blackberry picking.

We had to wear the right clothes so the thorns wouldn't hurt us as badly. We wanted my dog, Dino, to come blackberry picking so he could release his energy.

As soon as we arrived Dino ran off, and my dad said, "We will catch up with him later." We all went to the blackberry bushes. We didn't realize how thick the bushes were. They were so thick that we couldn't see through them. Then we started picking the bushes.

We stayed on the dirt road because blackberry bushes have a lot of thorns, and the thorns tore at our clothes. We wore jeans, but out shirts still ripped. We decided not to go into the bushes. I picked a blackberry right off the bush and ate it. It was delicious.

We picked buckets full of blackberries. As we were about to finish the next bucket, we heard a yelp.

We all ran to the scene, and had to go through the thorns as they ripped our shirts. When we made it to the scene, we saw Dino and a porcupine fighting! The porcupine was staring at him while Dino was biting at it. The porcupine didn't seem to mind. Dino kept trying to bite it, and the quills went into his mouth and nose. My dad grabbed onto Dino and told him to get away. The porcupine wandered off unharmed.

Once we went back to the road, my dad had to pull the quills out of Dino's nose as he cried in pain. Luckily, my dad didn't get stabbed by the porcupine. Dino had a small scar on his lip. He hasn't messed with a porcupine ever since.

The Jackson Hole Trip

In the story **THE JACKSON HOLE TRIP** *by* ***Zoe Chapman****, a girl gets stuck in the snow. Her dad is sent to save her. Little do they know their sister is not behind them. Who will the dad save first?*

"Hello!" a man in a lime green snow coat yelled. The man was standing at the airport entrance.

The man had a huge ball of hair on his head. My dad walked up to the man politely and said, "Hi, we are the Chapman family. Are you John?"

"Yes, that's me. I will be driving you to your hotel in the hills."

"So, John, where is the car?" my dad said loudly because his ears were still plugged from the long plane ride.

"In parking spot G at the south lot."

My family walked over to the car parked in spot G. We packed our bags into the trunk and hopped in the cold car.

On the ride to the hotel John was telling us what we would be seeing and doing in Jackson Hole. "Ok, thanks for the information," my dad said, yawning. The ride went quickly as we spent most of our time looking for caribou and elk out the car windows.

"This is the hotel you will be staying in," John said. We walked into the lobby and up the steps to our room.

"Wow," I said in amazement as I looked at the hand-carved, wooden, full-size bears all over the hotel.

"This is your room, number 209," John said. "Welcome."

"Bye, John. Have a nice day," my dad said, mumbling under his breath.

John left the room, and before the door closed the fighting began. "I call this bed."

"No, that is too small."

"No, that bed is mine," my sisters yelled.

"Hey, stop that racket!" my dad screamed. "You get that bed, Zoe. Ellie, you get the bed next to Zoe. Abby, you get the bed next to Ellie, and Mom and I will get the queen bed," my dad said in an angry voice.

We unpacked our things, and got right to bed.

"Good night," I said half asleep. I was very tired from the long day of travel and excited for what the morning would bring.

In the morning I was first to wake up, just waiting for the clock to turn eight o'clock so my parents could sleep, and then…

"Good morning!" I yelled. "Let's go snowboarding!"

"Yeah, let's go!" my sister Abby screamed.

Two hours later

"That was so awesome, Dad," I said, still trying to catch my breath from the slope we had just gone down. "Bye, Mom and Ellie."

Ellie and my mom were heading for the ski lodge.

My dad and I were in the line for the chairlift with my older sister, Abby. "Dad, how much longer until we get on the chairlift?" The words had barely gotten out of my mouth when…

"Sit!" my dad yelled at Abby and me.

We plopped our butts down on the chairlift. My dad is a picture guy, so we were not surprised when he said, "Smile for the camera."

"Cheese," my sister and I said.

After the bumpy ride we exited the chairlift and were on my favorite part of the mountain called Campground Trail. But that is when everything went downhill, and I mean downhill. "Let's go in the woods!" my sister hollered.

"No," I said.

"Why not?" Abby said.

"Because."

"Because why?"

"Well, what if I were to get hurt, Abby?"

"Well, then, Dad and I are going on our own in the woods!" Abby screamed.

"Fine. But I don't want to be alone so I am coming too."

"Well, then, come if you want."

It just hit me: We were in the woods, and Abby had just gotten what she wanted. Why won't she just board down the trails, and not in the woods? Oh, right, I remember: It does not look cool.

I just saw the sign. The woods were off-limits to skiers and snowboarders.

The sky became dark, and soon it became a huge blizzard. Before I knew it I was stuck. The snow was so deep, that I couldn't move.

I was stuck there under snow, and I have to say the snow was very deep, like five feet or something. Anyway, "Dad!" I yelled.

"Zoe?" my dad yelled. "Look to your left. No, your other left!"

"Dad I hear you, where are you? Dad, help me. I am stuck in the snow."

"Ok, um –Abby, stop!" my dad yelled. My dad unbuckled his snowboard, and pulled me out of the snow to safety.

My sister Abby went ahead of our dad, ignoring my dad's stop message. I knew we had to find Abby. We were skimming the horizon looking for a snowboarder in a bright blue snow suit. "Dad, I found her. Look over there by the yellow ski lift."

Swoosh, swoosh was all I heard. My dad was boarding down the hill. I jumped on the ski trail out of the woods and chased my dad down the hill.

I finally caught up with my dad and Abby at the base of the chairlift.

"Dad, when are we going to the ski lodge? I am tired from the runs," I said.

"I am, too, Zoe. Let's head in for the day."

The Next Day

"Good morning, Mom, Dad, Ellie, and Abby," I said, still sleepy.

Bang bang. "Good morning, Chapmans," a man said through the hotel room door.

My dad walked over to the door and opened it. "Hello, John. Always great to see you. Are you ready to drive us to the airport?" my dad asked.

"Yes I am. Why don't you and your family get your things together? We leave in a half hour at 8:30 for your plane ride home."

"That's good with me," my dad said.

We met John in the lobby and hopped on the bus parked outside the hotel. The bus was burning hot like an oven. John hopped on the bus and said, "How was your stay here in J-Hole?"

"It was great, thank you, John."

The bus rolled down the street, and in no time we were at the airport.

We walked into the airport though the front doors and down to security. Once we were done getting checked with security, my family and I walked to our terminal and got on the plane.

As my family and I were leaving the Detroit airport, we looked back at all the planes coming and going. We smiled, thinking about our next trip to Jackson Hole!

My Trip to The Homestead

A family trip makes memories that will last for a lifetime in **MY TRIP TO THE HOMESTEAD** *by Nick Scolaro.*

In July 2009, I went on a trip to The Homestead with my family. It's in Glen Arbor, Michigan. It is our family tradition to go every summer.

I really love it up there because there are so many fun things to do. I usually wake up and go play golf with my dad, which is really cool! Then we head down to the pool to hang out and have lunch. We also like to walk the beach looking for Petoskey stones and swim in Lake Michigan. In the evening, we go into town for dinner. There are a lot of different shops to go into that have cool things from the local area. We also take a drive to the Sleeping Bear Dunes to take a hike to the top. Then you can take the scenic drive where you can go to the lookout. It is really amazing.

But one of the best parts of my trip was meeting some new friends at the pool; one of them was a girl named Carly. She was so nice! We had such a blast hanging out at the water slide. That night we all went into town to have ice cream. We also went into one of my favorite shops called The Totem Pole.

The next morning we got the chance to all go swimming again before we had to pack up to go home. We always take one last drive by the beach before we head home.

The Homestead will always be one of my favorite places because it reminds me of being with my family and making friends I hope to know for a long time!

My Vacation to England

When an English boy goes back to England after being in the U.S.A for six years, everything seems different. Louis wonders how he will fit in in **MY VACATION TO ENGLAND** *by* ***Louis Parker***.

I was in England for the summer to see my family. I ate fish and chips that tasted good. Chips are actually French Fries.

One day I went to London. London is usually never full of people, but when I went it was packed. I was not in a very good mood in London because I was really hungry. I was happy when I got a McDonalds.

I saw all the famous places in London like Big Ben, the London Eye, Buckingham Palace and Horseguards Parade. My grandma worked there.

There were huge lines to stores, cafes, and restaurants. I waited fifteen minutes to get an ice cream. At the end of the day we got on the train and went back to my cousins' house.

One day we went to Blackpool. It is a seaside town. When we got there it was raining. We were disappointed, but since we were there we decided to carry on. Just as we bought fish and chips it stopped raining, so we sat on the beach and ate them out of paper.

After we finished eating we went to Pleasure Beach. It started raining again. My grandma couldn't come in because she had her dog and a sign said "No Dogs Allowed." We left her outside of Starbucks with her dog in a big bag to keep him dry and went into the theme park.

My mom said we had to go on five rides because she paid a lot of money to go in. We went on a boat ride that was inside so we didn't get wet. We also went on the biggest ride. It was a roller coaster. When we were going up the rain was pounding my face. It felt like hail. It made my face sting.

The ride was over, and my face hurt so badly, but luckily it was the fifth time, so we could go back to my grandma's. When we got home I lay down on the couch and watched TV till it was time to go to bed.

It was time to go back to America. It was nice to come back to the sun.

Surviving Cancer

In **SURVIVING CANCER** *by* ***Hunter Cornelius Lisabeth,*** *Spencer is diagnosed with cancer and is unsure if he will survive.*

There are multiple kinds of cancer. You can die from any one of them. All kinds of cancer are alike and different. In 2005, my brother, Spencer, was diagnosed with a type of cancer that occurs in the bone marrow. Our family was told it was leukemia and my brother had it.

I remember walking into the bedroom that Spencer was in. I saw the IV and all of the other strange cords that were hooked up to him. "Hi," I whispered. Spencer moaned something to me, but I couldn't hear what he said. I knelt down by Spencer's bed and asked him to repeat what he had just said.

Spencer whispered to me, "Hi, how are you?"

I whispered back, "So-so; how are you feeling?"

"Bad, my leg and stomach hurt a lot," Spencer moaned.

"Okay, I will see you later," I said. I felt like I had to leave the room because he looked like he was tired.

When I came home from the hospital I didn't know what to think about Spencer being in the hospital. I was only six years old. My mom and dad were worried about me. "What does Spencer have?" I questioned.

"He has leukemia," my mom and dad answered.

"What is leukemia?" I questioned again.

"Leukemia is a type of cancer," said my parents.

"Oh," I quietly moaned.

Spencer was in the hospital for two weeks. I had to spend some nights with different family members and friends while he was being treated. When Spencer came home, he had to have an IV of antibiotics for a month. First grade already began and Spencer missed the whole first grade. I missed him a lot.

For the first year of treatment, Spencer was in and out of the hospital many times. He had to take chemo and had to have his blood taken every week. One of the drugs he had to take was steroids, which made his cheeks and belly swell up. The steroids made him eat more because his taste buds changed to like different foods.

During the second year, Spencer was able to go to school a little more. He still had to have his chemo and have his blood taken, but he did not spend as much time in the hospital as the first year. Spencer had a major reaction to one of his drugs called PEG Aspirinagase. His heart rate went up to 160 beats per minute, his entire body broke out in hives, and he had a fever of 104 degrees. It took five days for his body to get rid of the medication in his body. It was very scary time for my family and me.

His last year of treatment was much better. He was able to go to school for most of the third grade. Spencer still needed his chemo, but did much better. On our ninth birthday, Spencer was granted a wish from Make-A-Wish. His wish was to go on a shopping spree to Best Buy. He bought a Wii, camera, laptop computer, and all the good stuff to go with his items. Spencer decided for my birthday that he was going to get me a PlayStation3 with games and controllers. For his birthday, I bought him a Pavel Datsyuk jersey.

When my family was told that Spencer had leukemia, we were shocked. It took some time to sink in but we came together as a family and fought through it. Since Spencer was so brave, our family had two huge celebrations when he finished treatment. One was in December of 2009 when Spencer took his last chemo drug. Thirteen members of my family spent New Year's Eve at the Splash Village in Dundee, Michigan. Six months later, we invited over 80 people that were family, friends, teachers, doctors and neighbors to a pool party in our backyard. There were games, food, and music by a DJ. My whole family is glad that Spencer survived his cancer.

World Beyond

1972

An ordinary gymnast is in for the ride of her life. A ghost is haunting the gym. Will the ghost leave her alone? Will she be okay, or face the consequences? Find out in **1972** *by* **Brooke Tushman**.

I was at gymnastics, and everyone was training for nationals. This is an optional meet, so we have all new routines to learn and perfect. Since I am recovering from an injury and in a walking cast, all I can do is condition work. My coach Jeunae is working on her computer. I was taking a break from conditioning and helping Jeunae. We were going through the list of people who got kicked out of the gym because they didn't pay. Then, I came to a name I knew. It said Kylie Cohen. Her file was completely empty. I typed in all the information that I knew about her. I told my coach I knew her, but she said it wasn't possible because she was a level 8 in 1972.

"I'm sure I know her. My mom can call her dad; she has his number."

Jeunae said, "That's impossible, Kylie isn't alive anymore."

I asked, "What happened to her?"

After she told me what happened to her she said, "It is too dangerous to let other people know what happened to Kylie in 1972, so don't say anything to anyone." Then the lights flickered off.

We all heard a girl screaming, "It's not true! It's not true!"

The words I had typed in under Kylie's name on the computer started to delete one by one. Was there a ghost in the building? I held my coach's arm as tightly as I could. I heard girls running to my coach. Jeunae told me she knew what to do because the same thing happened in 1972. She heard screaming back then when Kylie Cohen couldn't do her back tuck on the beam. I ran out the back door without anyone seeing me.

The next day I had to go to school, terrified that the ghost would follow me there. The year 1972 lingered in my mind. Upon seeing my best friend Nicole, I ran up to her. I told her all about what happened at the gym. I told her not to tell anyone because my coach would kill me. She followed me to the bathroom arguing with me about it because she didn't believe me. She opened the bathroom stall and there was the ghost.

I panicked. The ghost was pale, with a school uniform all shredded up, bright blue eyes and intense red hair. As we ran down the hall, Nicole told me she would now believe anything I told her. Mrs. Liel saw us running and immediately notified us that we would be receiving after-school detentions for running in the hall. Nicole tried to explain to her why we were breaking the rules by running in the halls, but I stopped her so that the teacher wouldn't find out about the ghost. I told Nicole after the detention we could investigate the ghost sighting ourselves. She agreed with me that it would be a good idea.

The detention wasn't so bad, besides snotty Emily being there. She is so mean; she thinks she's the most popular girl in school. After the detention, I saw Emily putting on white powder in the bathroom. When she came out she looked just like the ghost. We weren't scared because we knew it was Emily. Oddly enough, she must have overheard us discussing our upcoming detective work, and told us that she wanted in. She said she wanted to help because everyone hates her and she thought she needed to do a good deed to change people's view of her. I told her she couldn't tell anyone, and she agreed to stay and help. Again, oddly enough, it seemed as though she was turning out to be a nice person. We went looking, but we never found the ghost.

The next day after school, I went to gymnastics. I saw a big sword in my coach's hand. My coach told me I had to go to the bathroom and stab the ghost. My mind immediately filled with anxiety. I didn't argue with her because I could tell how serious she was about this. I went to the bathroom and there she was, the ghost of Kylie Cohen. I told her that I was sent in to kill her. She responded to me that she was sorry about scaring us, but all she wanted to do was apologize about what she did to Jeunae many years ago. I asked her what she had done that was so terrible, and she said she broke Jeunae's arm doing a back tuck on the beam. Kylie told me that Jeunae blamed her for the incident. "When everyone in the gym heard her blame me," Kylie said, "I started screaming, 'It's not true! It's not true!'"

Kylie's ghost then went on to say, "Well, it was true, because I set it up. I made sure she did all the work, and I kicked her arm. My conscience won't let me go back to heaven until I apologize."

Wow, what a story I found myself in the middle of! Kylie and I went back to Jeunae, and we told her all about our meeting. After several long moments, Jeunae decided to forgive her. As soon as this happened, Kylie's ghost smiled and disappeared. It seems like we now we have a new coach watching us from the skies.

Arizona's Adventures

Arizona dreams of going to Africa someday, but do his dreams go too far? Find out in **ARIZONA'S ADVENTURES** *by* **Hanna N. Baynham.**

Arizona was a little boy just looking for adventure. He was six years old and his favorite place to be was the zebra enclosure at the zoo. Arizona liked the zebra enclosure because he dreams of traveling to Africa someday. But, since he was so little, Arizona sometimes felt like an ant living in a beetle's city. Arizona was always an imaginative little boy. He would sit in his room for hours and imagine what it would be like to travel to Africa.

One night, Arizona had a dream that he was in Africa prancing with the zebras! He woke up to find out it was only a wonderful dream. He got up out of his racecar bed and it creaked louder than it ever creaked before. He walked downstairs to find his parents discussing, quite loudly, what seemed to be about money.

"Yes but Darrel, you have to get another job! I mean, it was completely your own fault you lost it," said Molly, Arizona's mother.

"Molly, calm down! I will find another job. Soon, I promise. And it wasn't my fault that I lost my job!" Darrel, Arizona's dad said.

Arizona hid behind his mother's gigantic, plump, palm tree. When his father looked (as it seemed) straight at him, Arizona fled from the room as fast as he could. He had a feeling that he wasn't supposed to hear a word of that little argument.

Once he got back into his small, compressed, little kid bed, he huffed to himself, "Why did Daddy lose his job? What does that mean?"

In the morning, Arizona looked at his clock. It had the numbers 4, 5, and 7. He couldn't read clocks so he laid his head back. He drifted off to sleep again and he dreamed of....

"Hee hee," laughed Arizona as he galloped with the zebras near a huge lake in Madagascar! Wait? He was in AFRICA! This was his very own dream come true! Arizona smiled in his sleep just thinking of being in Africa. Next, he played with the monkeys in the Bwindi Rainforest! This washed away his real life worry.

When he woke up from his fabulous dream, Arizona looked over to his clock but it wasn't his clock that was looking at him. It was a PEACOCK! He quickly looked around him and all he saw was green trees, 70 stories tall, and animals for miles and miles!

"Well, I don't think I'm in Tennessee anymore," Arizona said to himself.

He looked in the pocket of his favorite pajamas and there he found a map of Africa! There was a little red dot that said, "You are here." Even though he was only six, Arizona always knew how to read maps. He mumbled to himself, "Well if I'm here, then it's only two miles to the next town!"

He hiked for half an hour and finally found himself in a little town full of Africans with paint on their faces.

Arizona didn't know how to speak their language so; he mimicked, "Where am I," in his own way. They didn't seem to understand him so he walked back the way he had come. Arizona hiked another half an hour back to where he had started. He cleared back some brush and... he couldn't believe his very own eyes! There was a plain that had heaps of animals on it! Arizona kept running in and out of the endless peacocks, flamingos, and... ZEBRAS! There were at least 500 zebras snorting and galloping as if they were tiny gazelles leaping across a meadow. He loved this!

"Hey, Arizona," Arizona imagined, as if the zebras were actually talking to him.

"Hi," he replied.

This was his favorite day of the year so far. He was in Africa galloping with zebras!

"Wait," he mumbled to himself as his throat was dry. "Why am I in Africa? I was just in my bed at home with Mommy and Daddy protecting me." All of a sudden, Arizona broke down in the puddle he was standing in and cried. He couldn't stop crying. He then realized that he didn't belong in Africa with all the zebras and flamingos. "I just want to go home," he sobbed. "Please take me home."

He stood up and clicked his heels together. The next thing he knew he was awake in his bed with tears still in his eyes. His mother and father apparently heard him and ran to see what the matter was. He quickly gave them both a hug and sobbed the whole dream again. But he didn't mention where he went on this little adventure.

Mother and Father brought Arizona downstairs and fed him

some delicious, warm strawberry pancakes and told him, "Arizona, we have some big news for you! Daddy got a job offer!" Arizona's muscles tensed up and his teeth clenched really tight to keep himself from screaming. "We're moving to Africa."

Attack of the Man-Eating C.C.'s

In **ATTACK OF THE MAN-EATING C.C.'S** *by* **Noah Zacharias**, *Will and Rex come from outer space to Berkshire. They get bullied and turn into man-eating C.C.'s. Will Berkshire get invaded or will Berkshire win?*

It was year 2458, and everything was going fine at Berkshire Middle School until two kids, Will and Rex, came. No one knew this, but they were actual aliens from planet C.C. [Cupcake Land]. Everyone bullied them for about two days because they were new. Soon, they got mad and grew into man-eating cupcakes! They used their super powers to throw the bullies across the building and almost kill them. The kids had to go to the hospital. They each broke a leg, a wrist, and a finger.

The cupcakes were just going undercover. They just wanted to take over the world and not fit in. So they declared war against Berkshire. They only did it because they haven't had fighting experiences in a long time, and because they got bullied and were probably going to call the cops.

The principal called in the S.W.A.T. team and told everyone to go home, but they didn't so they could watch the battle. The Cupcakes got ready and called in their backups and King Cupcake. King Cupcake had the deadliest weapon ever—The Frosting Covered Sprinkle Gun! Their backups were Man-eating Doughnuts. They were no different from the Cupcakes. They were different by the body shape, but they still had the same strength. The S.W.A.T. came in, and the cupcakes got ready. The S.W.A.T. attacked and dominated with their riot shield and the weapons. The Cupcakes lost three-quarters of their men. The S.W.A.T. lost 20 of their men. King Cupcake surrendered, and the S.W.A.T. arrested them.

The kids ate the Doughnuts and Cupcakes with apple juice they had in the cafeteria. The S.W.A.T. saved the world and Berkshire from getting invaded! Berkshire had to set up a shield barrier that the S.W.A.T. gave to them to stop any kinds of extraterrestrials.

"But still the kids were scared, so with their super smart abilities they made a weapon called the bubble gum blower. All it does is build a mini shield around him or her," said Eric. "Everyone expects another attack. I think they'll bring more men next time.

"The kids at Berkshire made some weapons like the pencil launcher, the eraser grenade, and a desk tank. If you want my opinion, I think they're all set, so I'll continue with the rest of my story when I get home. I've got to go. It's almost time for bed," said Eric. "Mom, can we go? I want to go to bed."

"OK, honey," said his mom.

The Battle of Acadia

THE BATTLE OF ACADIA, *by **Brady Anderson**, is a harrowing tale of a boy's attempt to save his parents who were captured by the Knights of Acadia. Can Brady rely on his friend and cousin to help him save his parents?*

I saved my house from the evil genie lamp that almost blew my house into pieces. Not a big problem, right? Wrong! My parents were taken away by the Knights of Acadia. My name is Brady Anderson. I am an 11-year-old boy with brown hair and eyes. I am five feet five inches tall, I have a scar on my right eye, and this is my story.

After I walked the many miles to my friend Mark's house, I walked up to the door and knocked three times. It was our code, so he knew it was me.

He opened the door and said, "Dude, I just beat *Final Fantasy 19*!"

"I thought that game was impossible!" I replied.

"I know. So why you are here, man? There must be something bothering you."

"They got them, the Knights of Acadia stole them last night," I said in a panic.

"Got who?" he asked.

"My parents!" I replied.

"Then let's go get them."

"WE CAN'T JUST GO GET THEM! THEY ARE STUCK INSIDE THE CASTLE OF THE KNIGHTS OF ACADIA! THEY ARE GONE UNLESS WE SAVE THEM!" I yelled ferociously.

"Dude, calm down and we will get them back, I promise," Mark continued. "We just need to make a team of three and get some stuff to beat these guys."

"Fine," I said. "But it will be very hard to get past their long-range snipers and 14-foot wall."

"Let's head to the Blacksmith Shop now and get stuff we will need to defeat them."

"Perfect! Let's go!" I said.

So Mark and I headed over to the Blacksmith Shop near his house. We bought some swords, which I customized to shoot out mini tornadoes. We also bought some ninja stars that explode and a knife that explodes on impact when thrown. Mark thought that I was starting to go insane, but that's just me. I always think of how to make things explode!

"So, do we want to call my sister or what?" Mark wondered.

"No, we are going to call my cousin, Cameron," I replied calmly. "If he does not believe me, then I will ask my cousin, Claire, to help us out."

When I called, Cameron was playing *Call of Duty Modern Warfare 2* with his friend Jack. He said that he didn't believe my tall tale, but he would send Claire out to help. I can't believe that he thinks I am pranking him just to get him to come out and play. This is very frustrating. Finally, Claire came out and joined us.

"This better be important, Brady, because I'm missing my favorite show right now!" Claire said ferociously.

"This is very important," I replied seriously. "Here is a sword that I made. It shoots fire out of the blade. You need to use it for protection."

"Let's get this over with, then," said Claire.

"Why can't we just blow up their village and get on with it?" Mark wondered.

"Remember why you are here, you dingdong…to save my parents," I said, fighting off a few tears.

"Oh yeah, sorry," said Mark.

So we head over to the king's lair, and, of course, Claire was being her annoying self and was driving Mark crazy. Claire kept poking him and wouldn't stop. He looked like he could explode at any time.

Outside the wall of the Acadians, we could see they were stocked with bows and arrows. We talked for a long time about our plan of attack. Once we decided we laughed because we were reminded of the arrow roulette game from the movie *Grown Ups*. Once ready, we charged at their fortress. Within minutes, Claire and Mark were captured.

"Great, now I have to save them as well," I said.

When I found them, they were with my parents in a pit. They were warning me not to do something, but I was so excited to see them. "No, don't do it, it's a…" Before I knew it, the doors shut, leaving Mom, Dad, Mark, Claire, and me all alone in the dark, smelly pit.

The next thing I know, the doors opened and the pit flooded with light. I looked around and saw my family and friends. Even though I was captured, my dignity was intact.

The king of Acadia had decided to pay me a visit and present a challenge. My arms and bare legs were chained to a wall very tightly. I felt as if I was going to be killed in front of my family and friends right on the spot. I was being treated like an animal.

"Well, well, well, what have we here? A pitiful child all alone, chained like a very mad silverback gorilla," he said with a flick of his cape. "I have a deal for you, boy. I let you go, and then we fight in mortal combat. Then you can learn how we, the Kings of Acadia…"

"Kings?" I yelled. "What the blazes are you talking about? You are not a king. I will show you who is a king and accept your challenge. Winner takes all…"

"GUARDS, RELEASE THE PRISONER!" he yelled.

"No wonder people also call you King Acadia the Loud One," I said mockingly under my breath.

"EXCUSE ME, WHAT WAS THAT YOU SAID?" the king roared.

"Nothing," I said quietly. I followed him out to the yard where we would prepare for our match.

"Good! We will start in one hour, and, if you want your friends to live, you will be here."

The hour passed with me singing a song that I heard on a video game. It seemed to relax me and helped me to focus. I slowly ate lunch and tried to gather my strength.

I walked back into the yard where there was an evil zone filled with lava, lava stingrays, hammerhead sharks, zombies swimming like dolphins, and the weirdest of all the animals, a goldfish.

"What's up with the goldfish?" I said sarcastically. "I thought this was supposed be a fight, not sea world!"

Suddenly I heard, "Prepare to fight or your friends get it!" Finally, some excitement, I thought.

The king and I hit each other's swords with tremendous speed and strength. I almost fell on my butt. He got lucky and stayed on his feet.

"Showoff," I said under my breath. I didn't know that a guy this crazy would be this strong; this was going to take a while. I threw a ninja star, but missed him, and he flew toward me. I ducked, and everybody cheered for me.

I didn't think of it first, but Mark yelled, "Shoot him with a mini tornado!"

Wow! That is the first idea that Mark has had that did not almost get me beat up by the bad guy. I shot a tornado at him and he yelled, "AHHH!" as he threw up all over his favorite shirt.

As his rage grew, he went from mad to furious. I hit him with my back end of the sword on his head. That knocked him out. He started to sleep like a baby. I turned the lava to a hot stone with my tornado. As a shark tried to jump out of the lava, it froze in place.

I freed my friends and family. We left the castle and headed over to get some ice cream. Everybody thanked me for saving them. Claire left that night, and we dropped Mark off at home. We went to the hospital to fix my eye, which only took about 20 minutes. I went to bed that night, closed my sore eyes, and fell asleep with my dignity intact.

Berkshire Hobbits

It's one thing to move five times in four years. It's another to find out you're a hobbit, as in the story **BERKSHIRE HOBBITS** *by Cole Moore.*

It was the first day of school at Berkshire Middle School, and there was a new kid named Cole. He arrived at Berkshire with a chip on his shoulder. After all, it was his fourth school in five years. He had been moved around by his parents who couldn't seem to stay in one place. He didn't know what was in store for him, but he had perfected being quick on his feet.

As soon as he walked into math class, the teacher told him to go straight to the office. He asked why. He said, "I've been here five minutes, certainly not enough time to get into trouble, even for me." She said nothing. She just looked at him strangely. He then jumped up and went down to the principal's office not knowing what to expect.

He asked why he was there and, more importantly, who wanted him there. The secretary told him that no one had called him down, but then a little lady he had never seen before pointed her finger at him and yelled, "I called you, now get over here!"

She told him to step outside and for him not to be surprised at what she was about to tell him. She then quietly leaned over and whispered that he and she were not human, but were Hobbits. She went on to explain that his parents knew that if he had been found out that all of the Hobbits' enemies would come looking for him. After all, he wasn't just any Hobbit; he was Prince of the Hobbits.

Cole at once stepped back, thinking that this woman was crazy. He said, "Really? Then my mom must be a unicorn."

She did all she could to convince him and soon realized he needed proof. She took him into a secret room with two lockers and growled, "Step into the blue locker now!" Cole was curious and scared at the same time, but did what he was told. He stepped in, and there was no floor.

He fell for what seemed like hours. As he was falling, images of his birth mom and dad flashed before his eyes. This sparked memories of a lost childhood. His mom was in a garden planting hickleboogers, the most favorite food of Hobbits. His dad was using a quill, writing Cole's grandmother a letter for Christmas. Then Cole read the letter, and it was in the language of the Hobbits. To his surprise, he could understand every word. He screamed, "I am really a Hobbit!" He now knew why they moved so much. It was for his own protection.

He hit the bottom and fell to the ground. When he opened his eyes, he was in the most beautiful place he had ever seen. He was in the Shire. Berkshire was just a cover up for the land of the Hobbits. He had read about this place in the *Lord of the Rings* series, but never imagined he would wind up there himself.

The little lady he had first met in the principal's office came out of the second locker and smirked, "Are you convinced yet?" She no longer looked like the lady at all, but a fully-grown Hobbit, dressed in what appeared to be battle fatigues. He apologized and asked her why he was there. The lady he met ignored him and said, "Oh, yeah, my name is Mrs. Shopalop, your guardian angel. I have been protecting you until you were for ready for your mission."

What was his mission? Since he had just got to the sixth grade, this was the time to fulfill his destiny. He had to save his parents. His mission was to find his parents and rescue them from Prince Droll, the hated enemy of the Hobbits.

His parents had adopted him from his birth parents and raised him as a human. They came from a race of people whose sole purpose was to protect the Hobbits. Prince Droll had taken them. He had watched them for years, waiting for the exact moment to capture them to get to the Prince.

Cole knew what had to be done, but he was only one person. The lady told him that all he had to do was believe in himself and draw on his Hobbit strength to see him through.

She led him to the weapon room, and every time he touched a new weapon, he instantly became an expert with that weapon. He grabbed the bow, the arrows, and a bag full of other weapons and was soon on his way to take on the army of Prince Droll.

Prince Droll had an army of mutated mice and kittens and puppies. At first Cole brought out twin swords, but then he remembered that they used animals to guard the hobbits. Then Cole knew that if he could turn the animals on one another, he could sneak past them to find his parents.

He used his mind to transform the thoughts of the mice and kittens and puppies. Once he thought that where he came from kittens chased mice and puppies chased kittens, his transmitted thoughts made the army forget about him and begin chasing each other around and around.

He got by the army, but he still had to face Prince Droll. Cole took a special bow with a strong string on the end and shot an arrow at a hole in the castle. It spread apart so he could climb inside. As he got in Prince Droll was right there. Prince Droll wanted him dead so that he could take over the world.

The Prince warned Cole that if he came any closer, he would kill his parents. Cole asked him to let them go and take him instead. Prince Droll didn't know that Cole had tricked him. Cole pulled out his bow and arrow, and from one hundred yards away he shot Prince Droll, who fell from the window of his castle. As he was falling, to Cole's surprise, Prince Droll turned into a Hobbit. Prince Droll was Cole's brother. He was jealous that Cole was to become King of the Hobbits.

Cole kind of felt sad for his little brother because he was just jealous. Then it turned out that Cole had missed him.

When Cole first saw his parents he was so excited and overwhelmed at the same time, but he didn't have enough strength to speak. They said, "Cole, you are now the king. Our time here is over. We have loved you like our own son and we will miss you always." Just then, a light surrounded his parents, and in a flash they were gone.

Before his had time to cry, his guardian angel came to him and said, "Cole, you have to return to Berkshire. It is your destiny."

When he returned to the lockers, the angel told him to get in and close his eyes. Then he felt a wave of wind going around him that stopped almost as quickly as it had started.

He opened his eyes and was back in the principal's office. The secretary asked him why he was standing there and said, "No one called you, now go back to class."

When he returned to math class no time had expired. The teacher simply said, "Welcome, Cole; now get to work."

A Boy Like Me

A boy plays in his room. Then he looks in his mirror and realizes that there's another world in **A BOY LIKE ME***, by* ***Julian Hurt.***

One day, Joe was playing in his room. Then, he was looking in the mirror, and by touching it, his hand went *through* the mirror. He was surprised. He realized there was another world that looked like his, only the sky was red and everything was reversed. He went through the mirror, and he was in that world.

He saw someone who looked exactly like him. The other boy saw Joe and said, "Who are you and what are you doing here?" Joe said that he had come through the mirror. Joe asked the boy what his name was. He said his name was Ben. Then Ben asked what his name was, and Joe said his name.

Joe realized that Ben had a video game, and he recognized that it was his favorite game. He asked Ben if that game was his favorite game. Ben said yes. Then they played the video game for hours. When it was lunch time, Ben was having pizza. Joe said that pizza was his favorite food in the world. Ben said that pizza was *his* favorite food as well. Joe was happy that he met Ben. After they ate, they went back to playing video games and talked more about themselves.

The sun began to set. Joe said that his dinner was at 9:00. Then Ben said that his dinner was at 9:00 as well. Joe was surprised and glad.

Before Joe went back home, Ben told him his phone number. Amazingly, Joe's phone number was the same!

When Joe went back home, he ate dinner, and before he went to sleep, he asked the phone company to build a phone that can call anyone in the universe without getting a busy signal. Joe knew if he used the normal phone he would get a busy signal if he called Ben because they each had the same phone number. Luckily, he had the phone in less than five minutes, and then he went to sleep.

But while he was asleep, a bad guy robbed the house and broke the mirror. The burglar was so scared that Joe and his parents would wake up that he put everything back where he found it and ran away.

The next day, Joe saw that the mirror was broken. He was upset.

So after breakfast, he called Ben to say that he couldn't come over because his mirror was broken. Ben said that his mirror was broken as well when he was going to bed and accidentally stepped on it.

They were trying to fix the mirrors. But they kept getting finger cuts. They were thinking that they would have to give up. Then, Ben thought that he would get a mirror from the junkyard, and Joe decided to get a used mirror from a yard sale.

They got their new mirrors and tested them out. But they didn't work. They could not see each other. They figured out why the mirrors didn't work. They called each other, and after a few minutes realized what was wrong. They had the same mirrors, but the mirrors were made in different times.

Joe asked Ben on the phone, "How old is your mirror?" Ben said that his mirror was made in 1978. So Joe got a 1978 mirror and tested it. And it worked! Ben went through the mirror this time. And he was more amazed than when Joe went to his world. So they played outside with Joe's friends.

Camp

It's the first day of summer camp for Mary Mackey, her little sister Emma, and her best friend Alice. Camp Chippewa sounds like a normal camp, but it's not. It seems to have a ghost, and Mary will have to find out if this ghost is real in **CAMP** *by* ***L. Kapitanec.***

Present Day

Camp! Today is my first day of camp! I can't wait! Let me introduce myself. My name is Mary Mackey. I'm heading to Camp Chippewa. My little sister Emma is going to camp for the first time with me. There was a mountain of bags in the backseat of my mom's car. I got my luggage and headed for the bus.

"Mary, make sure Emma's bag gets on the bus too," my mom yells. "And make sure you keep an eye on your sister. Have a great time."

My mom said it was my job to show Emma around and keep her safe. She's a couple years younger than me so we are in the same cabin. Most of the kids that go to this camp live around here, so we have a school bus that takes us to camp. The bus was so noisy, my sister quickly found her friend, so I was alone. Then I saw a black, shiny Escalade pull up around the corner. It was Alice, my best friend. It must be her first year at this camp.

"Alice," I yelled.

"Oh, hi Mary," she said.

"I didn't know you went to this camp," I asked Alice.

"This is my first year, I'm a little bit nervous," replied Alice.

"Don't worry, I will show you around the camp," I stated.

We found seat three rows from the back. I saw some girls that were in my cabin a couple years ago, but they didn't recognize me. I haven't been to this camp for awhile. I waved goodbye to my mom and off we went. The drive was so boring. Thank goodness it's a short drive to Camp Chippewa. A head popped up from the seat in front of me. It was Miss Know-It-All Sally.

"What do you want, Sally?" I asked.

"Oh nothing, I just wanted to know how you been," replied Sally.

"I've been fine," I said.

"Good," said Sally.

"Why aren't there as many people as last time?" I asked.

"Haven't you heard of the ghost?" asked Sally.

Sally started telling the story of the ghost of Camp Chippewa. "Thirty years ago a girl was dared to walk around the camp wearing a blindfold on and she walked on the ice and fell through…"

30 Years Ago

Ella thought in her head, *Where am I? Which way is right, which way is left, where are the girls?* She could feel the heat of her breath on this snowy winter day. She tried to rip the bandana off her head, but she couldn't. It was too tight. It was pressing against her eyes. Ella walked in the snow for a while. She could hear the snow crunching, but then she couldn't hear crunching anymore.

"Okay take this off me now!" Ella yelled, but she heard no noise. She walked some more, and then heard a *crack*. Ella was on the lake and she had to get off. There was a *crack,* then a scream, and no girl.

Present

They finally arrived at camp. Mary was shocked! She was afraid to get off the bus. Alice had to pull her off. They found their cabin. It was getting dark and the counselor stopped by the cabin to tell them it was time to turn the lights off. All Mary could think about was what Sally had said on the bus. She couldn't sleep.

"Alice, Alice," whispered Mary. But Alice was sound asleep. Mary sat up in bed and looked outside the window. She saw a girl standing in the woods and thought she should be in bed because it was 12:00 o'clock A.M. *Maybe she's lost* thought Mary. Mary forgot her fears of Sally's story and grabbed her flashlight and walked slowly out of the cabin. The closer she got to the girl, the colder it got. Mary was now about a foot away. The girl had a bandana on her head. She had long blonde hair. The girl was wearing a white robe. Mary reached out to touch the girl and her hand went through her. Mary tried to scream but she couldn't. The girl was a ghost!

"Please don't be afraid," said the ghost. "I won't hurt you. I'm a friendly ghost." Mary was relieved to hear this. The girl looked so real!

"What's your name?" asked Mary.

"My name is Ella."

"What happened to you?" queried Mary.

"Thirty years ago, some girls dared me to walk around the camp with this bandana covering my eyes. I ended up on the lake and fell through the ice. I wander around at night now. I wish people wouldn't get scared off by me. I just want to have a friend."

Mary was not scared at all. She told the ghost that she'd convince the other girls that she was nice.

The Next Morning

Mary woke up in the cabin and couldn't see. There was something covering her eyes. She reached up and there was a bandana covering her eyes. Once she took off the bandana, she saw that all the girls were staring at her.

"Why do you have a bandana covering your eyes?" asked Alice.

"It must be Ella's bandana. I was with Ella, the ghost, last night. I saw a girl walking around last night and I went outside and followed her."

"There's no such thing!" said Sally.

"There was a ghost and she was real," exclaimed Mary. "She's a friendly ghost and wants people to stop being afraid of her."

Everyone except for Sally believed her. Well, Sally will just have to find out when she is sleeping tonight.

The Catastrophe
of the Science Fair

When disaster strikes at the science fair, two kids must keep the crowd from harm. In **THE CATASTROPHE OF THE SCIENCE FAIR** *by* **Natalie Rolf,** *a girl and her classmate will try to save the school from attack.*

It was a warm Friday evening, and I was in my room, lying on the bed with my eyes wide open. I was thinking about the events of last week's science fair. I was kind of glad about what happened. I had made a great new friend, but had lost an old one. Well, I guess Zee wasn't a great bunny. And it was at the science fair where I really discovered how destructive bunnies can actually be.

The trouble had started in between the judging and the awards ceremony. Keith Kindell (an annoying kid in my grade) was running up and down the school's halls, bragging about his invention to anyone who would listen. Unfortunately, I was one of those unlucky people who happened to be in the same hall as him at the time. I was at my locker grabbing my book for entertainment in between events (we had a whole hour before the awards ceremony started).

"Hey, Kate!" he yelled as he rounded the corner, and headed straight for me. "I bet my project's better than yours." I rolled my eyes, way up toward the ceiling. He noticed. "I'll prove it!" he said angrily and stomped down the hallway, and I saw him turn into the gymnasium. I followed him.

"This," he pointed to his masterpiece, "is the winning project, my invention. This is how it works. You open *this* little door, and insert some object you want changed, and you can change just about anything. For example, size, weight, or color. Let's see, how can I explain this better…" Then his hand reached out and grabbed…

"ZEE!" I stood where I was, frozen from shock and unable to move. By the time I had unfrozen, Zee was in Keith's invention with the door closed and locked. "Why harm an innocent little bunny?" I wailed. But he wouldn't listen.

"Exactly!" he said. "Bunnies are innocent. Even enlarged, bunnies can't do anything destructive. What do you want your 'new bunny' to look like?" he asked me.

"I want her just the way she was, don't change her at all!" but Keith paid no attention to me.

"I'm changing her height to fifteen feet," he said, and then pressed a little green button. There was a loud *CRACK,* and the town's power went out. Keith and I were left bumping into each other until we found the door. By the time I had found my flashlight and had looked around, Zee was gone. The only trace she had left was a huge hole in the ceiling.

Keith and I knew only one thing: we *had* to stop the bunny.

"All right, what should we do *now?*" I asked, emptying my backpack onto the carpeted floor. What had we done? We hadn't thought that changing something's height could make it evil, but we had just narrowly escaped a 15-foot evil bunny. Keith and I were sitting in the back of the empty library, in between two upturned shelves, but safe from evil bunnies. We looked at the contents of my backpack by flashlight, sizing them up.

"We've got a notebook, four pencils, a tissue, a science project, one pen, one rope, one paper airplane, my brother's plastic action figure, and a *flashlight,*" I said, waving our source of light around. "Oh! And I almost forgot the pack of Doctor Fruity's Sour Watermelon Gum." We generously helped ourselves. Once we were settled in, we came up with a brilliant plan involving a science project, a rope, a tissue, a pack of gum, and a flashlight. And then, it was time to put our plan into action.

We were about to put our plan into action when we were interrupted by Keith's strong feelings towards safety. He told me it was important that everyone is alert to the situation. I didn't personally feel the need to warn anyone.

"Fine, fine," I gave up. It was no use arguing with him. "But you're doing the talking." I followed him into the peaceful cafeteria, where the whole school was eating Mrs. Linton's (the old PTA president) watercress sandwiches by flashlight. "Wait here!" I commanded Keith, as I raced to the storage closet. I grabbed a microphone, and sprinted back with it under my arm. I plugged it in, tapped it, and stepped back. Keith stepped forward.

"Um, hi, everyone…uh…we just wanted to tell you all that…um," he looked down at his feet, mumbling through the microphone. Then his speech sped up rapidly. "That a giantandextremelyevilbunnyisontheloose." The crowd whispered and shrugged. Keith looked up at them, and then repeated.

"We just wanted to let you all know that," he raised his voice, "A GIANT, EVIL BUNNY IS ON THE LOOSE!" The muttering continued. The crowd must have thought that we were lying. They looked angry—like *really* angry. For a second or two, we just stood there, looking at them. Then finally, I unfroze.

"We should, uh…" I told Keith, pointing to the door.

"Good idea," he said, and we sprinted out of the cafeteria and headed back to the library. We grabbed all the equipment needed to put our plan into action. Then, by the light of my flashlight, we headed out to the playground in search of the bunny.

When we found (the once) Zee, she was tearing swings off their chains, and throwing them into a heaping pile.

"How did it get outside?" Keith asked, and I saw his eyes drift in the direction of the roof above the gym. There was a huge hole in the side of our school.

Great, I thought. *Now our gymnasium has built in air-conditioning.*

"Here we go!" Keith said, and threw me the flashlight. Then he sprinted off to the top of the play structure, after tying the rope from a tree to the play set. I then walked around the playground so the play structure was in between Zee and me. I threw the flashlight, as hard as I could, at the bunny. Normally, I would never have done anything so cruel to any pet of mine, but my bunny was evil, and I didn't care for her anymore. Even though my aim is lousy, I hit the bunny right between the eyes.

"Hey! Over here!" I yelled to the bunny. It turned its huge head, and saw me. It tossed a rusty old swing aside and headed for me. Luckily, it tripped over the rope Keith had tied. It fell to the ground with a loud *BOOM*. Then Keith and his invention jumped from the top of the play tower. They landed on Zee.

Keith shoved his project on top of Zee's ear, and twisted the dials. There was a loud *CRACK*, and the bunny got smaller and smaller. It kept shrinking and shrinking until it was no bigger than a small pebble. Then I spit my gum on Zee and wrapped him (and the gum) in the tissue. Then I walked over to the trash can, and threw it out. Keith and I walked in the direction of the school, and into the cafeteria.

It was a madhouse in the school cafeteria. They must have seen the bunny as it grew closer. The fourth-graders were standing wide-eyed around the windows whispering. The first-graders were screaming, crying, and peeing their pants. The sixth-grade girls were frantically redoing their hairstyles, while the boys were wrestling and throwing paper airplanes. The adults were trying to gain the attention of the crowd, but they were unsuccessful. It was so loud; nothing was audible, including the intercom system. But then, something amazing happened. Silence rang throughout the school as I ran into the cafeteria and onto the stage.

All at once, the audience began to chatter, and I had a brilliant idea... I plugged the microphone in, and tapped it. That got everyone's attention.

"Everyone!" I shouted. "Can I have your attention? I know there was an evil bunny on the loose, but it's all taken care of." Then Keith and I went into a long and tiring explanation. When they finally accepted that Zee was gone, everyone was very happy. We all munched on sandwiches (not the watercress, thank goodness – we had thrown those awful ones out and made good ones) and played games in the gym. Then Mrs. Hampston, our principal, returned from the pet store and gave me a brand new bunny!

The Curse of Blackhouse Inn

A.J. stumbles across an abandoned inn that people in the city say is haunted. Is the curse of Blackhouse inn real? The story **THE CURSE OF BLACKHOUSE INN** *by* ***Matt Power*** *will make you want to sleep with the lights on.*

I am a hobo. Seriously, I am homeless. I am A.J., Aaron James. I always walk by Blackhouse Inn, an old, abandoned, tall building; I guess it's about five stories high. It's kind of creepy if you ask me. I heard legends that this place is haunted, but I don't think that's true.

On the day that changed my life, I walked again past Blackhouse Inn. I thought, "Hey, I'm homeless, so why don't I just go in there and set up a place to stay?" I walked into Blackhouse Inn.

The place is all tattered, and furniture was ripped. Suddenly, I heard a little ghostly laugh. I turned around, and nothing was there. I said to myself, "Ah, forget it, that wasn't anything."

I went upstairs to find a bed, and then I heard another ghostly laugh. This time, I actually saw something. It was a large, *green* something…I think it was a GHOST!

I saw a room that might look good for a home, but it turned out I was wrong. When I looked into it, there were at least five green things motionless in the room. Suddenly, one of the things turned its head toward me, and I closed the door quickly.

I walked to yet another room where I saw a girl sitting in a chair. She looked human, so I went in to say hi and see if she had ever seen the green things before. But, instantly, she faded away. I turned to leave the room and there she was, standing in front of me.

What the heck is going on? This is REEEEEEEALYYYYY creepy.

I turned around and left for the door of the inn, but the door closed shut instantly. I tried to open the door, but it was stuck shut. This place *is* haunted!

The girl started walking down the stairs, with the green ghost minions behind her. Suddenly her skin turned from human to see-through pale.

"No one comes into this inn and lives," she said in a little soft voice.

I ran for another room. Yes! There was an open door. But guess what... it closed SHUT.

"KILL HIM!" I heard the girl scream. Instantly the green ghosts grabbed my arms, tight!

The girl walked toward me, and her skin went back to human. I punched the green ghosts square on. They screamed in pain. Wait a second. These things are ghosts. Ghosts hate sunlight! I opened a window and sunlight wooshed through the window. The ghosts and the girl screamed in agony. The green ghosts melted and disappeared, while the girl screamed, "NOOOOOO! I WILL NOT BE BEATEN BY A HOMELESS BRAT!"

I said, "Well, you just were."

The girl screamed, "NOOOOOOOOOOOOOOOOOOOOOO!" She melted and disappeared.

Next on the to-do list: Get out of here!

Dæmon Vs. Thief

An ancient evil is rising in the ancient kingdom of Sanjun. In **DÆMON VS. THIEF** *by* **Olivier Rochaix**, *an unlikely hero, a thief name Zack, is chosen to do the bidding of the gods and destroy it. Will Zack prevail?*

Sweat trickled down Zack's forehead. Zack's feet ached from running, but he kept on running because his life was at stake. Zack had tried to steal the royal crown and had gotten close to getting it, too; if only that pesky little princess hadn't seen his attempt. Now he had the whole of the guard on his tail, and they were gaining quite quickly.

Zack saw his chance and jumped into an open doorway. Zack quickly locked the door and slid the bolt. Zack turned to check out his surroundings. He turned out to be in a courtyard. It was almost like a miniature grove. In the center of the grove, Zack found a golden sword, implanted into a marble pedestal. The hilt was made of silver, with a very strong, red grip wrapped carefully around the edges. It was quite a masterpiece. Zack grabbed the hilt and slowly pulled the blade out of the pedestal. When it was fully out of the pedestal, Zack slid the sword into his belt. It was very dull.

Zack smiled. *At least there was something to gain from this escapade*, he thought, admiring the hilt. Then a small fissure cracked into the pedestal, glowing red-hot. A plume of golden-red flame shot out of the pedestal, taking a sharp curve when it was about a meter from the ground. The flame impaled Zack in the back before he could do anything to dodge it, sending him hurtling backward and into a big weeping willow. Zack's vision went blurry, and he blacked out.

Zack awoke with a searing pain in both his chest and his head. He remembered the crown, the sword, and the golden-red flame. Zack stood up, using the golden sword as a crutch. Then, the door leading to the courtyard started to splinter. Zack lurched upright. It was probably the royal guard! "Herrak!" Zack yelled the God of the Heaven's name in vain, looking for an escape route. *Boom!* One of the door's hinges broke. Then Zack found a way out of the situation.

Zack came to one of the trees and quickly climbed up it. When he was at the top, he jumped off the tree and grabbed onto the windowsill. He then pulled himself up and through the opened window. By the time he had slipped into the room above the courtyard, the room had been broken open and the courtyard filled with guardsmen. Zack then ran along the corridor, silently making his way out of the castle. Zack was about twenty or so feet from the gate when one of the guardsmen caught sight of him.

"There he is!" yelled the guardsman, pointing a finger in Zack's direction. Then multiple cries of "Get him!" and "For the King and Queen!" erupted from the crowd of guards as they rushed at him. Zack fought the urge to turn around and just destroy them. Even if he tried, he couldn't kill all of the guards.

As he came to the gate, the two gate guardsmen raised their hands and said, "Stop in the name of the law!" Zack had no time to fight them so he slipped in between them and headed for the portcullis.

Zack never made it past the portcullis. A plump guardsman managed to close it before Zack could get out. *I've never seen a man that fat move so fast*, thought Zack. Zack caught himself joking quickly. There was no time to fool around. Zack had about five minutes before the guards had him completely surrounded. Zack could find no other way out of this situation except for one, very difficult option. That option was to stall the guards long enough to find another choice. Now it was time to put this plan into action.

The mob of guards that were on Zack's tail in the beginning made it to the portcullis and started surrounding him, the guards had him in a bad position. An average guard made the first move and he came in flailing his weapon like there was no tomorrow. Zack jumped back and nimbly dodged all the blows from the man. Then a second guard jumped into the fight and connected a blow in the right arm of Zack. Everything stopped around Zack, the blood gently trickling around his arm.

Then a look of rage appeared on his face. Golden-red flames erupted from his body, sending forth pulses of energy. A look of horror appeared on the guard's face. Zack took the sword from his belt and charged at the helpless guard. He came down on his foe, and impaled the guard with a barrage of sword blows. He jumped onto his next foe and his sword penetrated the guard's heart. Every blow that connected left flames burning from their bodies. He dispatched the rest of the guards with ease, and only after he had killed the last guard did Zack think about what he had done.

Zack was afraid of what he had become. He had become a cold-blooded murderer. This was not what he had meant to do. He looked around and saw what he had inflicted upon the drawbridge. The portcullis was so badly damaged it couldn't have kept out a hamster. The moat was on fire, the clear water burning under the pure heat. And the wood of the drawbridge was decaying under the burning flames. Where had he gotten this kind of power?

Leaving the site of the wreckage, Zack ran as his long legs could carry him. He wanted to redeem himself before he would be brought to the afterlife. He wanted to walk once again on the path of good.

Zack slipped through alleyways, making his way to the Holy Herrak's head priest's home. He came to the door of the head priests dwelling and knocked three times.

"Who's there?" said a voice from the inside of the home.

"A man who seeks enlightenment," Zack said boldly.

The door opened and an old man came out. He took an astonished look at the sword on Zack's belt and ushered him in, motioning him to sit in a chair next to a small table.

"Do you know what that sword is?" questioned the old man while gesturing at the sword.

"What do you mean?" asked Zack, "It's just a golden sword."

"*It's just a golden sword,*" mocked the old man, "That sword contains a Dæmon so powerful it brought down even the most powerful empires, one by one. I want you to tell me how you found it, and leave not one single detail out."

With no other option, Zack told the old man about how he had stumbled onto the sword and how he had escaped from the castle. At the end of the story, the old man nodded.

"I'm sorry to say, but you might have only three days to live, or even less," said the old man.

"What do you mean, 'I might have three days to live'?" exclaimed Zack.

"Well, you see, the flame that came out of the pedestal, well that was the soul of the Dæmon. Its body was destroyed a long time ago, but its soul was imprisoned in this sword. If the flame hit you, well that means that it's fused itself within you," explained the old man.

"And…?" asked Zack.

"In three days, the Dæmon will take over your body and start rampaging again," finished the old man.

"I've already seen a show of that," said Zack.

"What do you mean, you've already seen a show of that?" inquired the old man. Zack told him about how he had massacred all the guards at the portcullis.

"Well, how do we stop it?" inquired Zack.

"There are two ways. One; you kill yourself, or two; you break the sword, and you might have a chance of surviving," recalled the old man.

"How do you destroy the sword?" pushed Zack.

"You have to break it over the sealing stone," said the old man.

Zack slumped, "This is just perfect, I going to have to do the bane of all thieves, return to the scene of crime," muttered Zack. Zack got out of his chair. "Well then, I'll be going. Oh, and by the way, I didn't quite catch your name."

The old man smiled, "You can call me Herrak."

Zack was trying to fit everything that had happened today into his head. Was the old man really Herrak, the God of the Heavens? Maybe it was all just a hoax. But the Dæmon was quite possibly real. He had to infiltrate that castle, but first he needed some rest.

The next morning was a sight to behold, for there was not one cloud in the sky. If people were looking for Zack, they would've found him hanging on the parapets of one of the towers. Zack retraced his steps to the grove inside the courtyard. Zack made his way to the pedestal in the center of the grove and pulled the golden sword out of his belt. Zack lifted the sword and struck down with all his force. The sword stopped an inch above the pedestal. The fusing process was starting. Zack swung again, but this time he swung harder and strained to fight off the resistance that kept him from destroying the sword. This time it worked, the sword shattered into a million pieces. Then, Zack felt weak all of a sudden, and all went black.

Zack awoke staring at his own body. He saw his body curled up on the ground, motionless. Then all faded into pure darkness. In the darkness, ahead of Zack, there was a fiery figure. Zack knew it as the Dæmon. The Dæmon seemed hurt.

"Why, Zack? Why didn't you save me?" asked the Dæmon, in a perfect impression of his sister.

Zack froze. Years before, the kingdom of Karrock had invaded his homeland, and this war had been started by the death of their high pope, which they had to blame on the nearest empire, the peaceful kingdom of Sanjun. The Karrockan warriors had poured into their cities, destroying everything in their path. Zack had been on a fishing trip with his father, away from any danger. When they came back, the city was in ruins. Everything the city had worked for was either charred or broken. When they came across their house, they found the remains of their family. Nothing was left except for bones and knives, one implanted in each family member's chest. Zack's dad killed himself the next day. He was found hanging from a tree with the same knives penetrating his body that had killed his fellow family members. Zack was the last of his family.

Zack was enraged that the Dæmon knew this painful secret. Zack charged the Dæmon with all his speed, striking his foe with his fists. His blows fell right through the Dæmon, since the demon was made completely of golden-red flames. Zack went tumbling through the Dæmon, catching on fire. After Zack patted the fire out, the Dæmon laughed, "Do you really think you could defeat me that way, you puny little mortal? This game was done when you destroyed the sword!" bellowed the Dæmon.

Zack smiled. Out from his pocket he drew a silver dagger, encrypted with ancient runes. Pricking his finger with the tip of his blade, blood trickled down the dagger and the runes started to glow.

"What is this spell? Please don't tell me it's a sealing spell! Those can't do anything to me now!" The Dæmon laughed enjoying toying with his prey.

"No, it's definitely not a sealing spell," muttered Zack to himself, and he charged the Dæmon yet again. This time, Zack struck with his dagger, and the dagger cut one of the Dæmon's fiery hands right off. The hand fell, and turned into hard stone, puffs of steam coming out from the Dæmon's hand. The Dæmon roared both surprised and angered at what Zack had done to his hand.

The Dæmon chuckled, "I haven't seen that spell used by a human in a long time, and you my friend, WILL PAY FOR WHAT YOU"VE DONE!" The Daemon struck at Zack, but Zack, ever so quick, dodged and sliced again, this time targeting the Dæmon's eye. The eye sliced open and hardened, releasing more steam. The Dæmon struck again, despite all the pain searing through him. Zack stabbed the Dæmon, this time striking the other eye, and brought the sword up and slashed the elbow of one the Dæmon. Finally, Zack knocked the Dæmon down with a blow to the chest. Then when the Dæmon was down, Zack issued the last blow, completely turning the whole Dæmon into stone.

What now? Thought Zack, *I have destroyed the Dæmon!* Zack saw another fiery figure in the distance. Surely it couldn't be the Dæmon; he had just destroyed it! As the fiery figure drew closer, Zack figured out it was just another fiery beast, its giant, crooked smile hanging on its fiery face.

"I see you have defeated my son. You're quite brave. You see, my son was never careful enough, always bent on revenge. You, a young boy, have beaten him even though many stronger and older men have tried. Then again, he was weakened by of his lack of physical anchor. Though I'd like to know how you knew that spell, it has never been written down," said the fiery beast, in its low, gruff voice.

Zack smiled maliciously, "That is not for you to know. Though you might know who told me the spell and gave me the blade," answered Zack carefully.

"Your father was a fool! How could he know that spell?" roared the angry figure.

"That's right! He didn't know the spell, but the blade was a family heritage, which was passed down through the family bloodline. An old man that lives in Sanjun told the spell to me. His name is Herrak," answered Zack, again.

"Well, I've got more pressing matters to attend to," he pointed his finger at Zack, "When we meet again, it shall be under different circumstances. These circumstances will be you bowing to my knees!" The figure smiled at this remark.

"Humph! We'll see about that!" scoffed Zack.

Then Zack felt a sickening sensation and he returned to the courtyard in which he had broken the sword. Zack was looking at his body, slumped against the pedestal. Zack merged with his body, and as he did so, he felt a sucking sensation, as if he as being pulled into another world. Pain seared through his body and he winced, closing his eyes. When his eyes opened, he backed in the courtyard, back in his own body.

"Ugh," said Zack. "I am never doing that again," muttered Zack while brushing sweat off his forehead, to no one in particular. Clearing a patch of hard ground next to one of the willows from the golden shards of the ancient blade, Zack sat down, laying his back on the hard wood of the willow. He then nodded off, a small smile, slowly curving up his lip. Zack was happy. He had cleared the land of an evil spirit and had done the will of the gods. The gods would surely repay him, right?

Dawn of a Legend

Who is Lily McNight, and what secret does she harbor that even she doesn't know? A spur-of-the-moment visit to the museum promises profound consequences for Lily in **DAWN OF A LEGEND**, *by* ***Sam Meinel.***

One fine spring morning in April, the flowers were blooming, the birds were singing…. It all was perfect: a bit too perfect. But that didn't bother Lily McNight, who was out for a stroll when she had a sudden impulse to go to the local museum. Even though she had been there on numerous occasions before, this time was different. She had no idea why; she just felt like something there was calling to her.

When she got to the museum, she noticed that there were very few people moving about. That was very odd, because it is always flooded with people. There, in the middle of the room, within a gold-trimmed glass case, was what she wanted to see: the proclaimed "magic" staff of imagination. She went up to the glass to get a closer look. The staff was a very deep sea green, about four feet long, with a lovely orange pattern going along it.

"Beautiful. Just beautiful," said Lily very calmly. Little did she know, as she pushed her face closer to the glass, that she was about to witness true power at work. As she withdrew her face from the glass, the staff began to glow a hot pink, which is the very opposite of the deep sea green it had just been.

"Hey! Get back!" yelled an unknown voice. Surprisingly enough, she listened to the voice and jumped back from the case. Right after she did, the case erupted with a glow that could've blinded her with one look. She turned her head away and was slightly stunned.

"What's going on here!" Lily yelled. "One minute ago this staff was normal and not alive, and now it is rampaging around the museum and destroying it!"

"Pick up the staff and imagine flowers," the mystery voice said.

"What do you mean! How do you know it won't attack me like the rest of the museum?" Lily replied.

"I don't," the voice said. As if the staff sensed her doubt about this, it soared over to her feet and fell still. She thought she was being silly by doing this; yet, she picked up the staff and did what the voice said. After a few seconds of concentrating hard, flowers emerged from the cracks in the ceiling tiles.

"Whoa! I don't believe it, this is incredible!"

"The power you now wield is unimaginable," said the voice. A figure stepped around from behind a pillar as the few remaining patrons scrambled for the exit. "The name's Gregory Gandora, but my friends call me Geo."

"Well, Geo, how did you know that the staff was going to erupt like that and that if I imagined flowers while holding it, flowers would appear? How did you know I would be here? I deserve some answers from you, Geo!" Lily hollered.

"I have been camping out, hiding amongst the exhibits, knowing that someone who could wield the staff would show themselves," Geo said. "About your other questions, I will just show you the answers with this."

He showed Lily another staff, slightly larger than the staff of imagination. It was midnight blue, engraved with an ancient writing that Lily couldn't make any sense of. "This is the staff of knowledge."

"You mean, *the* staff of knowledge?" Lily asked.

"Yes. This is the real deal," said Geo.

"But how did you..." Lily began to say as Geo touched her forehead with the staff and it engulfed her mind with images. This could only be described as an extremely fast slideshow movie.

"It's hard trying to find the right memory," she heard Geo say through the fog of pictures. "Ah, here it is," Geo said.

All of the pictures disappeared except for one that had seven staffs on them; two she recognized. The third from the right was the staff of imagination. The one on the far left was the staff of knowledge.

"What is all this?" she asked, even though she thought she knew the answer. She had learned about staffs in her archeology class in high school. This picture resembled the photos in her textbook.

"These are the seven staffs of the ancient world," Geo said.

"But what does this have to do with me?" Lily asked.

"Are you aware of the curse written in ancient hieroglyphics that no one could decipher?"

"Yeah."

"Well, it is that exact curse I'm now going to show you, and then we'll see if you are who I think you are," said Geo.

"But who is it you think I am?"

"All in due time, my new friend, all in due time."

As Lily stared blankly at the picture Geo was showing her, somehow she could understand the gibberish writing placed before her.

Suddenly Lily blurted out, "It says, 'Beware. The staffs seven thou shall not with intertwine. For if thou do, evil will spread like burning fire.' Geo, what does that mean?" Lily mumbled.

"If I knew, do you think I would still be searching for the rest of the people who can control the other five staffs?" Geo asked sarcastically.

"Why are you searching for the other five people, and how do you know I'm one?" Lily asked. That's exactly when the images disappeared and she was back in the room, which was now a field of flowers. "Did I do all this?" she asked as she gazed around at all the flowers.

"Yes. I am quite surprised at all the things your imagination can conjure already," Geo said with admiration.

"Wow. Wait a minute, I've visited this museum dozens of times before and the staff didn't ever do *this*!" Lily shouted, gesturing to the flowers.

"It does this now because I activated all the staffs at the central power source," Geo said.

"So does that mean that the rest of the staffs are rampaging around the world?" Lily inquired.

"They won't show their power except to the person they deem worthy to wield them," Geo responded. "I need you and the rest of the people who control the other staffs because someone has threatened the world. In order to stop this threat, the possessors of the staffs must work together."

"Please tell me about the rest of the staffs and how they work," Lily flatly stated, moving herself closer to what remained of the glass case.

"Fine," responded Geo, settling himself down on a bench right next to the shattered glass case that now had a vine of morning glories emerging from it. "In the beginning, there were seven ultimate weapons: power, healing, defense, wisdom, imagination, luck and knowledge. These "staffs," as people began calling them, were mysteriously hidden in seven ancient tombs. Over time," Geo continued, "through events of natural occurrence or man's creation, the tombs were discovered. Most of the staffs were unearthed and taken to museums or they became village artifacts spread throughout the world. Many believed the staffs had magical proprieties; they were right," Geo recalled.

"The staff of knowledge," Geo continued, "was the only staff to remain activated at all times in case something arose like the current situation." He then continued, "But we will get to our current situation in a moment. First I want to share with you how I came to acquire the staff of knowledge.

"Strangely, I was drawn to Stanford University when I was your age. I enrolled in the archeology program. After four years of constant study, this staff was passed down to me by my professor who was the head of the archeology department. As I closed in on my final days on campus and graduation was quickly approaching, one afternoon after class, I was drawn into the classroom's back room. Walking through the theater-type seating of the lecture hall, I approached the back room door. Once there, I cautiously eased the heavy oak door open. I peered into the dimly lit room, unsure of what I would see. Oddly enough, I didn't find anything except my professor and the staff. As soon as I walked into the room the staff flew to me and stuck itself into my hand. I didn't know it then, but it had just chosen me as its wielder. My professor explained to me that I could continue the legacy of watching over the rest of the staffs, or I could decline. Even though I was given the option, I felt as though I was meant to do this. So, I chose obviously, to continue the legacy.

"Now, back to your request. Let's begin with the one you control," Geo finished.

"OK," Lily responded with a hint of wonder in her voice.

"It is the staff of imagination, but you already know that. While you are holding the staff, you can conjure objects with the sheer power of your mind," he explained to Lily.

"Yeah, kinda got that part," Lily quipped.

"It is also a good idea to picture it as realistically as possible. Ideally, it would work best if you had seen the object just recently,"

Geo said. "A warning, though: If you haven't seen the object before, it may come out not as you intended."

"All right," Lily said.

Geo paused and took a look around the museum, but you could barely call it that because everything was covered in flowers.

"Next we have my staff, the staff of knowledge. It has many powers; its most common use is to help its controller see the past, present, or future in the form of images."

"Yeah, OK," Lily snidely remarked.

"It also has a few more uncommon powers. One of them is its ability to give advice."

"What about the rest of them?" Lily asked.

"I don't know very much about all of the others because I can only see the history of the staffs that are already wielded by a possessor," Geo explained.

"Oh. Well, why don't you just go to where the rest of them are located and find the people who are *the ones*?" Lily asked.

"Because it's not that simple. First, not all of the staffs are in museums, like yours. Some are village artifacts, some are owned by private collectors, and a few remain undiscovered. Second, the rest of the wielders are five out of seven billion people on Earth," Geo sighed. "So it may take a while. However, with your power of imagination I am hoping you can focus in on the other staffs and lead us to them. Since the staffs are activated by the true possessor of each staff's power they should be compelled to the staff just as you were drawn here to the museum."

Lily took her staff in her hand and looked intently into Geo's eyes. Taking a deep breath she said, "I'm ready. Let's begin."

As they took their staffs in hand and exited the flower garden that used to be the museum, they had embarked on an extremely difficult game of cat and mouse. Little did they know that they would be playing both roles.

There is more to the story!
Find the complete
Dawn of a Legend **by Sam Meinel**
at Amazon.com in January 2012.

A Destined Princess

When a normal girl finds herself in a nutty land inside her garage and has to save her parents' lives, she is put to the test to see if she is truly **A DESTINED PRINCESS** *in this story by* ***Sage Sanders***.

3/20/11
3:34 P.M.

Dear Diary,

I just arrived home from another boring day at school. I hate this stupid bus. The entire kids act like wild animals once they get here. And every day it's the same thing over and over. I get up, go to school, go to fencing class sometimes, then go home and do homework, go to sleep and do it all over again until the weekend. But the weekends are never fun either. I'm bored all day with nothing to do at home or I'm at work with my mom. I mean, I like school and all but I just wish that for once, I could do something actually fun in my life! Go to an amusement park, to the movies, or the mall. I never do that stuff anymore. It's just always the same old things every day, and my parents always seem so busy. They always hide things from me like where they are going when I stay home by myself or why they were so late for work. They are always too busy to ever do anything with me.

Crunch, crunch, crunch go the crisp autumn leaves as Madison shuffles her feet through them and crushes them up into pieces. "Mom, Dad, I'm home!" she yells, with her head tilted all the way back. No answer. Then Madison checks the kitchen, the living room, her parents' room, and even the basement. No one was there.

Oh, my, gosh! It's Friday and my parents aren't even here! They promised me that Friday would be family night. Well, I guess it's nothing to lose; we only play board games, she reminds herself while checking the library to see if her parents were in there. There was no one there. But she hadn't checked the garage yet.

When Madison entered the garage, she saw nothing but darkness. Then she turned on the light, and she heard a slight shudder. She quickly turned to the left, and then she saw a little brown door. "Whoa, where did that thing come from?" she said to herself. She was always so used to seeing her dad's golf stuff sitting right there all the time. Madison shrugged her shoulders and slowly walked closer to the door. Then she opened it and squeezed in there.

"Wow! What is this place?" She heard nothing but the chirping of birds and the trees whooshing in the slight breeze. It was so peaceful. There was beautiful, fresh green grass as far as she could see. There were beautiful, brightly colored flowers and fruit on every tree! It was such a sunny day. It really felt like summer! Madison then closed her eyes and inhaled some of the fresh air.

Suddenly, Madison heard something brush against some bushes. Then she saw something bright blue out of the corner of her eye. She followed it. She started to run down the path where she saw it, but she lost it.

Madison felt something soft rub against her chin. She looked, and there was a little, bright blue butterfly. He had beautiful decorated wings. He had a human body, though, kind of how they are in the cartoons. He looked quite young. His smile was pretty. He had all white human teeth! "Hello," the butterfly said. Madison jumped.

"Did you just talk?" she murmured to the butterfly.

"Why, yes, I did. This of course *is* the land of Mal," the tiny butterfly said with a wisecracking smirk on his face.

"Mal? Hey, those are the letters of my initials," she said, and then paused. "Oh my gosh, I'm talking to a butterfly! Oh, I must be in a dream." Madison closed her eyes and then opened them really fast. She was still there with the little butterfly just sitting there looking at her now with a really awkward stare. "Who are you?" Madison asks the small butterfly.

"I'm Sapphire. I'm- wait! Did you just say that the letters M.A.L are your initials?"

"Yea, big coincidence, huh?" Madison suggests.

"No, this is not a coincidence! Oh no! We are saved! We're saved! We're saved!" The microscopic creature started to dance very cheerfully upon Madison's shoulder.

"What do you mean?" Madison asks.

"You've finally come to rescue us!" answered Sapphire.

"What? I'm confused. Rescue who?"

"The people of Mal, of course, from Zorad. You're Princess Madison!"

"What! My name is Madison, but I AM NOT A PRINCESS, and who is 'Zorad,' and why am I the one to rescue people from him?"

"Well, it's a long story. Let's go to the castle and I'll explain everything on the way." Sapphire started to fly down a path. Madison followed. "So, you're Princess Madison!"

"I'm not!"

"Yes, you *are* Princess Madison. You were born here in Mal and your parents are Queen Annalisa and King Brock III. Zorad is the most evil, disgusting creature in the whole kingdom, and he has been jealous of your parents for years. He wants to be ruler of the kingdom, and as of right now, he is. Zorad kidnapped your parents and has kept them in the castle locked up.

"Only royalty can get in and out of the castle and that door you came through. That's why you've never seen me or any other Malanians. Usually no one but royalty can get in and out of the door, but for emergencies we have spare power to give to loyal people if something happens to your parents or you. When Zorad threatened to have his troops come into our home and assassinate us, we had no choice but to give it to him. That's how Zorad got into your house and kidnapped your parents. Zorad doesn't know that you exist, though. No one tells him because we all knew that Zorad was just a threat and one day, you might be our only hope. And today you are," Sapphire alleged.

"So I'm the only one that can save the kingdom?" Madison asked

"I'm afraid so."

Madison shook her head in confusion.

Sapphire and Madison were getting closer to the castle. "So how do I beat this Zorad? And why didn't my parents tell me about this kingdom a long time ago?" Madison questioned Sapphire.

"Well, your parents wanted you to have a normal life, but as soon as they changed their minds and wanted you to come to the kingdom, it was too late. You were already eight years old and hadn't had the proper training of a real princess, but then they got the idea that it was a good thing because maybe one day you would have to save us from danger," said Sapphire.

"Well, maybe I can prove to them that I really am a true princess by saving them."

"You really have no choice."

"I guess you're right. So how do I defeat Zorad?" asked Madison. They were finally at the castle. "Wow!" Madison whispered. She looked back. All she saw were bright green bushes with small red cherries on them.

After a long pause of looking at the castle, Sapphire finally said, "Follow me!" They snuck into the castle. As they stood behind a wall, Sapphire showed Zorad to Madison as he practiced fencing. "Hey, I fence," Madison whispered. Sapphire sat and thought for a while.

"Ha! I've got a great idea," Sapphire whispered. "You could have a fencing duel with Zorad to save the kingdom and your parents. Since he doesn't know you, then he won't know how good you are. In the real world humans are much more skilled than Malanians. He thinks that he's the best in the universe! But I bet you can beat him."

Madison thought about it for a long while. "Ok, I'll do it. Anything to save my parents and my kingdom," Madison replied.

"Great! Now you're talking like a real princess!"

Zorad was short and pudgy. But he was taller than Madison. He had an ugly, gray, wrinkled, face with a long, pointed nose. He had short legs and long, flat feet with long toenails. His mouth was large and really wide. His smile looked as if it was almost to his eyelids! He had a very mean smirk on his face, and his whole body was gray and wrinkly. He almost looked like an oversized rat!

He had sweat running down his face as he focused carefully at the other player. He moved fast, too fast. Madison just watched. She started to have second thoughts about doing this. "Here, I'll show you a secret room in the castle that Zorad doesn't even know about," Madison told Sapphire.

They snuck through long halls and pathways. Madison saw blown-up portraits of her yearbook pictures over the years on walls on almost every hall that they went down. "So how do you know so much about the castle and my family?" Madison asked Sapphire eagerly.

"Well, my wife used to be a dressmaker for your mother, and I used to shine your father's shoes for him."

"Wait, you have a wife? But you look so young!" Madison says.

"Well, no one in Mal looks *old*. There is so much healthy food and no depression or sadness. We all just stay young-looking. Anyway, I guess your parents felt close to us, so they told us all about you and the history of Mal. I know all about this castle and everything around it. This is even your very own hallway," Sapphire answered.

They finally came to a door. It was purple, Madison's favorite color. "You will be safe here. You should get some rest before the big duel tomorrow," Sapphire said.

"Wow, this room is magnificent!" Madison said.

"Your mother designed it just for you," said Sapphire. "Ok, now get some rest."

Madison walked into the room. She quickly turned around. "Sapphire, wait!"

"Yes, princess?"

Madison paused. She wasn't used to anyone calling her that. "Why did you and your wife stop working here?" she asked.

"Well, actually my wife died. She was very ill. After she died, your parents said that I could retire."

"Wow, I'm really sorry," Madison answered.

"It's fine, Princess. Just get some rest!" Sapphire said with a smile. He then left, and the door closed behind him.

Madison's room was purple and blue. Her bed was gigantic, and it had a purple canopy over it. Her bathroom had blue tile and purple curtains and walls. Her closet had purple carpet like her room and had blue polkadotted rugs. Her closet was filled with pretty, colorful dresses. After seeing the room, Madison finally plopped into her comfy bed and soon fell asleep.

"Wake up, sleeping beauty!" Sapphire whispered. "Today's the big day!"

Madison quickly opened her eyes. She was nervous. She got up. "Let's go," she said. She quickly hit the shower and changed and headed for the door. Sapphire led them to the fencing room where Zorad was practicing.

Zorad had big, ugly ears. He was dark gray with huge front teeth, he was muscular but very short, and he was good at fencing. Madison started to get more and more nervous. "Excuse me," Sapphire interrupted.

Zorad looked at him and Madison. "Who are you?" Zorad replied.

"I'm no one that you need to know of. I'm here to make a deal with you. You know that you're the best at fencing. But I want to ask you for a chance to save my kingdom. You, me, duel! If I win, you release the king and queen and let them be the rulers again. But if I lose," Madison sighed, "I'll be your slave forever."

"Well, I am the best, and I do need a new slave," he answered, and then paused to think for a while. "It's a deal!" Zorad replied with an evil smirk on his face.

It was time to fence. Zorad was good, but Madison was better. Zorad touched Madison twice. If he poked her again she would lose. She had only got him once, but she soon marked him in the chest again. It was tied up. But at the end, Madison got the last jab. Zorad lost. He was devastated and angry.

Madison's parents were free, and after the duel, her parents realized that Madison was ready to become a princess.

"Oh Madison, we are sorry we doubted you. You have showed us that you are definitely prepared to be princess, and someday, queen," her mom announced.

"Yes, we have decided that we will sell the house and permanently live here. I now declare you Princess Madison of the United Kingdom of Mal!" announced Madison's dad cheerfully.

A big ceremony was held with all of the citizens of Mal invited. Everyone watched Zorad go to the Malanian prison for life.

3/31/10
5:23 P.M.

Dear Diary,

I guess you can say that my family and I lived happily ever after. I'm very happy that I finally discovered Mal. This is the greatest place I've ever been to. I am now in what you can call "Princess School." I'm learning all the things there are to know about being a princess. Just the other day, I rewarded Sapphire with ten percent of royalty. He lives in the castle now. He's my best friend. Oh, and I have met some other people and animals here also. I've always known that I wasn't meant for a world like the one I was living in before. I guess I'm just a destined princess.

The Devil's Entry

THE DEVIL'S ENTRY, *by **Madison Shortridge**, is a story about a girl named Sara whose sister is captured by The Devil. She never thought her new house would have so many secrets.*

Long ago Heaven's brother, The Devil, was banished to the deepest part of hell. Over time The Devil has gotten stronger and has come back in some areas. My house was one of them.

"Sara," Mom yelled through her bedroom while finishing unpacking our clothes and shoes, "go check on Amy. She is wandering the mansion."

"Ok," I yelled back. Amy is my little seven-year-old sister that is always getting into trouble.

She has to be here somewhere, I thought to myself as I searched every room in the house. I was starting to get worried.

Earlier during the day I thought I heard screaming behind the bookcase in the abandoned hallway, but decided to wait till dark to investigate. As I approached the bookcase, I pulled the old green leather book. The bookcase opened. My mouth opened to scream for my mom, when I suddenly heard a quiet voice calling me. "Sara, come back. The Devil has got me."

At first I thought Amy was just playing, but then she didn't show up an hour later. Mom had asked me if she knew where she was. I had to lie to her. I told her she went over to Mary's house to sleep over. What was I to do? How do I save Amy? Should I have told my mom?

Later in the evening, I ran into the room that was going to be the new kitchen and stuffed a knife into the back pocket of my blue jeans. Slowly, I walked out of the kitchen and down the abandoned hallway to where the bookcase was. I pulled the same old green leather book. The bookcase opened slowly. There it was open all the way: The Devil's entry.

The ice cold wind blew through the fully-opened window. As I entered the room, every step I took made the floor creak. When I was fully through the bookcase doorway, the bookcase slammed shut. Panicked, I ran to the door, only to find it was locked.

As I turned around, the dimmest light shown from the room's closet. A staircase in the closet leading underground was suddenly visible. I had no choice of turning back.

There must have been a hundred steps, because once I was down to the bottom, all of the daylight was behind me. Finally, Amy was in sight, and so was the Devil himself!

Amy was in chains to the left across the room, and the Devil was to the right. Man, he was ugly! His eyes were glowing orange, his body was transparent, and his head was made of rotting flesh. Just the sight of him made me gag.

"Amy, Amy," I whispered. Amy turned my way and began yelling. Just as the Devil turned to look at what Amy had seen, I hid.

"What are you looking at, little girl?" the Devil asked Amy in a horrifying voice. Amy didn't answer. "Oh, fine. Don't answer me," the Devil growled. "It won't matter anyway, because I am giving you to the hungry souls of the dead tonight at midnight." The Devil turned and walked away down a hallway connected to the room.

I saw the perfect chance to save Amy. Running as fast I could, I grabbed the keys next to the entrance of the hallway and unlocked the chains around Amy's wrists and ankles. She hugged me so hard that I couldn't breathe.

Suddenly, we heard the sound of footsteps down the underground hallway. We scrambled up the steps to the closet door. Before we could completely shut the bookcase, a hand grabbed Amy. "Ahh!" Amy screamed.

Then I remembered the knife in my back pocket and began slicing at the Devil's hand repeatedly. I had to cut his hand off before he let go because dead people can't feel pain. Finally, the Devil let go of Amy, and we shut the door up tight. Amy started crying. I told her everything was going to be all right.

Amy and I decided not to tell our parents about the Devil. We both knew they wouldn't believe us. The room and hallway remained abandoned and hidden behind the bookcase. Never again would the devil bother anyone else. At least I hoped....

The Doll

When a doll looks good in a store, it doesn't always mean it will be the same way at home. In **THE DOLL** *by* ***Shawn Attisha****, a little girl gets an unexpected twist when she finally gets the doll of her dream for her birthday.*

The horror all started with Lucy saying, "Mommy, mommy, I want this doll." Lucy found a very worn-out doll that looked like it had been used before. It was a life-size doll with big black plastic eyes, long black hair, and a very weird and scary smile on her face, as if she was ready to kill someone. The doll was still in its box next to a trash can near an office.

"Well, ok, it is your ninth birthday in three days, so I'll get the doll for you, honey," said Lucy's mom.

Lucy and her mom went to the creepy cashier with long hair, a long beard, and circles underneath his eyes with pale skin. It almost looked like you could see his bones on his face as if he hadn't eaten for days. He started to ring up the doll since he was the only cashier open, but he stopped before doing it. He explained to Lucy and her mom in a creepy, deep voice, "Oh, I'm sorry, but that doll isn't on sale. It tends to do weird things on birthdays. Where did this little girl find it?"

Lucy replied, "But Mommy, I want it," interrupting him.

"I'll pay you $200 for that doll," Lucy's mother said.

The cashier replied, "I made this doll, and it's not like all the other dolls out there. This one is just different. I made a big mistake with it. You may think I am only a cashier, but I also make all the dolls here. This one is not a happy one like the rest! Your daughter will be in a lot of danger. It will try to kill her!" said the cashier in a frightening voice.

"Sir, are you fighting with a customer? I want that doll now. Don't be silly! A doll coming to life? Yeah, right. I will pay you triple the amount for this doll." The cashier could not turn down such a good offer and agreed with it in the end.

When Lucy and her mom got home, Lucy ran upstairs to her room to play with the doll. Lucy hadn't come out by dinner time, which was around six o'clock. "Lucy, come down for dinner," yelled Lucy's annoyed mom.

Lucy and her mom ate dinner. Her dad, of course, was running late from working in his office all day, so he could not eat with them.

The next day Lucy took her doll in for show-and-tell at her elementary school. She told them about all the doll's features, such as how you could feed it, dress it, comb its hair, change it, and just have fun with the doll as she had been doing.

After school Lucy came to her big white house with birthday balloons all over the place. She saw her mom wasn't feeling too well, so she called her dad right away. He came as fast as a race car on a track. He took Lucy's mom to the hospital, and then they dropped Lucy at her grandmother's house. Lucy was so scared for her mother that she didn't want to leave her, but her dad told her it was the best for her mother.

The next day Lucy and her dad went to check up on her mom at the hospital, and the doctor gave them good news, and bad news. The good news was Lucy's mom would be out of the hospital in three days, but the bad news was that she would not able to be there for Lucy's birthday, which was in two days.

Lucy's birthday was here, and her mom was still not well, so her dad went to the hospital to check on his wife. He left Lucy and her grandma home alone, which he regretted later on.

Meanwhile at the house, Lucy was upstairs playing with her other toys. Her grandma was sound asleep downstairs with the television on the highest volume, and nothing could wake her up.

The doll started to activate. It was programmed to kill the birthday girl on her birthday. The doll went to the kitchen and found a large meat-cutting knife with jagged edges, then started going up the long wooden stairs, and went up to Lucy's pink bedroom with posters all over her wall. The doll stared at her for about a minute with a grin on her face that you could never forget.

The doll took out the large knife, and began charging at Lucy with her eyes red like the devil, but with cat-like reflexes, Lucy smacked the huge knife out of the nasty doll's hand. Lucy picked it up as fast as she could before the doll got up and cut the doll's head off. Stuffing was coming out of the doll, and Lucy saw her eyes roll to the back of her head.

When Lucy's parents came home from the hospital, Lucy was shaking with so much fear she couldn't breathe, or even talk. Lucy's dad asked her, "Honey, what's wrong? It looks like you saw a monster," but Lucy was so scared she couldn't tell them what happened that late, dark night. She couldn't say one word. Lucy went right to sleep in her parents' arms.

Later on when she explained what happened to her parents, they took her to a psychiatrist and got rid of the doll for good. Still, to this day Lucy will never forget her ninth birthday.

Egypt

EGYPT, *by* **Nathan Higley**, *is a story about Kyle and his two brothers. They are stuck in Egypt and fight Serqet. Do they beat her?*

"Mom, hurry up! I found these weird symbols in this old book."

My name is Kyle, and I am one of the triplets in my family. Our parents are Egyptologists who won't stop working. I always call them workaholics. They say it will come in handy one day. Curt and Joe (my brothers) and I were walking to school and hawks kept following us. One of the hawks screeched and a big hole in front of us opened and sucked us into it. We awoke from the darkness in a desert. I asked if my brothers were okay and they said, "Yes."

We looked around and there was nothing in sight.

"The three hawks are still flying over us," Curt said. "We should follow them because they could lead us to civilization."

We followed the hawks until nightfall and the hawks flew into a pyramid. We walked into the pyramid too and rested for the night. The pyramid was lit with torches which was weird because the pyramid seemed abandoned. We went to bed so we would have energy for tomorrow. The next morning, Curt was reading hieroglyphics and Joe was turning invisible. And, there, right in front of me, was an old guy with long hair and he said that we were "The One."

"What do you mean we are 'The One'?" I asked.

"He thinks we are the people that have to beat the Egyptian Scorpion Goddess Serqet." Joe replied.

Then I just fainted. I awoke with a sword by my side and that guy was still there.

Joe continued, "We are 'The One' because I can turn invisible, Curt can read hieroglyphics, and you can handle a sword better than anyone. Together we are powerful."

"How do you know that, Joe?" I answered. "I've never even handled a sword before."

"Then you all should start training," said the guy.

And so we started training. The first thing I did was fighting air. The first thing Curt did was read hieroglyphics. And the first thing Joe did was play hide-and-go seek with the guy. After some time, we were told to rest since we had had a tough day practicing. We were going to fight a Serpopard tomorrow. He told us that a Serpopard is a leopard with a snake neck. We went to bed.

The next morning, we got up and ate then followed the guy to the secret chamber; the home of the Serpopard.

The guy said, "It is a tricky monster. Are you ready?"

We replied, "Yes!"

He let the monster out and it charged for Joe, but Joe disappeared. The monster stopped and went for Curt who made a word in hieroglyphics which turned into a fireball that was thrown at the monster. It sent the monster hurtling backwards into the wall. I threw my sword at the monster and it sliced his neck, but not completely. My sword stopped in mid-air, which was weird, but then I realized that Joe caught it and sliced the head off of the Serpopard.

"Good job!" said the guy.

"What is your name?" I asked.

"My name is Rashaad," said the man.

Then we heard a scream from the village so we ran as fast as we could to the village. And there, right in the middle of the village, was the most horrifying creature that I had ever seen. It was Serqet.

I yelled, "Split up!"

So Curt ran around the backside, I went up the middle, and Joe went on the right side of her. Rashaad ran off somewhere to hide.

"So you are "The One", I see." said Serqet.

A huge fire ball hit her in the back of the head which was thrown by Curt. But, the fire ball only burned the hood of her cape.

Then Serqet said, "Ah, brothers."

"And triplets," I said.

Serqet brought out her sword and screamed and a bunch of scorpions appeared. There seemed to be about a million of them. Curt started burning the scorpions and then I heard a scream so loud that I almost went deaf. It was Joe; he stabbed her in the back with a pitch fork. Serqet was dead.

We found Rashaad who was, surprisingly, with my parents. We thanked Rashaad for everything and went home safely and happily.

Ember Woods

When a boy who has lost a lot in his life discovers a hidden ability, his whole life changes. In **EMBER WOODS** *by* ***Nick Gullo***, *you can follow Kent on his adventure in discovering his powers.*

"Stop yelling at me, Mom!"

"Then stop disobeying me!"

"I didn't mean to. I… I didn't know."

"Go to your room, and don't come out until I tell you to."

Rinnnng ring.

Mrs. Darrel went to get the phone and picked it up, but never took her eyes off of Kent. Kent glared back at his mom. Suddenly their dog Ray came bolting down the stairs, barking and growling at his mom as if she were a stranger. She held her hand over the phone and whispered through gritted teeth, "Kent, get your dog out of here! NOW!"

The she put the phone back to her ear and continued with her conversation. All of a sudden her eyes widened, and she almost dropped the phone.

"I gotta go Kent. Stay here," Mrs. Darrel said, looking worried.

"I thought I was grounded."

"I've gotta go!" she stormed out the door.

It was probably a business crisis. Kent was sick of her stupid business. She thought it was so much to handle. That's why she exploded and grounded Kent when he used her "work computer" for homework. It can't be too hard to teach a kindergarten class of ten kids for four hours. The only kind of crisis that goes on around there is that someone needs their shoes tied or has to go potty.

Kent was 13 and hated life. Ever since his dad died last year, she'd been taking everything out on him.

Kent decided he wasn't going to "stay here," as his mom instructed. He was going to the beach. Kent knew his mom wouldn't have let them go to the beach alone, but he didn't care. He was angry at her and he wanted to tick her off! Kent locked the door and stormed off to the beach.

Kent took off his shirt and ran into the water. The cool breeze felt refreshing. Finally, peace and quiet.

"Hey, Kent!"

Kent looked around. He saw no one.

"Hey, Kent!" he heard again. "Look at me when I'm talking to you!"

Over on a lounge chair sat Zack Andrews, sunning his big white belly. Zack Andrews went to the same school as Kent and thought he was the coolest person in the world. Kent had been dealing with Zack's harassment since second grade. He would constantly tease Zack about his clothes, his brains, his hair, and anything else that would make Kent feel insecure.

As quickly as he could, Kent jumped up and ran. But Zack ran faster. Kent could hear Zack's feet kicking up sand behind him. Kent was hoping to lose him, but he wasn't fast enough. POW! He could taste the sand in his mouth. He turned onto his back, spitting the sand from his mouth.

"What is it, Zack?"

"I was talking to you, @$%#^%."

"What do you want?"

"You ta look at me when I'm…"

"Shut up," Kent interrupted.

"Excuse me, butthead?"

"I said shut up and go away!" Kent screamed.

Zack just laughed. Then he kicked Kent in the thigh as hard as he could and left without taking his eyes off of Kent. As Zack backed away laughing, Kent noticed that all the seagulls started to take flight. Were they afraid of something or just leaving? Zack walked with pride, strutting like a peacock, and no longer looking at Kent. The birds took off really fast in the same direction as Zack. Kent could no longer see Zack because the seagulls were swarming him. Kent could hear Zack screaming in terror. Kent lifted his arm to block the sun, and when he did all the birds flew up. He moved his arm back down for a second and all the birds darted back down.

Kent just stood there in the sand for a while and laughed, wishing that all the people in his school had been there to watch, too. *Why is everyone so stupid?* Kent thought to himself. *Maybe I'm just stupid.* Once he got the strength, Kent ran across the street and into the woods. He ran as fast and as far as he could without thinking about where he was going. *Why does no one like me, not even my family?* he asked himself. The pain in his thigh wasn't helping matters. Kent just wished he could disappear into thin air and all his worries would go away.

Out of breath, Kent stopped running and sank to the ground. He realized something. Being in the middle of the quiet, peaceful woods was like disappearing into thin air. It was just what he had asked for. It was like his sanctuary. There was no yelling, no screaming, and no one but Kent.

Kent finally had time to think to himself. He thought about everything that was going on. He thought about the past, the present and the future. He thought about his mom, and tried to understand her. He thought about his dad and really missed him. He thought about his goals, his accomplishments, and his dreams. He sat there and thought and thought and thought. He felt as if a huge load had been taken off of him and like all his stress was gone. Kent felt good. He felt comfortable in these woods.

Kent wasn't sure how long he'd been gone and thought he should get back. As he stood up and looked around, he realized he didn't know which way was back. The only sight was thick green trees. All the peace he was feeling left him. He started to panic. He was breathing short, quick breaths.

Kent noticed his shoes were all muddy and torn, and his head began to hurt, too. He let out a moan when he thought he heard something. Maybe it was his imagination. Kent stopped to look around. He now felt scared. He stood very still. There it was again. Now he knew he heard a noise, and he knew he wasn't going mad. Something was out there, and he didn't know what.

Kent sprang up and sprinted forward. He ran as fast as he could with his torn shoe. Kent felt like his feet were barely touching the ground as if some force were carrying him. He ran and ran until -- *splash!*

Kent had fallen in a river - a fast river! He was summersaulting over and over in the water, not knowing which way was up. Then his head hit a rock, and everything went black.

*   *   *

It was nice to be back in my nice warm bed, Kent thought to himself. *So soft, so warm, so comfortable.*

Kent heard the sound of rushing water. Then his eyes sprang open. He had been dreaming.

"Where the heck am I?"

Kent was in a one-room log cabin with lots of old paintings on the walls, a roaring fire in the fireplace, and an old wooden table in the center. The cabin looked weak and like it probably couldn't survive through the winter.

Kent started to remember running away from something. He sat up in the bed. He thought he should be afraid, but actually he liked the feeling of the small wooden house. He felt at peace here, but maybe this was just a dream.

Kent walked out of the log cabin. He took notice of his surroundings. There was a beautiful waterfall, a peaceful, streaming river, and an old man fishing on the river's edge. Kent's eyes widened when the man started to turn around. Kent swore it looked like he saw horns on the man's head. He flopped a big red hat on his head and started walking toward Kent.

"Well, good mornin', sunshine! You had a big nap there!" said the old man.

Kent said, "Uhh, where am I?"

"You do not know how long I been waitin' for ya."

"Ahhh, where am I?" Kent asked again.

"Well, you're in the Ember Woods, of course," the man replied. "How long did it take ya ta get 'ere, Barry?"

"I'm not Barry." Kent was now a little freaked out.

"Oh my gosh, Barry, do I have to take you to see the Lord or something? You seem confused!"

"The Lord?" Kent asked in a sort of irritated way.

"Okay, you *are* confused. Follow me!" Kent walked with the man, going up and down many long winding paths. They had been walking forever. Kent was tired and hungry, and it was starting to get dark.

"Excuse me, sir, how long 'til we…"

"We're 'ere!" interrupted the old man.

"There's nothing here!" Kent rolled his eyes while saying this.

"Be patient, boy! We have ta wait 'til sunset." As the sun lowered, a castle started to rise over the hills.

"Wow!" Kent was amazed by the huge castle. It had bright red roofing and a strong stone body. Even though the sun went down the castle gave off a faint glow.

Kent and the old man walked up to the big steel door. The castle door made him feel small and more like a kid. The old man pounded on the door (it was so thick that a simple knock couldn't have made a sound). The doors slowly swung open, revealing the most amazing room that Kent had ever seen. Everything was shiny and seemed to be made of gold, and the ceiling seemed to go on forever.

The old man moved quickly into the castle, knowing where he was going. He led Kent down a bright blue hallway with blue wallpaper, carpeting, and even blue doors. He led Kent to the bottom of the long hallway to a bright yellow door; it stood out from all the others. Inside of the door was an elevator, and not just any elevator. It was a stone elevator.

They climbed in the elevator, with Kent expecting it to break the lifting rope because of its weight. But it didn't. It took them probably three miles high until it finally stopped. It opened, revealing a green hallway.

Eventually Kent had gone through a blue, green, purple, red, pink, orange, and even a black hallway, all of which had a yellow door at the end. Finally they came to a white and red hallway (the last hallway). It had pictures of lions on the walls and seemed much more detailed than the others.

At the end of it there was a black door. Slowly walking up to it, Kent knew it was the last door; it just had to be. Kent was about to open the door when the old man stopped him and told him they had to knock on this one. Then they gave a nice, hard knock (not as hard as the one on the steel door).

"Come in!" a deep big voice shouted. They walked in the room. Kent felt both a little scared and a little excited. Kent was surprised to see a big white lion sitting on a throne.

"What do you want?" said the lion.

The old man bowed down, taking off his hat and revealing the horns that Kent thought he had seen.

"Uhh, uhh, I found this human boy floating along in da river, so I brought him out and dried him off and placed him in my bed. He calls himself Kent, but he's gotta be Barry." Things were starting to come back to Kent. He remembered falling in the water.

The lion spoke again in a louder voice than even before.

"This boy is human! How did he even get in here!"

"I don't know. I said he was just floating along in da river."

"You are not a sorcerer, boy; how did you get in here!" the lion shouted. Kent could tell that the lion wasn't having the best day.

"I fell in the river, and the river must have brought me here with its current," Kent replied in a soft voice.

"What is your name, boy?" said the lion, but this time in a nicer tone, understanding that Kent was scared.

"Kent Darrel."

"Now that explains it." The lion chuckled a little. "What is your mother's name?"

"Deborah. Why?" Kent was totally lost.

"Boy, do you realize you could disintegrate me right now if you wanted to?" The lion was now speaking with more respect to Kent.

"I'm not following, sir," said the old man.

"Charles, he is Deborah's son."

"Oh ma gosh, I was the first one to find Deborah's son! Yehaaaa!" The old man jumped in the air clacking his heals together.

"So what does this all mean?" Kent interrupted. He still feared the lion even though he was told he could disintegrate him if he wanted to.

"It means one day you will be Lord of Ember Woods," said the lion. Kent's jaw dropped, and his eyes widened.

"Seriously?" Kent doubted the lion.

"Boy, where have you been? You don't even know your mom is the most powerful sorcerer of the land?" The lion said this as if Kent was supposed to know these things.

"Wait, if she is most powerful, then how come you are Lord?"

"Because I am a male," the lion said with pride. "No, just joking! It is because your mother decided to leave Ember, and her responsibilities, to marry your father."

"Really?"

"It's too bad," said the lion, kind of chuckling.

"What's too bad?"

"Yeah, what could be bad?" said the old man. "I'm about to win my prize."

"You would have made such a great king," said the lion.

"Well, I might one day," said Kent in a confused tone.

"It was so easy. I didn't even have to come and find you." The lion started to make a choking noise but didn't look like he was choking.

"Kid, run!" screamed the old man. "RUN!"

The lion let out a roar and leaped off his throne at the same time the old man threw himself in front of Kent. Kent started to run and flung himself at the door. As Kent burst through the door, he could hear the old man screaming. It sounded horrible!

Instead of going through the door the lion broke the whole wall down. Kent jumped in the elevator and slammed the doors shut. It wasn't going very fast, but the lion couldn't get to him now. Kent heard a crushing sound above.

"Really? He's going to break the whole castle down!" said Kent. When the doors clicked open two guards were standing in Kent's way.

"Umm, hello," said Kent. "Who are you?" All of a sudden the two men jumped at Kent, plunging into the elevator. His first reaction was to scream. When he screamed, the men went flying back, plunging out of the elevator. Kent was about to keep moving when the lion crashed down from the ceiling above, crushing all the paintings and decorations.

"Boy, don't try anything funny!" yelled the lion. "We can do this the hard way or the easy way. You can let me eat you and get it over with or try to run and get yourself hurt before you die." Kent screamed, thinking the lion would go flying back, but he barely felt a thing.

"Fine, then," said the lion. The lion's rear end rose up in the air, and he was ready to pounce. The lion sprung up 20 feet high because the ceiling above was broken and he had room. He let out a mighty roar that you could have heard even if you weren't in the castle. Kent closed his eyes, and right when he should have felt terrible pain everything went silent.

When he opened his eyes, Kent saw not the lion but his mom, and the lion was gone. At first Kent thought he was dreaming or maybe even dead, but he knew he wasn't because he could feel the bruise that Zack had given him earlier.

"Mom!" Kent yelled.

"Honey, how did you get here?" his mom replied.

"How did you get here?" said Kent.

"The kitchen pantry, but that's another story."

Epilogue

Kent and his mom went home. Kent had to promise that he would never tell anyone about Ember Woods. His mom told him that he had to wait to be Lord. He must go through life always thinking of this and never forgetting his destiny.

She told him of her life in Ember, how she had fallen in love with a human and made the choice to leave after Kent was born. She had named him Barry at first (after his dad) but had changed his name so no one could use magic to find him.

His mom explained the old man, or rather, the creature of Ember who looked like an old man. The reason the old man had been so excited was because the Lion had offered a prize to anyone who could find "Barry," the future heir to the throne. He told everyone that he would be the only human that could get into Ember so it would not be hard to spot him. But the Lion had lied about the prize and his reason for wanting to find Barry. The lion had wanted Barry so he could kill him and keep the throne for himself.

Fearless

Nobody wants to face their biggest fear. A girl learns that facing her biggest fear is possible in **FEARLESS**, *by* **Jacqueline Hentschel**.

Tomorrow, *tomorrow, tomorrow, tomorrow*, was the only word that rang in my head. How was I supposed to fall asleep when I was going to be an adult tomorrow? My eyes closed, but as soon as they did, they popped back open again. When you are in bed staring at the ceiling time seems to slow down. I swiveled my head to the left to look at the clock on my bedside stand; it had been five minutes? Only five minutes had passed since I last looked at the clock? This happened for at least an hour. Finally, at I have no idea what time, my eyes drifted closed and I fell asleep.

I was suddenly jolted awake! Where was I? I was in a strange place. It looked like I was in a metal box. The room I was in was about the size of a gym, but everything, the walls and the floor, were metal.

Where was the clock? Maybe I was eighteen years old! LET ME SEE THE CLOCK! Wait a second. Shouldn't I be worrying about where I am! Where am I?

"Do you know where you are?" a voice that sounded like nails on a chalkboard screeched.

"N-n-n-nooo," I could barely utter.

"Well, you are facing your biggest fear," the same voice cooed.

"What are you even talking about?" I whispered less boldly than I thought it would come out.

"Before you turn eighteen, before you become an adult, you must face your biggest fear." There goes that voice again. At this point the voice was really getting me annoyed, and when I'm annoyed, I'm not exactly polite.

"Excuse me, I don't even know my biggest fear. Also I better not be missing my 18th birthday, because if I am, I'm going to come over there and slap you right smack across the face." I tried to speak boldly, but at this point I was just trying to hold back my tears.

"You will find out soon enough." The voice finally stopped.

This is just great, I thought to myself. *I'm at some strange place, missing my 18th birthday, and I'm about to cry. I haven't cried since I was six!*

"Get out of bed," a quiet but stern voice snapped.

Not only did I get out of bed, I jumped out of bed and yelled, "Sir, yes Sir." I know that seems dumb, but trust me: If you had heard that voice you would have done the exact same thing. This voice was different from the voice I first heard when I woke up in the metal box. It was not better, but different.

The person with the stern voice stepped into the room. His presence made the metal in the room seem a whole lot colder. This person had the palest face you have ever seen. His eyes, even though they were bloodshot, looked like they were shooting poison at you. The funny thing was I didn't even notice this person was only about three feet tall, until he started walking. I was so afraid of him that his small size didn't make him any less threatening. This person was so eerie. I was terrified of him.

"My name is Desdsl, I will be your guide through this process," the stern-voice-man commented like it was the worst thing in the world. "I hope you aren't one of those screamers; I already have a pounding headache and I might have to harm you physically and emotionally if you scream, or even talk above a whisper."

"OK, I have no idea what's going on. Can we just get whatever IS going on over with so I can go back to my house and get away from you crazy people?" I tried to whisper. I'm not sure why I was so afraid of Desdsl other than his appearance. Nothing else about him was that scary.

"OK, first thing first, we must attach these headphones to your head so we can find out what your biggest fear is," Desdsl stated. Then Desdsl pulled out the biggest pair of headphones I had ever seen in my life. The part that went on my ear was about as big as a tire.

"I'm afraid we're all out of modern headphones so we have to use the old-fashioned kind," Desdsl muttered.

"Just one more thing before you put those things on my head?" I questioned.

"OK, what?"

"Who was the man who first talked to me with that spine-tingling voice?" I could barely hiss. The man could have been watching me, and I know I wouldn't want to be known as the man with the spine-tingling voice.

"Oh, him? That's Mawuli. He is just there to scare you, so you don't do anything stupid like try to escape before I walk into the room," Desdsl said as a smug smile spread across his face.

"THAT'S POSSIBLY THE STUPIDEST THING I'VE EVER HEARD!" I exclaimed, even though I was only supposed to be whispering.

"But it worked," Desdsl said, and before I could scream anymore Desdsl shoved the headphones onto my head and everything went blank. My eyes closed, I stopped screaming, and every part on my body went limp. I was aware of what was going on, but just barely. After what seemed like forever, I woke up.

I wasn't in the metal room anymore. I was in a huge room, bigger then I had ever seen in my life! If I were in any other situation I would be running around this room doing cartwheels over and over and over again. But I wasn't in any other situation. I was in this one. Then Desdsl appeared out of nowhere.

"Did you enjoy your experience with the headphones?" Desdsl questioned.

"Ummmmm, I guess?" I replied.

"OK, then let's get started," Desdsl said in a very bored tone.

"Wait, where am I?" I said in what I imagine was a very confused tone.

"A church," Desdsl sighed.

"Wait, no, I'm..." Before I could finish the sentence my voice trailed off because all of a sudden, out of nowhere, things started swirling around me, like a tornado, only I wasn't being picked up by it. Anything that wasn't secured down flew in a spiral with the wind of the tornado. It was exactly like you see in movies.

Suddenly I was in a church. I looked around. There was nothing out of the ordinary.

My eyes focused on three caskets. I didn't know why they were there, but I went over to investigate. I had an idea, and my idea only got confirmed when I walked over there. Each had the name of someone I loved on it.

I tried to hold back my tears. I thought maybe if I didn't cry it would go away. It didn't go away.

I tried running out of the church, but the doors were locked. Tears were welling up inside my head. WHY WON'T THIS GO AWAY? I ran around. All the doors were locked. I didn't know why this was happening.

At this point there was no point in trying to hold back my tears. I started sobbing. *It's not real, it's not real,* I tried to tell myself through sobs. *It surely looks real,* a voice in the back of my head kept saying.

"SHUT UP, GO AWAY, THIS ISN'T REAL!" I yelled out loud, trying to convince myself. All of a sudden I stumbled out of that horrible place. I was back in the metal room. I saw my bed, and my blankets strewn all over the floor from when I jumped up to confront Desdsl. I climbed back into that bed. I had never wanted to be in any place so badly before.

After I had calmed down, wiped my tears, and thought about it for a second, I realized I had just faced my biggest fear! I could face anything now!

Right at that moment Desdsl walked in. In a monotone voice he said, "Congratulations, you have faced your biggest fear. Fall back asleep and you can go back to your home."

It's impossible to fall asleep when you are looking forward to something. But I did, just because I knew when I did I would be home safe and sound. This horrible night would go away. I would be an adult when I got home. Facing the thought of losing the people I love the most was my worst nightmare. After this experience I now know I don't have to be afraid, because I can always pull through, and everything will be okay.

Looking back at this strange experience I think the reason this happened to me was to show that as I become an adult, no matter what life throws at me, I will be able to handle it, and I will not be afraid of the future.

Freaky Night with Toys

A group of friends are held against their will. Now they must work together to save their families in **FREAKY NIGHT WITH TOYS** *by* ***Carson Kreitz***.

One night Jack, Sam, and I (Brandon) were shopping with our families at Toys R Us on a seemingly ordinary night. While we were checking out the video games, there was an electrical surge followed by the sound of thunder. The lights flickered, and the doors suddenly slammed shut and locked. The bikes started moving, Nerf guns were firing, and the Legos started building themselves. The toys were coming to life!

"Are they moving?" asked a puzzled shopper.

"Those are displays," said a worker, lying to prevent a panic.

"It's got Benny!" said a child in the action figure aisle, watching a Transformer drag his brother away.

So much for avoiding a panic, thought the worker.

Everyone in the store was freaking out. Soon the big electronic toys started capturing people. It was as if the microchips inside of them were brains, activated by the lightning.

Some customer managed to break out a window. The loud noise seemed to make everyone even more scared. They were so shocked they couldn't move. The toys sensed their new-found power and used it against us. They blocked the makeshift escape route and corralled people into a corner with baby gates. The giant plastic toy soldiers stood guard.

Luckily, we got away. We went to the employee break room, where the employees can relax and eat their lunches. There were five other people hiding there.

It was up to us to save everyone. We had to fight back. Sam saw a vending machine and got the idea to use sodas to hit the toys. He then punched it, and I picked up the bottle of Coke that fell out. I ran out into the toy store, shook it, and sprayed Coke at the toys.

"For Narnia!" I screamed to be dramatic.

I heard a couple of giggles from some younger shoppers. But Sam and Jack said, "It's no time for games" simultaneously. The

Coke actually malfunctioned three toys! After I saw what happened with the Coke, I picked up more.

"Hey, the Coke messes up the toys!" said a guy with excitement.

Everyone else saw and joined in. We even located Mentos in the checkout lanes and used them for greater firing range.

"Look for something that isn't possessed!" I shouted. We located fire extinguishers and shopping carts that were not toys and that did not seem to be possessed.

We had to free the prisoners and regain control of the store. Two other kids my age got behind an abandoned shelf along with me. I just went off and fought ten toys.

Also at one point a toy got ahold of a paint gun and fired at us. I got on top of a shelf and fired a fire extinguisher right into the heart of the toys.

After most of the toys were soda- and paint-soaked messes, broken down and out of commission, we corralled them in their own baby gate prison.

All of the human hostages were released. "But we're still locked in!" said a small girl.

I spotted a Buzz Lightyear toy that had been disabled because someone had taken the batteries out of it. I reinstalled the batteries and used the missile to blow open the glass doors of the store. We were free!

Everyone picked me up and carried me over their heads, singing "For He's a Jolly Good Fellow." Then they gave me a giant doughnut. I think I could get used to this hero thing.

Ghost

When someone dies, what do you do? Alison might find out when a spirit comes back from the past in **GHOST** *by* **Meghan Patricia Seneski***.*

When I was five years old, I had the best friend in the world who was Egyptian, just like me. We made our own legends and pretended like we were Ren, Ba, Ka, Sheut, and Ib (Egyptian ghosts). Her name was Amanda and we did everything together. She was my sister, or so I thought.

One day, Amanda and I were playing on the abandoned playground and we were swinging on the swing set, but when we were talking about what we were going to be when we were older, she said, "I'm not so sure that I'm going to be there when we are older." And then, she disappeared as if she was part of the fog around me.

Once all of that happened, I more or less forgot about it. Now, I'm 19 years old in my first year of college. Today, I decided to wear a piece of jewelry that I hadn't worn since I was five years old. I was grasping this amulet and thinking about Amanda. She was my best friend. These thoughts were running through my mind as I was walking to class, when suddenly, I was startled.

"Oh…, I'm sorry. I didn't mean to run into you. What's your name?" I asked.

"I-I-I-I don't know," she stuttered.

"What do you mean?" I asked, stunned.

"Where am I?" she asked, really confused.

"Campus. Why?" I said.

"Because I could have sworn I was just in the depths of the underworld," she replied.

"Excuse me? We need to get you to a doctor," I said.

"NO! NO! NOOOO!" she screamed.

"Calm down. People are starting to stare," I said.

"Who are you talking to?" my friend, Maloney asked.

"This girl. I don't know her name." I turned to look at the girl who I was talking to before, but she was gone. "Oh. Never mind," I said.

"Okay…." Maloney replied and walked away.

I headed to my next class, puzzled. I just realized that she looked exactly like Amanda, but 14 years later. Could this be Amanda? Where did she go? I was very confused. From out of nowhere, I heard her voice.

"So, do you know who I am?" Amanda asked.

"I think you're Amanda, aren't you?" I asked.

"I am?" she said, surprised.

"Well…you certainly look like her," I replied. I tried to put my hand on her shoulder, but it went right through. "Wait, my hand went through you and nobody can see you."

"Oh. That explains why nobody is talking to me," she explained. "Wait…I'm not Amanda. Memories of who I am are flooding through me right now."

"Who are you then?" I asked, stunned.

"Your mom thought I was your imaginary friend," she explained.

"YOU ARE AMANDA!" I screamed.

"No, I'm your 283rd generation grandmother. My name is Elizabeth. I was your friend when you were a kid, but more of your imaginary friend, and you liked the name Amanda, so that's what you called me. I was born in 2550 B.C. and was murdered in 2563 B.C., but nobody found my body," she said.

"Huh?' I asked more confused than ever.

"I never had the proper funeral. You are the one that can only see me because when you were five, you found a special Egyptian amulet of Anubis's head hidden in your attic. On the night I was murdered, I was taken from the house and I prayed that one of my family members that found it would have revealed where my body was. Unfortunately, the amulet must have been stored by someone who wasn't in the family," she explained. "When you found it, you were only five and couldn't help me, so I decided to take the shape of a five-year-old girl."

"Wait. Why were you gone all of those years?" I asked.

"Ma'at, the Egyptian Goddess of Justice, would weigh the hearts of the dead in the underworld against the weight of a feather to determine the worthiness of his or her soul. I had to be tested after all of those years and I never returned until you put the amulet on today," she explained.

"What do we do?" I asked.

"Find my body. Let your amulet guide you," she said.

"Ok. Why?" I asked.

"I need to have a proper funeral or else I will be here until the end of time," she explained.

"Fine," I said. We walked outside and I took off my amulet and it started to glow. I followed where it guided me and went into the woods. When we came to a patch of rough grass in the middle of the woods on the other side of town, I wished for a shovel. In my hand, there was a shovel a moment later. I started to dig and dig until I hit something hard. There was a gold tomb sitting there. I tried to open the tomb, but the lid was sealed tight. I looked at the side of the tomb and there was a lock. I used my bobby pin to pick the lock. The lock made a little click and fell to the bottomless hole. I opened the tomb and found the remains of her body.

"This is my body," she said.

"Ok. Now what?" I asked.

"Now, please plan a proper funeral and I can be at peace," she said.

"It will be done," I replied. She disappeared.

The funeral took about a week. My mother and grandmother were surprised that a family tragedy was resolved from thousands of years ago, like an old family mystery. They said that they never told me because they thought that I would never understand. By the end of the ceremony, something felt strange. To me, everything and everyone disappeared. My vision went black.

Someone dragged me to their house and trapped me there.

When I woke up, I was tied up to a chair and all I could hear was the droning sound of water. Then, I could see the face of an animal with the shape of a human body. I saw Anubis. I don't know why the God of the Underworld was there, but I had a feeling that it had something to do with me seeing a ghost.

"What's going on?" I said.

"Oh, so you woke up?" he asked. "I'm sorry that I have to do this, but our secrets must be kept. Understand that you are the chosen one," he said. Then he threw God's wine (a magical legendary Egyptian wine) all over my face. I fell into a deep sleep.

After that, I stopped breathing. I died.

I knew why I had to go to the depths of the underworld. All of the secrets had to be kept, because if these secrets weren't kept, all of the worlds would collide and everybody would be in danger, especially my family. After all, I am the chosen one.

Gnome World

When a kid accidentally discovers a magical world, he tells his friend, and they're up for an adventure. In **GNOME WORLD** *by Jacques Vos, will these two kids put Gnome World in danger, or will they save it?*

*W*hoosh, zippity zap. Spencer appeared in a little house and was approached by a one foot- tall man who looked like Santa Claus in his little overalls and pointy red hat. The man asked Spencer why he was in his house. Spencer told him, "I saw a shiny, purple, mysterious-looking helix when I was cleaning out the basement. I went to touch it, and I ended up here." The gnome tried to look surprised, but Spencer wasn't convinced that the man didn't know what the purple, shiny helix was.

Just then Spencer realized he was the same height as the man and was surprised he hadn't realized it earlier. Spencer asked, "Why am I so small?"

The little man sighed and said, "The purple helix is a teleporter to Gnome World, where we are now talking. Using the teleporter means if you are too big to fit in a house you become small enough to fit in one." The gnome then said, "My name is Floyd."

Spencer tried to take in all this information, but it was too much. He was thinking it was a dream, but it was very real. Spencer began to panic. What if he was stuck in Gnome World for the rest of his life? He asked, "How do I get home?"

The gnome simply replied, "Over there." He was pointing to a purple helix just like the one Spencer had come through. As Spencer walked through it, he heard a low echo of Floyd's voice. "Don't tell anyone about Gnome World, and never come back!"

When he was home he ran up the basement stairs, out the front door, and across the street to his best friend John's house, and said, "Dude, you are never going to believe this!" He told his best friend about the gnome and how a purple helix transports people to Gnome World.

His friend John said, "Yeah, right, you liar. That so did not happen!"

A minute later Spencer brought John down into his basement and proved it to him. Spencer said, "I dare you to touch that helix thing." John did it, and they were sucked into Gnome World. They arrived in Floyd's house, and he was furious.

He said, "I told you not to tell anyone and to never come back!"

"But what is going on?" Spencer asked.

Floyd said, "There is a legend that one day the gnome emperor grew sick and could only get his medicine from the humans. So the gnomes somehow built a teleporter to the human world to get his medicine. That is why we have these teleporters." Floyd also said, "If anyone else comes with either of you boys back to Gnome World again I'll have your heads. Got it? Since you're here I will make you a deal, too. You can see Gnome World if you never come back."

The boys then both squeaked, "Yes, Floyd."

John was in awe as he walked out of Floyd's front door and saw the noisy city: There were mile-high skyscrapers connected by glass catwalks, blinking digital screens like billboards, and gnomes bustling in all directions. Who knew gnomes were so modern? With their funny little outfits and long white beards, John had imagined them living in little huts scattered through a forest.

Floyd pointed to a bank across the street and explained that they would be able to change some money there for gnomesons so they could go explore the city. They went to check it out.

Something was very strange inside the bank. Before they knew it, they were tearing up. It smelled like onions everywhere in the bank, and a little canister that looked like a smoke bomb had transparent gas coming out of it.

John and Spencer's vision was so blurred that they could barely see what was happening. They heard some shouts and realized a gnome was robbing the bank! Before they could even react a gnome dressed all in black wearing a gas mask crashed into them. Coins spilled everywhere, and the gnome slipped on the coins, giving the boys an opportunity to grab him.

The police exploded through the doors and took the gnome away. The bank manager thanked them over and over again, and assigned one of his senior partners to take the boys out to tour the city and have a huge meal.

The gnome king was overwhelmed with gratitude and impressed with the boy's bravery. He named streets after the boys, and said, "You will always be welcome in our world, as long as you do not tell others about us."

Spencer and John thought it was so cool to be secret heroes of Gnome World and didn't want to make the king mad, so they gladly kept their adventure a secret.

The Halloween Nightmare

Dan has a dream, but doesn't realize that it is actually a terrible nightmare. Find out about the nightmare in **THE HALLOWEEN NIGHTMARE** *by* ***Youssef Abdalla***.

Dan had a dream. The dream was about a time when Dan's family bought a new house in the middle of nowhere. His family settled in the house and Dan's cousin, Max, came over for Halloween. Max's parents let him stay overnight. Dan and Max played in Dan's new cornfield. They didn't fall asleep until midnight.

Although Dan fell asleep late, he woke up at 4:00 A.M. to some loud, screaming voices. He saw a few blood tracks on the floor. He was extremely terrified. In his mind, something was telling him to go to the cornfield. Dan saw Max's body in the hands of a scarecrow.

The voice in his head told him to go back home to the kitchen. Dan did not want to go, but now the voice was controlling his body. Suddenly, he went maximum speed straight to the oven. He opened his eyes and saw stars, planets, and even the black hole. He was in space. Dan tried to wake himself up from this nightmare by pinching himself, but all it did was give him a bruise. He was actually already awake but in space.

The voices came back and the universe disappeared. Dan fell hard on the kitchen floor which made a big *BOOM*! The scarecrow appeared in front of him and opened its mouth. Words started coming out of the scarecrow's mouth. "If you want your cousin back, you must listen to my exact direction," said the scarecrow.

Dan became terrified. The scarecrow was telling him to go back to the cornfield. Dan had to go since he still couldn't control his body.

"If you want your cousin back, you have to do me one favor," the scarecrow continued. "You will burn the house and run away!"

Dan didn't know what to do. He wanted to tell his parents about the whole night, but he was scared that the scarecrow would hear him.

Dan finally decided that he was going to do what the scarecrow told him to do. He was scared, but that was his only choice. After he finished setting his house on fire, he waited for the voice to come back. To his surprise, he was slowly and painfully waking up.

When he woke up, he was not in a dream. He was back in Philadelphia, Pennsylvania where he actually lived. He went over to his parents and gave them the hug of their lives. For the first time in many years, he was actually happy to see his parents again.

Halloween Scare

In this story, Lizzy and Rebecca walk to a house in Rock Creek that is unlike any other. Will they survive? Find out in **HALLOWEEN SCARE**, *by* ***Brianna Staten***.

It was a special Halloween night in October on Hoopla Null Street. A six-year-old named Lizzy and her cousin Rebecca were going trick-or-treating. After walking to a few houses and getting treats, Lizzy said, "I'm getting tired of carrying my bag."

Rebecca responded, "We're almost home. Just keep carrying your bag."

They saw a big house on the street called Rock Creek with a lot of lights and decorations. They thought that they were going to get a lot of candy. While Rebecca waited near the street, Lizzy walked up to the door. A wolf popped out! It grabbed her, went inside the house, and set her in the bad people room. Lizzy got captured because she bullied the man's son at school. After the wolf popped up, he never was seen again.

Rebecca was still waiting for Lizzy. After about three minutes, Rebecca went up the driveway and looked for Lizzy, but nobody was there. Rebecca rang the doorbell, and the door opened on its own.

Rebecca didn't see anything. She checked at least 50 rooms in 60 minutes. She was really tired, and she thought to herself, "I really need to find Lizzy or I'm really busted." She saw all different types of rooms. She panicked, and was really scared and creeped out. She also saw flying bats and spider webs all around the house.

A few minutes later she heard a girl screaming. There were a lot of flying bats left.

Rebecca saw a big red button that said, "Self-destruct and take-off." Rebecca pressed the button down. The machine said, "Self-destruct in 10, 9, 8, 7, 6, 5, 4, 3, 2, 1." The whole house collapsed. Pieces were all falling in, and water was everywhere. It would have been a complete disaster except that she saw Lizzy!

Rebecca was so happy that she found Lizzy and that they didn't die. She grabbed Lizzy by the hand, and they ran out of the house as fast as they could. Lizzy explained what happened and that she wasn't hurt. She also explained how scared it was to be next to pointy things and never knew how she got there.

They walked back home and were safe. They told their mother what happened, and her mom made a story about the situation and made sure everybody was fine. After that night, Lizzy's mother will never let them go down Rock Creek again.

Heroes of Dwarfenheimer

Two humble miners go on a mission for the king in **HEROES OF DWARFENHEIMER** *by* ***JP Culbertson***. *They hope to come back as saviors of their city—if they make it back at all.*

Dwarfenheimer is a small city with tiny houses walled by mountains that existed in the Middle Ages. It is inhabited by kind, war-skilled dwarfs. These dwarfs live simple lives, and have simple jobs. They are farmers, miners, hunters, and lumberjacks. One special dwarf is named Rafele. He is a skilled miner who finds himself one day on a heroic mission.

That one day started out like any other. Rafele was out mining in the caverns with his best friend, Folstag, when the King of Dwarfenheimer suddenly appeared. He said, "Rafele and Folstag, you must join my army to hunt down the enemy troll king named Dufarge in the neighboring village."

"Sire, why do we need to kill him?" asked Rafele.

"Well, he has been sending troops to raid our farms," said the dwarf king. Rafele and Folstag understood, and their quest began.

Rafele and Folstag hunted through the forest of the troll's village in search of the king. "People say these trails are dangerous," said Rafele.

"Why?" said Folstag.

"Because they are full of crooks and bandits and crazy magicians," said Rafele. Rafele and Folstag were glad they were together.

As they were walking along, they met someone named Magi. He told them that he was a time traveler and that he could take them on a journey with him to the future. Both Rafele and Folstag were suspicious of him because he looked like a troll. Before they could react, Magi transported them to the 21st century, and they were no longer in the forest of the trolls. They were in the halls of Berkshire Middle School! Being dwarfs, they looked a lot like sixth-graders (with added beards!).

They ran through the halls looking for Magi. They found him in the gymnasium hiding under the bleachers. What they found was

Magi talking into a glass ball. "Sire, my mission was a success, and I really should go back to our time," said Magi.

"Very well," sighed Dufarge. While Magi was talking to Dufarge and had his back turned, Rafele quietly picked up Magi's staff.

"Surrender, Magi!" said Folstag. Magi just realized his staff was in the hands of Rafele. Folstag and Rafele summoned the power of the staff by saying the word "Home."

"Oh, come on," sighed Magi. Just like that, Rafele and Folstag were back in the forest.

It was not long before they found Dufarge and his men. They were in the forest going to see if Magi had returned. Rafele and Folstag battled the troll king's guards in a sword fight. "Foolish dwarfs, you can't win with your puny strength and courage," said Dufarge. That sentence made Rafele so mad he killed the guards in his rage of anger. Dufarge started running but tripped on his cloak. Rafele, still in a rage, ran at Dufarge and fulfilled his quest. Rafele and Folstag came out victorious—the troll king was dead!

The two dwarfs returned to Dwarfenheimer. They let the dwarfs of the city know they were safe from the trolls and the troll king. The farms would also be safe from troll raids. Rafele and Folstag became heroes of Dwarfenheimer. They knew that they couldn't have done it without each other.

"Well," said Folstag.

"Well what?" said Rafele.

"Dwarfenheimer wouldn't be safe without you…," said Folstag.

"Dude, I could've died if you weren't here," said Rafele.

"When?" said Folstag.

"When I took Magi's wand," said Rafele.

"Oh, sorry, I forgot," said Folstag. "Thanks for being a great friend."

"Well, see you later," said Rafele.

Just like that, the sun went down in Dwarfenheimer.

The Hero's Sands

In the story **THE HERO'S SANDS** *by* ***Zach Heaton***, *a young man must defeat the evil god of chaos and save Egypt. But can Mark fulfill his destiny and destroy Ordel forever?*

Deep in the heart of the Sahara Desert, far from any civilizations, a lone man collapsed in the sand. He made no sound, and even if he had, the blistering winds would have blocked it out. He thought to himself, *I can't survive out here. I haven't had food or water for days, and there are no oases for as far as the eye can see.* He managed to climb back onto his knees, as the sand began to pelt his bare chest. He stood, and shuffled onward into the blinding winds.

Several hours later, the sandstorm began to subside, and he could barely make out the outline of a temple. He wandered over to the building and stared at it. *Where did this come from?* he thought. *Who built it and why?* But his sense of survival overcame his caution and he walked inside.

His surroundings amazed him. The middle of the room was mainly unoccupied, save for the blade resting on a pedestal, which he took the time to remove and place in his belt. The man then walked around the room examining the walls, which were lined with unreadable inscriptions and looming statues. One in particular sparked his interest. It was a massive monument of a man holding an eerie scepter. The whole body was made of some sort of black marble. He reached out to touch the statue's hand. As his fingertips made contact with the stone, he felt electricity surge through them and he blacked out.

When he awoke, the man was confused. *Where am I? Who am I?* Then he remembered that his name was Mark and he was a traveler who had been brutally beaten by a criminal he refused to let by him in a market. He had wandered into the desert to escape and stayed there for many days. He had finally found sanctuary inside the temple. The temple! He stood, and then looked around, wondering what the lightning on his fingertips had done. As he continued his observation, he fell backwards with a start. The inside of the temple was exactly the same, but this one had no walls! All around, a battle raged. Mark saw a warrior, possibly Egyptian, run up to a massive monster with the head of a cobra and the body of a man, only to be swatted away by the beast's mighty hand. He walked out onto the battle field and drew his sword. Another monster, this one with the legs of a goat and one eye, saw him and charged. He steadied himself, braced for impact, and at the last moment, thrust his sword through the monster's eye. It collapsed, moaning in a mix of rage and pain, and then lay still.

Mark stared at his kill, wondering just what that electricity had done to him. He could never have done that before. Other than an occasional bird or the bugs under his feet, he had never killed anything, and definitely nothing of this size.

I must be dreaming, he thought. *That would explain it. All of these monsters aren't real.* But then, a venomous liquid flew through the air next to him, and he knew now was not the time to ponder that. Adrenaline coursed through his veins as he sprinted behind a nearby wall, ducking down to avoid being seen by one of his hideous foes. He took this moment of safety to examine the blade he had found in the temple. Its handle was ornately carved and decorated with colors and inscriptions. The grip was made of red cloth. Mark looked at the blade. It stuck out from the hilt three feet, and started curving off to the side two inches. It kept this curve until the end, where it straightened into a sharp point.

Amazing, he thought. He heard an intense howl and wondered whether it was made by a dying creature, or an angry one. He got his answer when his wall shook and he looked up. Standing on the thin slab of rock crouched a beast unlike any he had ever seen. Its stature was human, but the resemblance stopped there. Its head was that of a ferocious jackal, and its legs were of black dogs. Its muscular chest rippled as it growled and slashed with its clawed hands.

Mark leapt back, but one of the claws tore his shirt and hit flesh. He cried out as blood dripped from the wound, but the beast continued its assault. Seeing its enemy's retreat, it made a massive leap and landed behind Mark. He turned around, just in time, for he managed to dodge the incoming claws. He rolled along the ground, and sliced his blade through the air, catching the beast on its arm. It howled, only to be silenced by an arrow to the head.

Mark looked in the direction the arrow had come and saw another warrior, clad in red armor, holding a long bow.

"Looked like you needed some help," he said, chuckling.

"I had it all covered."

"Tell that to the gods."

"Gods? Where are we?" Mark asked.

The warrior relaxed his muscles, easing the bowstring back to its original position. "You don't know? Obviously, you're new here. This is Egypt! Look around you. Can't you see?"

"All I see is a bunch of sand and human bodies. Is that what I'm supposed to see?"

"No, not exactly. Come on, I'll take you to my little house on the canyon. I'll explain more there." And with that, he walked off into the trees and rocks. Mark, not wanting to be left an easy target for monsters, stood and hurried after him.

As they neared the little clearing of trees on the edge of the canyon, Mark saw what the warrior meant by a "little" house. It was so small; it couldn't even be considered a house. More like a hut or a shack. It was one room with one window and a door. He wondered how the warrior could live like this. They walked inside with Mark having to bend down so that he could get in. The warrior then pulled up two chairs for them to sit down in. *Why two chairs?* he thought. This man could hardly get any visitors. When he sat, the other man began to talk almost immediately.

"I always knew you would come. I have foreseen your arrival for several decades. The gods told me of it. They said 'A time will come when a being of great power and a pure heart will appear from a bolt of fire, and he will vanquish the coming evil.' Months later, as the gods had said, an evil beyond any all of Egypt had ever seen arrived. This evil had one name: Ordel. He was once one of the elder gods, but he had been punished for his injustices. He is a massive being, made up entirely of black marble."

So that was the statue of Ordel in the temple. No wonder it teleported me to this dimension, or whatever it is, Mark thought.

The man continued to tell him his story. "I decided to become a warrior in this battle of good versus evil, and for years that is what I was. But then, not that long ago, I was approached by the God of Creation, Ptah, who promised me immortality if I would remain forever in their service. I took his offer and I have not aged since. And I have held my end of the bargain as well. I have fought for the gods for 50 years. And I have never wavered in my loyalty."

"But then, today, I was fighting Ordel's monsters when I saw a stream of fire shoot from the clouds. That is when I knew the prophecy was correct. Your arrival was real. I vowed that I would train you until the time was right for you to destroy Ordel."

"Wait, you expect me to defeat this Ordel character?" Mark exclaimed.

"No, not now at least, you would last 15 seconds at the most before he incinerated you. That is why I have prepared to train you. By the way, your first test is now. I hope you can outrun me to the training center."

"What?"

"Always expect that your opponent has an opening move. That is the first tip. Second tip: Climb with great agility, for if you fall, you die."

"Great tip. Now I know where the training center is at least."

"Yes, but I know where the footholds are."

"We'll see."

Mark trained for months and his physical abilities were at their fittest. He could outrun the old warrior, and climb the canyon better than a bug with glue on its feet. Even the old man was impressed, which Mark had learned was hard to do. Then, one day, everything changed.

"It is time," the warrior said.

"Huh?"

"It is time for you to face Ordel."

"But I'm not ready. I've only trained for five months."

"You have no choice. One good thing about immortality is that you figure out the signs that tell about future events. And I have seen many."

"What do you mean?" Mark was getting confused.

"I mean, now is my time to leave you. I have taught you all I can. And you must learn to stand on your own two feet." And with that, a dark shadow swirled around the old warrior and carried him into the sky.

Mark realized he was alone. This feeling was unfamiliar, as he had lived with the old man for five months. He also realized he felt sad. The warrior had become like family to Mark and it hurt to have him taken away like that. Mark decided that his friend was right. He needed to face the evil. That was the only way he could save Egypt and the old warrior.

So, Mark walked through the forest from which he had come five long months ago. As he got further along, he picked up his pace until he broke into a run. He ran and ran, as fast as he could, all the way to the edge of the trees. There, he slowed into a walk and crossed onto the battlefield where he had met the old man.

It was deserted. There were no bodies or warriors or monsters. Nothing. Just empty sand. Mark scanned all around, looking for any sign of danger, when he spotted the citadel. It was immense. The walls were made up of a mixture of black marble and the substance that had taken the warrior. Even though he hadn't seen its interior, Mark knew it was evil. Just because of one fact. The citadel was floating. And it wasn't a trick of the light. It was just hovering, suspended in mid-air. There was only one thing that could do that. Ordel. As Mark watched, a wave of orange and black energy erupted from the sides of the citadel. With this wave came a gravelly voice.

"Ah, look at our little hero. Come to save your friend? Or maybe all of this land? Or possibly both? Well, don't think it will be easy. I have some surprises in wait for you," the voice said.

But Mark, undisturbed by the voice's threat, just watched the citadel. It continued on like this for several moments, until he decided it was a waste of time to watch the building and moved towards the stronghold.

As he got closer, he felt an invisible barrier repelling him from his destination. But he persevered, and he was fifty meters from the space below the citadel when another energy wave erupted, followed by a surge of pain that ran through his body. It was the pain he had felt five months ago when he had first arrived in this land, only much greater in intensity. Mark felt his willpower being sapped from his body and his strength depleting. Suddenly, he was just like the Mark who he had come to this land; weak, ignorant, and nervous.

But he realized that if he gave up now, he would never defeat Ordel and save Egypt. So he fought the drain, and felt his strength returning and his willpower growing. He stood, making his way into a shuffle, still fighting the pain that threatened to consume him. Then he again heard that dark, gravelly voice, telling him to give in, to quit. But Mark would never give up. He continued to walk until he was right underneath the citadel.

For his efforts, the citadel rewarded him. A spiraling staircase lowered itself down so that he could climb aboard. *Strange,* Mark thought. *It's as if Ordel wants me to come in.* Pushing that thought away, he walked up the stairs and onto a ledge. As soon as he reached the top, he felt the barrier dissipate.

He came to a stone door, which he blew to smithereens with the sword he had found. *Such power,* Mark thought. *The sword could never do that before.* Then he walked into a long hallway. At the end of the hallway, he saw the old warrior hanging upside down from the ceiling.

Mark began to walk down the hall, but then paused. *This is too easy. It must be a trap,* he thought. And as if on cue, the tiles on the floor behind him collapsed, leaving him stranded. *I guess the only way to go is forward.*

He continued to walk down the hall, but felt a slight tingling as he neared the halfway point. He instinctively ducked as a burning arrow flew straight over his head, just merely an inch from his face. The tingling continued, and more arrows flew across the hall. But each time Mark dodged, and eventually he made it to the end of the hall.

Even though it appeared that no more arrows were coming, the tingling didn't stop. Suddenly it intensified, and he spun around, and just in time, too. Several black-marble arrows were headed straight for him, and there was no time to dodge. Knowing this was the end, he knelt, admitting defeat. But suddenly, he moved faster than he had ever moved before. He brought his sword up and began to deflect the arrows. Mark moved so fast his arms were a blur. Soon all of the arrows were in ruins on the ground. He turned around and continued through the citadel.

Mark walked until he came across another door. He opened this one, expecting the worst, but found nothing. So he continued walking. That is, until he found out that some of the tiles burst into flames. From then on, he proceeded with caution. Eventually, after a seared hand and two burnt feet later, he made it to yet another door. Without warning, the tingling sensation he had felt earlier started up, and the door swung open.

From inside, a booming voice shouted "Welcome to Hell! So, you made it past my three tests. Congratulations! You have made it far. But too bad. For it will all be in vain once I incinerate you!" the voice boomed.

Undeterred, Mark yelled, "If you are so powerful, why don't you show yourself!"

"Oh, a feisty one, eh? This means I will feel even more pleasure in destroying you." And with that, the floor began to rumble and crack, bursting into multiple fragments of rock. And within the gaping hole in the ground came the most vile and evil creature imaginable. It rose into the air, surrounded by a black and orange vortex of energy.

Its features were humanoid, except that it had no nose. Its hands were clawed and its chest rippled with muscles. Its skin was made of black marble. And all along its body ran cracks filled with molten rock.

"Ordel," Mark exclaimed.

"At your service! Or, rather, you will be at mine if I choose not to kill you!" the god roared.

"Well, then. Are we going to battle?"

"Oh yes, we shall battle," Ordel boomed.

His fist exploded in flames, and he slammed it into the ground behind Mark. The floor collapsed, leaving no escape route. Then he reared back and readied to crush the young hero. But at just the last moment, Mark leapt out of the way, barely escaping a painful demise.

"Stand still, vermin," Ordel bellowed loudly, and the elder god breathed fire all around the chamber, attempting to fry Mark. He dodged the flames and crawled onto Ordel's arm, which was still imbedded in the floor. He ran up the appendage and stood firmly on the beast's shoulder. Suddenly, the massive arm that had been left in the ground became unstuck, and it slapped at Mark, who easily dodged the blow. Then he slammed his sword into the shoulder and jumped off as the arm cracked and blew apart.

In tremendous pain, Ordel screamed in agony as he flailed about, sending rubble raining everywhere. This just caused him further pain. "Oh, that was a terrible mistake, mortal!"

With his remaining hand, the god grabbed one of the columns supporting the roof and swung it at Mark, who was also trying to dodge the falling debris. But despite this he managed to duck under the clumsy attack and threw his sword into his enemy's eye. The eye cracked and exploded, and the sword flew back to Mark.

By now, Ordel was practically incapacitated. Half of his head was missing and he was without one of his arms. As rock rained down around them, he moaned and shifted, shaking the ground.

"I may not be able to fight you now, but I'm not finished yet." As he said this, his body began to grow spiky rock protrusions to protect him. Mark, having not the slightest idea what he should do, ran circles around the beast, looking for a chink in the armor. In the end, his back seemed like the only place that he could hit, and, knowing he might have only one shot before Ordel recovered, sprinted right over the edge, jumping at the last moment. As he flew through the air, he felt time slowing, and he knew all his life had been leading up to this moment. In the second before he drove his sword into his enemy's back, he felt content. He had finally found his purpose.

Mark then found himself again plummeting onto the spiky back of the elder god of chaos, Ordel. As he neared his target, he felt the protrusions that had been erected puncturing his flesh. Before he had a moment to think about the pain, he was there, driving his sword into Ordel's back. The god bellowed, but was silenced when he exploded in enormous fragments of stone. Mark barely had time to cover himself before the entire building exploded in gas and energy. He landed on the ground below where the citadel had been. As the sound of the explosion quieted, thoughts crossed his mind. *I won,* and *Now what?*

As he pondered these thoughts, he did not notice the wisp of black smoke swirl down behind him and drop a small figure. "Don't care to see your teacher, eh?"

"What? It's you!" Mark exclaimed.

"Of course it's me. Who did you expect?"

"No one, in fact. I thought you were dead!"

"Not dead, just extremely proud that I taught the warrior who killed Ordel! I never would have said that was possible before now. I left you knowing that your chance of success was slim. Yet here you are."

"Here I am."

"By the way, what happened to…," he never got to finish. As he said those words, Mark's knees buckled and he collapsed into the old warriors arms.

"MARK!" he shouted. Mark's skin was turning pale and his eyes were glazing over. "What happened?"

But Mark didn't know. Then he remembered. The gas! It must have been some sort of nerve toxin! "Th-the gas… from the explosion. It was poison." But then he lost consciousness and died.

The warrior sobbed for many minutes, and then he too fell to the gas's ef

As Mark and the old warrior passed from the physical world to the Afterlife, they could almost hear Ordel's laugh. He laughed and laughed and laughed, all the way until the pair reached the gates of the Afterlife. There, they met a tall man. He wore Egyptian garb and looked at them with great satisfaction.

"I am Ptah, God of creation. You two have proven yourselves worthy in the face of overwhelming evil. This is your reward." As he said that, the gates opened, and a great light filled Mark's vision. "WELCOME, MIGHTY WARRIORS, TO THE AFTERLIFE!"

Kala's Quest

A girl is granted an unusual power in **KALA'S QUEST** *by* ***Eliana McComas**. Suddenly her power isn't so great when she gets an interesting assignment. In this story Kala goes on a journey to help solve the unnatural obstacle planted in her path.*

I added the last curve to the mini unicorn's horn. Then I heard a pop, a fizzing sound, and a sucking sound all at once. I jumped out of my chair, knocking it over. I glanced all around my room to see what was happening. There was nothing outside my room, and nothing in my room was happening.

All that time the sounds had been getting louder and louder. Soon it sounded like a tornado was in my room. I jumped onto my bed and buried myself under the covers trying to get away from all the noise.

All of a sudden the noise stopped. I peered out from under my covers to see what had happened. Nothing was out of place… until I glanced at my drawing desk. There, prancing on top of my desk, was the mini unicorn I had just drawn. I raced to my paper to see if my eyes were just playing tricks on me. My lead drawing was still there, but now colored in with watercolor.

"That's just what I planned to do! Color this in with watercolor!" I breathed.

The colors were perfectly how I had imagined them except more realistic than I had thought to draw it.

I pulled out another sheet of paper and drew three leaves on it, this time with a graphite pencil. Three perfectly formed leaves appeared-this time with less noise.

"Red, orange, and brown…with pastels. Just how I thought to draw them," I said in amazement.

Glancing around I saw a door in my wall that had never been there before. I threw in the unicorn and leaves, not really thinking. Then the door disappeared, showing that that room would only hold my magic drawings.

This is what happened five years before, in a certain bedroom of a certain house.

* * *

"Good morning! Are you ready for art?" boomed Mr. C.

"Yeah!" the class roared.

"Today we are going to start a new project. We are going to do pencil sketches…"

I jumped in my seat. "**Pencil** sketches?" I thought to myself.

"…of your own fantasy monster."

My eyes widened. "F-f-fantasy **monster**?" I said in a hoarse whisper. I gasped and started breathing heavily. "MONSTER, MONSTER, MONSTER…" was screaming in my head.

After school when Amica and I were walking home together, I stopped, turned, and faced Amica.

"Amica, I need to tell you something."

"Yeah, what?"

"Do you promise not to laugh or tell anybody?"

"I'm your BFF! Do you think I would?"

"OK, well, whenever I draw anything with a pencil it, umm, well… it comes to life," I said unhappily.

"What?"

"Yeah, all of my drawings come to life! I don't know how it happens. It just does!"

"This is *so* odd! I mean like, no one else has a power that I know of! Can you show me? Like, here and now?"

"Yeah…" I pulled out a scrap piece of paper and a pencil, and drew a daisy. It popped out into my hand. "See!"

"Wow!"

"I've tried basically every type of pencil that exists! And I have **no** idea of what I can do to get out of the art project so that I don't have to create a monster!"

"Let's go to your house. We can come up with solutions there."

"OK."

At my house Amica and I made chocolate chip cookies while thinking over my problem.

"There's no way out of it!" said Amica. "With Mr. C.'s strictness, and you being such a good drawer, he won't accept **any** excuse!"

"I know, and that is the problem."

Bing! beeped the oven, signaling to us that our cookies were done.

"I'll get the oven," I said. While I was pulling the cookies out of the oven I wondered aloud, "Maybe we should go to our secret meeting spot in the woods. It would be a good quiet place to think."

"What about the cookies?"

"Huh?" I said, not realizing I had said my thoughts out loud. "Oh! I guess we'll just bring them along."

Crunch, crunch, crunch went the leaves as we traveled along the path into the woods.

"Brrr! It's getting chilly! I hope it snows soon," Amica said.

"Hopefully we won't stay here long. It's cold," I said. "But the cookies will warm us up!" As I unwrapped the basket of cookies a delightful smell of chocolate wafted through the air. "Mmmm!"

"Yummy!"

We sat in silence for a while just munching on our crispy-on-the-outside, but gooey-on-the-inside chocolate chip cookies, and listening to the wind howl through the trees.

We started discussing my problem again, when a beggar woman stepped into the clearing.

"Hello, girls," the beggar woman said.

Amica gulped, "Hi?"

"I'm sorry if I'm bothering you girls. I just smelled the cookies and was wondering if I could have some."

"Sure, umm, take however many as you want," I said. I gawked at the beggar woman in surprise.

"Oh, thank you, dearies."

"Uh, you're welcome," said Amica.

The beggar woman sat down and ate her fill of the cookies. By the time that she was done there were only four cookies left.

"Oh you were so kind to me, so I will reward you…"

"What?" we both said, looking at the beggar woman and then at each other in confusion.

All of a sudden, the wind picked up, and a tornado of leaves formed around the beggar. The birds in the trees flew around the tornado. Then the tornado settled down, and instead of a beggar woman, inside of the leaves was a beautiful fairy. The birds settled down on top of the fairy's shoulders. The fairy was wearing a pale blue dress that looked like snow falling and shimmered whenever she moved. She had four bracelets, each themed with a different season. Her shoes were made from blossoming flowers. She had a circlet made of sunbeams, and in her hair were brightly-colored leaves. "I heard you saying that you had a problem. Did I not?" she said smiling. "My name's Chandi."

"Whoa," we both gasped.

"What? Are you surprised that I'm a fairy?" Chandi said giggling.

"Yeah! It's not like every day that you see a fairy," I said.

"Well, I guess that's true," said Chandi with a smirk. "I guess that we don't just turn up and show ourselves every day. But those chocolate chip cookies were good!"

"We made them ourselves," said Amica.

"I figured you did. Now to the point- I heard you saying that you had a problem. I can help fix problems. So what's your problem?"

"Well I… uh… whenever I draw something with a pencil it comes to life. I have, well, also Amica, we have an art assignment to draw a monster…with a pencil. I have **no** way to get out of it!" I said.

"My, my. You do have a problem… One sec." Chandi pulled out an odd-looking purple phone and called somebody. "Hey… Yeah… Order of giving number 18, it was chocolate chip cookies. So how… One has this problem… That's what I was getting at! Whatever! Whatever she draws comes to life… has this assignment… No! To draw a monster! What? OK. Sure… Thanks! Yeah, got it all here. Bye!"

"What was that about?" asked Amica.

"Oh, I was calling a more advanced fairy to see what you had to do to fix your problem."

"It's that hard?" I asked.

"Be quiet I want to hear what she's going to say!" Amica whispered into my ear.

"So, yeah, first you have to retrieve two pieces of wood from the Thorniage Troll Bridge in the middle of the forest. Then you have to go to the Whispering Meadow and collect a Silent Snowfall blossom. After that you have to go to the Flaming Fire Pits of Thorniage and light one of the pieces of wood you brought in one of the fire pits. If you put this in the pack it will stay lit. Finally you have to go to the Babbling Brook's source, the Waterfall of Wrath, and soak this cloth in its water. Then you come to my palace, and I make the potion to cure you. After that you go home."

"What did you just say?"

"She said we would have to go to the Thorniage Troll Bridge, the Whispering Meadow, the Flaming Fire Pits of Thorniage, and the Waterfall of Wrath and get stuff from them." I replied, a little confused myself.

"But... those aren't real places," said Amica.

"That's what I thought, too!" I replied. "Aren't they just legends? And so much stuff?" I asked Chandi.

"Do we really have to go to the Flaming Fire Pits, and the Waterfall of Wrath?" asked Amica.

"First off, yes, they aren't real places to you but... Well, I'm going to transport you to another world. There you'll be able to talk to all creatures, and most of those legends are true. Nobody there has probably ever seen humans before, so... OK. I will cast a spell on you to make you look like fairies; you will be able to fly. Secondly, I'm sorry, you have to go to the fire pits and the waterfall! I can tell you what you'll need to survive, though. Umm... Hey, if you have anything you want from home, tell me now so that you can start your journey now!"

"Whoa! Now? As in now?"

"Shouldn't we tell our parents?"

"Yes, right now, and nope! Your parents wouldn't believe you if you told them!"

"You're right. Well, I want my warmest pajamas, not the footies..." Amica continued listing items for a while.

I asked some questions, and Chandi said she would provide us with a mini oven that worked, a freezer box that would contain whatever food they wanted, the softest tents imaginable, running water, a map, a box to contain the items we collected, and a box that contained whatever clothes they needed for the day inside.

"I'll leave a note and cast a spell to make your parents not worry. OK?" said Chandi. "One last thing, everyone knows that the tradition in Thorniage is to help those on a true quest. Many, even dangerous beings, follow this custom. But, beware! Some care nothing for such manners and will try to hurt you greatly if they can."

"OK!" we replied and braced ourselves for the whirlwind Chandi sent at us.

When I opened my eyes we were in a completely new and different place, and a map was glittering from fairy dust in my hand, and a pack was glittering next to my feet on the ground. I glanced around for Amica and saw that she and I both had glistening wings on our backs. Our hair was done differently, and we had very different clothes on. "We really are fairies now," we murmured almost in unison.

"Chandi told me that before getting the wood from the troll bridge we should bake some chocolate chip cookies and place them far away so that the trolls would leave to eat the cookies," I told Amica.

"Sounds great to me," replied Amica sleepily.

In the morning I baked the cookies, and Amica scouted out where we were. She came back after an hour to tell me that the bridge was a half hour's walk away, but if we flew it would take twenty minutes. We decided to walk the first half of the way, so the trolls wouldn't be as close to the bridge when we got there. Then we would fly the second half of the way. We set out at once, telling a blue jay to uncover the basket of cookies in ten minutes.

Ten minutes had passed, we were about halfway to our destination, and the smell of fresh-baked cookies was in the air. Five minutes later we saw two hulking trolls coming down the path toward us. We ducked off the path while they passed.

"You know, Cahir, that I hate leaving the bridge unattended," the bigger of the two trolls said.

"Seriously, Ryan, we've guarded the bridge for years and no one has ever come by except for squirrels, rabbits, and other creatures like them. If we leave our post for a few minutes to eat those good-smelling cookies, nobody will care!" the second troll answered.

Once the two trolls were out of earshot I whispered to Amica, "Let's fly now!"

We flew down the path away from the trolls. When we reached the bridge I set to work prying off two pieces of wood from the bridge while Amica stood guard. After a couple of minutes of pulling with all my might I succeeded in getting two smaller planks from the bridge. We hurriedly stuffed them into the pouch Chandi had given us. We glanced around to see if the trolls were coming, and we heard their voices. We flew quickly across the bridge into the woods on the other side.

Once we were safely away from the bridge Amica asked me, "What do we have to collect next?"

"She said to collect a Silent Snowfall blossom from the Whispering Meadow," I answered.

"What do they look like?"

"Well, I think they look like snowflakes with silver dots on them if you look at them from above. They are shaped like lilies and grow in small clusters."

"Really?"

"That's what Chandi told me while you were sleeping earlier."

"Speaking of sleep, we should get some now!"

"OK. I'm tired myself."

The next day we set off for the Whispering Meadow. We arrived in good time and immediately started looking for the flower.

"I don't like it here. People say it's haunted, and there's so much mist!" Amica complained.

After five minutes of searching we heard a voice. "Stop! What are you doing?" said the voice.

Both Amica and I screamed.

"Stop screaming! You're hurting my ears!"

Amica frowned while I said in a hoarse whisper, "Show yourself."

Out of the mist came a green blob that slowly materialized, as it got closer, into a pixie.

"I guard this place. Now get your fairy butts outta here or tell me whatcha' doin'," the pixie said to us.

"We're on this quest thingy-ma-bob and have to get a Silent Snowfall blossom from here," Amica said impertinently.

"Well, well," the pixie said smugly.

"Are you going to let us or not?" demanded Amica.

The pixie, not knowing if they were powerful or bluffing, played it safe. "Of course I am! Silent Snowfalls are our most popular flower this time of year."

"Then can we get one?"

"Of course; go ahead. Just remember I'll be watching you if you take any other flower."

When we left I whispered to Amica, "I'm glad he didn't see through Chandi's disguise.

We gathered the flower and went all the way to the pits. Right before we entered the pits I pulled out one of the pieces of wood we had gotten from the bridge.

"Ready to go in?" I asked.

"Yeah," Amica answered.

We entered the Flaming Fire Pits expecting the demons and devils, goblins and ghouls, spirits and sprites, and all the other nasty magical creatures the Flaming Fire Pits would hold. Once inside we could swear we heard the smoke whispering to us, "Come this way."

"Hold it right there!" yelled a voice from within the flames and smoke. "Now who are you?" the voice said more cunningly.

"No one of consequence!" I said, a little snootily, to him.

"No one of consequence, eh? Well then, would you care to join me, no-one-of-consequence? On an outing?" the voice carried on, drawing beautiful scenes in my head. "You would be a queen. We would dance by the fire, and everything would be all right. The pits would blaze to our dance. I could make you a wreath of ashes to adorn your head…"

I started to walk toward the voice, mesmerized by the beautiful scenes he had planted in my head.

"NO!" Amica screamed. "NO, NO, NO! Don't go with him. He's evil!" Amica screamed and pulled me back.

"You little devil… We were just having fun."

"You're calling me a little devil? Why, you're probably a devil yourself!"

"And you're right. How did you guess?"

"Oh! You make me so mad! Calm down, calm down, and calm down! OK. We need some of your fire 'Mr. Devil' so *may* we get some from your pits?"

"Ha! It's 'Mr.' Pratt to you. Why do you need my fire, Miss No-one-of-consequence?"

"So Pratt is your name… Well, we need fire because we're on a quest!"

"A quest… Well, well, I guess I'll have to let my little adventurers go. Although we had a great time together!"

"Come on! Let's go!" Amica said to me.

We started to tiptoe toward the pits when a devil distracted us. Then other goblins, ghouls, and spirits started attacking us! We had been unexpectedly surrounded and there was no apparent escape. Flaming arrows were flying through the air, several came so close they singed my hair and wings. Other beasts were on foot with daggers and javelins, and not a few had maces. Magic spells were hurled toward us and we dodged them the best we could. Behind us we saw creatures suddenly frozen, turned into toads, and disappearing in a puff of smoke—all those who caught the full force of the fiendish spells we barely avoided. Finally I saw an opening among the throng, grabbed Amica and darted toward the gap, lugging Amica all the way. If not for all the confusion, *and* our fairy wings, we never would have had a chance.

Finally we dashed through the air to the closest pit before anyone could delay us any longer. Once the piece of wood caught fire we stuffed it into our bag. Then we flew at full speed out of the Flaming Fire Pits of Thorniage and up the coast.

The next day we tramped over to the waterfall. Once we got there we were amazed at what we saw. Unlike the myths telling the dangers of the Waterfall of Wrath, the waterfall looked like paradise. The waterfall bubbled over with rainbow-colored water, and had jungles on either side. We snuck through the forest and up to the waterfall's edge. There was no one around except for a crab and two rainbow trout splashing in the water.

"It's so amazing," I breathed, reaching down with the cloth to soak up the water.

"And soon that'll be all ya know," said a voice from behind me.

I jumped around, and in the crab's place was a human boy with a knife in his hand. I gasped confusedly and then murmured, "Changeling. It has to be." I then turned and whispered to Amica, "Changelings are probably the most vicious type of magic being when they are determined to do or get something"

"Aye, you're right. Now whatcha' doin' round here with my water?" the changeling asked furiously.

"Well, we're on a quest, and we need some of your water," I said timidly.

"What's so important 'bout dis quest?" the changeling said, more curiously this time, but still mad.

"I have this power and umm... well... I need the water to control it."

"Yer guys are comin' with me!" the changeling said, shoving the knife at my throat and dragging Amica along behind him.

We entered a sparking cave filled with gems of so many different colors, there were even more colors than all the colors of the rainbow. The changeling strode through the opening and into a back corridor. He then led us though several dark and damp winding passages, and we ended up in a small room. The changeling gave us some food, handed us a candle, and said that he would be back in a couple of hours with more food. Then the changeling left the room, and we heard the click of the lock once the changeling closed the door.

"What was that about? He almost killed you! Are you OK? He almost killed you! Did you see he had a knife? He almost killed you with it! That boy is creepy. What do you think about him? Creepiness can kill people! Did you know that? I'm confused! Weren't things supposed to go smoothly and easily? I'm hungry! We might get killed if we eat the food. Do you think we should eat the food? To eat or to stay alive is the question. Do you think it's poisoned? I hope not because I'm hungry," Amica said hurriedly.

"Slow down!" I laughed. "What did you just say-ask-exclaim to me? And didn't you, like, repeat that he almost killed me a lot?"

Amica asked her questions again, and I replied, telling her that his knife was obviously very blunt, that I would just eat the food, and that I thought he was weird. The food turned out to not be poisoned or drugged, but we still slept fitfully.

The next day he questioned us for hours, and he finally saw we meant no harm and were on a true quest. We had lunch there, and then he led us out to where we had come from. We paused in the jewel-filled cavern, and he let us take a couple of the jewels.

"Sorry! 'Course you can take some! If that's all you 'bout," the changeling said, its scowl now a smile. "I had to just check. Ya never know these days! People jus wannin to have all dat power!" While we walked through the passages he explained, "Err, err, sorry 'gain! That's just my act if somer-body comes round, wannin' to steal all dis water. Ya know? It would make his self be more powerful than me so he can go and steal the cup of eternal life."

"Interesting story," I said while soaking the cloth with some disbelief. (If his story *was* true, though, I might want to come back here someday.)

Soon we were on our way to Chandi's palace. We flew and ran to Chandi's palace, and entered gasping for breath…. We were welcomed in right away, and once Chandi came to us she took the ingredients and set to work. After about two hours Chandi came out of the room she was working in with a purple bottle.

Chandi told me to drink it all right now. Right before I draw anything I have to think "on" if I want it to come to life, and "off" if I want it to just be a drawing. She also gave me a purple sparkly feather. The feather would make my drawings that came to life disappear.

When I got home I thought "on" and drew a daisy. It came to life. Then I thought "off" and drew a tulip. The tulip didn't come to life. I was so excited! The potion worked, and now I wouldn't have to worry about art assignments anymore! Right away I thought "off" and set to work drawing my monster. It was the most magnificent thing I have ever drawn. I remember staring at its beauty right before I finished it. Trembling, I brought my hand down to make the last stroke. "What if the potion didn't work? What if it all goes wrong?" I thought to myself. Gulping, I set my pencil to the task of finishing the "beast" I had drawn. I lifted the pencil off of the paper and nothing happened! I was so happy and proud of myself!

The next day I couldn't wait until art. When it was time for art I handed in my drawing first thing.

"What a beautiful monster!" Mr. C said. "I was thinking most people would draw ogres, dragons, and sea-serpent type things. But you exceeded my expectations once again! I shall show your drawing to **all** of my classes!"

I smiled to myself. It was going to be a good year in art. I know because my beastie proved that (which was a mix of dragon, whale, horse, tiger and sphinx). I was so glad; now I have a magical power that **I** can control.

I added the last curve to the mini unicorn's horn. Then I heard a pop, a fizzing sound, and a sucking sound all at once. There, prancing on top of my desk was the mini unicorn I had just drawn. I raced to my paper to see if my eyes were just playing tricks on me. There my lead drawing still was, but now colored in with watercolor.

This is what happened five years before, in a certain bedroom of a certain house.

That house is my house. That bedroom is my bedroom. That power of creating drawings that come to life is my power. Except now I can do more things with my power. I can control it, and maybe expand its use. I will use it for the greater good of the world!

"Like that's ever going to happen!" exclaimed Amica.

I have my drawing power, and Amica has her own power. Her power is the power to talk anyone into anything. We both have another power between us, though. It's the power of friendship.

Kaos

In normal suburbia an abnormal event occurs. A teenager named Eric releases a demon lord and must stop it before it kills everyone he loves. The horror awaits you within the words of **KAOS** *by* ***Alexander Trombley.***

The Neanderthals approached the shining black shrine. The black temple had been there as long as they could remember. They grew restless, as the adrenaline pumped through their veins, one decided this was enough wait and rushed into the temple. It seemed as if the temple reacted to the oncoming warrior and dropped one of its pillars to block the attempt at invasion. The pillar crushed the Neanderthal and this angered his brethren. They attacked the temple itself with such ferocity that it could have left the strongest man in all the lands curled up in ball shivering with fear, but alas the temple was not affected. They sent wave after wave of men to destroy this temple of godly power but each of them fell to their knees with exhaustion or dead from the various revolts of the temple. At some point, among the chaos, a man of great religion spoke to his fellow tribe members, saying that this was a shrine to the gods and that they must stop their attempt at defacement unless they wished to anger the gods to whom they loved and prayed. The man was wrong. This wasn't a shrine at all; it was a prison to a creature which man later deemed the devil.

The ranting and attacks went on for centuries with the original people dying, leaving fewer relatives until the population dropped to almost nothing. One man thought that if the building were indestructible, it would make the perfect weapon, and so he set off to gather pieces of rubble left behind by the prison's attacks and crafted a sword.

The sword has passed through the tribe for five hundred years, and it rests in the hands of an irresponsible young man by the name of Eric Ment. Eric has had an uneventful life, and has been feuding with his best friend over the fact that Eric's old girlfriend was now his friend's girlfriend.

Eric strode into his dreadfully empty house wearing his black shirt and a plaid overshirt strewn open and flowing in the wind. He wore jeans with tears on his knees and frayed hems. His black Converse were splattered with mud. Eric threw his blue book bag on the ground, intent on releasing his fury. *Why would my best friend do this to me? Why would he betray my trust?* he thought. He saw what he would do to release his anger immediately, when he looked up from his current fascination with kicking his mom's metal vase, when he saw an obsidian sword resting in a glass case. He broke the glass and took the sword, swinging it down and shattering it upon the floor. Eric felt power shoot through his arms and fell to the floor gasping in pain. He struggled to get up, but the force that shot through him had him pinned to the floor. Eventually, the pain subsided and so did the force, leaving him lying on the floor exhausted from his struggle and lying next to a shard of obsidian that had cut a gash in his head.

Eric felt like a god; his body tingled with the power of anyone and everyone who had ever died, it felt like he could do anything even though blood was pooling around his head. Eric peeled himself off the ground and discovered to his dismay the sword that had been broken mere seconds before had regained its original shape. Eric felt compelled to grab the sword. His flesh melted at the touch of the handle. Eric screamed with pain. He released his grip on the handle and watched it fall to the ground as though the only thing capable of handling it was gravity. Eric looked at his hand and found carved into his flesh was the symbol known as the pentagon. Eric went to bed strangely exhausted by this encounter, yet still exhilarated by the power.

Eric wondered when his parents would be getting back from their business trip. The next morning he woke up and continued his weekly schedule: waking up, dressing, eating, running as fast as he could to catch the bus as it turned the corner driving away, and riding his bike the lonely five miles to school. Eric found himself wondering when his parents were going to come back so that he didn't have to be "babysat" by his house sitter. Since he shattered the sword about three weeks ago his five closest friends had disappeared. During the fourth week the principal made an announcement at an assembly. Five students, his closest friends, had been either injured by bizarre incidents or stricken ill with some new strange disease.

Eric called his friends but none answered. Finally, he decided to visit each of his friends. Each time he found a jarred door, which swung open placidly upon his arrival, and each time he found that all that was left to greet him were scorch marks and signs of struggle.

Eventually, he found himself standing at the last house left and found bullet shells and burn marks that looked like feet. Eric smelt the rancid odor of death. He rounded the corner to his friend's room and found the bed shredded. Before he registered that he was moving, he was at the bed. He found himself looking at a rope. Eric reached for the rope, grabbed it, and pulled on it. The moment that Eric pulled the rope dummies swung down, hung by their feet. The dummies were made to look like his friends; one had its throat cut with stuffing falling out, one lacked all of its limbs, one seemed as pale as a ghost with fake bile dribbling down his shirt. The dummies twisted around the rope turning unnaturally until it reached the fifth body, it stopped there with a real person, a dead person, looking at him. The body hung by its throat, its eyes rolled back in his head, spit dribbled out of its mouth and that is when things became even worse. Invisible blades seemed to stab the body through its chest. Blood started to bleed through its white shirt. Eric fell back and scrambled to the opposite wall. He was puking in the corner on the other side of the room. He heard footsteps walking towards him. He yelled, "Who are you, what are you, why do you taunt me?" Eric started to cry, tears gushing out of his eyes, "Why are you doing this to me, why are you killing my friends?" Eric wailed at the lifeless room.

"Eric, I stalk you because you are going to kill me, and as a last thought for you, what makes you think I only killed your friends? When was the last time you spoke with your parents?"

The words echoed around Eric's head. The house burst into flames. Eric ran down the hallway, fire burning his hair off at the roots. He grabbed a knife from the kitchen and ran out the door. Thinking he was the specter coming to finish his work, Eric attacked a pedestrian and ran. Eric felt the gush of warm air hit his bare, burnt back. Eric sprinted home. He called the motel his parents were staying at and heard that his parents had had an accident. All that was found was a rounded, smooth, glassy piece of obsidian.

Eric crawled into his bed, burn marks covering his body. He cocooned himself in blankets and went to sleep. He heard voices calling him in his dreams. A dark shroud circled his unconscious body. Eric gasped as the darkness plunged into his chest.

The next day, Eric went to school with only one glove. He was dressed in a dark jean jacket; he wore a black Pixies shirt under that. He wore pitch-black jeans and black Converse. When he walked through the giant glass double-door he was confronted with his "friend." His ex-best friend attempted to start a conversation with Eric. "Hello, Eri…"

Eric cut him short, "Don't attempt to talk to me! The damage is done and you have caused it."

As Eric strode away his former friend called out, "What have you got to be angry about? Last time I checked, you two broke up."

Eric nearly broke the door as he threw it aside in his frustration.

As the day progressed, Eric became more and more flustered as he thought of how the young man he talked to hours before had caused the deaths of his five closest friends, indirectly or not. After all, it was his anger at this child that caused him to break the sword.

At the end of the day, Eric hid in the shrubbery at the park near his friend's house. As his friend walked around the corner, Eric drew a knife from its sheath hidden under his jacket. Eric pounced on the lad and stabbed him in the back, making sure to hide his face from his victim. As Eric ran away leaving the young man sprawled on the ground with blood seeping out of his back, a dark cloud seeped out of his body and formed into the shape of a man.

Eric arrived home out of breath. He rested on the couch turning the bloodied knife over in his hand. He felt the need to run. He ran out the door and found that his feet carried themselves in the direction of his former-best friend's house. As he neared the house, his feet carried him towards the doorway faster and faster until he was tripping on every step. Eric plunged through the front door. It seems that his feet had done their job and it was his hands' turn to work, for they reached out for the handle to the living room. As his hands got closer to the diamond doorknob, a heat started to build until he felt like his hands were on fire. Eric twisted the doorknob and found that a man in a dark uniform awaited him.

The man was no man at all; he was a half-god. Eric fell back to the door, felt for the handle, and felt melted metal instead. Eric then recalled two things; one was that he had been told stories of a demon lord that had tried to kill his earlier kinsfolk. The other was that the handle on this side of the door was pure gold. Eric cursed at the stupor at which the family held themselves, believing that they should have nothing but perfection. If the creature facing him had created the flames that melted the handle, then he was the lord named Kaos who set out to kill his kinsfolk to claim the name of a god. Eric had to test his theory though because he could not kill an innocent man.

Eric inched along the wall to the glass window surrounded by steel. Eric felt for the latch. His hand gripped the latch and it melted. Eric charged at Kaos and found the obsidian sword in his hand. The creature dodged leaving Eric off-balance. Kaos returned the favor and attacked in a flurry of movements, traveling too fast for the human eye to see. Eric felt the knee before he saw it. He was sent flying by a knee cloaked in a shroud of darkness. Eric's ribs were crushed, but he somehow managed to stand up. He sent the sword hurling through the air. The sword struck Kaos square in the chest. Kaos fell to the floor.

The end of Kaos was not as expected of a demon lord. He did not spew flames from his mouth or melt; he simply fell over and disappeared. Eric felt raw power tingling surge through his body. He then left the plane of existence; his body was engulfed in a cloak of darkness. He emerged sitting on glassy, black, stone throne. Eric now knew that he had absorbed Kaos and that the sole meaning of his existence was to defeat and become the Lord of Demons.

Living in a Daydream

Anne, a lonely sixth-grader attending Berkshire Middle School, lived in her daydream world. All she wanted was some peace and quiet, but she got more than she hoped for. Find out how her dream went wrong in **LIVING IN A DAYDREAM** *by* **Samantha Zerafa**.

Anne was the kind of person who sat in a corner in school all day and daydreamed. She always visited her imaginary world in her mind where her life was perfect, or at least what she thought was perfect. She thought her actual life was terrible and cruel. She believed life, as a sixth-grader at Berkshire, was torture. She got bad grades, she didn't have any real friends, and she thought everyone hated her. The only reason her life was like this is because she never tried, she just fixed it in her fake world and pretended it was all better. In Anne's world, she was the most popular person in school, and all of the teachers adored her. Comparing that life to her real life is like comparing copper to gold, good but not amazing, to gold, expensive and perfect.

It was one of the first nice days of the school year. The sun was glaring, all the snow had turned into puddles, and we were allowed to go outside for noon recess. Anne had just finished her lunch and was rushing to the library with her head down in her book. She didn't like reading, she liked writing, but she used the book to pretend to read when she was lost in her daydream world. She entered the library and rushed to a chair in the corner where she sat alone every day. "Hi Anne," said a girl named Mary. She always tried to talk to Anne and be her friend, but Anne was too busy feeling bad for herself to notice.

Anne looked up and quietly said, "Hi."

"Do you want to go outside with me?" Mary asked. "It's really warm."

Anne looked back down at her book and the girl walked away. *I wish that everyone would just leave so I can daydream in peace. I hate how teachers always tell me to focus. They don't get it! Neither do my parents; no one understands what it's like to be me,* Anne thought.

Anne sighed and went back to her daydream. She wished that everyone would just disappear so she could have space to think without interruption. She stayed in her mind for a long time, thinking about how school would be if she were popular.

After awhile Anne peered at the clock and saw that it was time to go to her next class. She quickly walked to her math class so she wouldn't be late. She was too busy thinking about how unfair homework was and she didn't notice that nobody was in the hall. When she walked into the class, nobody was there either, but this time she noticed. "I bet they just misbehaved and were held outside for bad behavior," she said out loud.

Anne waited and waited and waited, but she didn't see one person. "I didn't want this!" she screamed. "I just wanted some time to think. I just wanted to go to my perfect world where I have friends."

She walked outside the library to try to find someone, anyone, but of course no one was there. All of it finally caught up to her. The realization of what she had done hit her with full force like a kick in the stomach. She felt dizzy and sick as she noticed the world around her, empty and alone. Even the smell in the air was empty. It didn't smell like students or teachers, it just smelled like plain old air.

She walked out the front doors of the school. The world outside was scary and unwelcoming as cold air blew in her face, but the worst part of it was the sound. Dead silence, no children playing, no birds chirping, not one thing could be heard.

"It isn't true, it just can't be," Anne shrieked, shattering the silence.

She ran as fast as she could down the street and didn't stop. She knocked on every door, rang every bell, and looked in every back yard, with no success. She turned corner after corner, and kept running and searching. She was so frustrated and so sad at the same time that she hadn't noticed how far she had run.

Anne didn't stop running until she tripped on a branch, hurt her foot and hit her head really hard. She was at least three miles away from the school and had no idea where she was. She was lost in a silent, empty world with no one to help her. She felt something warm running down her cheek and she wasn't sure if it were blood or tears. She thought, *This makes me realize that I depend on my dreams too much. I need to make real friends and try in school instead of pushing it aside when something goes wrong. I deserved this punishment.* Anne's head hurt terribly, and she was sure her ankle was broken. She decided to rest, so she lay down and silently cried herself to sleep.

She heard a faint noise in her dream that said, "You have now learned," but that was her only dream.

Anne woke up in a dark room and started screaming at the top of her lungs because she had no idea where she was. The lights turned on fast and several people rushed to her side. She saw her mom, her dad, Mary, and a nurse. "What happened?" she demanded, still very confused.

Anne looked around and found out that she was in a hospital room with one of those long gowns on. She had a bandage on her ankle and her forehead. She felt sore when she moved so Anne lay back against the pillow. Anne's mom explained that Mary had gone to the office when she didn't see Anne in math class, so they went searching and found me a few miles north laying on the ground bleeding. Anne explained to them that she had wished everyone had left the earth and it came true, so she went looking for people then tripped and fell. Of course no one believed her, but she knew it happened.

A few months later, Anne was being counseled to help her with schoolwork, and because her parents think that she has issues because of the hospital accident. Anne and Mary are now best friends, and Anne has given up daydreaming for good. She is now a writer, who wrote a very true story called "Living in a Daydream."

The Lost Tomb

In **THE LOST TOMB** *by* ***Chester Rogers***, *two students go inside a pyramid to find King Khufu's tomb to see what he really looks like.*

Mrs. Babich's sixth hour class went on a field trip to Egypt. A student named Corey had a crush on a classmate named Rosa. She was half-Egyptian. Ever since the fourth grade, Corey thought Rosa was fascinating and beautiful. Corey even picked flowers for Rosa so he could tell her how he felt about her. He had forgotten to water the flowers, so Rosa didn't think he liked her.

While they were taking a tour with Mr. Baruti in Cairo, Corey grabbed her hand and said, "Let's go find King Khufu's tomb."

She had always wanted to find it, so she said, "Okay." While they were looking for it they found this large pyramid and Rosa said, "This is it." Since Rosa learned and understood what Egyptian words were, she found a sign with Egyptian letters on it that read, "Khufu the Great Pyramid Builder." After she had spoken those words out loud, the large doors opened and they held hands as they entered the pyramid.

Next, Corey and Rosa found a small room with gold and treasure inside. It was a tomb. They were so excited that they were so close to touching the beautiful jewels. Rosa gently picked up a necklace with hieroglyphs that read, "If you find this necklace, you will have wealth in your family." Suddenly, they heard a rumbling sound coming from the ceiling. Just then, huge skeleton bodies fell down upon them.

Rosa screamed, "Ahhh!"

Corey, trying to be brave said, "Follow me, Rosa!"

Corey grabbed a silver sword and he slashed his way through the skeletons. The guards had found him escaping and they had swords also. Then, they started to fight against Corey, so he tried to get Rosa out of the tomb and he did by running through the doorway. The skeleton bodies followed them and suddenly, the door closed after Corey and Rosa had left the tomb. So the skeleton bodies were crushed as the door closed upon them.

Rosa and Corey continued walking through tunnels, finding more rooms with artifacts, and finally saw a light at the end of the tunnel. But off to the side was a sarcophagus that read, "Khufu the Great and Mighty Pharaoh." They opened it and they saw Khufu's mummy. They saw another sarcophagus; it was small, so it could have been his unknown child or friend. So they closed it up and headed out of the pyramid. As they got out of the pyramid, Rosa kissed Corey, and he was now Rosa's boyfriend.

Michael and the Mysterious Hole

When a boy discovers that his mother is gone his life gets changed forever. In **MICHAEL AND THE MYSTERIOUS HOLE** *by* **Malia White***, the boy does not know if this is real or not.*

Michael was coming home from Stroh's Middle School. The bus dropped him off right at his house. *Boom! Crash! Bang!* He heard loud noises coming from his house, and he ran inside. When Michael got into the house he saw that the house was all messy. He was very frightened. Michael shouted, "Mom, where are you?" There was no answer, so he tried again, "Mom!" There was still no answer, so he cautiously looked around the house. Michael could not find his mom anywhere, and he started to panic.

Michael decided to look outside. He looked around his backyard and had no luck. He needed to think calmly, so he sat against a tree, and in a few minutes he fell right through the ground! The tree had a sensor in it that detected his movement. It made the ground open up.

Michael found himself underground, which looked exactly like the same place he fell from. The sky was gray in the underworld and blue in the real world. He said, "That was really weird!" as his voice trembled and his body shook. He started to look around with a confused look on his face.

The sky turned a darker gray. Thunder and lightning started, and then heavy rain poured down. He could see something coming at him. It looked like it was flying at first. When it got closer, he could see that it was huge and walking on many legs.

Michael was terrified. His heart raced faster, and he started to shiver from the cold rain. He was afraid the thing that was getting bigger was going to kill him. He looked down to see if there was something to use as a weapon and couldn't find anything. Michael looked up again and found that the thing was getting closer and closer to him.

He found out that "the thing" was a huge robot. Its body was shiny silver aluminum, and it had two black eyes. It had six legs and claws instead of hands. The robot was over two stories high.

Michael needed a weapon. He remembered his great grandpa's sword in their garage and raced to get it. He ran from the garage and shouted, "I have a weapon and I'm not afraid to use it!"

The robot was coming faster and faster. Michael looked up and saw how huge the robot was. He told himself to be brave and looked for what made the robot function. He saw red, blue, and green cords which he thought could provide power for the robot. Michael knew he couldn't reach the cords. He would have to find another way to fight the robot.

The robot said, "Rahhhhhhhhhhh!" just as Michael chopped off two of the robot's legs. The robot got really angry and slashed at Michael. He ducked just in time and cut off one more leg. He could see electricity coming out of the robot's legs. The robot's legs jerked, and it sparked electricity at Michael. He blocked it with his sword. The electricity bounced off the sword and went right back to the robot, and he went down, down, down. The robot was dead. The robot had sparks of electricity coming out of it.

Michael ran away from the robot as fast as he could and when he looked back he ran into a pole! He was unconscious....

Michael woke up in a forest and had no idea how he had gotten there. He felt that someone had helped him. But who? The forest looked like no other forest. It was all dark and foggy. The sky was gray, the trees had no leaves, and there were a lot of owls. He got up and looked around.

In the distance he saw something big and white. Michael slowly walked toward an object in the fog. When he finally reached the big white object, Michael discovered that it was a building. Michael opened the door and walked in. He looked around. He walked down a long hallway, saw a window, and could not help looking in.

Michael was surprised to see his mother tied to a chair and a man watching her. He heard the man watching his mother say, "I have you trapped now and the boy will never find you."

Michael looked around to find an entrance to the room where he wouldn't be caught. He found a vent that he could climb through to enter the room. Michael climbed onto a ledge and into the vent. He started to crawl in order to find the room where his mother was. Finally he found the room when he heard her voice and peeked through the grate. He started listening to what the man was saying. When the man left, Michael climbed down from the vent, which startled his mother. She looked relieved when he started to untie his mother.

He asked his mother what had happened, and she said, "The man captured me when you were coming home from school. Furniture and dishes were crashing as I fought to get away. He brought me here to get his revenge."

Michael whispered, "Why would he want to get revenge?"

His mother whispered, "Don't you remember that your dad is on a secret mission in India to keep something safe? He wouldn't tell us for our safety."

"Finally, I got you untied; now let's get out of here!" Michael whispered.

Before they could even get to the door, the man came back and said, "Where do you think you are going, little boy?" The man punched Michael extremely hard in the gut, and Michael fell. He could not get up for a while. The man laughed at Michael and turned around. At that moment Michael's mother hit him in the head with the chair she had been tied to. The man fell hard, and Michael and his mother thought he was unconscious. They started to run for their lives.

When they looked back they saw an army of men chasing them! They ran faster and faster. They ran into a dead-end hallway and started to panic. They started to bang and kick the wall, but nothing happened. The army was getting closer and closer to them. They leaned against the wall when the army was about one yard away. The wall rotated, and they fell into a dark tube.

They landed in the yard of their house! Michael's mother said, "That was really weird. One moment we were being chased by an army, and now we are back at home."

While his mother was talking, Michael looked in the distance. He thought he saw something moving. After Michael turned around his mother screamed, and then fainted. Michael saw that another robot had followed them. It looked exactly the same as the first one.

"I know how to deal with you!" Michael shouted. He grabbed his sword and started to chop off the robot's legs. The robot swung two of his legs at Michael and missed him. Michael ran under the robot's legs and cut off four of them. Down the robot fell, and sparks went flying.

Michael ran to his mother and took her inside the house. She woke up and asked what happened. Michael said, "A robot came and chased us and I killed the robot, but don't worry about it."

There was a huge swirl of dust outside about the size of their roof. The kidnapper popped up from the hole in the ground by the tree. He was holding a spear and told Michael to give his mother back to him. Michael screamed, "No!"

The kidnapper said, "Well, in that case," and threw the spear at them. Michael caught the spear in midair and dropped it. He then pushed the man down.

Something weird happened. There was a whirlpool that sucked the kidnapper down into the ground. At that moment, a friendly-looking man popped up from the hole next to the tree and said, "Do not be alarmed. I am Eric, a friend of your dad's. I helped you along your journey. My mission was to only help you, Michael. I carried you to the forest that would lead you to your mother. Then I went back to kill the rest of the robots. In order for you and your mother to be safe we need to cut down that tree. Whenever the sensor on the tree sees movement it opens the entrance to the underworld. Cutting down that tree will seal the evil underworld forever. You did a good job, Michael. Your dad would be really proud of you."

Missing

*In **MISSING** by **Alison Rhen**, will Nicki's friends find her in time, or will her kidnapper get to her first?*

Nicki was the type who didn't say much. One Saturday night she was supposed to hang out with her best friends in the whole world, Alexis and Joanna. It was night time as she was driving to go meet them at a club. When Nicki got to a four-way stop, instead of taking a left she took a right. About a mile and a half down the bumpy unpaved road Nicki noticed that she was coming up to something that looked like a warehouse. She hopped out and went to check it out.

As she was walking up and down the empty street, she saw a little flicker of light. She decided to try and find it. She walked faster and faster until she found the light. It led her to a door, but the door was locked. Nicki reached up to her hair, pulled out a bobby pin, and tried to pick the lock. Even that did not work.

She had seen boxes under the window. She thought she would climb up them and see what was inside. After her eyes met the window she pressed her face to the cool glass.

She saw two men. At that moment she recalled a newscast she and her mom had watched. It was a breaking news alert. Two men had broken into the historical museum and taken a necklace. She had also seen the video of the two taking it, and realized that was them. Without thinking she screamed as loud as she could.

The two men ran out and tried to grab her. She was running as fast as a lion. She hopped in her car and drove off at around 150 miles an hour, and was soon reunited with her friends.

These three were close. They did everything together, but she never told about what happened.

One March day, the three girls were walking home with a big group of 11th-graders. Alexis, Joanna, and Nicki were in the back of the group when Alexis heard a car following them. As she turned around two men fully dressed in black started walking towards them. The girls (out of complete fright) ran to the front of the pack of people.

BANG! One of the men had a gun. He shot and hurt two of the kids, and he stopped at nothing to get to Nicki. He kidnapped Nicki and one other 11th-grader. The other person was named Joe Green. Joe looked like something straight out of a surfer's magazine. He had long dark golden hair, not far off from Nicki's. From the back not many people could tell them apart, which is why the man in black grabbed them both.

One year later to the day Nicki had been taken, Alexis, Joanna, and their mothers all went over to Nicki's mom's house. Her mom, Emma, had been very lonely since Nicki's dad left her the last year. When they arrived, Mrs. Lone was drenched in tears.

They were normally very polite girls, but today they ran right past her and went straight up to Nicki's old bedroom. As they swung open the door, they saw dust everywhere. Apparently from the look of things Mrs. Lone was too upset to go up there.

As Joanna was looking at her clothes she heard a noise coming for the wall. She looked over and saw something being engraved in the wall. Joanna ran out of the room screaming. Alexis walked over to where Joanna had been the second before to see what was being written. When Joanna came back in, the two read out loud, "Your friend is ok, go to this place at this time, or she won't be." The place was Ireland, and the time was the following Monday. It was one week away. Monday was fast approaching. All they could think about was the lie they were going to say.

As the night grew darker the two girls sped as fast as they could down to the railroad tracks. When their tires meet the rusty tracks they stood and waited for the train to slow down just enough so that they could jump on. They could hear the *click clack* of the wheels hitting the side of the tracks. The train was going around 35 miles per hour (which is slow for a train; it must have just been at a stop, and was starting up again). As the train grew near the two hopped off their bikes and got ready for a big leap on. "Ready, 1, 2, 3!" Alexis shouted, and at that moment they bent down as far as they could. Then they jumped for an open train car.

They both landed on their side. The car was so small that their feet had to hang out of the side. From then it was smooth sailing, or so they thought.

When the train arrived near their destination they grabbed their stuff and ran as fast as they could to where the message had instructed. It was a sea cave.

Joanna started freaking out. She turned around and started to run the other way. But Alexis pulled her back, and they walked slowly into the cave. Thanks to Joanna acting like a runaway two-year-old, the flashlight had fallen out of Joanna's backpack and broken.

As they got farther in, the cave got darker. Walking side by side, they tripped over something. The "thing" had long golden hair like Nicki, a small nose like her, and the same little heart-shaped birthmark just left of her chin. Alexis screamed, "NICKI IS THAT YOU?"

All of a sudden the body moved. "What, who is that?"

"Nicki, it's us, Alexis and Joanna."

"Oh, guys, you found me!"

"Yeah, thanks to that ghost writing," Joanna said.

"I know what that was; it was the other guy the dude took, but he killed him like a week ago."

Alexis butted in, "So his spirit must have come to warn us so the same thing didn't happen to you."

"Well, that's nice and all, but I want to get out here," Joanna said with a hint of sarcasm. So all three got up and ran out and back to the train station.

15 hours later

"Are you ready?" Alexis asked.

"Yup! All I want is to be with my mom."

When they walked in the door all three moms ran to them. "Where were you? Are you ok? Wait, is that NICKI!"

After they all calmed down, Alexis and Joanna were grounded for life, but that didn't matter. The three of them were together for life, grounded or not.

Monster Hospital

An unintentional accident leaves Sloan fighting for her life and for the survival of the hospital. She is faced with the most challenging episode of her life. Will the hospital be saved? Find out in **MONSTER HOSPITAL**, *by **Sloan Kanat**.*

Sloan was hanging out with her friends in her living room. She went in the kitchen to make some popcorn for herself and her friends when her friends heard, "Oooooowwwww my lip!"

"Are you all right?" Sloan's friend called.

"No! Go get my parents right now!" Sloan cried.

Her other friend came running in. "Oh what happened?" she asked.

Sloan yelled, "Where are my parents?"

Her parents came running down the stairs. Sloan's mom said, "Girls, I am going to need you to go home now. Sloan's dad will take you. Please go and get into the car."

Sloan and her mom arrived at the hospital with Sloan's dad arriving about ten minutes after them. They were waiting in the ER when a doctor ushered Sloan to a room behind two double doors and told her parents they were not allowed to come back under any circumstances. The door to the room had number 19823764500IUVSRT, which was very unusual for a hospital. The room was a lifeless tan color. There was a stethoscope and a few other medical instruments sitting lifelessly on the counter. There were no windows, just the counter with the simple tools. Then she looked behind her. The creepiest thing she had ever seen was a giant needle the size of a hockey stick.

The next thing she knew she was about to be poked with the monstrous needle right into her forehead. She screamed and ran away from the gigantic needle. Then she crept into an empty room, or so she thought. She took two steps into the room and then—*boom*! She dropped through the floor into a trap.

Then she turned around and standing there was the boss of all the evil doctors, Ignolio. He was the most evil doctor in the entire universe. People shiver at the sound of his name and now Sloan knew why. All he said was, "Why are you in my lair?"

Sloan barely could speak but managed to sputter these few words out, "I just ran in here and I fell through the door."

"I can see that," he said.

"I'm sorry," she stammered. "I...I will be leaving now."

"Not so fast," he declared. "I will be watching you. Here is the door."

She bolted out the door. The door shut behind her. She ran even though she had no clue where she was going. Finally, she needed to stop and take a breath. She looked down, up, to the right, then the left, in front, and behind her. There was nothing. She was relieved, and then she heard a faint noise coming from under the floor. Sloan put her ear to the ground and listened. It sounded like struggling and yelling. She knocked on the floor and all the noise stopped. It was silent, too silent.

She looked up and what she saw was scarier than Ignolio. It was a swarm of angry zombies who looked very, very, hungry. They must have been part of the Ignolio clan, sent out to take over the whole hospital. She stood up hoping they wouldn't notice her, but to her bad luck they started after her. She sprinted around every single turn there was, until she ran into a door that was locked. She hummed to try to get the bad thoughts out of her head, it worked until she turned around and saw the zombies were gaining on her, and she could do nothing except hope the door would open. She pounded and screamed hoping someone would hear her.

To her surprise the door magically creaked open, but what she saw was not even close to what she expected. There were tons of doctors tied with rope around their hands and feet and duct tape over their mouths. She started rummaging through everything in the room until she found the only thing in the whole room that would work, a pair of scissors that looked like they had been used by a bunch of kindergarteners. It would have to do. She started sawing away at the rope tied around some of the doctor's hands and then those doctors found some scalpels and started to help her. Before they knew it all of the doctors were free from the ropes and duct tape.

Then Sloan asked the question that had been gnawing away at her since she found the doctors. "Who are you and how did you get in here?" she asked.

One doctor stood up to answer, "We are the real doctors of this hospital and we were just going about our daily routines. Suddenly, these horrible people came through our doors. Before we knew it, they forced us all down here together and then had those zombies watching us. As you can see, they aren't doing a very good job. They had us all down here wrapped in the rope and duct tape."

"I am sorry to hear that, but I think I know how we can get out of here," she said. "All we have to do is pound on the door and see if those zombies are paying any attention. Then when they open the door to see what all the commotion is about, we charge and run through them and knock them all to the ground. Then we run up back to Ignolio's lair, tie rope around his hands and feet, and wrap duct tape over his mouth. We lock him down there and crawl through the hole above him and at last we will be out of the basement." She couldn't believe she thought of that devious plan.

"But what will we do after that?" one lone voice exclaimed in the background.

"I haven't thought of that yet," she replied, "but I think I have an idea. First, after we get past Ignolio, then we will have to locate all of the evil doctors. Then we charge with the monstrous needles and anything else we can find. We will fight to the death."

"How do you know that is going to work?" asked that same lone voice.

"I don't know," Sloan replied. "I just have a gut feeling there is a weak point in Ignolio's army. We must go before it gets too late," Sloan said. "Now who's with me?" There was no reply. "I said, 'Who's with me?'" with all of the breath she had left.

"ME!" everyone proclaimed.

"What are you all just standing around here for; we have a hospital to save!"

So they got to it. The doctors grabbed everything they might need out of the basement and crept to the door. *BANG! POUND! BANG! POUND! BANG! POUND! BANG! POUND!* They all were pounding and banging on the door. The door started to crack open like someone was unlocking it, but it wasn't locked which only meant one thing. The zombies were coming to see what all of the commotion was about. As soon as Sloan thought all of the zombies were behind the door, she kicked it down knocking several zombies with it. Everyone rushed out and trampled the closest zombies and threw whatever they had at the ones in the back. Before they knew it, all of the zombies were either playing dead or really, honestly, truly dead. Sadly, one real doctor was lying with them all spread out among the floor. All of the doctors said goodbye to the friend and walked silently away.

When they reached the entrance to Ignolio's lair they heard footsteps behind the door. Everyone held their breath. But it was no use, Ignolio opened the door and the expression on his face was pure amazement.

Ignolio said, "How in the world did you get out of the basement? I had those zombies guarding the door." Everyone looked behind them and Ignolio stopped at the sight of all of the zombies lying on the floor. He announced frustrated, "Don't ever hire zombies to do the dirty work. They will just let you down." He pointed to the zombies for emphasis.

"You should have chosen better guards," one person replied.

"I would not talk back at me if I were you!" Ignolio said sounding determined for defeat.

"What, are you going to have your zombie mob to come and take me away? Or should I say ex-zombie mob." Sloan said sarcastically.

"Charge!" another man said in the background.

"What? Wait!" Ignolio pleaded for help. Everyone came charging towards him. One woman stuck the needle right into his forehead and he dropped to the ground without a sound. He disappeared without a trace. Everyone ran out of his lair like nothing ever happened.

"Follow me," Sloan said. "I know where we should go next." Everyone followed her. She led them right to the ambulance and they all crammed into it and drove right to the entrance of the ER. Immediately, the doctor imposters came rushing out, but what they found when they opened the back doors were 27 people crammed into this small ambulance. So almost all of the people fell out and onto the doctor imposters. Most of the doctors were crushed and unable to move. But they all got up and several real doctors stayed back to keep an eye on the doctor imposters so they wouldn't get back up and fight.

Then the rest of the doctors and Sloan rushed inside to defeat the "other" doctors. They barged through the door with weapons they had found hidden in a supply closet. Then one person called out, "There I see them." Everyone followed the man and he led them right to the other doctors. This was war. There were people falling down left and right, giant needles the size of cars were being flung around the room until all of the imposters were on the ground.

The real doctors had won the battle; the hospital was theirs again. All that was left was cleaning up and fixing Sloan's lip.

Muffled Screams

An innocent trip to a haunted house leads Coco Zihama into mind-twisting circumstance. Years later a young girl named Kylee is pressured into going into that same house. Will Kylee meet the same fate as Coco? Find out in **MUFFLED SCREAMS** *by* ***Katy McNarney***.

Wednesday, October 29, 2001

"Yeah, let's go. It will be fun," Coco suggested to her friends.

"Go where?" asked Bartina Martezz.

"To the haunted house," exclaimed Demia Garten.

"Awwww, I hate that house," whined Tristy Weston. "It's so creepy."

"Oh, it's not that bad. Haunted houses are supposed to be creepy," Coco argued.

The next thing they knew, Coco Zihama and her friends were at the well-known Second Street Haunted House. The two-story home was abandoned before they turned it into a haunted house. Coco and her friends purchased their tickets and went inside. Tristy didn't have the strength to stay in there for a minimum of one minute. So, the first room they went in, she panicked. It was time for her to leave. Demia and Bartina lasted through half the house, but after that they couldn't take it, so they left.

Coco was left alone, but she didn't care. She loved haunted houses and she was determined to make it through. She heard a strange noise like someone whispering the name Annie. She just kept walking. She kept hearing the noises, this time getting a little creeped out. She decided to leave and try coming back another day, but right when she turned around someone grabbed her! She started to scream. It was useless; the person had already covered her mouth. She panicked, kicking and swinging her arms, but the stranger wouldn't let go. Coco Zihama had been kidnapped!

Meanwhile, Coco's friends grew worried that she wasn't coming out. They called the police, but the police couldn't find her. What they hadn't realized was that there was a trick wall that opened into a long hall. At the end of the hall, there was a trick door that led to the room in which Coco was hidden. There were two other doors that led into other rooms. These rooms would help trick anyone who found the hall. Her parents were also called by the police. They wanted to go in the house to search for her, but the police wouldn't let anyone go in after the incident. The people running the haunted house went into questioning. They were not charged with any crime.

Friday, October 15, 2005

Kylee Verona was walking down the hall at Rose Middle School, right after break ended, when Nadia Lufa, Rita Chin, and Lola Tate were talking in front of Rita's locker.

"Hey, Kylee, come here," Nadia cheered. Kylee walked over to Rita's locker. She was excited to see her friends after a long break.

"So we were thinking you could do something," Rita claimed. "We were thinking you could go into that house. You know the one on Second Street? It's abandoned. We really want to see what's inside."

"No, I don't think it's a very good idea," Kylee murmured.

"Oh come on, please," Rita groaned.

"Why can't you go in the house?" asked Kylee.

"Please?" whined Rita.

"Fine," mumbled Kylee.

"Great," chirped Rita. "We will be there tomorrow at five to watch."

Kylee was so desperate for friends. She decided to go to the house.

Saturday, October 16, 2005

Kylee went to Second Street.

"Hey Kylee nice to see you," Nadia mumbled.

Kylee stood in front of the house studying it. It was a decent sized two story home. The wood was a faded brown with hints of green. The house looked unsteady.

"Go in already," Lola instructed. Kylee walked in the house. It was cold, damp, dirty and just plain old creepy. Kylee felt like somebody was watching her.

It couldn't be, the house is abandoned, Kylee thought nervously. She walked around the house. Somebody grabbed her by the arm. She stood very still thinking that if she didn't panic, the person wouldn't be as tempted to take her. She was wrong! The person wasn't letting go; in fact the person was pulling her toward "itself." She started to scream but nobody could hear her. She was in the back of the house. Kylee felt something hit her head; she blacked out.

Friday, October 18, 2005

Kylee woke up. Her hands and feet were tied. A man was staring at her. From what she could see, he had long, dirty brown hair. He had blue eyes and a short beard. He smelled of must and mold. He was dressed in a blue denim shirt with worn black jeans. The room was oddly shaped. There was one long wall and the other three walls were short. The paint was peeling. There were spots of tan but most of the walls were a dark brown color. It was hard to tell if the walls were brown or tan. She was sitting in the opposite corner between one of the short walls and the long wall.

"Why did you take me?" Kylee asked. The man didn't answer.

"He just does," a voice said from the corner. Kylee saw a shadow walking toward her. "He did the same to me."

"Who are you?" Kylee said. This mysterious voice turned on a lamp across the room. Kylee saw a girl that looked about nineteen years old. She was extremely thin. She had long, wavy blond hair. She was dirty and smelly, but not as smelly as the man. She had vivid green eyes. She was wearing jeans and a purple long sleeve shirt.

"My name is Coco Zihama."

"You're the girl that disappeared four years ago!"

"Yep."

"Who is this man? Where is he?"

"See those stairs?" Kylee nodded her head. "The stairs lead to a small room. That's where he sleeps and eats and cooks. But I'm not quite sure who he is. All I know is that he's my kidnapper."

"Oh."

"Don't be sad, you get used to it after a while." Kylee didn't say anything. The man walked over to Kylee and Coco and gave them a single piece of bread with butter on it, some canned green beans and some canned tuna.

"Is this what we have to eat?" Kylee asked the man.

"You know, he won't answer."

"Why not?"

"I don't know. He just has never spoken. He's never said anything to me."

"Oh."

"So is this what we get to eat?" Kylee asked.

"Yeah, this is pretty much it. We get this every Monday, Wednesday, and Saturday. On Tuesday Thursday, and Sunday we get a piece of bread with butter, canned corn and cold chicken soup. Fridays are my favorite. We get two pieces of bread with butter, canned green beans, cold ravioli, and some canned tuna."

"What do we get to drink?"

"See that faucet over there?"

"Yeah."

"Well that's our water. Here let me untie you."

"Why didn't you try to escape already?"

"I did."

"What happened?"

"Well let's just say he had a knife. See this scar?" Kylee was shocked. This scar was on Coco's arm. It was slim yet long.

"Oh my gosh."

"Yeah I know. I was shocked when he did it too. He took care of me after he did it though. Just don't get into that kind of situation okay?"

"Okay." Coco walked back to her corner. Kylee walked around the room.

"Coco, look at this."

"What?"

"It's a loose floor board."

"So? This house is old. I wouldn't be surprised if you found a loose wall."

"But there's something in it. I can see it."

"Fine, let me see." Kylee and Coco pulled the floor board off the floor.

"OH. MY. GOD." Coco said.

"Those are pictures right?"

"Yeah, those are pictures."

"Who are these people?"

"Well the little girl looks like his daughter and so does this one."

"Look, a jump rope."

"And a letter."

> *Dear my little Sophie and my Annie,*
> *I'm sorry I let you die. I should have gone with you on the plane; that way we would still be together dead or alive. I want you to know that I will always love you and that I am writing this letter on September 11th, 2001. I have pictures to remember you two and our favorite jump rope. So don't worry I will remember you two. I will, I promise.*
> *Love,*
> *Daddy,*
> *Jr. Kuningham.*

"Oh my gosh, that's so sad."

"Yeah, I know. They must have died on 9/11."

"Wait, are the walls as old as the floors?"

"What do you think? And why does it matter?"

"'Cause if we find a hole in the wall we could finally get out of here!"

"How are we going to sneak out?"

"Well, I will sneak out and go get help while you cover for me."

"Now, how are we going to do that?"

"Uh…we could both sneak out."

"I told you the story, so that won't work either."

"If he comes at us then we will hit him with the board."

"Ok, I guess that will work."

"Let's do it tonight."

That Night

"Where is he?" Kylee asked.

"Not sure but if we don't see him, now is the time to do this." Kylee and Coco found a hole in the long wall and started to crawl out. Coco went first as Kylee followed behind. Kylee felt somebody grab her foot so she screamed.

"Hit him with the board!" Coco yelled. Kylee smacked him across the head with the board. As Kylee crawled on she could see that the board had knocked him out but hadn't drawn any blood. They crawled through the wall and into the main entry way. They ran out the door.

"I'm so excited. I finally got out of there," Kylee exclaimed.

"Ahhhhh, fresh air," Coco said.

"Yeah fresh air!" Kylee and Coco went to the police. Coco had seen where Jr. had taken her, so she could show them where to find him. They finally found Jr. He saw a psychologist and finally started to speak. He told them about his two daughters. He gave the psychologist the letter and the pictures, which pretty much explained everything, other than why he took Kylee and Coco.

"I didn't mean to hurt anyone. I really didn't. I just wanted my two daughters back and with them living with me. I did," Jr. explained. "Coco reminded me of Annie and Kylee reminded me of Sophie."

Epilogue

Jr. Kuningham spent about seven years in rehab. After that, he met a woman named Lela and had three boys. The oldest was named Billy. The middle child was named Bob and the youngest was named Joe. He soon became a therapist. Coco was reunited with her family. Her family was so happy to see their "dead" daughter alive. She became a doctor. Kylee also was reunited with her family. She became a veterinarian. Kylee and Coco became great friends and appreciated what they had done for each other.

Multiverse

When a girl doesn't clean up her room she somehow ends up in the television. In **MULTIVERSE** *by* **Brooke Goodwin**, *a girl will have to find her way out.*

My story is a very interesting one. It is a story that you, of course, have not heard. The best thing is my entire story is true. Oops, I'm starting to get off track. I should have started the story by now. Well, just to tell you, my name is Luna, and this is my story about how I got stuck in the television.

A few days ago my dad was asking me to clean my room. I soon forgot and decided to watch TV. My television wasn't working when I pushed the "on" button on the remote. I soon got angry and started bashing in all of the buttons on the remote. All of a sudden I saw this great wide morph of colors like I was in a kaleidoscope or something. Then quickly everything went blank.

After I could see things again I noticed that I was not back in my house. I was in the TV show *Tom & Jerry*. Tom (the cat) started chasing me all around the house until the channel changed. I couldn't help but wonder who got the TV to work.

Next I was in *Spongebob Squarepants*. Spongebob thought I was Patrick (his best friend) and asked me if I wanted to go jellyfishing. I had always wanted to do that ever since I first saw the show, so I said yes. Once I got the net it was HORRIBLE. Each time I tried to catch a jellyfish I got caught in the net and got stung by a whole bunch of jellyfish. I felt like I got shocked by a million Tasers. I had to hold back the tears because I didn't want Spongebob to come and talk to me. Spongebob can get on my nerves sometimes when I'm watching the show, so there's no way I'm gonna talk to him.

Before I got stung by any more jellyfish the channel changed. I was on the Wii channel, and someone was playing *Super Mario Galaxy*. Mario was trying to stomp on me because that's the way you kill enemies in the game. So, I think he thought I was one of his enemies. I had to run away from him so I wouldn't get stomped on. Luckily I didn't. Then, the game turned off, and someone turned off the TV.

Mario went inside of the game's library because he knew the game had ended and he didn't have to play anymore. Suddenly as I turned around I saw Princess Rosalina, the queen of the stars on the game. She told me that she knew that I wanted to get out of the TV and there was a way to get out. But when I asked her what the way was she said that I should look inside myself and sooner or later I'd find out. Rosalina left, and I got so angry when she left because she knew there was a way to get out, but she wouldn't tell me.

I turned around and I saw a catapult (most likely it was from Rosalina). I thought about how to use the catapult to help myself. I thought maybe I could shoot myself out of the television. So, I jumped on the catapult and pulled the string. Sure enough, I was out of the TV.

I told my family, and none of them believed me! But the worst thing about my whole adventure was that no one noticed I was even gone! They thought I was still cleaning my room.

I also know you're wondering if I liked my voyage into the TV. Well, yeah, of course I did. It was so fun. Oh, and by the way, I was being sarcastic. I hope that doesn't happen to me EVER again!

The Mysterious Island

Harry and Olivia go to a weird world they had never even heard about. Will they find their way home in **THE MYSTERIOUS ISLAND** *by* **Hannah Kelly?**

One August, there was a sister and brother, Olivia and Harry, who were playing outside. Harry and Olivia were close. They did everything together like playing and being bored and being happy together. They did everything else you can think of. They had just finished playing a round of soccer, and they had had a long day.

Harry and Olivia were getting sleepy. They figured that they might as well fall asleep. As Harry and Olivia were sleeping, Olivia was talking. She was saying over and over, "Get away from me…get away from me…" She was tossing and turning, and finally Harry woke up.

He looked over at Olivia and saw that she was okay, and then he turned back over to go to sleep. That was when he looked up and saw…a monkey.

He shot up and looked around. Behind them was a river, but before they fell asleep the house was behind them. Harry was freaking out not knowing what to do, so he panicked and splashed water in his face to make sure that he was seeing clearly. Harry finally calmed down after throwing water in his face.

Harry tried waking up Olivia. He tried a lot of things, like shaking her and splashing her with water. Finally he walked up to Olivia and he shouted in her ear. "Who are you talking to?"

"AHHH! Harry, what was that for? I am going to hurt you!"

"Sorry, but I had to wake you up. I mean, just look where we are!"

"Oh my gosh, where are we?"

"I don't know. That's why I woke you up. We need to find our way out of here."

"Okay, let's go."

Before they left, they searched the place to see what it was like. Olivia was finding a lot of unusual things. Harry was, too. They found flying trees, butterfly chairs, and miniature people made of moss and grass. All the while they continued their journey to find their way out.

As the two walked around they found a house with leaves, vines, and flowers. They thought someone lived there, so they went to check. Harry knocked on the door. No one answered the first knock; he knocked the second time, and no one answered. After the third knock with no answer, Harry lifted his hand to knock again. But as he swished his hand forward, a very old man came to the door.

He had wrinkles all over him. He had a hunched-over back and a cane to walk with. He had overalls on like he was a farmer. "What do you guys want?" he asked rudely.

"Well...." Harry and Olivia looked at each other and shrugged.

"Wait; let me guess.... Did you guys get here while sleeping?

"Yeah, how did you...?"

"Come inside and I'll tell you all about it, and how I got here, too." He cut them off before Harry could finish his sentence.

They walked into his house. It was much nicer on the inside than the outside. It was warm and comfy. They sat on the couch. The old man told them all about his journey.

"When I was a little kid about your age, I got here the same way you guys did, and I didn't know how to get out. I was stuck for a long time. Many people have come here, but only one knew how to get out. I followed every single kid until that one person discovered how to get out. I decided to stay here just in case some kids like you landed here, in order to help. So if you would like to get out of here, I know how."

"Sure! One question, though...what happened to the other people?" asked Olivia.

"Well, let's just say they didn't get past the giant octopus very well. So now that I've told you guys, let's get moving."

"WOW! Did you say 'giant octopus'?" asked Harry.

"Yes, I did say 'giant octopus.' Now can we go?"

"Yeah, sorry, that just shocked me!" Harry exclaimed.

Their journey through many adventures began with giant monkeys. They had to find bananas to get past the giant monkeys only to find giant spiders awaiting them. It was then that they discovered why the old man had flies on him. He threw the flies into the giant web, which got them past the giant spiders safely.

Finally they got to the very end. "This is the hard one to get by," the old man told them as they approached the giant octopus. There was only one way to get through the portal, and that was with the sleeping berries.

The old man told Harry where to get the sleeping berries because he knew Harry would be fast enough. The portal closed every three hours, and there were only four minutes left. Harry ran back, got the berries, and came back with two minutes left to spare. Harry threw the berries in the octopus's mouth, and—*BAM*—the octopus was asleep!

Harry and Olivia turned and waved to the old man. They walked through the portal and found themselves awake in their chairs. Before they told their parents everything, they remembered that they had never asked the old man's name. They felt very bad about that.

They ran to their parents and told them the whole story about the flying trees, butterfly chairs, and miniature moss and grass people. Their parents pretended to go along with their children's story.

As the summer passed, Harry and Olivia ended up going back again because they found it so interesting. Then they finally figured out what the old guy's name was: Patrick! Every time they went back they visited Patrick, and together they would go on new adventures and discover what they hadn't seen before.

And that is my interesting story about Olivia and Harry's adventure to the mysterious island.

The Night
of the Evil Snowman

"Uh oh, we're trapped!" is all Alicia and Calvin could think in the story **THE NIGHT OF THE EVIL SNOWMAN** *by **Aaliyah Sesi**. An innocent day turns into a snowy nightmare.*

As the snow had fallen to the ground
On the street there was no sound
The days of summer and fall had passed
It was winter at last
As the flakes flew through the air
A sense of magic would soon
bring DESPAIR...

"Where are my gloves?" yelled Alicia.

"They are in your bin," said Calvin.

As fast as they could, they got their snow gear on, ready to start the day.

"Don't be away too long," their mother yelled out the door.

"Okay!" they both said in sync.

At the park there were kids sledding down the hill, doing snow angels, making snowballs, and making snowmen. "What do you want to do?" asked Alicia, as excited as can be.

"I want to make a snowman, too!" answered Calvin.

"Sounds good to me," said Alicia. "I'll start on the bottom!"

"Then I'll make the middle!"

As time passed, the kids finished their snowman and did many other things, like sledding.

They noticed that it was getting late. The two kids started on their way home.

The snowman they just made had magical sticks as arms. They had found his arms by a vending machine. He had an old red hat on, and his nose was a rotted carrot they found by the trash. But as day turned into night an eerie feeling came over them. That feeling went over their snowman, too, causing him to come to life as an EVIL snowman. First his head, then his sticks, and last his lower body came alive.

The wind started to gust, and snow whirled through the air, enclosing the kids in a circle of white. Alicia grabbed Calvin and held him tight. "What is happening?" they both exclaimed. As they looked forward with terror, the snowman that they had just created was coming at them with great strides. The coal that the children put for his eyes burned like fire. The sticks he had for arms turned into stakes, and as he came close he started to raise them, grabbing at the children.

As the snowman was coming towards Alicia and Calvin, they heard a loud scraping on the road. *Shhhhhhhhhhhhhhhhhhh, shhhhhhhhhhhhhhhhh.*

"Do you hear that?" asked Alicia.

"Yeah, what is it?" Calvin asked back.

"I think it is a snow plow."

"Oh no, here it comes!" exclaimed Calvin.

The sound also was heard by the evil snowman. He was so mesmerized by it that he forgot about the children, even though he was only an arm's length away. Alicia and Calvin saw that the snowman was distracted, so they ran to the sidewalk as fast as they could. As for the snowman, he ran towards the snow plow with curiosity.

As the plow came closer, though, the snowman realized too late that there was a death trap right in front of his big, round, snow head. He tried to get away, but the sound lured him back and crushed him like the snow that he was.

The kids ran four blocks without looking back at the snow that once made up their creature. They arrived at their house, amazed at how their creation had come to life.

"This was one of the most exciting days of my life!" exclaimed Alicia.

"This was the most exciting day for me!" Calvin said, sounding out of breath.

"Home sweet home," they both said. "Mom, we're here!"

"Hi, how was your day?"

"We have the strangest story to tell you!"

Night's Journal

Have you ever thought that night could be a person? Well, neither did Alex, until she got a visit. In **NIGHT'S JOURNAL** *by* **Nicole Yost**, *she finds that a friend can come from anything.*

Dear Journal,
It happened again. I was just doing my job, when another kid went screaming into the night. Sheesh! I'm just doing my job. You can't have day without the Night. It's hard enough working all through the night, and now I have to deal with all the screaming kids? You think it's easy, my job?

Night was writing in the attic of an old abandoned house and sitting on an old sofa. She peered over the journal, hoping no one would come, since she wasn't allowed to be there because it was unsafe.

It's hard being a twelve-year-old girl and having to stand up to your family's traditions. I mean, who knew that Night had traditions?

"Still writing in that journal?"
Night jumped up in the air when she saw her father was there.
"You know, we got that journal when you were just a shadow. You learned to write early," her dad said as he walked over to an old chair. Night was sitting with her legs stretched out.
"So?" she said with a confused look on her face.
"Well, you are still writing in it! I can't believe that there is still room to write in that thing."
"Whatever," she said as she stood up and walked over to the door. "What did you want to ask me?"

Fanning away the dust and coughing, Dad said, "I wanted to tell you (*cough, cough*) that there's five minutes 'til we have to get out there."

Every night it was Night's job to watch the children in a house in one neighborhood. Her family would stay in the same neighborhood for two years, but switch houses each night. It was lonely work, watching children sleep. It was even worse when they woke up afraid. Tonight's job is in the Barkers' household. Night is in charge of watching over twelve-year-old Alex. She partly enjoyed it, because they were the same age. Night wondered if Alex's life was anything like hers. Moving around to new places all the time made it hard to meet others like herself; that is, until she turns thirteen.

That night, as her mom, dad, and brother were busy, Night sat there by the closet, writing.

I can't believe it! Every night, I'm stuck here writing in my journal! It's starting to get boring. I can't wait 'til I'm thirteen! Then I will have more freedom without parents watching over my shoulder, and I can change it up.

Then she heard Alex waking up. *Oh man, I'll be so busted!* But it was too late. *This girl is going to wake up and scream.* Luckily she couldn't because she was so scared.

As Alex rushed to the light switch, Night rushed to the closet. Alex flipped on the light switch, and heaved a huge sigh of relief. The dark shadow that she thought she saw earlier had left. Then she saw a book lying by the closet. *What is a book doing right there?* she pondered for a while. Then it was like a little light bulb went off in her head. *The thing that I saw must have left this. I wonder what could be inside. Maybe if I take a little peek, I'll know what it was doing here and why.* With that settled, she walked back to her bed. But it wasn't settled, was it? *Time for a little light reading,* Alex thought.

She opened the book, and saw that it was a journal. It was written by a twelve-year-old girl, just like her! *Wait a second,* Alex thought, *I didn't see any girl, only a mere shadow. Boy, this is getting eerie, but I'm too tired to worry about it.* She turned on her old butterfly night light, which she hadn't used since she was little, and went to bed.

Night had to leave, too. It was almost dawn, and she had to get back to the abandoned house where her family stayed during the day. Night wondered, *How am I going to get my journal back?*

The next day, Night's father told them that they were going to a different house. "But, Dad," Night exclaimed, "why can't we do the same house?"

Then her father explained, "Not until you're thirteen!"

"Come on, Dad, can't I please start early? My birthday is only in one week!" said Night, using her best puppy dog face.

"All right," said Dad, "I guess one week before thirteen is long enough."

Whew! That was a close one, thought Night as she went back to the girl's room. She searched the room but could not find her journal. The only place she hadn't checked was the bookshelf, which was next to Alex's bed. *No,* Night thought, *it's too risky! But I have to try.* Night pulled gently on the journal. *Almost there,* she thought. Just then, the book slipped from her hand!

"Who's there?" Alex woke with a start. "I know you want your book back, so please, tell me who you are!" Alex was trying to sound brave, but she was shivering inside.

Night didn't know what to do, so she stood up.

Alex said, "I saw that! You moved! Now who are you?" She was not really afraid, but more curious, especially after her reading.

"I'm here to get my journal back," Night said softly. "You won't believe me when I tell you who I am."

"Try me," said Alex.

Night took a deep breath. "I'm the night." She paused. "I mean, I'm not a person like you. I'm a dark shadow that comes when the lights are out. I give you a reason to rest after your long day. I make sure things are quiet and soft. But I'm also a twelve-year-old girl who writes in a journal. My name is Night."

Alex had many questions, but she startled Night by blurting out, "I read your journal! And from all your adventures, I've decided to keep one, too. My stories won't be as exciting as watching little kids in Italy, but they are the true stories of my life."

Night was surprised and embarrassed. Someone else had read her innermost thoughts! She knew it was impossible. How could a girl like Alex understand?

"Wait," said Alex, as she got out of bed and walked toward Night. "We're not that different. We both have fears and hopes. For one thing, I'm afraid of the dark!"

"Well," said Night, "I'm afraid of the day!"

Both girls burst out laughing at the same time. How funny that it should come to this! Is it possible for a human and the night to become friends? The two girls sat and talked for the rest of the night. As the dawn came, Alex held Night's shadowy hand.

"That wasn't so bad," said Alex. "I'll look forward to the next time you come."

"Me too," said Night.

"You'll need this," Alex said as she handed back Night's journal. "And next time you can read from mine."

"I'll look forward to that," said Night. "I never had a friend before. It's nice. It's nice to have someone to talk to, and not just a page."

Over the years, they met on different nights, each one sharing the fun they had. They both learned that by facing their fears together, it wasn't so bad.

There is a world of possibilities, and it's nice to share it with someone.

And with that thought, Night finished off the last page of her journal.

The Saviors of Time

A monster from a once powerful clan is forced to embark on a journey to save himself and his clan. As his journey moves forward, he meets new friends that will help him along the way. Will he be able to complete his race against time? Find out in **THE SAVIORS OF TIME**, *by* ***Cal Cerny****.*

Thousands of years ago, the Tarks were a strong clan of ancient beings unknown to the Humans. But that all changed when a group of human discovered our Clan's home. They brought an army of Humans with their most advanced technology that they had at the time. We were sent out into hiding after they burned our home to the ground. The myths that you have heard, The Yeti, Bigfoot, the Loch Ness Monster, they are all once a part of the Tark clan, adapted to the environments that they live in. Now we are forced into hiding in the last undiscovered place on Earth, The Hole.

The Humans know of its existence but believe that it is too deep to ever reach the bottom where we live. It is a haven. Long ago, a group of monsters went on a search for a human warlock that could cast a time spell that would send them back in time and stop the Humans from destroying their village. The Humans have always hated the Tark Clan, for they thought that they were a curse brought to the Earth by an evil demon. But the other Humans found out about their own kind plotting against them, and the warlock was executed. The Tark clan was sent into hiding for the rest of eternity, but now a small group of 21st century monsters are trying to replicate what their ancestors had.

Qwarty strode the jut along the cliff side up to the surface. He was one of the monsters that would soon be on a journey to save his clan, but he did not know that yet. Qwarty had always been fascinated with the surface world, one thing that put him apart from the rest of his clan. His leader, Tark had persuaded the others in his clan to hate the Humans and make it their duty to wipe them out from the face of the Earth. Tark sees the humans as horrible creatures that had taken the Earth from them and twisted it into their own dreams. Once Qwarty had made it to the surface; he headed about a half-mile away to the shoreline that provided the clan with water. He would stay there until the day came to an end.

Down in the labs Eternity, Terik was about to test his Anti – Shock device for the first time. But as soon as he was about to pull the lever, the bell rang for the end of class. Terik was in the 14th year, or as the humans called it, college. He had invented a machine called an Anti – Shock device. The machine could send out a shock wave to cancel out the shock sent from a dynamite explosion. As the monsters clan became older, and the Human technology had become more advanced, the Humans had ruined the world with their pollution and mining. A couple years back, the humans had blown almost half of the monster population away in their search of gold. Luckily, they survived and migrated to our city, Eternity. Terik was an inventor not a hater and that would be one thing that would bring him together with Qwarty.

A year later, Qwarty and Terik had both discovered that there was a way to stop the humans from discovering their home. Qwarty had found a book held in by the roots of a tree and read it day and night until he knew everything about the people that came before him. Terik had found out about the people and how to save his home from a human computer that he obtained from an abandoned house. The humans thought that a monster finding a warlock and going back in time was a folktale, but Terik knew better.

Qwarty and Terik had both set out in search for a human warlock when they met each other for the first time. They had both asked each other what they were doing out here, because going outside of the city was strictly forbidden. They both told the truth and had found out that they were each in search of a warlock. So together they traveled through snow, rain, ice, and wind. But one night, in a blizzard in northern Canada, they saw a small shack with smoke billowing out of the chimney.

"This snowstorm will wipe us off of the face of the Earth if we don't take refuge!" said Qwarty.

"But it will give away our cover!" followed Terik.

"If we don't, we'll die!" protested Qwarty.

"Only if we have to, but if we are found by the surface patrol, I'm blaming this all on you!" said Terik.

The two friends slowly made their way over to the small cottage and knocked on the rotted door. The door opened a crack and they heard the sound of an old, raspy voice.

"Who are you? What do you want?" the voice asked.

"We are in search of shelter and this cottage was the nearest refuge we could find!" yelled Qwarty against the howling wind.

"If you say so, you may come in," said the voice.

"My name is John Maying and what would yours be?" asked John.

"My name is Terik and I proudly make my home in the Tarks' clan."

"Shut up! He does not know of the Tark clan!" hissed Qwarty under his breath.

"Ah, I see. You two are from the ancient clan of the Tarks. And by the looks of it, you're off doing something you shouldn't be," said John.

"How do you know of us? I thought that we were unknown to the humans!" screeched Qwarty

"Well, I also have something hidden from the humans. I am a Warlock," admitted John.

"No!" Terik and Qwarty both gasped.

"Now that we all know who we are, what are two ancient beings doing out in the middle of a blizzard?" asked John.

"We were in search of a warlock. And now I guess we've found you," said Qwarty.

"We need you to cast us a time spell so that we may go back in tome and stop your race from finding our home," said Terik.

John thought to himself and finally said, "I can cast you a time spell, but it will only last for a day or so."

"We won't even need that much," replied Qwarty.

As John cast the time spell, a large swirling portal opened up from the middle of nowhere. John said, "Get in! I can't hold it any longer!" The two monsters stepped in, and so did John.

The three beings were forcefully spewed out onto the cold, hard ground. It was winter and they could see the glow from torches over the hill. They soon realized that the group was headed towards them.

"We need to take cover!" yelled Terik.

"No! We first need to change the humans' path so they won't find our home! When Terik noticed that they had been shot out near a large pile of rocks, he had an idea.

"Push those rocks over the hill to block their path!" he yelled over the advancing army. Once the group of Humans had noticed that their path had been blocked, they turned back to head to their village. Once the army had left, John opened a portal and sent them whisking back in time.

When the team had fully recovered from the travel though the time stream, they went to look at the world without any discovery of the Tarks home. But as they walked along Qwarty said, "Oh no, this can't be happening." The land that used to be the city of Eternity was a barren wasteland of vast nothingness.

"It looks as though we have changed the world as we know it," said Terik. A large stone to the right of the group had a description of some sort. Qwarty read:

> *For we have defeated the Human Empire,*
> *and as for those who fought in this long*
> *war we value greatly. And as for those*
> *who died for our reign over the Human*
> *world, our world will be valued forever.*

"It is a plaque of some sort," said John. "The Human race was defeated by the Tarks and they now rule the world."

100 Years Ago

The Tarks had seen the Humans' fiery torches pass their home; they knew that they were in search of their homes and must be destroyed. The Tarks marched out to face the oncoming humans. The humans were strong, but the Tarks were stronger. Once the Tarks had wiped out the humans in the marching army, they went on to major cities and set them burning to the ground along with the human inhabits. The Tark army had grown strong with every city they destroyed. After the human race was gone, the Tarks set up major cities where the Humans had been. Once the fires had spread from the war, the world was now a barren wasteland of vast nothingness. The Tarks hoped to rule the world for as long as their clan could hold it and never let it go.

Present Day

Every member of the group knew that they would have to go back in time to prevent themselves from stopping the humans. Qwarty thought to himself *I know that I don't want the humans to find my home, but I don't want the world to look like this. We must go back and stop ourselves.* John knew what must be done and zapped them back to the time where the Humans found his friend's home without asking. Qwarty and Terik went without struggle because they knew that the world couldn't stay like this. As soon as they got to the right time period, they instantly saw themselves before they stopped the advancing army. The three sprinted out and grabbed themselves before they could push the boulders off of the ledge. The advancing army passed without a problem and as John flashed them home Qwarty could swear he heard the screaming of his ancestors.

Once they had gotten home, the group all went their separate ways. Qwarty continued as a human life researcher. Terik became an expert in machine making and the Human Defense Department hired him. This department specializes in defending the Tark Clan from Humans. John went back to living in his little cabin in the snowy woods of northern Canada. The Tark Clan will forever live in peace, thanks to the time and effort put in by these three people.

Scary Dolls Come Alive

In **SCARY DOLLS COME ALIVE** *by* ***Tayler Lenard***, *a young girl and her family have to defend their lives from little plastic terrors!*

There were once three dolls on Maria's bed. They looked mean. They all had this weird grin on their faces. They were mad on the inside, but they couldn't show it. They were unplayed with and broken. When I say they were broken, I mean they had only three fingers and no hair.

One rainy day, Marcia left her toys outside. There they were struck by a lightning bolt. The dolls became alive as they screamed. Their faces began to turn pale white, and their fingers began to grow. Their hair started to grow. They were all redheads.

They began to remember the bad times they had spent with that little girl Marcia. She used to throw them on the floor! They had had enough of that.

The dolls had to work together to open the door. I mean, they were only two feet tall. They finally got in one hour later.

One by one they ran upstairs! The dolls creaked the door open. They grabbed Marcia by her hair. Marcia screamed and tried to fight back, but the dolls had strength.

It was a good thing the mother heard an unusual noise. She began to call Marcia's name.

"Mom, help!" Marcia screamed, crying.

"Shut up!" one of the dolls said.

The dolls looked at each other. They hadn't known they could talk, but it just came out of him. They were surprised because not only could they hear, but they could talk, too!

"I'm coming, sweetie. Don't worry," Kerrie, the mother, said.

But the dolls had a plan to tie the mom up. The dolls searched the rooms. "I found something," one of the dolls said repeatedly. "It is rope. Come on. Let's tie her up."

But what they didn't know was that while they were doing that, the mom got something of her own. It was a gun. The mom didn't know that they were dolls. The mom ran upstairs, but didn't quite see the dolls. Remember that the dolls were only two feet tall.

Dad came home. He noticed that the house didn't look right. "Kerrie! Marcia! Are you home?" Dad called.

"Yes, be quiet," Kerrie said. But the dad saw the doll. The doll tied the rope around the mother's ankles.

"Watch out!" the dad said. "There's something behind you!" The dad grabbed the gun off the stairs. The gun trembled in his hand.

"Help!" Kerrie said.

"I'm coming, baby!" He shot all three of the dolls.

They heard sounds coming out of the closet.

They saw black hair. It was their daughter. They took the duct tape off of Marcia's mouth, and they grabbed each one of the dolls by their hair and walked to the Dumpster. They stared and stared for about five minutes after throwing them in.

Three days later the garbage truck came while the dad was jogging by the Dumpster. He told the garbage man to be careful. Then Dad looked in the garbage.

The dolls were gone.

Shipwreck

Beck and Amy were looking forward to a relaxing cruise until an unexpected person appears on the cruise ship. Amy discovers some interesting things in **SHIPWRECK**, *by* ***Jordan Tripp***.

Beck

The day we set foot on the boat was one of the greatest feelings ever! The ocean breeze in my face, the sound of the waves: Nothing could be better.

"Okay, first thing on our agenda is…water skiing!" Amy said with both hands in the air. "Or, maybe we can play shuffleboard."

I looked at Amy with a look on my face that said, "You're crazy." She knew what I was thinking, so we just walked into our cabin and set our stuff down. Then, Amy ran out of the cabin and down the stairs.

"C'mon Beck, you know that we're not just going to be staying in that boring old cabin all day. So let's go climb the rock wall, ok?" I did want to climb the rock wall, and I knew it wouldn't be a vacation if we just sat in a cabin. So I ran down the stairs and joined her. We held hands as we walked to the rock wall.

The rest of the day was fantastic.

At about 7:00 o'clock, we went to dance in the ballroom. The music was slow and quiet. It was a black tie event. So Amy was still getting ready. Me? I just put on my best suit and left. I turned around and saw Amy walking into the ballroom. She was wearing her red dress, and her hair was pinned in a bun. But the thing that made her stand out the most was her tiara that she had worn on our wedding day. I took her by the hand and we danced to the slow music. "Wow! Now I see what took you so long to get ready," I said. "You look great!" She blushed as I spun her around in a circle.

"I wanted to look the best in the room," she replied. "Oh, that sounded rude. I'm sorry." Her face turned red.

"It's fine. And you do look the best," I said with a grin that spread on my face. She looked at me with her bright blue eyes, and she smiled too.

"Hey, I'm starving, let's get some food." I nodded and we walked to the café down the hall. The room smelled like candy and coffee. Amy and I both got a coffee with whipped cream and cinnamon sprinkled on the top. Then we got two ham and cheese sandwiches. We sat down at the little tables seated by the window. We talked about our vacation and what we were going to do when we got home.

"So, how's the night going so far?" Amy asked. "You've been really quiet." She did not make eye contact when she asked.

"I have a bad feeling about this whole vacation. Something, there's something that's bugging me. I don't know what it is, I just don't know." I looked down to my watch; it was 12:00 midnight. "We should head back to the cabin, it's late."

We got up and walked out the door. Amy had her head on my shoulder and we were holding hands. This was one of the best nights we ever had.

Amy

I woke up the next morning at about 9:00 o'clock. Beck was still sleeping, so I got dressed and decided to walk around the ship. When I arrived at the pool, I sat down in one of the beach chairs.

"Guess who?" It was Molly. She was my best friend, and I hadn't seen her in two years. I stood up, surprised to see her with black hair, a leather vest, and black makeup. Molly used to be the kind of person who had pink shirts with white skirts and sparkly flip flops. But she still kept with the white skirt.

"Oh my gosh, what are you doing here!" I said as I ran and gave her a hug. "You told me you moved to Peru." She was shocked that I remembered.

"Well, Peru got boring," she replied. "So, I wanted to take a break, move back to the states and go on a cruise and chill. So, what are you doing here?"

"I'm on vacation with Beck," I said as a little grin developed on Amy's face.

"C'mon, I want to talk to you." She pulled me to the side of the spa. "You want to be rich?" Molly said.

"I'm already rich." I said. Molly looked irritated.

"No, richer then you are already. Since you're married to Beck, he has all the money, right? So if he somehow died, you could get all the money. Then you would be richer than you ever imagined!"

I looked at her like she was crazy. Where did my best friend go? Why was she saying this to me? "No!" I screamed. "I'm not killing him! I love him. But you can't see that. Now just stay away from me…and Beck!" As I walked away, she said something that shocked me the most.

"Fine, if you don't, I will!" Molly said with an evil voice.

"No, you're going to stay away from him."

Suddenly, Beck walked right in front of Amy.

"It's time for you to go, Moll," Beck said with a blank but angry look on his face.

I could see that Molly wasn't going to leave, so I took Beck by the hand and pulled him back to the cabin. Beck wouldn't look me in the eye. His eyes were sunk down.

"Don't worry about it, she's crazy," I said. I opened the door to the cabin and sat down in the office chair.

"We have to get off this boat or something is going to happen; something bad," Beck said. "We must go now!" Then he put our suitcases on the bed and began packing our clothes, books, and everything else we brought.

"Beck, calm down! Our vacation is not going to be ruined because of some stupid lunatic who thinks she can do what she wants!" Beck looked at me again, and then looked at the thrown clothes all over the room.

"Can you help me pick up these clothes?" I walked over to him, gave him a hug and helped him with the clothes.

When was it going to happen? Beck was surprisingly happy. I guess he thought nothing was going to happen. But I did. Molly never acted like that. I was always by Beck's side when we were out of the cabin.

"Beck, you're not telling me the truth." I looked at him and he looked at me and didn't say anything.

"What am I not telling you?" he finally asked with such a fierce, but flat, look and voice. I didn't know what to say.

"How does Molly even know you?" I asked. Molly couldn't come to the wedding because she was in Peru and the next flight out would have been a year after the wedding. But now that that I think about it, how did she get on this boat if the next flight took so long?

"Okay, I'll tell you, but I can't talk about it right here," Beck said quietly. "We need to go back to the cabin, right now, if you want to know." I nodded and he took me by the hand and pulled me back to the cabin.

"So, what's the big secret?" I sat down on the freshly made bed. I noticed the chocolate fall off the pillow and onto the bed. Beck sat down next to me.

"Before I tell you, I am sorry for not telling you sooner," Beck started. "I didn't know how you would take it." Beck hesitated for a moment and then continued. "Okay, Molly was never like this and you know that. But I know that she moved to Peru. I know that because she told me." How could be had known about Molly? I never introduced them.

"But, how?" I asked. "How do you know her?" I was getting annoyed. I was trying to stay calm.

"My brother, Eddy, sent her to kill me. He was, and still is, insane enough to want to kill me. He sent me a letter saying that I should start writing my will because Molly is going to kill me. I don't know why he would send that. He's crazy; there's something wrong with him. If Molly doesn't kill me, then she is going to be sent into a dark abyss," he explained while looking down at the ugly carpet.

"Why does your brother want to kill you?" I was less annoyed with the fact that he might die at any given moment.

"Since I was born, my brother hated me. My father loved me. He was some type of king or something. He had powers which could do just about everything. When he passed away, he granted me his powers. I still have them. I just don't use them. If I die, then my brother gets the powers. So, he sent Molly to kill me."

I didn't know what to do. I wanted to cry, but I couldn't find the energy to do it. So I just leaned over and gave Beck a hug. He kissed the top of my head, and, without saying a word, we headed out for dinner.

Molly

I crept into the Captain's control room. Dang! He was sitting right there in his flamingo office chair. Can I ever catch a break? Guess not. He turned around.

"Who's there?" the Captain asked.

"Your, uh, room service" I said enthusiastically. "You won a free dessert!" I hate being nice to people.

"Cool!" the Captain replied.

But it wasn't dessert. It was a blade with his name on it! Okay, it didn't technically have his name on it. I entered the room, approached him from behind, and cracked his neck. The Captain was dead. Then I took the blade and stabbed the control panel until it exploded! Nothing new, but still super cool! I turned around to leave and noticed Beck in the doorway.

"You're not going to get away with this, Molly," Beck said with an angry face.

"What are you going to about it?" I asked. "Kill your baby sister?"

"I sure am," Beck said flatly. I was a bit scared, which is not a familiar feeling to me.

Luckily, Beck only broke my arm. The rescue team came and got me from the sinking ship. Without telling anyone, I went to Las Vegas.

Beck

The ship was sinking. I could see that Amy was frozen in terror. I grabbed her hand and took her to the ballroom. When I was waiting for her the night we danced, I began to look around the ballroom. I told Amy to look at the big purple bird flying around the ballroom asking for a cracker. There wasn't a bird, but I had to distract her. I shrunk the boat down and put it in my pocket.

"Let's go!" I had to scream so she could hear me.

"Where did the boat go?" she cried in shock.

"I put it in my pocket!" I simply replied. She gave me a weird look as I took her to the edge of the boat. I made two ropes to lower the boat into the water. I hooked the boat to the ropes and rolled it down. I grabbed Amy and jumped into the boat. I pulled the life jackets out of my pocket and enlarged them. I gave one to Amy and I put on the other one. I gathered up enough wind to push us away from the sinking ship.

"Molly did this, didn't she?" Amy finally managed to ask. "She wanted to kill you!" Tears ran down her face, and I felt horrible that I had put her through all this. Amy didn't deserve this. I hugged her close as we sat in that boat together.

Amy and I were rescued by a helicopter. Eventually, Eddy found out that I wasn't dead and that Molly was sent to the abyss. Surprisingly, no one else came to kill me.

We were finally home and began to unpack.

"Hey," Amy yelled. "Molly never gave me my designer tank top back!" We both laughed, and that's when we knew that everything was going to be okay.

Skye's Adventure to California

In **SKYE'S ADVENTURE TO CALIFORNIA** *by* ***Skye Johnson,*** *Skye's sister, Jaquelyn, leaves for L.A. for her acting career. Skye becomes depressed that she left and wants to do something about it. Will Skye ever get her sister back?*

"I don't want to leave!" Jaquelyn cried. "I want to stay here, with my family!" Jaquelyn was just about to leave to go home to her small apartment in L.A. She had to do a bunch of shows and auditions for her career because Jaquelyn is an actress. She is 24 years old.

"I know that you don't want to go, but who is going to take care of your cats?" her mom said. The conversation went on and on for a long time, but finally, Jaquelyn was forced to leave, so she said her goodbyes to everybody, and soon she was in the airport getting on the plane.

Meanwhile...

Skye, Jaquelyn's younger sister, was very, very sad. She complained to her mom.

"MOM! GET IN HERE NOW!" Skye sobbed violently. Her mom rushed in the door of her room. Inside was her daughter crying in a cozy green bed. Skye lived in a beautiful castle. On the cold stone walls there were paintings that showed the former leaders of the castle. Her room was at the very top of the castle. Skye had super long blond hair, and icy blue eyes to match.

"What's wrong, honey?" Her mom panted from running up the long staircase. It was late at night.

Skye cried, "Why did she leave?" She buried her face into her mom's purple shirt, her tears staining the cotton.

"Who?" her mom asked.

"You know who! Jaquelyn! Why did she leave?"

"She has a better life there, and you know it. Now go to bed. Goodnight, honey. See you in the morning," her mom replied as she left the room.

Skye spent the night dreaming about her beloved sister. She dreamed that they were laughing, flying above the clouds, bouncing, and having fun. Then she woke up to her mom saying, "Get up. Get up, Skye. It's time for school. I have pancakes cooking on the stove and I laid out your prettiest dress." So Skye got ready for the day, and when she got to school, she complained to all of her friends. They felt really bad for her. She was too sad to eat and had run out of tears.

Days, weeks, and months passed. Each day Skye grew sadder and sadder, and the days seemed worse and worse for her. Then one day after school, she was sitting on her bed, and she created a plan. "Mom, can I have $5,000?" Skye pleaded.

Since her mom could see that she was in need, she said, "Sure, Skye." (Her family is very, *very* rich, and $5,000 dollars was like a cent to them.)

That night, the moon was shining brighter than ever. And since she had no other choice, well, that is if she didn't want to wake up her mom or the guards in front of the castle, Skye tied her extremely long hair to the top of the castle, opened up the window as wide as it could go, and jumped. It was a long way down. It hurt her ears but it was totally worth it. She closed her eyes as the wind blew through her hair, and it felt like the dream that she had. Then she hit the ground with a large thump. She quickly scrambled up and called her private jet pilot (Uncle Zoom). He was in her sparkly driveway in a matter of five minutes with the small jet in the trunk. Skye made him promise not to tell her mom about all this.

They hopped into the jet and Skye said, "Go to Los Angeles, California, please." It was a long ride, four whole hours! She talked with her uncle about how it was there, because he had been there before. It seemed like a beautiful place. They finally got closer and closer to the airport. It was really early in the morning, so it was still dark, and Skye could see some beautiful lights over the city.

Once they landed in the airport, she stopped at a restaurant to eat some Dairy Queen. She got a chocolate ice cream dipped in warm chocolate. After she was done eating, she called her limo driver, Uncle Seth Bob. He knew where to go and on the way there she talked about her jet ride. When she arrived, she hopped out of the limousine and yelled out, "Thank you!" Skye ran as fast as the wind up the stairs (even though she tripped a couple of times) and burst open the door to Jaquelyn's apartment. She walked in to see Jaquelyn crying, her face buried in between the cushions.

Jax didn't notice her, as she was too busy crying. So Skye crept up on her and yelled "SURPRISE!" Jaquelyn's looked up. Her face was red, and her jaw dropped. She had one eye open and one eye not."

"OMG! SKYE! DO MOM AND DAD KNOW?" Jaquelyn screamed.

"UUUh…" Skye said nervously.

"Awww, you're becoming more and more like me!" Jax squealed. They hugged a super long hug, and Fozzy, Jaquelyn's cat, rubbed up against them, his long black fur tickling their legs.

That night they had ice cream galore and watched *The Lion King*. Then Skye jumped out of her seat. "Oh my gosh! I forgot! I lost a tooth today and when dad and mom come up to give me money, they will know that I flew here for sure!" Jaquelyn was terrified. After about ten minutes of talking it over, Jax and Skye both decided that they would come home while their parents were still sleeping. Skye had just remembered that the whole reason that she wanted the 5,000 dollars was because she wanted to build a secret room inside of her closet for Jaquelyn once she finally convinced her to come home. And convincing Jax was probably the easiest thing to do in the world, so Skye knew she was going to need the money.

The room had to be a secret, because if Skye took Jaquelyn home and she had nowhere to sleep but with Skye, their mom might sneak in on them and see Jaquelyn at home. That would make their mom really mad because she wanted Jaquelyn to make more money for them in California. Skye told Jaquelyn, and she got really excited. Skye wanted it to be a surprise what the room looked like so she didn't even give her a hint!

Uncle Seth Bob drove them to the airport where they got first class seats together. It was long but worth it! Jaquelyn fell asleep listening to the flight attendant saying, "We will be landing in two hours…we will be landing in an hour and thirty minutes…we will be landing in an hour."

When the flight was over, Jaquelyn and Skye rode home in a black limo, so they would blend in. They said a farewell to their limo driver. Skye led the way to the castle. They turned and dashed and sprinted through the black night. Jaquelyn said, "Wait, I think I hear something." They heard a small rustle, and whipped their heads around. There they saw a black figure dashing towards them. They sprinted away and in the heat of the moment, a potato sack captured both of them.

"What's happening?" Skye whispered.

"I don't know, just keep calm," Jaquelyn replied.

Soon they heard the creaking of long stairs, and then felt themselves being thrown onto the bed. The sack was opened, and through a little hole, they saw their mom staring at them with an angry face. She started to use their full names, and that was never a good thing. "Jaquelyn Amanda Johnson! Skye Evangeline Rose Johnson! How could you do this?"

"How'd you know?" Jax said.

"Well, I figured that you had gone when you weren't there when I came up to put money under your pillow. I got very scared because I couldn't find you anywhere. Then I remembered how you were so sad that Jaquelyn had gone. The next thing that hit me is that you had just asked me for $5,000 earlier. When I put all the pieces together, I just knew that you had gone to find your sister," she said to Skye.

"And you," she bellowed to Jaquelyn. "I can't believe you would let your sister do this!"

"Sorry, Mom," Jaquelyn whispered.

"So I got into black clothes and waited for you to come home, so I could capture the both of you," Skye and Jaquelyn's mom said.

"Um, as long as we're all confessing, I made a secret room for Jaquelyn to stay in when she got here. Wanna see?" Skye said. Their mom just grumbled and left the room.

They rushed into the secret room, and it was the best room ever! It was equipped with fuzzy aqua wall paper, an egg chair, a disco ball hanging from the periwinkle ceiling, a fuzzy aqua rug, an aqua radio, a bubble maker, and best of all, A BOBBY JACK BED! "Do you like it?" Skye said. Jaquelyn was speechless. She just fainted. Skye said to herself, "I'll take that as a yes!" Skye dragged Jaquelyn onto her bed and walked out of the secret room, and back into her own green room. This time she laughed herself to sleep.

Jaquelyn stayed there, and they were as happy as could be. Fozzy, Olive, and Zappa, all three of Jaquelyn's cats, stayed there, too, and each had its own fuzzy little bed. And of course, each had an aqua play structure. Jaquelyn and Skye spent the rest of their lives together, and every night they took turns reading a good mystery book to each other. They had vanilla ice cream every day, and even though Jaquelyn loved California, she loves home even more.

Stick Wars Force Unleashed

When the three most powerful weapons of creation are stolen, the three brave heroes must go retrieve them in **STICK WARS FORCE UNLEASHED** *by La Mar H.*

One day in the animated land of Stick World, the Diamond of Life was stolen. The Diamond of Life was so important because it allowed the stick figures to do the things humans could not do in real life. It has a system that only allows non-criminals could use it. Also, it kept the Three Weapons of Creation apart because if they were put together they could blow up the whole universe. Therefore, the master of all ninjas hid it with the Fire Sword, Ice Kunai and the Lighting Shuriken many years ago. If any one of them were found, the person would be the richest and greatest person in the world. When the ninja tribe found out that the Diamond of Life was stolen, they sent their men to go retrieve it; but no one could find it. So then, they sent their best three ninjas out one more time to get the Three Weapons of Creation so that the underworld wouldn't take over the world.

The three ninjas had powers like lightning, earth and air. These powers were given to them from training and hard work. So the chief, Sweet and Sour Chicken, asked Wan, San and Bon to retrieve the three weapons. He believed that his evil skeleton brother, Sour and Sweet Turkey, might have been planning to steal the Three Weapons of Creation. Bon, San, and Wan argued with the chief because they did not want the dangerous task of retrieving the weapons.

"Yes, I know this, but remember that you come from a worthy family. You are as sneaky as cats and fast as cheetahs. Compared to the three of you, your enemies are like three-toed sloths. You are wise like the owl and even without the Diamond of Life, you are still very powerful!" professed Master Sweet and Sour Chicken. So Wan, San, Bon agreed and set out to find the three missing weapons.

They took with them food for three days, dirt bikes and the map they hoped would lead them to all three weapons that the Sour and Sweet Turkey had hidden. Hours into their journey, they finally arrived at their first destination. The Ice Kingdom was hard, rocky, cold and totally slick. You could smell fear in the air as San, Wan and Bon entered.

"Wow," Wan said as he gazed up at the midway point of the ceiling floating in midair. "Is that the ice kunai?" Wan was mistaken by the Ice Knight from the Underworld as an intruder and was attacked. The Ice Knight pulled out his sword that had a diamond tipped edge. It could cut through anything.

Meanwhile, five warriors surrounded Bon. Bon tried to tell them that he wasn't trying to fight, but they didn't listen. So, he did battle with the five warriors: an Archer, a Swordsman, a Wizard, a Viking and a Spartan. The archer shot one arrow at the three ninjas, but Bon cut it in half the long way and then kicked him in the face. Next, the wizard tried to defeat Bon, but as soon as he realized how powerful Bon was you could hear a SSSSS sound as he ran away. The Viking threw his axe but missed and Bon hollered out to him, "I am not the enemy! The one who stole the Diamond of Life is who you should be fighting." The Swordsman ignored Bon and due to his pride, got his head sliced off. Wan, San and Bon defeated all five warriors and headed towards their next destination, The Tower.

"Roughly 2000 feet up," Wan said, being the group nerd. When Wan, San, Bon got closer to the tower, they were shocked at the height and the feel of it. It force field felt like the zap from a static electric shock. They could smell the sweat of the warriors and could see little sparks of electricity running up down and across the tower. It looked like an immense show of fireworks. Not knowing Sour and Sweet Turkey's evil henchmen were following them from the underworld, they began to climb up the tower.

Zzzzzz. A strange noise filled the air.

"Do you hear that?" Wan asked. It was the Lighting Archers!

"Climb faster," demanded Bon.

Wan could clearly see the Lighting Shuriken, but out of nowhere an archer grabbed his leg. "Get off of me!" he yelled as he kicked the archer off of him then grabbed the Shuriken. Together, he and his brothers jumped and with their ninja cloaks acting as wings, safely landed to a grassy clearing in the woods.

"Two down, one to go!" declared Bon. The brothers celebrated. They were kicking evil butt! They gobbled up some grub and went to bed except for Bon. He had been having these crazy nightmares, so he decided to take a jog. At about half a mile, he saw a dojo. It was burning and he could feel the intense heat. Like any typical warrior, Bon bravely stepped inside. There he saw the final weapon with an enormous fire-breathing dragon guarding it.

Knowing he had fire powers, Bon rose above the fire like it was nothing. He tried to hit the dragon but all he did was lure it to him. He ran toward the sword, but was struck to the ground by the dragon's tail. With lightning speed, he reached for the sword and cut its head with one blow. He ran as fast as he could back to the group. The others were shocked, but they packed their bags and headed home.

After the news was spread, the village assembled Spartans, Mukluks, Janissary, Bellmen, Boyars, Knights Templar, Navy, Comanche, Mongol Ming Warrior, Musketeers, Sun Tzu, KGB, CIA, Celts, Somali, SWAT, and a GSG-9. They also gathered M4A1s, FAMASs, SCAR-Hs, TAR-21s, FAL, M16s, A4s, F2000s, and AK-47s. The Rounder World declared war. San, Wan, Bon had the most powerful weapons in the war.

Ready for war they had their weapons at their side and properly attired in armor. Their duty was to acquire the Diamond of Life. The people in the air were to either bomb or to act as a lookout. People in tanks had to be in the front to shield and, everyone else had to get San, Wan, and Bon to the Diamond of Life safely. As the army moved into the evil territory, it was the first bomber who bombed the castle. They did not see it coming. The castle crumbed and the ground opened up allowing San, Wan, and Bon to slither under the remains of the castle where they discovered the evil master Sour and Sweet Chicken guarding the Diamond of Life.

"Why do you even want to steal the Diamond of Life anyway?" Wan, San and Bon said at the same time.

"The reason I want the Diamond of Life is that when I was about your age, my brother and I both wanted the old ninja master to grant one of us the Diamond of Life. I thought I was going to be chosen, but my father denied me this honor because he saw anger in me. He then banished me to the Underworld."

"That's your big reason? That stinks!" Wan declared. Then San gave the tribe the attack signal, and they banished the evil ones to the Underworld forever. So that's the story.

Stuck in a DS

When a young boy, Danny, clicks a button on his DS, something weird happens to him. In **STUCK IN A DS** *by* **Christo Seman***, find out what happens to Danny.*

"Dad, can you please get me the Super Mario Brothers Four, please?" Danny asked. "Please, Dad?"

"Okay, we might be able to get you a DSI XL too," his dad replied. Danny and his dad went to buy the game at the video game store.

While Danny was playing his new Nintendo DS, he always wondered about a weird button on the system. The button was labeled "DNT." Danny checked the manual which said that it meant "Do Not Touch." He really didn't care, so he clicked the button and suddenly he appeared inside his DS. He was in the middle of his game, and didn't know how to get out!

"Where am I?" Danny asked.

"You are in your Nintendo DS!" a mystery voice replied.

"Who said that?" Danny yelled.

"I am your Nintendo DS!"

How is my Nintendo DS talking to me? Danny wondered to himself. "If I am inside my DS, how do I get out?"

"There are two ways," said the voice. "First, you can turn off the game without saving; the second way is to beat the whole game." Danny chose to turn off the game, but it was too late. He couldn't turn off the game, so Danny had to beat the whole game.

Danny asked his Nintendo DS where to find the game, and the system showed him the way to a portal. Danny was suddenly in the game. He had to start at World One, so he was thinking about how to get to World Ten as fast as possible.

Danny remembered that in the classic Super Mario Brothers you could jump to different worlds. So that is what he decided to do. In about two minutes, Danny was in World Ten. He had to beat all the levels in World Ten, but the Boss Battle was not that easy. Danny had to jump on Bowser three times. He had lost at that point, but good thing he had a checkpoint. He won the battle on the last attempt without getting hurt.

He felt like he was teleported out of the game and out of the DS. Danny was so happy that he got out, but also a little sad. He would miss the adventure: It was the best adventure he had ever been a part of. He started checking out his other game systems for a "DNT" button. Danny was hoping for a similar adventure in the Nintendo Wii.

Super Josh

A curious dog named Josh unknowingly drops his owner's experiment while in his lab. At first it's all fun and games, until Josh's dad gets in trouble! Will he save his "dad" in **SUPER JOSH**, by **Sophie C.**?

Hi, I'm Josh; my dad is a scientist freak. He never pays any attention to me because he is always in his lab working on some type of experiment. This is the story of how I became known as a Super Hero, well a Super Dog.

Boom! The door slammed shut. I ran over to the window as my master's (dad's) car faded away as it drove down the street. I heard a creaking noise as the door of my dad's lab opened. I was curious to see what experiment my dad was working on now. I knew I wasn't supposed to go in there, but I couldn't resist it! As I walked into the lab, I saw different colored liquids in shiny glass bottles. I started to sniff and walk around and then there was a crash.

Oh no, I thought to myself. I knocked down a table with my tail! I saw all of these different colored liquids and shattered glass bottles fall to the floor.

"My dad is going to kill me," I barked. I walked around the lab to see how bad the damage was. "Ouch!" I whined.

I stepped on a piece of glass that was covered with a grassy green liquid. *Boom! Bang! Bam!* A tornado formed around me. It lifted me off the ground and carried me somewhere. Then the tornado just dropped me with a loud thud! Then everything went black.

When I woke up, it was morning. I couldn't remember a thing about last night. I walked into my dad's bedroom like I always do in the morning. Oddly, he wasn't there and the TV was on. I checked his lab but he wasn't in there either! I caught a glimpse of something moving out of the corner of my eye when I walked by the mirror. As I walked closer, I realized the creature was copying every movement I did. It had long, curly, golden blond fur, green piercing eyes and a small black nose. It took me awhile to finally realize that the weird looking creature was myself.

422 • THERE'S NO APP FOR THIS

I looked so different! Then suddenly, I remembered last night. *The tornado must have done this* to *me,* I thought. *I was really ripped! I had some muscle before, but now my biceps were huge! The ladies can't resist this. I also got much taller, and I could see better and even smell better. Just then, I noticed a red and blue cape around me. It had the initials SJ on it. I guess I got smarter too because I realized it stood for Super Josh! Wait....that must mean I'm a super hero!* I got really excited! Now, I could fly, run fast, and save people or animals from horrible villains.

With my new super powers, I went to search for my dad. As I was walking down the street sniffing for my owner, I saw the TV on at a restaurant and it showed a picture of my dad. As soon as I saw him on the TV I knew something bad happened to him. I ran like lighting through the streets picking up any scent I could of my dad's car. My nose led me to a dark, black abandoned building. Through a broken window, I could see my dad strapped tightly into a wooden chair. I flew up and peeked closer through the window and saw that my dad's eyes were shut and that he had a bunch of cuts and bruises all over him. In the corner of the room were two big guys. I quietly crept into the building just as the two, huge men turned around to face me. I karate kicked them both in the head. The guys fell to the ground with a loud thump. Then, I ran over to my dad and untied him from the chair. I threw him over my back, flew back to our house, and then I laid him gently down on his bed.

When he woke up the next day, he didn't have a clue about what had happened to him. As he yawned, he walked into his lab, which was surprisingly spotless. It was as if he had forgotten about the whole thing, I played along and acted innocent while he finished up some experiments.

My dad never noticed my super powers. So now, when I go off on missions, he thinks I just need to go to the bathroom. And from that day forward, I continue to save people's and animals' lives.

The Super Power

No need to fear; family is here. This story is about a super-powered boy whose family has been killed—or so he thinks. In **THE SUPER POWER** *by* **Iniko Williams**, *is flying better than family?*

One spring day, two friends, Bubble and Gum, were on their way home from school. While they were walking, Bubble said to Gum, "Hey, let's go down Hayworth Street!"

"Are you kidding?" Gum replied. "Nobody goes there. That street is totally haunted and, not to mention, creepy!"

"C'mon, it is daytime, and it will be fun," pleaded Bubble. Against his better intentions, Gum reluctantly agreed, and they turned down the dreaded Hayworth Street. *Nothing unusual,* thought Gum. *There are nice houses and lots of kids.*

"Hey, there is Mr. Jefferson from school!" shouted Bubble. But Mr. Jefferson never looked up as the two boys shouted their hellos and waved. "He is always so nice at school," said Bubble. "Oh well, two more blocks and we are home free, and then we can tell our friends we conquered Hayworth Street!"

Their fun free feeling was cut short soon when, without warning, it got very dark. The kids that had been there we suddenly gone! Gum began to feel scared. "Bubble, d-did you see that?" stuttered Gum.

"What?" asked Bubble.

Slowly both boys turned to see a mysterious dark figure hurrying toward them with a loud screech. "Run!" they both shouted.

Gum was running as fast as his legs could carry him, but before long he realized that he was running alone. Scared and confused, he turned back to see where his friend could be. In a flash of light he saw something that even he could not have imagined. It was Bubble! Super Bubble! He and the dark figure were in a heated battle. With guns blazing and flashes of light, it was almost like a video game or a space movie. Just when the figure had Bubble to the ground and all Gum's hope of ever seeing his friend again seemed gone, Bubble quickly moved with the speed of a panther to blast the figure one last time as it fell to the ground. Then there was silence.

Gum quickly ran to his friend. Although he had a million questions, he was not quite sure where to begin. The first question was of course who is this masked figure and why was he chasing them? Bubble kneeled down and with razor-like precision removed the mask from the cloaked figure. What he saw was unbelievable: Mr. Johnson! "Why? Why would you do this? We thought you were just an old man."

Mr. Johnson began to speak. "You think with your eyes, child. Therefore you are easy to fool. My real name is Krylon, and this street belongs to my people. Many years ago we came to this planet looking for intelligent life and to study the strange creatures you call humans. We also came looking for our lost prince."

"Lost prince?" both boys asked.

The next few words he spoke were almost unbelievable. "Bubble, your real name is Kaldar, and you were one of two sons born to King Sycon and Queen Islish. When our planet was destroyed, we all had to get away very fast. Your mother gave birth to the both of you here on planet Earth."

"Both of us?" asked Bubble.

"Yes. You and your brother Kangon."

"Where is my brother and why did I all of a sudden have the power to fight you?" asked Bubble

Krylon sighed and asked the boys to wait a minute while he explained. "Kaldar, when you were born we were at war, and your mother hid you and your brother with human friends to make sure you were safe. She trusted that after the war we would find you and you could be with us. She never made it back to get you, for she was lost in battle. I vowed that I would find you and reunite you with your brother."

"Krylon, I understand, but where is my brother? I need to know."

"Please allow me to finish. You are the older of the brothers. Therefore your powers are manifesting now. You may think that you are only an eleven-year-old boy, but you are much older. Your brother Kangon is very gifted. He will possess the power of wisdom and light. You are a warrior. Together you can bring compassion and understanding where there is war. I never thought that I would find you together here with your brother Kangon."

"My brother!" exclaimed Bubble.

"He's my brother?" asked Gum.

"Yes, this is why you two were immediately drawn to each other. I have watched you over the years and waited for the correct time to bring you together. I came after the two of you because it was time to let Kaldar manifest his power. As I dreamed, Kaldar, you are a warrior of epic greatness. Kangon, your cautiousness has kept your brother safe. You both are in need of more training, which we will begin soon. Welcome home."

As they left Krylon (AKA Mr. Johnson), they were so glad to find that not only are they best friends, they are also brothers— brothers with the Super Power.

There's More in New York than the Yankees

Dreams hold warnings and challenge one boy to extraordinary actions in **THERE'S MORE IN NEW YORK THAN THE YANKEES**, *by **Miriam S. Goldstein**.*

*Y*ou *know when things seem good at the time but end up terribly in the end?* That's the first thing that popped into my thoughts when I woke up in the hospital, but I didn't know why I was there. "Chad! Dr. Gerginsmith! Nurse! He's awake!" a voice cried. It was my mother's voice.

"M-Mo-Mom?" I say feebly.

"Yes, honey?" I was about to say, "Why am I here?" but then it all came back to me…..

She came to me in a dream. She was standing in the corner of a dark, dark, room. A light hung above her head. She was wearing a dress made of everything beautiful about the Earth. I saw trees and vines, flowers and fruits. But in the center of her dress, there was a black blob. I stood on the other side of the room, staring at her. "I'm dying," she said calmly. She looked about my age.

"Who are you?" I say.

"I am the spirit of Earth. I am all of nature and human spirit. As long as I live, the Earth lives with me. But everyone forgot about me. They're polluting my soul, killing my creatures. I am the spirit of the Earth, not the cities with pollution and violence," she says. I see a tear rolling down her cheek.

"Why are you telling me this?" I didn't know at all. I'm just twelve-year-old Chad Smith. I live in Brooklyn and eat at McDonalds. I went hunting with my Uncle Chuck last summer. Why did she want me?

She says, "Chad—"

"Wait, how do you know my name?" I interrupt.

She calmly replies, "I know everyone's name, and everything about every person. I know your parents are divorced, you live with your mother, play football, have OCD; you have a cat named Lucy and a dog named Max. I also know you are the only one who can save me. All the other humans have lost sight of all peace and something called Maru. Maru is the connection between nature and me. I need you, Chad, I need you…" She faded away, still saying, "I need you."

I woke up in a cold sweat. "Wow, oh my god," I said aloud. Lucy, my cat who sleeps at the bottom of my bed, stirred and meowed. I petted her, still thinking about the girl in my dream. "You know," I said to my cat, "she was kind of cute, but if she's the spirit of the Earth, she's probably, like, a *billion* years old. Why did she look so young?" My cat purred in response.

I checked my clock. It was only one o'clock in the morning. I went back to sleep. As soon as I closed my eyes, I was back in the room. She smiled. "You're back," she whispered.

"I will help you," I said. "But first I need to ask you a few questions. First, where am I?"

"You're wherever you think you are or where *I* want you to be," she replied.

"Holy poop!" I shout. "Okay, back to my questions." My tone went serious again. "Now, what's your name?"

"My name is Shudras Makiu, but you may call me Sara," she said with a gorgeous, twinkly laugh. "Well, all right, Sara, two questions left," I say with my wannabe serious tone.

Sara looks behind her. "No time now!" she says. "If we talk too long in this way, it will do serious damage to your brain, but every time you dream, I will be with you. Good-bye, Chad."

She kisses my forehead, and I shout: "WAIT!" but she only fades away.

I wake up saying, "Wait, wait, wait." I realize I'm awake and say, "I need to get back to sleep!" I toss and turn for an hour, under the blanket my big sister made for me before she went to college last summer.

My mom comes in and says, "Happy Saturday Chad-y. I made chocolate French toast."

I pop out of bed and say, "Oh yeah!"

I run down the hall of our three-room apartment in my favorite Transformer pajamas. I know I'm too old for them, but I can't outgrow the soft fleece, no matter how hard I try. On Saturdays mom lets me eat in the living room so I can watch TV on the couch. I grab the chocolaty goodness that is my mom's cooking and then turn on *Full House*.

After breakfast, I go to the house of my best friends, John and Joanne. They're twins, and they live in the apartment next door to me. We do the usual: play videogames, then go to Central Park and play football.

I came back and had almost forgotten about the dreams and Sara until that night after my mom and I spend an evening together. Again, it's the usual, pizza, and it was her week to choose the movie. We watched *It's Kind of a Funny Story* for the fifth time, and mom started crying for the fifth time at the end.

When I went to bed, I remembered the dream, and then thought *Oh, it was probably my imagination*. Boy, was I wrong. The whole thing started up again as soon as I closed my eyes.

I was in the room again. "Welcome back, Chad," said Sara. The black blob on her dress was bigger.

"Sara, I've got loads of questions!" I say eagerly.

"Well, then, I have a feeling that they must stay *unanswered* questions," she says with a smirk.

"Why, why?" I whine.

"Would you like some cheese with that whine? Some things here *must* be kept a secret. But, don't worry, everything will work out fine—" her tone darkened "—*if* you do exactly as I say. Goodbye, Chad." Then I wake up.

"Oh, come on!" I shout. I kick the covers, and Lucy stirs in her sleep and meows. "Sorry, Lucy," I say, "I'm just a little annoyed at Sara right now. She was sassier than I remember." I get out of bed and get ready for church.

During the middle of a prayer, the world got dizzy and fuzzy. There was a sound much like a bee in my ear. *Wheeeeee* went the noise. Then everything went black.

I was in the room, but it was falling apart, "Chad! Thank goodness you're here!" shouts Sara. She runs into my arms, crying. "Sara, what the heck is going on here!" I shout above the noise of the room breaking. Tears are pouring out of her eyes, only they are black and oily.

"I-It's t-t-t-oo late, Chad, I'm almost dead," she sputters.

"How can I save you, Sara?" I stay surprisingly calm.

"I-I-it's too hard, Chad, too hard for you. You're only a mortal… Too hard for me, too, and I'm *immortal.* I'm sorry. So, so, so very sorry. But *you* are the only one who can do this. It's all up to *you.*"

A year later

I have no idea what happened that night: none; zero; zilch; nada. I wish I did, though. No matter how hard I think, I can't remember. It's a shame. I just know that what I did was big, huge, gigantic, GINORMOUS! It was on the news for months, my mom tells me. I didn't get to see it, though, because I was in a coma for two months with a broken leg and minor concussion. I asked my mom. She said that the paramedics found me underneath a tree in the middle of Central Park with blood from my brain oozing out my ears. When I woke up, I kept asking if Sara was okay, and then they thought I became schizophrenic. By the time I woke up, the news had moved on to the disappearance of a girl named Alison in Rosewood, Pennsylvania. Weird, huh? It was a good thing my coma started in the summer so I didn't miss school.

But a few days before the last day of school, I remembered a few things about that night. There were me and Sara in the Dream World, and I'm just guessing here, but I think I did something to her to prevent the idiocy of humans and the way they treat her from hurting her anymore. I really wish I knew. It's killing me!

But now it's time for me to graduate from elementary school. (Mine goes K-6, not K-5.) We did a run around the blacktop, pied the principal…the things I saw older kids do every year before me, and now *I'm* doing them. I feel old. At the party that Mrs. Jenkins, Paul's mom, throws, I see Sara in the corner, standing with someone else. The black blob on her dress is gone. I've got a feeling it's time for another adventure. I've got three months until junior high: three months to save the world—again. But this time, I'm ready. I'll see you on the news!

Trapped in a Snow Globe

In **TRAPPED IN A SNOW GLOBE** *by* ***Alexander Moss,*** *a girl wishing to live in Chicago has her dream come true. But she gets trapped in a snow globe and needs to get out before her big swim meet!*

One rainy, soggy day in Zurich, Kansas a girl named Marissa was in her room wondering, *I wish I lived in a big city like Chicago, New York or even Los Angeles.* Marissa looked at her collection of snow globes. She had more than Albert Einstein could count, but her favorite one was the snow globe of Chicago. Marissa always asked her mom, "Why can't we live in a bigger city like Chicago?"

Her mom always had the same answer, "Sorry honey we just don't have the money to live in such a big city."

Right when Marissa's mom was about to leave she said, "Honey, your friend Loraine is coming over soon. You should get ready."

"Oh, I totally forgot about that, Marissa admitted. "Thanks for reminding me."

About 20 minutes later, Loraine came over and they ran up to Marissa's room. They were talking about school for a while. Then the two girls were looking at Marissa's snow globes they began talking about their swim meet tomorrow. "I can't wait for the meet," Loraine mentioned. "Plus, you are the best on our team."

"You don't have to say that. You are really good, too."

"Yeah, but not as good as you. You swam a one hundred meter in a minute and eight seconds!"

"Yeah I did!"

"So I was just wondering, which snow globe is your favorite?" Loraine asked.

"My Chicago one. I love it. I've always wanted to live there.

"Why can't you?"

"We just moved here a little less than a year ago, and my mom doesn't want to move again."

"Oh, well it's time for me to go. See you at the meet tomorrow Marissa"

After Loraine left, Marissa was looking into her Chicago snow globe. Suddenly she felt a tingly feeling. She felt her shoes getting bigger. She looked down and her feet were tiny. Then it felt like her body was way too big for her head, and it was! Her head was shrinking. Then her body! Before she knew it she was two inches tall! Then she had a thought, *What if I could somehow find a way into the snow globe.* She remembered there was an opening at the top, but thought it was hard to open. With this body she probably wouldn't be able to open it.

First, she had to climb up the side. That's what's going to be hard though because she needed to climb up a circular side. She ran as fast as she could to grab a stuffed animal to use as a trampoline to get in top of the snow globe. Once she got the stuffed animal over by the snow globe she started jumping. On the fourth try, she almost got up there, but she slipped off. She walked onto the stuffed animal. She took three small jumps then… she was on top of the snow globe.

The next task was to open the little slit. She tried and tried to open the slit but it wouldn't budge. She tried to stick her foot under it. Her foot was under and the slit was ajar. She bent down and pulled. She pulled and pulled and pulled until it opened. The slit was opened and she was ready to jump in. She leaned over the ledge. All she could see was black. She bent her knees and jumped.

"AHHHHHHHHHHHH!" she was screaming for almost five minutes. In the corner of her eye she saw a building. Then she noticed she had a parachute with her. She pulled the string and she was floating in the air just like a butterfly. It took about three more minutes until she landed. Once she got out of the parachute she knew where she was.

Marissa stopped in amazement. She saw skyscrapers with windows scaling them. She could smell the fresh hot dogs coming off the grill. She could hear the honking of cars in traffic. She could feel the rush of people walking in and out of department stores.

"I'm in Chicago!" she exclaimed.

"Yes, you are," said a man.

Marissa saw the man and asked, "What's your name?"

"My name is Tom, but you can call me Tommy," he replied.

Marissa and Tommy talked for a little while longer. "Where did you come from?" Tommy asked.

"I live in Zurich, Kansas. It's a very, very small town."

"So how'd you get here?"

"Well, this is my snow globe. I shrunk down and jumped into my snow globe."

"Oh, this is a snow globe?" Tommy asked disappointed.

"Well yes, but once you get inside it seems like this is a real live city."

"Yes, I guess. I was wondering where you're staying?" Tommy asked

"Nowhere, right now."

"You can stay at my house. My friend has an extra room and anything to help you who fell from the sky."

"Thanks a lot," Marissa proclaimed.

Then Tommy asked her to come to his apartment for some food and a drink. Marissa said yes and they headed off to Tommy's apartment. When they got there Marissa couldn't believe her eyes. He had everything- a large leather couch, a 70 inch flat screen TV, the biggest kitchen she has ever seen and, her favorite of them all, a little puppy dog. "Oh my gosh. That puppy is the cutest dog I've ever seen!" Marissa exclaimed.

"I found him on the street. He looked lonely so I adopted him," Tommy asserted.

Once Marissa was done looking around Tommy's monstrous apartment, she walked outside and started to walk around the city. She started to look at the Sears Tower. She remembered that she had read that it was the tallest building in the USA. After she looked around the Sears Tower she made her way to the Shedd Aquarium. She saw otters, octopus, whales, penguins and lizards. She couldn't believe how many different animals they could have. Marissa thought, *Why is my mom not letting me see this? It's amazing and wonderful.* Then Marissa made her way to the Chicago Institute of Art. Stepping inside she was astonished over the many pieces of art there. Her favorite part was the African exhibit. She had always loved the masks and artistic colors and shapes on the mask. She especially liked the Thorne Rooms though, with all the designs in such a small place.

When Marissa was done at the museum, it was about 5:00. As she walked out of the museum she remembered, *Oh my gosh. I have a swim meet tomorrow and it's one of the biggest in my life. I can't miss it.*

Marissa sprinted to Tommy's apartment, rushed in and exclaimed, "How do I get out of here!"

"What are you talking about?" Tommy asked.

"I have the biggest swim meet of my life tomorrow and I need to get out of here," Marissa proclaimed.

"I have a friend who owns hot air balloons. Maybe I can get one. You said you fell from the sky, and that there was an opening. Maybe if we can get close enough you can jump out of here."

"That sounds like a great idea!" Marissa shouted.

That night Marissa fell asleep wondering if she would miss her meet. She was worried that she would, but she would have to trust Tommy. As she lay back on her pillow she fell asleep worrying.

The next day Marissa woke up at 8:50 A.M. ready to get back home. When she walked outside she saw a big hot air balloon. Tommy was standing in it, "Ready to go?" he announced.

Marissa shook her head, got into the hot air balloon and they were off. After about ten minutes in the hot air balloon, Marissa could see a small opening in the sky. She knew that was her way back home. She got onto the ledge of the hot air balloon. "I guess this is it," Marissa proclaimed.

"Yeah I guess it is," Tommy said.

"Next time we have to go to a Cubs game!" Marissa said excitedly.

"Sure thing," Tommy answered.

In a flash Marissa jumped out of the hot air balloon with her eyes closed and as she opened her eyes she was back in her room. A minute later her mom walked in and said, "Are you ready for your meet?"

"Yes, I am ready mom," Marissa confirmed. "Mom I was talking to a friend last night and they said Chicago was a great city."

"Well we will have to wait honey," her mom said.

As Marissa was about to walk out the door from her big swim meet, she looked at the Chicago snow globe. In the distance of the snow globe she could see Tommy waving and smiling. Marissa smiled and waved back.

Travel to Elasqush

In **TRAVEL TO ELASQUSH** *by* **D. Johnson**, *Jack decides to play a video game called* Evil Royalty. *He is soon sucked into the evil world of Elasqush. With his new friend, Jake discovers the king has an evil secret.*

It's Saturday, and Jack was so excited because he got a new video game. It was called *Evil Royalty*. It was about ruling nations all around world. Jack found something weird when the game menu said, "Pick a country." There was a new country called Elasqush. He clicked on Elasqush and the strangest thing happened. The words on his screen said, "Welcome to Elasqush." Then there was a loud *BOOM*! He soon realized that he was sucked into the video game!

Where am I? thought Jack.

"Squeak ook squawk."

"Ahhhhhhhh!" Jack said. "Who the heck are you?"

"Hi, my name is Scribbles."

"What kind of name is Scribbles?" inquired Jack.

"Everybody's name is Scribbles in Elasqush."

"How do I get out of here?"

"Don't ask me, ask the king." said Scribbles. "Follow me!" Then they were off on their way to see the king.

"Hear ye, hear ye," said the king. "Today we take over America." Cheers emerged from the crowd of people surrounding the king.

"Now I get it. Wait a second; did he say America?" Jack shouted.

"We have sent our mighty army to destroy those ugly people," continued the king.

"Okay, now it's on!" roared Jack angrily.

Jack marched up to the king and said, "Listen here, you."

"Who dare disturb the king?" yelled the king.

"Jack is my name, but that doesn't matter! The thing is you can't destroy America."

"Why can't I do that?" said the king.

"You can't do that because America is my country!"

"Come on Jack, let's just go," said Scribbles.

"I also meant to say you are a dummy!" Jack screamed at the king. The crowd was silent not letting out a peep. No one had ever said those words to the king before.

"How dare you insult the king? You two shall be destroyed as soon as possible!" roared the king.

"Oh no, oh no, our goose is cooked now!" said Scribbles.

The king demanded that Jack and Scribbles be destroyed. They ran as fast as they could to flee the palace.

"Guards, get those evil people!" demanded the king.

"Let's go before his guards find us," whispered Scribbles.

"I'm with you on that one," agreed Jack.

"Quick, over here! Let's hide behind this huge rock." Then Jack and Scribbles jumped behind the rock, and said, "That was a close one. Wait, why do I feel all fuzzy?" asked Jack.

"Me too," said Scribbles. "It kind of feels like we are getting transported," concluded Scribbles.

"What's happening? I think we might be getting out of here. Wait, I think my mom turned off the game," said Jack surprised.

Then Jack and Scribbles started jumping for joy. Then there was a loud *BOOM* just like when he entered this strange, yet cool place. Finally, Jack realized he was back home. All seemed to be well, until Jack's mom knocked on his door.

"Hi, sweetie. How was school?"

"Good, why?"

"I just wanted to know, wait one second," she said slowly.

"What's the matter?"

"Nothing, except today is Saturday and you don't have school on Saturday," his mom replied.

"Well I…" Jack stuttered.

"What about your new friend?" Jack's mom interrupted. Her hands rested on her hips as her foot tapped the floor.

"What new friend?" Jack said, trying to act surprised.

You would think Jack would have finally come clean to his mom about Scribbles. However, Jack's mom easily discovered him after she heard a loud sneeze come from the closet. She looked in and saw a white colored monster with red stripes; she knew it was from the game.

The good part was Jack actually got to keep Scribbles. The bad part was that Jack was grounded for two weeks because he did not tell his mom about Scribbles in the first place.

Well, that is what happens when you take a trip to Elasqush.

The Troll Adventure

Jason, Eliza, and Harry go on a cool adventure to find their parents but they run into some nasty encounters. Find out about their adventure and if they find their parents in **THE TROLL ADVENTURE**, *by* ***Hannah Major.***

There's this thing: It's called telling the truth. My friend, Harry, should try it. Oh, I forgot to tell you my name is Jason. Have you ever had a friend lie to you?

I have, all the time. And I'm getting tired of it, so I'm going to tell Harry to his face.

But, this story is not only about friendship and telling the truth; it's about an adventure. So listen close. This story will blow your mind.

"Hey, Harry, what are you doing?" I asked.

"Oh nothing," Harry replied.

"Cool! You want to hang out later?"

"Maybe," said Harry.

"Okay, bye," I continued. "Hey, Eliza!"

"Sorry, Jason, I can't talk now," replied Eliza. "I'm looking for someone."

"Oh, okay," I said. "Bye."

"Hi Jason!" my mom yelled when I came in the door. "How was school today?"

"It was okay," I replied.

The next day at school was crazy. The teachers acted like they were under a spell; but, they only acted that way toward me and my friends. I was kind of freaked out! I tried to ask what was going on, but they all said nothing, just like everything was the same.

When I got home, my parents were gone. I called for my dad, but he didn't answer. Then I tried calling for my mom, but she didn't answer either. Something is going on, and I'm going to find out.

I called Harry and told him that my parents had disappeared. He said that his parents were gone and so were Eliza's parents. We decided that we would wait a day and if they were still gone in the morning, we would go looking for them after school.

The next morning, I still couldn't find my parents so I called Harry and Eliza. They said that their parents were still missing too.

So, they came over and we got ready to go looking for our parents. First, we had to pack. We made three grilled cheese sandwiches and packed six sodas, a couple of cookies, a flashlight, and a tent. We all made sure that we had our cell phones.

We set out into the cold, dark night. We searched for hours, but our parents were nowhere to be found. It was getting really dark, so we set up the tent and decided to continue our search in the morning.

I was the first one to wake up; I woke to the feeling of movement. I got up and looked around, but we weren't in our tent anymore.

"Oh good, you're up," a strange voice said.

"Who said that?" I asked nervously.

"It's me," said a voice from the driver's seat.

"Who are you?" I asked nervously.

"I didn't think you would remember me," continued the voice. "I am your cousin, Jake. You met me once, but you were only two years old."

He told me that my parents went on a quest and got captured by a troll named Bob. My parents sent Jake to protect me. Suddenly, a rumble came through the floor and Harry and Eliza both woke up. I looked through the back window and saw a giant one-footed troll with five eyes, eight arms, and a big nose.

"Step on it!" I yelled as Jake smashed on the gas and we zoomed down the street. Harry was screaming.

"Harry, be quiet!" I yelled, but he just kept screaming. I couldn't blame him. I was about to scream and then—*Boom!*— everything went dark.

"Jason, wake up!" Harry yelled.

"What happened?" I asked.

Harry told me that I had fainted. I rubbed my head because it hurt. When I fainted, I must have hit my head on the car door or window.

But the good news is that we lost the troll, Bob, for now.

"Where to next?" My cousin, Jake handed me a map.

"Where did you get this?" I asked.

"I grabbed it when I was leaving to find you guys."

As we looked at the map I noticed that the writing didn't make sense.

"What language is this?" I asked.

"It's Greek," Jason said.

"Can anybody read Greek?" I asked.

"Not me!" Harry said.

"Not me!" Eliza said.

"Well, I don't think I can either," I said. "Jake, can you read Greek?"

"Just a little, but luckily I brought my Greek translator."

"Why do you have a Greek translator?" I asked.

"For times like this, of course!" he replied.

Anyway, we finally got there. But don't ask me where "there" is because I don't even know. It was dark, very dark, with scary people. The buildings were very old and worn down. We walked into a restaurant called Bob's Burgers. I was scared to go in because of the name.

"Hey guys," I asked. "Do you think Bob, the troll, owns this place?"

"No," Jake said. "We lost him. He's long gone."

So we walked in, and of course, it was just as I thought. Our parents were tied to a chair and Bob the troll was standing in front of them.

"Let them go!" I yelled.

"Okay," Bob said. Then he let them go and we all went home.

Wow! That was easy. My mom said that Bob was actually really nice. "He gave us soup and a cookie. We played Scrabble and we had a good time." My mom said that she even had Bob on speed dial. Wow! Now, that's weird.

"Take him off of speed dial," I said.

"Why?" my mom wondered. "He's my friend."

"Okay, Mom," I replied. "But, when he tries to eat you or kidnap you again, don't come crying to me!"

"Don't worry!" my mom replied with a smile. "I won't.

The Unknown End

A father raises a crossbreed between a Demon and a Human. When he is ordered to war, Ren is sent to a military camp to find a power like no other. Will he control it or lose it in **THE UNKNOWN END** *by* ***Ryan Larson?***

If you are hearing this that means the end of your world is near. The creatures that are coming for your world are called Humans. The Humans are ruthless and cunning with their modern technology and weapons. They are creatures that have soft skin and weak bones. We are demons that can spike their power when we attack to give it some extra kick. Some have this special energy called Chakra, which gives them the ability to use special attacks. We live in a place called the Demon Paradox. The Paradox has an energy called Chaos Energy. The Humans are stealing the Chaos Energy from the Demon Paradox because they are running out of power and energy for their growing population. They also destroy other populations on other worlds. They do this to spread fear and to show how strong they are as well.

My name is Ren. I am not just a regular Demon. I am actually a crossbreed between a Human and Demon. I am 15 years old, just a teenager. Our leader during this dark time is Tex, who happens to be the devil. "I need to make a plan," he muttered to himself in his almost pitch black office that was only lit by a half a dozen candles.

The next day he spoke to the rest of the Demon counsel about his idea. He described how he believed that we could take our Chaos Energy and supplies back from the Humans. It depended on sending a massive attack to their front door. The counsel liked his idea. Just as the counsel was about to discuss the details on who to send as general…*Qchhhh.* "The portal; it's opening!" yelled a soldier. Human soldiers were rushing in firing their AK-47s and RPG's. There were Demon soldiers doing their best to fight and topple the Human force. I couldn't see much because there was an immense cloud of dust around the battle. The battle was fierce, and the Demons managed to fend off the Humans.

The next morning my father was sent to war and I was sent to military camp. Camp was not a place you would go with your family. It had turrets ready and electrical fencing with barbed wire on top all around the complex. When I was let in, I saw older Demons in the battle center, and younger Demons practicing battle moves and strategies. When the general walked up and down looking at us new recruits, it felt as if the life was sucked right out of me. The general yelled, "Is this it, a bunch of kids?" He laughed, and then told us to run the obstacle course.

The course had rock walls, lava pits, spikes and more. "I cannot believe that he made us do that with no training whatsoever," I yelled as I finished the course. Then at that moment, as if he had been listening, the general walked up into the finish area.

"Attention!" yelled the general spitting while doing so. "I will not accept flunkeys, babies, tattletales or wimps!"

Two months later, he gave us a real hard test. We had to fight team on team. It was until you're <u>really</u> down. It was near the end of the test and it was Rex and I fighting. We were pretty evenly matched considering the amount of damage we both had taken. I jumped up in the air because Rex's wings were damaged earlier in the battle. I had a clear shot so I took it. I used my new move Flair Blitz. Whoosh! I was engulfed in fire and shot down at him like a fiery bullet. Rex tried to dodge it, but he was too badly wounded. It was a direct hit and Rex was too weak to get up.

When I returned to my quarters, the general came in to congratulate me for passing the test. Then he told the others to retake the test tomorrow. I was happy that I passed. The next three weeks were tough both physically and mentally. It was the most intense for me because the general said, "Since you're a crossbreed, you can unlock a power so powerful, it could end the war." After that, I was determined to become a Super Demon. After three and a half long years of training and hard work, I finally became a Super Demon.

The next day, I was allowed to go home. I had just started the trip back home when – *BOOM!* I was under attack. I fought for a while, sending attacks down onto the Human forces. After they retreated, I followed and learned that they had captured my friends. After I heard that, I was furious. I traveled to their base, but I had to follow them in the shadows and could only wander at night, but even then I had to be careful.

I quietly made my way into the area where my friends were being held. They were knocked out. With them like that, how could I get them out? I went over and tried to wake them up, but to no success. I broke the lock and that woke them up. I told them that we were going to get out. They asked how they would get out of there. I told them that I would make a distraction by going Super Demon. "We need to be quick because the Human troops are closing in," I yelled over the noise of tanks and weapons firing.

We got back to the homeland. My father and our head general met us there. Before we could start to talk Human soldiers started to arrive. We were under attack again. They must have followed us back home. I went Super Demon and my friends readied themselves. I used my Flair Blitz move, which took out a good portion of them. My friends took out the rest of them, while I tried to convince the Human General to surrender and give up the Chaos Energy. The General said, "I will not surrender the energy unless you defeat me".

"I was hoping you would say that," I said. I used my new move, Iraquen, and took him down. He gave us our energy back and left our Paradox forever. So now my story is over and yours begins. GOOD LUCK!

The Unknown Witch

Ashley was certain her parents were going to throw her a surprise party for her birthday. She heard them whispering night after night for weeks! Little did she know the surprise would change her life forever in **THE UNKNOWN WITCH** *by* ***Joclyn Mitchell.***

Ashley was a regular teen with regular parents, regular friends and regular grades. All this would soon change. One snowy Saturday, Ashley woke up to the sound of her TV. It was her 15th birthday! Her parents were downstairs cooking her favorite meal-salad and pizza. She rushed down the stairs to see her mom and dad. Ashley came into the kitchen and her parents yelled, "Happy birthday!"

"Aww, seems only yesterday I was changing your diaper. Now you're fifteen years old," her mother cried.

"Mom," Ashley cried.

Her dad started crying, "I'm sorry. You're just my baby and I feel you don't know who you are."

"I know who I am dad. Don't worry."

"Let's eat!" her mother cried over her father. "Come on, I'm starving and I think you are too. Ashley can take the first bite before we eat. Wait Paul, can you go wake Melissa up please? How can she sleep on her big sister's birthday?"

When her dad was gone Ashley turned to her mother and said, "What did Dad mean when he said I don't know myself?"

"Oh, your father was just upset. That's all."

"But Mom."

"Ashley, don't worry about it," her mother interrupted her. It's your birthday! Now, how much do you want on your plate?"

But it wasn't ok. Ashley knew that something was wrong, the way her dad and mom had been whispering the night before. All she could make out of what they were saying is they needed to tell her or they had waited too long or she can't harness them forever. It was strange. Ashley finally decided that maybe it was just better if she pretended like it hadn't happened. When her sister came rushing down the stairs, Ashley lost her train of thought.

Her sister yelled, "Happy birthday! I'm so sorry I was not awake. I must have hit snooze when I was sleeping."

"It's fine," Ashley said to her sister. "You're here now."

"Let's eat," her mother called behind her. "Now for your 15th birthday, your father and I took the liberty and had your friends plan your party for you. They said they had everything under control. We are supposed to be meeting them at 12:30. So after breakfast go and hop in the shower and get dressed."

"Ok," Ashley replied. "Wow, I wonder what they're going to do for me?"

As Ashley walked up the stairs she thought about her five best friends: Massy, Amber, Alexis, Maggie and Emily. "Wow, I wonder what they're planning for my birthday? Is it a carnival, or ooh…maybe a party at school when school is out? I can't believe that my parents are letting them do this. Wow, my parents are finally getting cool."

When she arrived at the party, she could not believe her eyes. They changed the school into a carnival! Everywhere she looked there were games, a dance floor full of people in masks and her favorite band Paramour! When she saw her friends, she screamed and gave them a hug. Massy was wearing a shimmer blue dress with an ocean blue mask. Alexis was wearing a hot pink dress with a dark pink mask. They all looked amazing. It was a perfect party, the party of her dreams. "I can't believe you guys did this! How you get the school?" Ashley asked.

"I had to make a little bargain with Mr. Grow, but it all worked out," said Molly.

"Wow, I'm not properly dressed for this," Ashley said looking around.

"We didn't you tell what to wear. Sorry, but we wanted it to be a surprise," said Erica. "We have a dress for you in Mrs. Hendrickson's room. Go put it on in there. We will be in the gym where the dance is so you can hang with us and dance."

"Ok guys." When she got to the room she saw her dress lying there. It was the most beautiful thing she had ever seen. It was a red dress, but it was no ordinary red dress. She put it on quickly. When she looked in the mirror, she almost didn't recognize herself. It was like she was a different person.

When she entered the gym, she saw her friends in the middle of the dance floor dancing away. She walked over to them. Massy yelled, "You look amazing. I mean you look awesome! I knew that red dress would look good on you!"

"Hey, have you seen my parents?" Ashley said. "I can't find them anywhere. Have you seen them?"

"No, sorry. Look over there."

As Ashley turned, she heard a whish sound behind her and when she turned Massey's way again, she was gone!

Ok then, Ashley thought to herself. *That was weird.*

"Hey," a voice called behind her.

"Oh hey Maggie, have you seen Massy? She just left a second ago.

"No; hey, are you ok, Ashley?"

She saw an odd look in Maggie's eyes. She had seen this look before and it wasn't good. She was usually upset about something or worse.

"We need to leave," Maggie said finally. "Where's Alexis and Emily? We need them. I told them this was a bad idea."

"What are you talking about?" Ashley yelled over Maggie. "Why do we have to find Alexis and Emily? What's going on?" Ashley screamed.

"Come on," Maggie yelled. Maggie pulled Ashley in as tightly as possible. Maggie wasn't wasting any time. She hurried over to the downstairs locker room where Emily and Alexis had been standing. Maggie rushed to them and yelled, "We have to go," Maggie announced. They all exchanged looks.

"What is going on? "Ashley yelled in frustration to her friends. "I'm not going anywhere without an answer." They all looked at each other. Alexis whispered to Emily. They all shook their heads.

Emily walked up to Ashley and said, "You are going to come with us to the car and we are going to leave. You won't miss anybody. Your parents already know you're gone. We are going to a place that is top secret and on the way there, you won't ask questions about where we are going. It will be a normal car ride, got it?"

"Ok," Ashley replied. "What's everybody standing around here for? Let's go to the car!

As Ashley and her friends drove, Ashley noticed that something wasn't right. "Alexis, stop the car!" But she just sped up more.

"Lex, you're going to get pulled over! Slow down," Emily screamed.

Ashley felt a sensation in her body. She put her hands out and the road in front of them cracked in two.

"Oh, this is just great," Emily screamed. "They don't tell her so she doesn't know how to control it. Then they stick us with the responsibility."

"Em, calm down. Her parents wanted to tell her. You know that," Alexis replied.

As the girls continued, Ashley thought, *What the heck is going on? Why won't anyone tell me what just happened? Why they are treating me like an outsider?"*

"I know it's hard, but come on," Maggie said trying to calm Emily. "Let's set the other drivers straight. Alexis, do you want to go with me?"

"Sure, anything to avoid the tension in this car."

As Alexis and Maggie stepped out of the car, Maggie said over her shoulder, "Em, calm down. She didn't mean to. You know that. Just don't bite off her head. Ok?"

"I'll try not to," Emily said.

"Now someone really has to tell me what is going on here! Why won't anyone tell me? Come on," Ashley demanded.

Emily turned around to Ashley and said, "I don't know how to tell you this, but you're a witch."

Vampire Disses

When a Goth girl is planning revenge, she finds out that she has to compromise because everything isn't what it seems to her. In **VAMPIRE DISSES** *by* **Meagan Sikorski***, she finds out the one she wanted was her worst nightmare.*

She cried out, "But please." Lander paid no attention to her drama-queen fit. He had better things to focus on than a screaming Vee Materson.

Vee wasn't the crying type, but she did have a reason to cry, for she was not liked by her crush Phoenix Slater, who was, of course, a vampire. Vee is a punk with an edge of goth in her, and there was a part of her that loved Phoenix. But the part of Phoenix did not like Vee back. Sure, he liked her as a friend, but never anything more. But indeed a broken heart is worth crying for.

Phoenix quickly turned around and swiftly said, "Shut up. I like somebody else."

Vee's expression turned from sad to angry. She was so angry her snow-white skin turned lava red. She replied back just as harshly to him, "You'll pay for this," with a bit of scream in her voice. Then she stormed off.

Phoenix had never wanted to make Vee cry or hate him, but it wasn't his fault that he liked another girl. It was clearly the feelings going around in his head. Phoenix walked up the long driveway to his mansion. He thought, "What chance does a mere mortal have against a half vampire?" He can only drink animal blood, and he has regular teeth because he's a half vampire. He can be out in sunlight, plus he can also see his reflection in the mirror for the same reason.

Vee got home soaking wet. Instantly after she said those threatening words to Phoenix, it started raining like the whole world was sad. Her gothic makeup was smudged down her eyes and cheeks. She let out a yell—a yell so loud she woke up her pit bull, Sweet Dream, upstairs. She went upstairs and started sobbing uncontrollably. Vee thought to herself, "I'm going to get him good." With Phoenix's vampire secret she could do anything to him, or so she thought.

A few days later, Vee discovered she couldn't do anything to

Phoenix. Because he was a half vampire, the full vampire effects don't work on him, like his burning in the sunlight and drinking blood and seeing his reflection in the mirror. The whole town thought she was loony and cruel for putting a fair citizen through all the long, annoying tests she did on him. But one person thought she wasn't loony, and that was a super-hot jock, Trevor. He was in love with Vee.

Two weeks later Trevor and Vee got together, and Phoenix and his crush Zena got married and moved to Bucharest, Romania. Of course, Zena was a full vampire. She bit Phoenix, and he became a whole vampire, too.

The Velvet Elevator

THE VELVET ELEVATOR, *by **Jenna Woodrow**, is about four middle school boys who are visiting a dad's office. The boys will need to put on their smarty pants if they want lunch in this century.*

"Can we go now?" exclaimed Mason.

"Yeah, I'm starving!" added Zeke

"Oh, c'mon guys, it's not that bad, is it?"

"Are you kidding, Justin! This is terrible!" Alex blurted.

"OK, OK, fine. Let me ask. HEY DAD, CAN WE GO TO THE SUB SHOP NOW?"

"Justin! Don't yell in the office!"

"Sorry, Dad. But can we please go?"

"I still have some work to do, but you can go eat and bring something back for me. OK?"

"Yes! Food, here I come!"

"Hold on! Here is 40 bucks. Bring me back the change, and don't use all of it!"

"We know, Dad!"

"Be good. Just because it's bring your kid to work day for the office and I let you bring a few friends doesn't mean that you get to run around and act like wild animals. I love you, stay safe," Dad said as he kissed Justin on the head.

Justin stared at his dad with embarrassment in his eyes and mouthed the words, "Not in front of my friends, Dad!"

"Oh, sorry. Well, go on, I thought you were hungry," he replied.

"Bye, Dad."

"OK. Bye," said Justin's dad.

The boys walked down the never-ending hallway running their fingers across the smooth marble walls with Justin in the lead. Justin turned a corner.

"Where are we going, Justin?" asked Zeke.

"To the office lobby. They redesigned it so it's not as old and dingy-looking as it used to be, and it looks really cool now!"

The four of them went through the double doors ahead of them and looked around the room with the new leather couches and the perfectly polished tables. Justin scanned the pictures of special people that founded the Reinhold Deetrie Olson PC Law Firm where his dad worked. When he got to Mr. William Reinhold, the main founding father, the picture seemed to scowl at him. Justin got a creepy feeling and a shiver down his spine every time he saw the picture, and the eyes seem to follow you. Every time Justin talked to Mr. Reinhold, Mr. Reinhold didn't ever smile but acted all prim and proper. And judging by the stories told by his dad at home, Mr. Reinhold was no nice guy!

"Justin, it's not that this isn't cool, but I'm hungry," said Alex.

"Yeah, dude, maybe we can come back," added Mason.

"'Kay, let's go," said Justin, still eyeing the picture. They went out the doors and into the never-ending hallway. They walked gazing at the marble walls and deep mahogany wood. They walked until they reached the carved, brass elevator doors. Zeke pressed the down arrow and immediately, the doors opened.

They walked in and were left breathless. It was the fanciest elevator they had ever seen. There were red velvet walls and golden handles on them. It also seemed a bit smaller than before. "Must have redone the elevators, too," said Justin.

"I guess so," Mason managed to say as he pressed the "ONE" button with a star on it. As soon as the button was pressed, the doors closed with a bang and the elevator plunged down. Zeke got dizzy and fell to the floor, Alex became nauseous as he hit the floor, and Mason and Justin clutched the hand rails right before they hit bottom. The doors slowly opened as Alex said, "Well, that was weird."

"Yeah, really weird," said Mason. Justin was staring at Zeke who was still on the floor moaning and groaning.

"Mmmmm, I caaannnn't feeeeel mmmmyy toooes. Mmmmm," he groaned.

"Well, then, you're going to Joe's Sub Shop with numb toes. Now, get up. I'm hungry!" shouted Alex.

The lobby was busy and packed. Justin helped Zeke up, and they made their way through the swimming pool of people. When they got to the fancy glass doors to the street, a tall man in a red and gold uniform opened them and said, "Have a nice day, boys."

"You, too," said Mason.

"That's funny. I don't remember a doorman being there before," Justin said looking over his shoulder.

"It doesn't matter! Let's go! I'm going to die if I don't eat soon!" exclaimed Alex.

The boys walked a few blocks and realized that they did not recognize any of the stores that they had passed. They walked back toward the office building. "This is where I thought Joe's was," said Justin. Instead of a sign that said, "Joe's Sub Shop," there was a sign that said, "Sanders."

"Well, obviously it's somewhere else. What the heck is Sanders anyway?"

"Ummm, I'm not sure," Justin replied. "Let's go back to my dad. Maybe he can help us!"

"Good idea!" said Mason, sounding worried.

They started running down the street when Zeke accidentally bumped into a man who was buying a paper at a corner newsstand and knocked his paper out of his hands. They didn't remember the newsstand being there, either.

"Oh, I'm so sorry!" Zeke pleaded.

Mason leaned down to pick up the newspaper. It read:

The Detroit News   Wednesday, August 28, 1968
DETROIT TIGERS IN WORLD SERIES!

"1968?" Mason thought to himself. "How can it say 1968?"

Then he saw it. All of the cars were old-fashioned, or what Justin's dad called "classics," and all of the men wore suits and hats. That's why there was a newsstand at the corner and a store called "Sanders" instead of "Joe's Sub Shop."

"Here you go, Sir," said Mason as he handed the paper to the man.

"Why, thank you, young man," he said in return in a prim, proper, and polite way.

"I've seen that man before," thought Justin. "Where have I seen him?"

"So where are you fine boys going?" the man interrupted.

"Oh, just down the street. That building, to be exact," Alex pointed.

"Is that so," the man said. "You know, I just opened my new office there."

"Oh, really," said Justin.

"Yes. My name is Mr. Reinhold. I'll walk with you," he said.

Justin swallowed hard and saw the resemblance. "He looks just like the guy in the office lobby," he thought.

Mason whispered to his friends, "Guys, look at all the cars and what the people are wearing!"

They looked around, and they, too, saw the old cars and strange clothing.

"What's going on?" whispered Zeke.

"It's 1968," Mason replied. "I saw the date on the newspaper."

"But, how?" asked Alex.

"Well, I'm not really sure!" Mason replied. "But, we need to get back to your dad, Justin!"

"He's right. Let's go!" said Justin. The boys started to run down the street.

"Wait up, boys! I'm not that fast!" they heard Mr. Reinhold yell from behind.

Zeke turned around and said, "Sorry, Mr. Reinhold, but we're in a bit of a hurry!"

When the boys got to the entrance of the building, the doorman greeted them and opened the door. They pushed and shoved their way through the crowd to get to the elevators. They got in the same one that they came down in, and Alex pressed the number 42. Instead of going fast as lightning, the elevator was going as slow as molasses this time.

"How many years ago was 1968, Mason?" Justin asked in a shaky voice.

"Umm, let me think. I believe 42," he replied quickly and with a voice that said "I'm the smart guy."

"Guys," Justin said, "do you know what just happened!"

"Uh, oh!" Zeke exclaimed.

"What?" screeched Alex, who felt as if he was being tortured.

"Relax, Dude!" Mason said with the weirdest look on his face.

"Focus, guys!" Justin encouraged.

"OK," said Mason.

"So, we went back 42 years, right?"

"Yeah," answered Zeke.

"Well, my dad works on the 42nd floor," Justin announced.

"Freaky!" said Alex.

"Do you think it's this funky elevator?" said Justin. "I am never going on this elevator again!"

"Neither am I," the rest of them said.

"What are we going to tell your dad, Justin?" Zeke asked.

Justin replied, "Just let me do the talking."

As the elevator opened and they got out, a short man entered.

"Good luck, man," Zeke said.

"You're going to need it," Mason added.

The man made a puzzled look and entered mumbling, "Kids...."

They ran to Justin's dad's office. "Did you forget about me?" Justin's dad said. "Where's my lunch?"

"No, Dad. You see, we got lost and could not find the sub shop!"

"What are you talking about?" his dad turned to look out the window. "I can see it from here. Well, I can take a break now, so let's go together. Justin, walk ahead and tell Nicole I'm going to lunch. That way she knows to take messages for me. We'll meet you at the elevators."

"OK, Dad." Justin walked down the hall towards his dad's secretary's desk. "Nicole, Dad wants you to know he is taking us to lunch."

"Thanks, Justin. Have a good afternoon," she replied.

As Justin was walking back toward the elevator, he heard his name called from an office. He stopped and, with hesitation, popped his head into the doorway. Sitting at a large desk sat Mr. Reinhold. "Uuuhh, hi, Mr. Reinhold. Did you call me?"

"Yes. I did call you. How is your afternoon at Dad's work?"

"Well, it's been sort of...unusual, to tell you the truth. I can't really describe it."

"I know exactly what you're talking about," he said as a huge smile spread across his face. "Get along now, your dad is probably waiting," Mr. Reinhold said with a wink.

Justin left the room and went to the elevators. His dad and his friends were waiting for him. "Where have you been?" Dad asked as pressed the button on the time-traveling elevator.

"Ummm, Dad, let's go on the other elevator," Justin said, holding his breath.

"This one is fine, Jus," Dad replied.

"No, Dad. Trust me. You don't want to go on that one!" Justin said in a panic.

"Jus, what's gotten into you?" he asked as he walked behind the boys to the other elevator.

"Just trust me, Dad," Justin said with a grin.

We Swear on Our Jellybeans

A crazy class of first-graders learns in the end not to mess with the principal. Find out what happens to these kids in **WE SWEAR ON OUR JELLYBEANS,** *by* ***Grace Manion.***

"Becky, stop biting her!" I yelled as Becky was sinking her little first-grader teeth into the arm of her classmate's dark green jacket.

"Where did that noodle come from, Timmy?" I asked, very eager to know where he got the neon orange foam pool noodle from.

"Give me back my elephant, Lily!" shrieked Lindsay while riding on Lily's back and throwing her arms around her neck. Lindsay was trying to get the big, new, and aqua-colored elephant from her before Lily could enjoy it.

This is pretty much a typical day of teaching for me. Usually after lunch and recess I return to this. I closed my eyes and listened to the noises, trying to pick out every sound in room filled with powerful voices from insane first-graders with colorful toys that give off a positive energy until they hit the walls and fell to the floor. But today the sound was louder. Although not by much, I could still tell it was. Also I couldn't pick out the sounds like I usually can. I was so mad that every time I would walk back from a talkative lunch with the other teachers I would come into an ear-piercing room. I felt I just had to do something, so I did what any frantic teacher would do: discipline.

What I did was somewhat similar to discipline in your mind, but discipline to me is this. I stood on a school-bus-colored chair and yelled as loud as I could, "If everyone doesn't stop this now, I will shove the class pet, Hammy the Hamster, in the toilet!"

Everyone looked around at each other biting their bottom lips. Every kid was sweating, and I bet they would have wished they were wearing shorts and t-shirts. They were all hot from moving so much. But at least, for once, it was silent in Miss Mazie's classroom. I told everyone to sit in their seats so we could start class.

After about two hours of doing crafts and reading them a part of a book, they went to gym class and then went home with not a peep.

The next day I walked into a quiet classroom that was full of whispers and the word "jellybean." I took a deep breath and mouthed the words "thank you" as a sign of relief.

All the kids were huddled in a really small and enclosed circle at the left of the room by the cubbies, whispering. They didn't notice me. This was so weird because they usually are attacking each other by now with toys and fists. Were they being nice to each other for once?

I got closer and closer. I tried to make them not notice me. It was hard because I was wearing my very high, bright scarlet red high heels that were clicking on the floor and my tight, gray skirt that made it impossibly hard for me to take big steps.

I crouched down behind the kids so they wouldn't see me. I could start to hear what they were saying. I moved my head closer and closer. My back was toward them, and I looked out of the corner of my eye toward the circle. My straight, long, blonde hair was brushing up against some students. Now I could hear every word that came out of their little mouths.

"Does everyone swear that they will never be nice to our teacher, Miss Mazie, ever again? And if anyone breaks their promise they will have to give each student ten jellybeans."

"We swear on our jellybeans," whispered all the kids but one.

"Well, I swear never to be mean to our teacher ever again," snapped Abby.

"Why would you be on her side? She flushed Hammy down the toilet," asked a little boy.

"No, she didn't. She just wanted us to be quiet!" said Abby, a little annoyed that they believed that.

"I'm with Abby on this one," I whispered, acting like I was one of the kids.

"It's the hamster shover!" whispered a kid.

"Why are we still whispering?" whispered Max.

"I didn't flush Hammy!" I said in a normal voice while standing back up.

"Hey, I have a great idea! Let's all attack Abby and Miss Mazie!" yelled a random kid.

The kids all started hitting me and Abby with pool noodles, blocks, stuffed animals, and whatever they could get their greedy little hands on. It just looked like a big blurred rainbow because they hit my glasses off. I scrambled for my glossy red glasses (that surprisingly match my shoes), put them on, and saw Abby standing by the closet with finger paintings, gesturing for me to come her way. Once we finally were safe in the closet we took some time to catch our breath. That was plenty of time for Abby to realize something.

"Wait, if the light isn't on, then why is it bright in here?" asked Abby while looking around.

"A window!" I said, pointing at it and standing up. "Pile up the boxes with me, Abby. We're getting out of here!"

It didn't take long to pile up the boxes, mostly because some were piled already. We just had to move them around. Then we climbed up and out.

"I'm so hungry, Miss Mazie. I didn't have any breakfast," whined Abby.

"Well, there's that cupcake store, Give Me Cupcakes, just down the road, and my car is right there."

"Do you mean the store that is painted crazy with half the store neon green and the other half neon pink so it can get people's attention?" clarified Abby.

"That's the one with the new pet store next to it," I answered.

"So I get to ride in my teacher's pink car, eat cupcakes, and ditch school?" Abby asked excited.

"Pretty much," I answered.

"Well, then, what are we waiting for?" Abby asked me like I was a crazy person. We drove all the way there with the wind kissing each of our long bright blonde hairs. The only smell was the cold yet humid air hitting our noses.

We opened the door and got out of the car. We walked into the cupcake store, bought the cupcakes, and sat down. Abby got a vanilla cupcake with vanilla frosting and rainbow sprinkles. I got a chocolate cupcake with chocolate frosting and chocolate sprinkles. We sat down at a reddish orange table with dark navy blue chairs and two, small, golden star stickers right next to each other on the table.

We started talking about what the kids might be doing. "I think the kids opened the closet door, saw we escaped, and went home," I told Abby.

"Well, I think they ate each other. They're like animals!" Abby told me.

"They are the craziest class I have ever taught," I told Abby.

"Or maybe a teacher was walking by and saw them fighting and called the police," laughed Abby.

"If you finish your cupcake we can check," I told her. So she bit a big chunk out of her cupcake. Seconds later I was walking out of there with Abby next to me with her frosted-and-sprinkled face.

When we got back to the school we tippy-toed through the hallways and into the classroom quietly, so no one would know that we had left. When we peered into the classroom the principal was in there. *Busted*, I thought. What I didn't notice was the principal had a broom in her hand and was putting toys away. And the kids were gone! It was so weird!

"I told you they would eat each other," said Abby to me, slightly whispering.

"Hello, ladies, how are you doing?" asked the principal, Mrs. Molly, like there wasn't a problem at all.

"We're fine, but...where are they?" I said, scanning the room.

"Where are who? Oh, you mean the kids!" said Mrs. Molly. Then I heard mumbling coming from the closet, and Abby and I turned our heads in that direction. Abby and I walked slowly to the closet with five finger paintings on it. I opened the door and saw all 22 kids had been taped together and thrown into the closet!

"Did you do this?" I asked Mrs. Molly.

"Yeah," answered Mrs. Molly like there still wasn't a problem.

"Why?" I asked her.

"Well, I had to do something," said the principal. "They were walking in circles and staring at each other like animals ready to attack their prey."

"See, I told you they were going to eat each other," Abby said.

"Exactly, they looked like they were going to eat each other," Mrs. Molly agreed.

"All I know is that these kids are creeps," I said finally.

Since that day the kids never were bad ever again. Doctors also had a new discovery: the phobia of getting taped and thrown into a closet by psychotic principals.

Witch

Did you ever think that your teacher could be a witch? In **WITCH** *by* ***Keith Harris**, a boy believes that his teacher is a witch. But, nobody believes him.*

One day, I noticed that my teacher had a blue mouth. I thought she must be a witch. I remembered that witches have blue mouths. When school was over, I hid in her car as she drove to her house. When I snuck into her house, I saw some potions all over the house. I dropped my backpack and ran as fast as I could.

The next day, the office called me down. My teacher, Mrs. Straub, and the principal, Mr. Miller, wanted to speak with me. When I went into the office, I noticed my backpack that I had dropped at her house.

Mrs. Straub asked me why I had followed her to her house. "I thought you were a witch," I replied nervously. "Why did you have gloves?"

"Because I was cold," replied Mrs. Straub.

"Then why do you have potions all over your house?" I asked.

"Those are not potions," Mrs. Straub laughed. "They are perfume bottles."

"Oh," I said.

"If this happens again, you're going to be in big trouble, young man," Mrs. Straub said. "And I'll quit!"

"Please, do not quit," said the principal, Mr. Miller. "You have been working here for a very long time."

"Now is my time to say good bye, Mr. Miller," Mrs. Straub said.

"I'm sorry," I said.

"Thank you, Keith," Mrs. Straub continued. "I was about to quit anyway. Now I have a good reason."

Mr. Miller was really mad. He told me that I was suspended for a whole month. And the next time that I get in trouble, I will have a detention every day.

"Or, Keith," Mr. Miller continued, "if you can get Mrs. Straub to come back, then you will not be suspended."

I went out to look for Mrs. Straub, and I hid in her car again. When she got in her car, she took off her wig, shoes, and gloves. I ran out of the car and told Mr. Miller what I had seen. He looked out the window and saw her.

Mr. Miller called the police and ran outside to catch Mrs. Straub. He threw water on her and she melted. When the police arrived, they asked what had happened. I told them that they do not want to know.

The Wonders

In **THE WONDERS** *by* ***Torry Charnas**, a hidden world is revealed. Perhaps fairy tales can be real.*

I bet you don't know my stories about wizards. Wizards are fairly nice. But like people, some are good, and some are bad. They have powers, but they cannot do a lot of things. Each magical creature can do its own thing. Some can do more than others. Wizards are pretty lucky when it comes to that. They are pretty powerful, but one thing is they cannot fly.

Some people think witches and wizards are the same, but they are not. Witches are the ones who fly! They are completely different in so many ways, but that's a different story.

Wizards cannot control other creatures, but they can do magic on humans, so watch out!

Now that you know about the wizards, let me tell you about the Flowers. They are the most powerful creature ever! There are five of them. They are in a group or whatever you want to call it. A lot of creatures go to ask them for wishes, but they will probably die because they are really asking to rule the world. The Flowers know what they are going to do with the power.

It's lucky for you that the Flowers exist! You would probably be slaves right now if not for them. You may not know this, but they protect you!

Now, they were not always together. Sam, the main member of the Flowers, knew he had the wisdom to save the world, but he did not know how to do it. One day he was just taking a walk in the park when he tripped over a book. It ended up being a book of magic. Sam was truly amazed by the detail in the book. On the first page it said clearly in dull text, "Whoever will open this book: Your wishes will come true. But beware: The power in this book is stronger than you think!" The book continued, "And there are all together five powerful ones."

Sam knows who three of the others are. There is one more, but they do not know who or what it is. They will know when they see it. Could it be you?

Zombies!

ZOMBIES! *by **Andrew Saad** is about a group of friends who are chased by zombies and have to save humanity. They find themselves making decisions to defeat the zombies.*

Imagine a bunch of zombies chasing you and your friends around school! I never did until it actually happened.

It was a usual day until we arrived at school. We all sat down in class and waited for the teacher, but instead of Mr. Z walking in, a zombie rushed into the room! We knew it was a zombie because it said, "I am a zombie here to capture you." The zombie had two different-colored eyes and wore jeans and a short-sleeved shirt. Weirdest of all, he was green and yellow.

We were shocked, so we started running around the school. We realized there were lots of zombies because as we were trying to escape more of them would start following us.

In all the chaos, we tackled a zombie and took it hostage. Jack yelled, "Why are you chasing us?"

The zombie said, "We only like Berkshire kids to come to our base."

First we ran to the gym. Next we went to Mrs. Rivera's room. After that we went to Mr. Phillips's room. What was weird about his room was that there was a spaceship right in the middle!

Out of nowhere, 11 zombies crawled into the room and forced us into the spaceship! Scared out of our minds, we tried to figure out what the zombies wanted from us, but we were unsuccessful. What appeared to be the leader of the zombies stood in front of us and told us we were being taken as prisoners on our way to the moon! He instructed everyone to put spacesuits on. We were told we would have to wear spacesuits to breathe until we were transformed into zombies.

On the way to the moon he told us once we were zombies it would be our job to capture more students and bring them back on these spaceships. He also said that the head zombie was formed in an acid spill on Earth where he stole a spaceship and flew to the moon!

After a successful landing, hundreds of zombies surrounded the spaceship. They stared us down as we were rushed off the spaceship. They forced us to jail and made us wear these ultramodern electronic handcuffs.

Soon after we got to jail, we thought of a plan to escape. We decided that we would ask to go to the bathroom and then tackle the guard. So Jack asked to go to the bathroom, and John and I tackled the guard. As soon as we had the guard subdued, we ran out of the jail.

The zombies spotted us and started chasing us. We found moon vehicles, and we quickly got into one of them. We sped off as the zombies chased us.

As we got into darker territories, the zombies seemed to slow down. The deeper we got into the darkness, the fewer zombies chased us. We concluded that the dark side of the moon was forbidden to them, and it was a good hiding spot for us.

On the dark side of the moon, we found some type of shiny pink and green rocks. The rock glowed in the dark, so we thought we would take it to help us see our way back. We didn't know what it was, but each of us took a piece of it anyway.

We ran behind a zombie and knocked him out by hitting him on the head with the rock, and we quickly realized that the rock froze him and turned him back into a human. The man didn't know what he was doing, but he led us back to the spaceship anyway. We ran to the ship hoping none of the other zombies were watching.

We saw the three zombies guarding the craft, so one of us went behind each of them, and we hit them on the back of the head with a rock. With the power of the rock we took the zombies' craft and scrambled to find out how to get back to Earth. As we were frantically searching, I saw a lever that had a strange symbol on it. I pulled the lever, and a navigation screen shot out of the wall. I found Berkshire Middle School on it, and I hit the pilot button. This set us on our way back to Earth.

Once we landed at Berkshire, we realized that the zombies had followed us. As their ships started to land we began throwing the rocks at the zombies, and they turned to humans. Our group was getting bigger and bigger, so we were able to find the zombies more easily and turn them back into humans. At this point, we got all of the spacecrafts and we decided to fly back to the moon to rescue all the others.

When we got back to the moon, we all went to the dark side to collect more rocks. After we got into our spaceships, we chased after the zombies and started dropping rocks onto them. The only problem was that when we got to a big zombie kingdom, we saw a giant zombie that the rock couldn't freeze.

We all went back to the dark side to think of another plan to defeat the huge zombie. First, somebody suggested we hit him with a spacecraft, but nobody else liked that idea. Then, someone else proposed that we run up and start fighting him, but everybody thought that he would beat us. Finally, somebody suggested that we sneak into the kingdom and see if we could find his weakness. We had a democracy, and 12 out of the 20 people voted to do that.

We left for the kingdom. Once we got there, we saw a map in the back entrance. We decided we would figure out his weakness if we knew what chemicals changed him into the zombie. We ran through the building, freezing all the zombies we saw, until there were none left.

When we got to the giant's office there was a lock on the door. We threw a rock at it, and it fell off. We walked into the office and started looking on his laptop until we found an article on him. We printed the paper and took it to his laboratory. We opened up the cabinet and took all the acids that hurt him and made a mixture! Then we took some of our rocks and covered them in the mixture so we could attack him easier.

We ran outside and taunted the zombie. Then we all started throwing little pieces of the rock at him. They were burning him but not killing him. So two people went up to him and poured the acid on him. It burnt him to ash. We checked the moon two more times for other zombies, and then we headed back to Earth.

We were so excited to be heading back home. As soon as we got to Berkshire, thousands of people including parents, teachers, and students were waiting for us, and were so happy for our safe return. They also thanked us for stopping the zombies from taking over our world. All of our parents were worried sick, but were very proud when the principal presented us with a bravery award. What a great feeling it was to be home again.

Index of Authors and Titles

Made in the USA
Charleston, SC
25 May 2011